Kim Lawrence lives on a [...] her university lecturer husb[...] arrived as strays and never [...] one or both of her boomerang sons. When she's not writing she loves to be outdoors gardening, or walking on one of the beaches for which the island is famous—along with being the place where Prince William and Catherine made their first home!

USA TODAY bestselling author **Trish Morey** just loves happy endings. Now that her four heroines-in-training have grown up and flown the nest, Trish is enjoying her own happy ending—the one where you downsize, end up living in an idyllic coastal region with the guy you married and, better still, realise you still love each other. There's a happy-ever-after right there. Or a happy new beginning! Trish loves to hear from her readers—you can email her at trish@trishmorey.com.

RULES OF ENGAGEMENT

KIM LAWRENCE

TRISH MOREY

MILLS & BOON

First published in Great Britain 2025
by Mills & Boon, an imprint of HarperCollins*Publishers* Ltd,
1 London Bridge Street, London, SE1 9GF

www.harpercollins.co.uk

HarperCollins*Publishers*, Macken House, 39/40 Mayor Street Upper,
Dublin 1, D01 C9W8, Ireland

Rules of Engagement © 2025 Harlequin Enterprises ULC

Engaged in Deception © 2025 Kim Jones

After-Hours Proposal © 2025 Trish Morey

ISBN: 978-0-263-34453-0

02/25

This book contains FSC™ certified paper
and other controlled sources to ensure responsible forest management.

For more information visit www.harpercollins.co.uk/green.

Printed and Bound in the UK using 100% Renewable Electricity
at CPI Group (UK) Ltd, Croydon, CR0 4YY

ENGAGED IN DECEPTION

KIM LAWRENCE

MILLS & BOON

To my loyal writing companion, chocolate.
And my husband, who brings me the chocolate!

CHAPTER ONE

THE FOOTSTEPS CLEMMIE registered as she was halfway down the narrow alley—a shortcut from the library to the main road—did not have her quickening her pace. The clip-clop-clatter of the senior librarian's favourite spiky ankle boots was unmistakable.

Clemmie turned and waited.

'Clem, I caught you!'

The older woman paused to catch her breath as she pressed one hand to her dramatically heaving chest and the other to her pink-streaked bleached crop to protect it from the wind. Clemmie's boss was waging a one-woman war against the mousy librarian stereotype and, as she liked to boast, she was winning!

With a questioning shake of her head Clemmie waited for her to catch her breath. To make Lily run in those heels it had to be a problem.

'You were catching the train home tonight?'

Still puzzled, Clemmie nodded and shivered. The alley was a wind tunnel.

'I haven't packed yet,' she admitted ruefully as she pulled her hood up protectively over her red curls. 'But hopefully I'll get a late train tonight, or if not first thing...' A possible reason for the chase occurred to her. 'Has Prue called in sick? I thought she looked a bit off this morning.

Do you want me to do a shift tomorrow morning? I could if you're pushed, and leave later,' she offered.

'Prue was just hungover,' her boss inserted drily. 'I despair of you—you are such a pushover. I know you swapped shifts with Prue last week. She takes advantage.'

'I didn't mind. So, what is…?'

'I wanted to give you a heads-up in case you were heading straight for the station. It's the trains.'

'What about the trains?'

'There aren't any—its rail Armageddon!' she declared dramatically. 'All over the news. I just heard there's a major points failure and a goods train derailment. No casualties, thankfully. And apparently the strike talks have broken down again.'

Clemmie pushed out a sigh, her breath turning misty white in the cold, damp air. 'Just what I need.'

'You could hire a car? Wait…can you drive?'

'I haven't driven since I passed my test, and that was eleven years ago.'

She couldn't afford to run a car, or for that matter hire one. A depressing thought had she been the sort of person who allowed herself to be worried about such things.

'But don't worry. I'll think of something. You go indoors; you'll freeze to death,' she added as an extra-strong gust blew her hood off. For several seconds she was blinded by her red curls.

'Well, good luck—and have a good holiday.'

Clemmie made her goodbyes and, hunching her shoulders, set off for the walk home. That was one of the advantages of the house-share. She saved on transport costs. The house she occupied with ten other people, who in the agent's details had been described as young professionals, was within easy walking distance of work.

Another was that against the odds they got on reasonably well—though not all were so young, and 'professional' was stretching the point. She spent the ten-minute walk considering this obstacle to her holiday, and by the time she had reached the house and let herself in she had a possible solution in mind.

The house was in darkness, the last of her housemates having left the previous evening. They had all made what the landlord had termed *'alternative arrangements'* for the next fortnight—which was how long the landlord had said the decorators would be in.

She reached for the light switch and fished out her phone, unfastening her coat but leaving it on as she walked through to the kitchen.

It was a biggish house—high ceilings, three floors. The sort that had once boasted a cook and a maid. There were few original features remaining, but it did still retain the odd creaking board and dark corner, which were more noticeable when it was empty—like now.

Not an issue for Clemmie. who was not spooked by creaking boards. For the first eight years of her life she had lived in a much bigger and older house, with multiple creaks and even a reputed ghost. She didn't believe in ghosts and she quite liked creaks.

Someone had left the radio playing, and the invisible news reader, sounding irritatingly upbeat about the situation, was outlining the combination of events that threatened train services this weekend.

Figuring the chances of the weather report offering any light relief were slim, she switched off the news channel and turned to her phone, scrolling until she reached the name Joaquin Perez and smiled to herself.

It wasn't often that a librarian assistant's list of contacts included a billionaire hedge fund boss who, among his accomplishments, was the founder of the Perez Investment House.

It was just as well she had his private number and also, just in case, that of his PA, because without them, access to the handsome, newsworthy and much lusted-after billionaire was virtually impossible. Members of the general public did not gain access to Joaquin without being screened by multiple layers of protective security.

It didn't stop his fans trying. His perfect profile and other parts of his anatomy were frequently the subject of debate among his league of devoted online followers, who often shared crazy fantasies about him. They all seemed to share one fantasy—namely that they were the perfect woman for him and one night spent with them would make him realise this.

Clemmie had shared a night with him.

She had been eleven at the time, and Joaquin a lanky thirteen.

Her expression softened when the memory of him climbing in through her bedroom window slid through her head.

He had responded to her wail of *'It should have been me, not Chrissie!'* by telling her she was being an idiot, before pulling the covers up to her chin and lying down beside her while she sobbed herself to sleep.

The next morning he had been gone before she woke and, going downstairs, found her mum asleep, her head on the kitchen table beside an empty wine bottle.

The anniversary of her twin's death was still tough for them both—it always would be—but these days they got together and shared their memories of Chrissie. There were tears, but there was also laughter.

She was jolted back to the present by *a deep* voice with an almost tactile 'shiver down the spine' quality.

'Hold on. I'll be with you in a minute.'

She hung on. She couldn't hear what Joaquin was saying but, even muffled, his delivery suggested that any fools within a fifty-yard radius should take cover.

This was a Joaquin that she did not know; she wasn't sure she'd want to. He was a supremely self-confident person. He had a self-confidence that bordered on arrogance...and actually crossed the line frequently.

You couldn't simply correlate his confidence with the social position and wealth he had been born into, or the fortune he had made. It was more about self-belief and his total commitment to following through with something he thought strongly about.

He didn't appear to need the approval of anyone.

More of a people-pleaser, Clemmie envied him sometimes.

'Bad time?' she asked.

'No, Clemmie. I'm all yours.'

Those were words that she could imagine quite a few women heard in their dreams—in a different context, obviously. Because she and Joaquin were not friends with benefits—just friends.

And she liked it that way.

Her brow furrowed as she put her phone on speaker and laid it on the table, freeing up her hands to remove the annoying strands of untameable hair from her face.

'Are you back from New York?'

She knew that he'd been based there for the last four months, although why remained a little vague to her, but she imagined that it involved him becoming even more wealthy than he already was.

How rich did a person need to be?

Clemmie answered her own question, because she suspected that Joaquin didn't need to be rich. Oh, he spoke about the freedom that money gave him, but money was not a goal in itself. He enjoyed, perhaps *needed* the challenge of pitting himself against the odds and winning.

An image of him climbing a seemingly smooth rock face and punching the air in triumph when he reached the top flashed into her head. She had chickened out before she'd gone a few feet and slithered clumsily back to the ground. Chrissie had always been the brave one. Like Joaquin, her twin had been hooked on the adrenalin rush.

If her twin had lived, would she have ended up being Joaquin's best friend?

Feeling immediately guilty for the thought, she gave a shamed grimace.

'Got back last night,' he said.

'Your text...'

'The one you never replied to?'

She ignored the wry interruption and passed on an explanation. 'Are you still going to Maplehurst this weekend?'

'I am.'

'Me too—and I'm a bit stranded.'

'You need a lift?' He spoke into the pause. 'You just nodded, didn't you?'

She laughed. 'I nodded *enthusiastically*.' She paused. 'And you just smiled, didn't you?'

His short burst of laughter was warm and deep.

'I had planned to go back tonight, or tomorrow morning,' she said. 'But obviously I can fit in with you.'

'I'll pick you up in...an hour and a half?'

'Am I being a nuisance?'

'Why change the habit of a lifetime? Address?'

As soon as she had given it he hung up, and her phone immediately began to shrill again. She glanced at the caller ID.

'Hello, Mum.'

'The trains! So when will you get home? You will be here to meet Harry?'

Clemmie pictured her parent, looking effortlessly chic in something she had just thrown on, rubbing fretfully at the gold locket she always wore—the one that had a photo of herself as a baby in one half and her sister in the other.

'Calm down, Mum, I've got it sorted,' she said, ignoring the voice in her head that pointed out the benefits of *not* getting home. 'I've got a lift.'

It wasn't that she didn't love visits home—she did. But this time it would not just be her and her mum. It would be her, her mum and her mum's new boyfriend, the latest in a long line of losers that had followed the biggest loser of all—her dad.

The difference was that her mum was engaged to this one, and she couldn't wait for Clemmie to meet the man who, according to her mum, was 'perfect'. But then all the men in her mother's life had at some stage been perfect—until they were revealed as not!

Her mum, capable and sensible in all other ways, had a blind spot when it came to men and their faults. To make things worse, she fell in love so easily—but maybe that was because she was falling in love for two, because Clemmie didn't fall in love at all.

She didn't believe it was about *falling*. That made it seem accidental, and Clemmie was always in control of her decisions and her hormones. She had no intention of *falling* for someone who would swear eternal devotion one minute and betray her the next.

'Someone I know…a boyfriend?' Ruth Leith continued, not giving her daughter a chance to interrupt. 'Would he like to stay over? We could…'

'Mum, I didn't say it was a "he"?'

There was a slight hesitation before her mum reacted to the teasing interruption. Then, 'So long as you are happy, Clemmie.'

'Oh, Mum. I'm not gay! And I know you wouldn't care if I was. Actually, it is a "he", but don't get excited. It's Joaquin; he's spending a couple of weeks at the manor.'

This was information that even her mum couldn't spin into anything romantic. Aside from her belief in true love, her mum was too much of a realist.

The Joaquins of this world did not date women who were short, skinny and had red hair that refused to be tamed no matter how much product got poured on it.

'Oh, right. It's good that you have a lift, but since when was he coming here? No one told me. The house is closed up—and what about catering?'

Maplehurst Manor was normally closed at this time of year. Joaquin's mother, who owned the place—a gift, apparently, from her husband—wasn't keen on British winters, and every February the Perez family had a ritual en masse get-together in their Spanish castle.

The manor hadn't always been closed up in the winter. Clemmie could recall sitting at one of the windows, rubbing a space in the frosted pane to watch the snow fall. She could even still recall her last Christmas there, when it had still been her family home.

She suspected she might have romanticised the memories. February snow had meant freezing to death, because the heating had never worked. But she still got a nostalgic ache, thinking about the logs spitting in the smoky, massive inglenooks of the Elizabethan mansion deep in the Dorset countryside that her father's family had called home for centuries. That was before her dad had gambled it and pretty much everything else away.

Her handsome dad was not sentimental about the Leith family's ancient seat. He wasn't sentimental, full stop. He was charismatic, and charming, and when she had been too young to know better Clemmie had adored him, competing for his attention—which had been a waste of time and effort.

He had always preferred Chrissie.

His attempts to stay in touch with his only living daughter now involved the occasional postcard from wherever he was in the world.

She hadn't seen him in years, and she knew that he'd never paid a penny of the child support he'd been meant to to her mum—who, since the divorce, had lived in the gatehouse that came with her new job: housekeeper in her old home. He had taken off when Chrissie was diagnosed, leaving a note saying it was 'doing his head in' and he couldn't bear to see his pretty daughter lose her hair.

He had said he would come for the funeral, and Clemmie had rather stupidly believed him, but he hadn't turned up.

'I was looking forward to spending my time with you and Harry,' her mother said now.

It was a lie, but not the sort that hurt people—the sort that Clemmie could never forgive.

She could see why her mum sounded disgruntled. When the house was empty her workload as housekeeper was light, but if any family member was in residence she was kept busy and often brought in casual local labour to help, along with outside catering firms to cope with social events.

'It's only Joaquin, as far as I know, so I'm sure you still can.'

'Is he bringing anyone? A *girlfriend*?'

Clemmie, who knew her mum's appetite for celebrity gossip well—especially when she knew the celebrity personally, and had once regularly fed him at her kitchen table—stemmed the flow of speculation.

'I haven't the foggiest, Mum.'

As children, she and Joaquin had enjoyed an unexpected friendship. Unexpected when you considered that Joaquin and his family had lived in the grand house she had once called home while her mum, no longer lady of the manor, had become housekeeper to the new owners.

A perfect solution, her mum had said, because it came with the gatehouse cottage and Clemmie wouldn't have the added disruption of changing schools.

Her mum had been pretty upbeat about what most people would consider a huge downgrade, pointing out that the roof didn't leak and the plumbing was not ancient.

Clemmie had been less philosophical, but she'd pretended to be okay with the arrangement for her mum's sake, while secretly she longed for her old room with the leaking roof.

The room she had shared with her twin, Chrissie.

Her mum, perhaps sensing how she felt, or maybe on the suggestion of the counsellor who had been part of Clemmie's life for a couple years, had moved a second bed into her tiny new room at the gatehouse, and nobody had said anything when she'd arranged all Chrissie's stuffed toys on it in the exact way that her twin had left them.

She had, however, hated Joaquin before she'd even known his name.

Her first encounter with the boy who had *stolen* her home had been in the woods that surrounded the manor. Clemmie had still thought of them as *her* woods, even though they were owned by this new family. That day she had climbed a tree to rescue a cat. The cat had rescued itself, which had left Clemmie hanging from a branch by her snagged cardigan.

Rescued by the new boy from the manor, she had responded by kicking him when he'd said, with the lofty superiority of ten years to her eight, that girls could not climb and told her she was trespassing.

It hadn't been the most promising of starts, but things had thawed during that first long summer holiday, and then they had bonded over their respective parents' disastrous unions and a mutual determination not *ever* to marry, because marriage was for idiots.

'At least you have one good parent. Both of mine are rubbish,' he had told her during one of their early exchanges, and she had realised he was right: she *was* lucky.

Her dad might be a nightmare but her mum, despite her bad taste in men, was fantastic. His family might be loaded—the Perez family were old money *and* new money, his grandfather having built a second fortune when he'd invested in a computer firm that soon became a global brand, and all Joaquin had to do was ask and he got anything he asked for—but *both his* parents *were* awful!

In fact, the entire Perez family were snobbish. They were the sort of people who guarded the family name and were willing to go to great lengths to maintain the illusion of being the *perfect* family. Their name might be synonymous with philanthropy, but they were ruthless when it came to preserving their own good name.

It helped if you had the money to buy yourself out of trouble—and they did. A Perez didn't divorce, Joaquin had explained to her. They stayed unhappily married. Although according to him his own parents might have broken with that particular tradition.

His dad had bought his mother Maplehurst Manor. And after that gift his mother had conveniently forgotten his dad's pregnant girlfriend—the one who had killed herself. There would be no baby to embarrass the Perez family and the girl had not had any relatives.

Ironic, really, that his family cared about their family name too much while her own dad didn't care about his at all.

Despite the fact they had both grown up and changed as their lives had taken very different paths—though Joaquin's contempt for marriage remained—their friendship had lasted.

Hence Clemmie came to have a billionaire hedge fund boss listed in the contacts on her phone.

They made a point of texting weekly, and sometimes it was more, but it was eighteen months since she had last seen him face to face, and their exchanges did not include the salacious details her mum craved. Like everyone else, Clemmie got her gossip from social media and news outlets, which seemed to suggest Joaquin was on the point of matrimony on a weekly basis.

She supposed it was inevitable that they would grow apart, and that the process would speed up once he did settle for one partner. Girlfriends or wives might not like their man texting another woman at two in the morning—

though to be fair it hadn't been that time where he was—
no matter how innocuous the text.

That time she had turned over and gone back to sleep,
meaning to respond the next morning. She was going to
miss those selfish texts…

She shrugged off the heavy, self-indulgent weight of
self-pity before it could claim her. What was the point of
getting down about something that hadn't happened yet
and might not?

Her lips twisted into a small self-mocking smile. It
could be she was flattering herself, because not even her
mother, who frequently called her 'pretty', would claim
she was the sort of woman beautiful women felt threatened by. And Clemmie herself was too much of a realist
to make that claim.

She was philosophical about her lack of looks. It wasn't
that she was plain, precisely, but her features were not
symmetrical enough for conventional beauty, or even pret-
tiness. Her mouth was too big for her small triangular face,
and her colouring was not to everyone's taste. Though the
combination of creamy freckled skin, red hair and pale
green eyes did make her stand out from the crowd.

'Well, if he does turn up with some woman in tow give
me a text.'

'I will,' promised Clemmie, who until that moment had
not even thought of such a possibility.

Now, as she climbed the stairs to finish packing, it
was *all* she could think of. That and the low-level nau-
sea churning in her stomach. She really shouldn't have
skipped lunch.

There was no reason he shouldn't be bringing his latest lover, and no reason he should tell her if he was. She
had never allowed herself to foster any romantic feelings

for Joaquin, even when it had occurred to her that there was a very good reason that conversations stopped when he walked into a room.

He was, of course, an off-the-scale gorgeous and sinfully sexy man. Way back she had had a few breath-catching, skin-tingling moments that she had probably been too inexperienced to hide from him, but he'd pretended not to notice. Or maybe the brutal truth was he genuinely hadn't?

She had no intention of finding out. She valued their friendship too much for that to happen. Besides, she had observed from a distance the casual, often callous way he treated his lovers, and it was definitely better to remain his friend—which was a much more permanent position.

Luckily, she hadn't fallen in any real way—which, if her mum was any measure, meant being *in lurve* involved being totally oblivious to a man's faults.

Clemmie was well aware of Joaquin's faults, and she wasn't about to allow herself the self-indulgence of filling up space in her head with unrequited lust. Life was too short for self-induced unhappiness.

Besides, not only was she not his type—which seemed to involve having curves, endless legs and a pout—sometimes men were just so *predictable*—he was definitely not her type. He couldn't be, because there was still a big question mark over her 'type'.

She had met men who ticked all the boxes on her list—the list in her head…it wasn't as if she had a spreadsheet or anything. She was prepared to be flexible—just not the sort of flexible that got her lumbered with a compulsive liar like her dad. Unfortunately, all the men who seemed suitable, and also fancied her, did absolutely nothing for Clemmie—not even a tingle.

She didn't really count the kiss she'd shared with Joaquin on her eighteenth. Well, she couldn't. That had only been a birthday kiss, and they'd both laughed about it the next day—him more than her.

But then he hadn't instigated the kiss, had he? Though in her defence wine had been involved. The bottle he had packed in the luxury picnic basket he had pulled from the boot of his sports car when they had arrived at her favourite lakeside spot.

The sun had shone...it had been a perfect day. The wine and the sun had made her sleepy and she had lain down on the blanket, a hand lifted to her face to protect her eyes from the sun, and fallen asleep.

At first she had swatted at the grass tickling her nose, and then, when she had opened her eyes, she had seen the hand holding the grass belonged to Joaquin, who was stretched out beside her. He had long left behind being skinny and lanky by that time; he had filled out in all the right places.

She had said something rude and pulled the strand of grass from his fingers, and he had grinned his 'fallen angel on steroids' grin.

It had been a purely spontaneous gesture when she had raised herself onto one elbow and pressed her mouth to his. He hadn't moved, but she had, reacting to the wine or to something more basic as her lips moved across his.

She remembered feeling warm...and dizzy. Then her confusion had been followed by deep mortification as he'd removed her hands, which had found their way around his neck.

The rejection had felt like someone throwing a bucket of ice water over her. If she could have crawled out of her skin she would have.

'Too much wine,' he'd said, and his lazy, relaxed attitude had not lowered her embarrassment level, but at least he hadn't laughed.

That was the day she had acknowledged her crush and it had died a death.

Joaquin sat in the lay-by he had pulled in to so he could answer a call. It didn't require a long conversation, just a decision, and decision-making was not something he struggled with.

He took the opportunity to check in with his PA, Rose, to whom he had left the task of rearranging his calendar. He had planned to go down to Maplehurst tomorrow, but the shift in his diary was not too onerous, and his PA was excellent. She would not appreciate any attempt on his part to micro-manage her.

His confidence was rewarded. There were no issues, and there was nothing preventing him having an extra day at Maplehurst. He had always liked the place, but it was where his mother based herself for a portion of the year—not the perfect situation. He frequently wished that she was as distant and remote now as she had been when he was a child.

Of course he knew it wasn't maternal love that made her so attentive these days. It was the fact that he could be appealed to for extra funds to supplement her position of 'near penury'.

He knew full well this wasn't the case—she received a more than generous allowance from his father, and frequent top-ups when her errant husband was caught doing something embarrassing with one of his youthful social secretaries, physiotherapists or wellness gurus.

It had been a year since Joaquin had been to the manor, and that had been for a party his mother had thrown—

some sort of charity thing. Clemmie had not been there, so he'd been bored out of his mind—especially as his mother had invited a few candidates to be the mother of the grandchildren she was longing for. He found the aforementioned *'longing'* a bit strange, considering the fact that when he was a child having him in the same room as her for more than five minutes at a stretch had brought up the subject of her 'delicate nerves'.

This time his mother wouldn't be there. She, along with the rest of his extended family, would be gathered at the *castillo*, the official reason being the annual dinner party they gave, which was meant to celebrate his parents' and his grandparents' joint wedding anniversaries—a celebration so embedded in family tradition that even his grandfather's death had not stopped it happening.

He seemed to be the only person who appreciated the irony and the sheer hypocrisy of celebrating two marriages which, by anyone's measure, were absolute disasters. And it wasn't just a night. He could have coped with a single night of hypocrisy, but over the years the celebration had morphed into a fortnight of family togetherness, which translated as half of his February involving extended sniping and back-biting. Though on one subject the disparate sections of his extended family were all of one mind—it was time he got married. It was his *duty*.

Duty was overrated, but it wasn't even duty that made him turn up each February. There was a large element of sheer laziness involved. Bottom line: *not* going required more effort than turning up.

Over the years he had perfected the art of tuning out the nagging, and it actually amused him that they thought they could influence him, that they wielded any power at all over him. But that was his family, and their collective ego was vast.

However, his tolerance had limits, and his grandmother had recently pushed it beyond that limit.

Talk about insulting his intelligence!

Her manipulation hadn't even been subtle. It had been about as subtle as the monster of an ugly engagement ring she had sent him, with the attached message that she was sending this *'precious ring'* to him now because she wouldn't live to see it on his bride's finger. The ink had even been artistically smudged—presumably by her heartbroken tears falling on the paper.

He knew for a fact that the ring had sat in a bank vault for years, because it had belonged to his grandmother's mother-in-law, whom she had loathed.

Remembering the damned thing was still in his pocket, he fished it out and put it in the glovebox before starting up the car.

Joaquin had no worries over his grandparent's imminent demise—she had just returned from a sponsored trek up Kilimanjaro and left the film crew who had been recording the event for a TV show entitled *Eighty is the New Fifty* in her wake.

But her stunt *had* had an effect—though not the one she had intended. It had brought home to him the hell he was voluntarily walking into.

He was an adult who wielded power, commanded respect and on occasion fear, and yet here he was, meekly submitting every year to a week of moral blackmail and nagging. His family had clearly taken his indifference for pliability.

But he had a professional reputation for being remote and inaccessible—a reputation that was pretty much well-earned. It was about time he lived up to that reputation. In no other aspect of his life would he have allowed such a situation to continue.

It was time he broke the cycle—and there was no time like the present.

He had responded to his grandmother by text.

I have made alternative plans for next week.

He had re-read the text, to make sure there was no hint of an excuse, and that no element of humouring could be read into the stark sentence, and pressed 'send'.

It was only then that he'd wondered about the 'alternative plans' he had boasted of. For some reason he'd thought of Maplehurst. Although he spent every summer there, he'd never been there at this time of year. He remembered that one year Clemmie had sent him pictures of the manor covered in snow, and the image had stayed with him.

His mother spent large sections of the year at Maplehurst, playing lady of the manor and hosting charity events. It was a comfortable way to avoid her husband, who spent his time moving from one fashionable spot to another with a variety of nubile youthful *'assistants'* in tow, to cater to all his needs. But she was never there during the winter months, and after Christmas she went straight from their ski lodge to the *castillo*. After that she made the return trip, with a short detour for a detox at her favourite exclusive Swiss spa.

He hadn't shared the details of his alternative arrangements with anyone except in the text he had sent Clemmie, who hadn't got back to him.

That hadn't rung alarm bells.

There would be a reason.

He had speculated briefly about what that might be…a new job…or a new boyfriend?

The idea seemed…

He felt the weariness he had experienced of late settling over him and pushed both it and the question away. For a friendship to last into adulthood there were unspoken boundaries which had to be maintained, and he wanted that friendship to last. Actually, probably *needed* it to, he acknowledged.

His thoughts drifted to that moment when he had come close to overstepping that boundary. When Clemmie had been just eighteen, and a little bit tipsy, he had watched her sleep, her lashes fluttering on her cheeks, her breasts rising and falling. He'd just been thinking about adjusting the parasol to protect her face from the sun when she'd given a little cry in her sleep, her arms thrashing as she fought off some invisible demon in her daymare.

Did she still have the nightmare she had once told him about? he'd wondered. The one where she tried to save her sister but found there was a choice: she could save her sister or herself. She always woke up crying in shame, feeling irrationally responsible for her twin's death.

She had reacted to the tickle of his piece of grass on her face and opened her eyes, and in that moment, before she was even fully awake, she had kissed him.

He still didn't know how he had not responded, when every instinct in his body had been urging him to explore the warm lips being offered up to him, to push her back on to the rug and…

But a small corner of his brain had kept repeating, *This is Clemmie…this is Clemmie.*

And it had been Clemmie—but not the Clemmie who was his.

Clemmie was a constant in his life. She was the anti-
dote to his adulatory press releases and to all the people
telling him how brilliant he was. Sometimes her outlook
on life left him anxious for her; she had an ability to view
the world through rose-coloured lenses—though maybe
that should be green. Clemmie possessed the most extraordinary aquamarine eyes that could smile without moving
any other muscle in her expressive face. Despite her pale
colouring and pre-Raphaelite mass of red curls, her lashes
were naturally dark, as were her straight brows.

He was thinking of her face when he arrived on the
street where she apparently now lived. It was long, with no
defining features to make it seem any different from several of the roads he had driven through to get here, lined
with tall houses mostly split into apartments.

He scanned the area for a parking space. Some of the
redbrick Victorian houses had their original wrought-iron
fences, but most had knocked the walls down and con-
creted over the tiny gardens to create parking spaces. He
was about to give in when an MPV beside a builders' skip
pulled out and he neatly pulled into the space.

He located the number that Clemmie had given him,
but before he could hit the doorbell it suddenly opened,
revealing a long, narrow hallway painted in an anonymous discoloured cream. The only colour came from the
original encaustic tiles on the floor.

CHAPTER TWO

'Hi!'

There was a long pause while she stared at him as if she was in a desert and he was a cool, deep pool of water. She was struggling to elevate her gaze from his mouth. On one level she knew what she was doing, and that she must look like an idiot, but she couldn't stop any more than she could stop breathing.

This made no sense!

She wanted to kiss him—and not in a warm and friendly way.

Her lashes flickered as she struggled to make some sort of logical sense of the jumbled thoughts that slid through her head.

Nothing was different. He was still the same Joaquin—just eighteen months older than the Joaquin she had shared a fish and chip supper with, sitting on a bench while he talked with animation about his new literacy programme, sounding committed and caring, and so genuinely angry that some children lived in homes without books that she had wanted to hug him. She'd had no issue at all in following through with the impulse, laughing when he had complained she'd got grease on his suit.

So what had changed? It wasn't as if she didn't already know he exuded a pheromone cloud that could poleaxe a woman at fifty paces. He was even dressed similarly today, because like on that evening he had come straight from a meeting. He was wearing a dark suit, a pale shirt, his narrow silk tie providing the only splash of colour. His hair was a similar length—short, but starting to curl on his neck the way it did when he needed a trim.

His skin still had that golden glow, with the faint shadow of stubble on his jaw an earthy addition to the miracle of symmetry that was his face. All strong angles and intriguing hollows, with penetrating dark, heavy-lidded eyes set beneath thick brows and framed by long, curling lashes any woman would have killed for. He possessed a sinfully fascinating mouth that combined lushness in the full lower lip with control in the sensually sculpted upper.

In short, he was chiselled perfection, then and now, but now she wanted to kiss him.

She *really* did.

These thoughts raced through her head as she tried to breathe through the moment, before managing a creaky inhalation and painting on a smile just this side of inane.

Asking herself *why* was for later. Now was the moment to stop looking like a total drooling fool!

'Hi, back,' she said brightly, breaking through the paralysis.

She didn't want to think about the instinct that had bypassed her brain and nearly pushed her into action.

Luckily it had passed.

Blame it on his mouth, she thought—and, yes, that worked, she decided as her eyes lingered on the sensual outline of his lips. That sinfully sexy curve had probably given rise to many a forbidden fantasy, and her relatively tame one was going to stay safely locked in her head.

So it was all good, she soothed herself.

Joaquin's wide brow indented in an interrogative frown. 'Everything okay?'

Her feathery brows lifted as she shrugged and smiled, allowing her gaze to float away from his stare. 'Having a bad hair day. And if you say *every* day is a bad hair day for me...'

The jokey warning drew his glance to the red-gold cloud of curls that surrounded her small face like a fiery nimbus, spilling down her slender back in a wild tangle of curls that looked bright against the black cotton top she wore underneath a green oversized shirt, unbuttoned, with the sleeves rolled up to the elbows.

She withstood his scrutiny, the only hint that she was not relaxed the shadow of wariness reflected in her wide-spaced pale green eyes.

'I didn't like to text while you were driving, but parking is impossible.' She held her hair back with one elbow and craned her neck to look down the street.

'I found a space.'

She pulled her head back in and gave her hair an irritated pat. 'Of course you did,' she murmured drily.

Still standing on the step, he arched a questioning brow.

'Sorry—come in,' she said, moving to one side to allow him inside without a collision. It was a very narrow hallway, and he was not a narrow man—lean, definitely, but his shoulders took up quite a lot of space.

She made herself as small as possible.

Joaquin shrugged and walked past her—no point overthinking the unaccustomed awkwardness he'd picked up on. Eighteen months was a long time...

But despite his pragmatic attitude he still couldn't shake

the impression that there had been a shift—that some dynamic between them had changed.

He was still the same, which meant that *she* had changed?

He found he resented the possibility.

He had wanted to relax, and Clemmie was always uncomplicated good company.

'I saw you from upstairs.'

She bit her lip and stopped speaking a sentence too late. But at least he couldn't see her face, which she was sure must have guilt written across it.

Not that there was any need for guilt. It had just been a slightly over-the-top reaction to her first sight of the tall, unmistakably broad-shouldered and long-legged figure.

She blinked away the image floating in her head and dismissed the visceral surge of tangled emotions that for a split second had made her brain shut down.

As he had reached the path in front of the house and paused to look up, she had found herself quite stupidly ducking down, out of sight.

His dark lean face had looked hauntingly beautiful—not something that was open to debate, just a fact—and as she'd looked at it the inevitable tummy quiver had been there. But within normal levels. Because she was no longer a smitten eighteen-year-old and they had something much more precious than sex. They had something that lasted and she was not going to blow it.

Or make a fool of herself.

'You *sure* you are all right?' he asked.

'Fine.'

And she was, she decided, cutting herself some slack. In eighteen months she had simply forgotten the sheer scale of his physical presence—but on purely aesthetic grounds alone he deserved a tummy-quiver and a dry mouth.

The idea of not having Joaquin in her life was something she was not willing to contemplate.

She didn't want things to change.

Her small chin firmed; it didn't have to. She took a deep, sustaining breath and her nostrils flared—not to smell the damp winter air that had entered the hallway, but the crisp, masculine scent that clung to his tall, lean person.

She paused to allow her heartbeat to return to normal and the skittering tingle in her belly to vanish, the tendrils of heat under her skin to cool. None of these things happened, but she stubbornly clung to the belief that they would.

'Are you ready?'

She was ready, but his impatience triggered a belligerent defiance in her—because his impatience belonged to a man for whom people were never late. It was the impatience that came with having people arrive early—she was betting he didn't notice—and the impatience that came when people were always eager to please.

She really hoped that when he did marry it would be to someone who would not encourage these traits, though it probably wouldn't be. He'd marry someone who told him he was perfect; that was the way of the world. Oh, she knew he'd said he would never marry, and with his parents as an example she understood where he was coming from, but she was sure that one day he'd meet someone who would shake his certainty. Someone he would walk through fire to be with.

She repressed a little sigh and lifted her chin. Before

the inevitable perfect, pouting wife turned up he was still her best friend.

'Actually, no,' she lied, embracing the illusion of control as she slanted a sweet smile up at his startled face.

She watched as his initial shock slid into a semi-amused dark, appreciative glitter that said he knew she might be and probably was winding him up. They'd always verbally fenced, and until she'd felt it again she hadn't realised how much she had missed the buzz that was now in her blood.

At the foot of the stairs she paused and swung back, very aware of the eyes that were following her. Her bouncing curls followed her impetuous action before falling across one narrow shoulder.

'I am grateful,' she blurted suddenly.

His brows lifted and a lazy half-smile tugged one corner of his mouth into a fascinating smile. 'It doesn't show.'

'Allow for the fact I've just put everything in the wrong recycling boxes.'

His brow arched. 'Deliberately?'

She pushed out a scornful snort. 'Don't tell me you'd know a recycling box if it bit you on your...'

Her eyes dropped and she felt the scorch of heat on her cheeks before she fixed him with a glower, to show she had not been thinking about his excellent behind.

'Consider this a learning experience,' she told him. 'Imagine that not everyone has people arriving early with smiles fixed on their faces, saying what they want to hear...it will make you a better person, Joaquin. Seriously, though, this is a nice thing for you to do. You are really helping me out of a bind.'

'I feel sure you would have worked something out.'

'Yes,' she agreed. 'I would have. But travelling with you beats hitching.' The dimple in her right cheek deepened.

* * *

Before he could ask if she was actually serious about the idea of hitching—he'd put nothing past her—she had whisked away, taking the stairs three at a time.

She hadn't lost weight—she'd always been slim and she still was—but the curves of her body seemed more defined than he remembered. She was, he decided, searching for the right word and finding it, *sleeker*.

She made him think of a sleek cat, all supple curves and claws. The rear view of her bottom was pretty spectacular too, he observed objectively.

'Go through!' she yelled over her shoulder.

After a moment, he did. The options were limited. The only open door was at the end of the narrow tiled corridor, all the other doors along the way were closed, complete with locks.

He had walked the length of the kitchen he'd found himself in when she reappeared, breathless, fighting her way into a boxy quilted jacket. She was showing a different view of the jeans, and also a tiny sliver of smooth belly as she got her arm stuck half in and half out of the sleeve as it tangled with the oversized blouse.

'Let me,' he snapped out, annoyed at the effort it took to raise his eyes from that satiny sliver of bare flesh.

Her eyes lifted as she shook her head to dislodge the curls, revealing her green eyes, pale aquamarine. 'I can manage.'

He arched a brow and shrugged.

Clemmie always had been incredibly stubborn—to an irritating degree. And that much at least had clearly not changed. His wide brow furrowed as he tried to pin down what the elusive change was.

Nothing as obvious as her skin, which was still translucently pale. Her stubborn little chin was still stubborn, and her mouth was still too wide for her small heart-shaped face. The green eyes, their irises rimmed by black that defined the colour, were still slightly slanted.

The awkward silence stretched.

'Good-sized kitchen.'

His attempt to say something nice about the room made the dimple in her right cheek appear.

'It doesn't seem that way when all ten of us are trying to cook a meal.'

His brows hit his hairline. *'Ten!'*

'More when you include girlfriends and boyfriends,' she said, openly amused by his shock. 'Think of it as a free lesson in how the other half live.'

Her amusement vanished when his dark eyes swivelled her way.

'Including yours?'

'Including my what?' she said, feigning ignorance.

'Boyfriend.'

'Oh…' She had frequently teased him about his well-documented love life, which he insisted was half fiction—that left an awful lot of non-fiction—but he had never once previously asked her if she was dating. It had been one of their unspoken no-go areas—not that she had realised it until now, as he ignored the *Keep Out* signs.

For a brief moment she was tempted to invent a boyfriend, to make her life sound more interesting than it was, or more complicated. The thought brought a stab of shame. She was not her mum, who thought a woman needed a man—a mindset that had always struck Clemmie as weird, because her mum was a competent and together woman, who could turn her hand to anything. She had been a brilliant single parent and, thanks to her elegant French grandmother, could make a cheap outfit look designer just because of the casual confidence she wore it with. She ought to be the last woman to feel the sort of self-doubt she did after a love affair ended badly.

Clemmie could not imagine ever putting herself in that position...laying herself open to that sort of hurt.

'Oh, I'm not planning on settling down for a long time yet.'

Which told him absolutely nothing and instantly made him curious.

'But in the meantime you are enjoying yourself?' he asked, then stopped, aware that he was starting to sound unhealthily interested in her sex life. 'This place suits you?' he added, changing the subject.

'You mean I look at home against a backdrop of peeling wallpaper and flaking paint?'

He laughed, an attractive sound—but then everything about him was attractive. She searched his face, looking for some flaw, and found that he looked tired—well, you would if you spent your days making millions and your nights falling out of nightclubs. Not that she had ever seen photographic evidence of the falling.

The same could not be said of all his companions, she thought sourly.

She had never seen him the worse for drink—not even on her eighteenth birthday. He'd been glazed, she decided, thinking about the smoky hot look in his eyes before he had removed her hands from around his neck.

'It was a question, not a statement. I *meant* do you like sharing? You wouldn't prefer a place of your own?'

Clemmie laughed.

Looking bemused by her reaction, he pressed, 'You don't mind sharing?'

Rumour had it that some women did not mind sharing Joaquin… Clemmie gave her head a tiny shake, to banish the lurid images that rode the coat-tails of that thought.

'It's not about preference. With London rents and my salary I don't really have an option,' she responded, her heated cheeks the only clue to her mental gymnastics. 'And there is always company. You're never alone.'

'That doesn't mean you can't be lonely.'

The idea of Clemmie being lonely in this place, with its peeling paint and, having noticed the tangle of exposed wires along the ceiling, what he suspected were botched electrics, brought a rush of furious anger quite out of proportion with the circumstances.

Oblivious to the anger he was experiencing, Clemmie grinned, treating the comment as a joke 'Earplugs are a must, but when I need some "me time" there is a park within walking distance.'

'You could always come and work for me, you know. There is always a place for someone smart who can think outside the box. You are capable of so much more…'

He realised it was way past the moment when he should have shut his mouth and stopped speaking. Clemmie never had disproved the 'redheads and temper' theory. Anger swelled over her like a dark cloud.

'I am not a charity case. I happen to love my job, and if money mattered to me I wouldn't have gone into it to begin with.'

Actually, she had more fallen into it than chosen it, after a holiday job before she started uni had gone so well that she had been offered a full-time post.

'I know you consider I'm a failure, and you can't understand someone who doesn't care about money and *things*. I didn't have a five-year plan, and as for fulfilling my potential—what makes you think this isn't my potential?'

The horror of what she had just said hit her with the force of a sledgehammer.

His expression was thoughtful as he looked at her, which made Clemmie think she had just exposed her soul, or at least her inadequacies, to him.

'When did I say any of those things?' he asked eventually, not reacting with the anger she had anticipated to her outburst.

She gave a guilty little grimace. 'Never,' she admitted gruffly.

'I never had a five-year plan either—that would be too limiting. Plans equate with tunnel vision; they blind you to the opportunities that fall your way and they stifle ingenuity. That's not to say I would opt for chaos, but routine and consistency are the enemy of innovation.'

'Well, no one would ever accuse you of being consistent. You change the rules depending on your mood.'

'And there is the secret of my success.' He elevated a satirical brow. 'Are you ready *now*? If it helps, you have totally put me in my place.' He executed an elegant mock bow. 'I am humble.'

She gave a snort of amused disbelief. 'Sure you are.'

Some of the tension in the air between them seemed to have dissolved, and she felt more comfortable. The tingly stuff was still there, but in the background.

'Yes, and I am a supermodel,' she retorted, adopting a catwalk pose and pouting.

His smile faded. Her action had lengthened the sliver of flesh to a section of creamy perfection, and lifted her small breasts under their layers in a way that could make a man who was not him think about peeling them away to reveal what was underneath.

Sleek.

From the ether the word came into his head again as he struggled to straitjacket the hormonal surge of his imagination.

He said the most lust-dampening thing he could think of.

'You do know that your fridge is growing things that might be a jungle by the time you get back?'

'It's a salad tray—it's meant to be green,' she retorted. 'And what were you doing in our fridge anyhow?'

'I was looking for some water.'

'We don't do designer water—but we do have a tap.'

'I'll pass.'

He stood waiting impatiently for her to join him, carrying the extra bag she had apparently forgotten.

This time they got fifty feet down the road before she stopped.

'Did I lock the door...? I'll have to check.'

By the time she got to the car—it hadn't been hard to locate the only long, low, luxury car on the block—Joaquin was already loading her bags into the boot.

Clemmie threw her handbag on the back seat and straightened up, one hand still on the passenger door handle of the soft-topped car.

'I had locked it. I should text Mum and tell her when we'll be arriving. She didn't have a clue you were coming, you know.'

He dismissed the criticism with a quick sideways glance and a shake of his head. 'My presence need not impact your mother's break. I am quite capable of looking after myself.'

'So you'll be having beans on toast next door while we enjoy something delicious Mum knocked up? Are you angling for an invite, Joaquin? Actually,' she continued, not giving him an opportunity to respond, 'I wouldn't mind you being there on Saturday. That is the big reveal of Mum's new boyfriend and I have to be on my best be-haviour. She thinks he's a saint.'

'And if he is will you mind that?'

Her brows drew into a frowning line over the bridge of her small, neat nose. 'Why would I mind? I don't want him to be another loser.'

'Well, you and your mum have always been a team.'

'I'm not jealous, if that's what you are suggesting, I'm just…'

'Own it—you don't like sharing.'

'I hate seeing my mum hurt.'

'She hasn't allowed experience to make her bitter. She is a warm, open woman who—'

'Unlike me, you mean.'

He swore under his breath. 'What is it with you today, Clemmie? You are so touchy.'

'It's not me. It's you and your…'

Her voice trailed away. The truth was that although she had always been aware of the male aura he projected, she had never been so skin-peelingly focussed on it, and the anticipation of how it was going to feel in the enclosed space of the interior of the car did not improve her mood.

She inhaled and pinned on a forced smile. 'Sorry. It's been a long day. I do want Mum to be happy, but I hate her being unhappy. I just wish she wouldn't do it to herself.'

'I know, Clemmie, but you can't expect her to be celibate.'

Some of us manage quite well.

Clemmie shook her head. 'I know that, but why would anyone put themselves out there like that? Risk having their heart stomped on? You know, sometimes I understand totally why people go for anonymous sex. It doesn't have the power to hurt.'

'I agree. But though it's great in the short term, it can get a bit bland and samey. It can leave you with a hunger for something just out of reach.'

She stared as he slid into the driver's seat.

After a pause he murmured, 'Take it from someone who knows.'

Things had only just got back to normal and he was talking about sex... How did that happen?

She shifted uneasily in her seat and turned her head sharply, as if the cars they were passing were fascinating, after a moment redirecting the conversation into safer channels.

'So why *are* you here? Shouldn't you be in Spain, for the traditional Perez anniversary celebrations?'

'I should.'

She glanced curiously at his profile, taking in the tautness of his jaw. 'Have you fallen out?'

'I have never fallen in.'

She grunted, well able to understand this. 'Your mum is a bit of a cow...' Her eyes widened. 'I said that out loud, didn't I? Sorry.'

'No apologies necessary for speaking the truth. She is.'

'They still think you are their route to Perez immortality?'

'I am not interested in immortality.' His eyes briefly flickered her way. 'The name ends with me.'

'You might change your mind when you meet—'

'Not you too!' he exploded in irritation. 'I will never change my mind. Marriage and happy-for-ever-after is not on my five-year plan,' he mocked.

'Except you don't have one. All right, all right!' she tacked on quickly, when his expression slid from irritated to thunderous. Marriage was not a subject he was capable of joking about. 'I think—'

Before she could complete her placatory sentence the tickle in her nose exploded into a full-blown sneeze that was quickly followed by another. One hand pressed to her face, she reached into her bag for a tissue. The contents were in her lap, minus any tissues, when she heard the exasperated click of Joaquin's tongue.

'The glovebox.'

She nodded and reached forward. The tissues fell out, along with a small leather box. The gold tooled letters in the aged leather made her brows lift.

His eyes swivelled sideways, and before he could tell her to leave it alone she had opened the box and was viewing the ring that lay inside the cushioned velvet.

Was this why he had overreacted? she wondered. He was already secretly engaged? Or on the point of becoming engaged? Did he not want the world, including her, to know before he popped the question?

'I wouldn't have told anyone. I *won't* tell anyone,' she mumbled, putting the pain in her chest down to the fact that he hadn't trusted her with his secret. In fact, he had lied.

'Tell anyone what?'

'That you are engaged—or about to be.'

'Did you not hear a word I have been saying? I am not getting engaged. Will you put the damned thing back?' he growled.

'All right...all right,' she returned, examining the ring, which she had slid onto her finger. 'She must have very slim fingers,' she said, hating the unknown woman.

He sighed, barely clinging to his temper. 'I am not getting engaged.'

'I'm not going to blab.'

'Take it off, Clemmie.'

There was a small pause, interrupted only by her frantic huffing. 'I'm trying to... Butter... Have you got any butter?'

'Butter?'

'To grease my finger. Or ice.'

'For God's sake!' he ground out. 'Just leave it. I'll—'

Joaquin never got to finish his sentence.

His life didn't flash before his eyes, but time did seem to go into slow motion. Conversely, his thought processes seemed to speed up, evaluating his options with a cool logic devoid of emotion as the lorry that had careered across the central reservation up ahead maintained its head-on collision course with them and picked up speed.

There was not going to be any last-minute reprieve unless he effected it.

He registered a squeak from the passenger seat. No scream—just a quick, breathy, 'I'm fine.'

Was that in response to a question he didn't recall voicing? There was no time to speculate, just sift through the alternatives.

They were limited.

Do nothing. Drive into the steady stream of vehicles

on the opposite side of the road. Or hope there was a soft landing beyond the hedge that skirted the embankment.

It turned out there was a ditch.

The car lay at a forty-five-degree angle, its back wheels spinning, the sound loud above the drumming in his ears. He'd turned to Clemmie, with a grin that was fifty percent adrenaline and fifty percent relief on his face, when there was a deafening thunder as the lorry crashed about fifty yards north of them.

He didn't look to see where. He could see Clemmie's face and she wasn't grinning back. She was unconscious, her blood-streaked face ashen.

A hundred lessons in what to do when dealing with a casualty slid through his head. They were instantly discarded. This was not a casualty—this was Clemmie. He struggled to push the emotion away and deal with the facts.

Spinal injuries—do not move. Maintain airway. Recovery position.

Which came first?

And then priority didn't matter, as his nostrils flared at the acrid smell of fuel. An audible hiss added urgency, and then he saw the first lick of flame.

'Leave it, mate! Save yourself! It's going explode!' yelled a distant voice above the roar. 'She's probably gone anyway.'

She's alive, he said inside his head, because he didn't have time to waste in voicing his fury.

Leave her...?

That was not an option—less of an option than a world without Clemmie in it.

He closed off the line of thought. It was an action now and think later scenario, and he just had to hope and pray, as he gave up on opening the door and dragged Clemmie's limp body through the smashed window, that he was not doing any damage to her.

As he pushed his way through the hedge, away from the car and onto the road, he saw a crowd had gathered around a figure sitting hunched on the road, near where the lorry had hit a tree.

Someone was yelling something that Joaquin couldn't hear, but whatever it was had spurred the small group into action. Supporting the man between them, two members of the group began to move away.

Joaquin only noted this with the five percent of his brain that wasn't focused on the pale, blood-streaked face of the woman he carried. Everything in his chest had contracted into an icy fist, but he pushed through the fear, knowing that this was not the time for emotion.

Her face was illuminated as the lorry went up in flames, lifting off the ground in an explosion that deafened him. The scene now looked like a war zone, but Joaquin just carried on running as there was a second explosion—presumably his car.

'You can put her down, mate. We have it now.'

Joaquin carried on running, initially not registering the words or the presence of the two uniformed figures who were jogging along on either side of him.

Then, as consciousness of the hand on his shoulder registered, he slowed.

'I can't hear...' he said, feeling as though he was speaking into an echo chamber.

'It'll pass.'

The paramedic nodded to the stretcher that had appeared beside them and Joaquin released Clemmie to the care of the professionals. He stood there feeling helpless, and more terrified than he had ever felt in his life.

'Let's get a line in...her SATS are good.'

They allowed him to go in the air ambulance with her, where he sat back, feeling comforted by the cool efficiency and thumbs-up signals of the emergency staff.

Clemmie felt herself rising through layer upon and layer of clinging grey cotton wool. She reached the surface and the noise hit her. She knew that something had happened—something bad that she didn't really want to remember. The pain was something to focus on, not remembering. And then she saw Joaquin and it all came back.

He was getting married! And he didn't trust her—he had lied.

She groaned.

'Clemmie, it's okay. You're going to be fine.' He turned away. 'She's awake, she's in pain—give her something.'

Clemmie closed her eyes—they felt too heavy to keep open. She felt a sudden rush, and the pain she had been clinging to receded.

She forced her eyes open again, unsure how long they'd been closed.

'It's stuck, Joaquin. I'm so sorry. They might have to amputate... No, I'm joking.' She really didn't feel like joking. 'Don't let them take my finger.'

'She's passed out!' Joaquin yelled accusingly as he felt panic ripping through him.

'Her SATS are fine—don't worry.'

'Don't worry' in these circumstances had to be the most insane thing he had ever heard.

The flight might have lasted five minutes or five hours. It had been surreal. And the sensation continued now, as they entered the hospital. He kept up with the trolley until suddenly double doors opened and then closed in his face. Clemmie was whisked away into the white corridor distance.

'Sir, you need to be checked out. The burns...'

Joaquin shrugged dismissively. He didn't need to be a medical expert to diagnose that the pinkness of his skin under the sooty grime was superficial.

'I'm fine,' he responded, ignoring their frustration as he channelled his inner 'billionaire in charge' persona. It was a relief to step away from the unaccustomed feeling of helplessness, or at least to smother it.

He repeated his demand to see Clemmie, to be told what was going on, until people stopped looking sympathetic and nervously directed him to sit in the waiting area until they got someone more senior to speak to him.

Fighting the clutch of dread in the pit of his belly, feeling by turns furious and terrified, Joaquin was oblivious to the attention his physical presence, along with the cuts and grazes, the blackened face and singed clothes, was attracting. Even more attention came his way when the large TV screen on the wall playing silently was suddenly lit up with images of a tall man backlit by fire carrying a red-head. A red circle appeared on the screen, to highlight the sparkle of a ring on the unconscious figure's finger.

It began to play again, on a loop, as the newsreader at the top of the screen spoke and the commentary scrolled across the screen, putting words to the action that he assumed had been recorded on someone's phone.

The third replay filtered into his consciousness.

He swore under his breath. Just what he needed. He was now a billionaire hero who was engaged. To prove the point there was now an enlarged picture of the ring on Clemmie's finger.

He was suddenly conscious of several phones being turned his way, recording images that would no doubt be added to the rubbish already out there.

His jaw set, Joaquin got to his feet as a man appeared, his sleeves rolled up to the elbow and his tie tucked into his shirt. At last—someone with the authority to make a damned decision.

CHAPTER THREE

TEN MINUTES LATER Joaquin walked into a room with the medic, who was explaining that his fiancée was asleep.

On the point of correcting him, Joaquin paused. It seemed worth playing the fiancée card…the risk that came with denying it might restrict the access he had finally been granted.

Would he live to regret his split-second decision?

That was not a question he asked himself.

'Your fiancée has sustained some bruises and grazes, and a head injury, but other than that she is fine.'

Joaquin glossed over the fiancée reference once more—that was a correction for the future. His focus was the fact that Clemmie did not look fine to him at all.

He voiced his opinion. And then it was one of those occasions when his identity had gone before him. Because moments later—or at least it felt that way—the suits arrived.

He quickly separated the medics from the managers and addressed his questions to the medics, making it clear that he did not wish to patronised.

The replies he received were soothing, but it didn't change the sick feeling of anxiety in the pit of his belly that he couldn't even pretend was not fear. Not that this inner fear showed on his face; he had perfected his mask a long time ago and few people could see beyond it.

Clemmie could—but then he didn't have to disguise things around her. She was a rare someone who would never exploit a weakness.

He controlled his impatience and listened to the doctor who had brought him here explaining the situation. Irritatingly, he was clearly of the mindset that favoured never using one word when ten would do and throwing in a few technical terms to baffle his audience.

But when he took away the word salad it seemed to Joaquin that the main concern was Clemmie's head injury. His stomach contracted viciously as his dark, silvered glance slid to the line of neat stitches on Clemmie's brow, surrounded by a darkened swelling that was half hidden by her red hair. Someone had made a passing attempt to wash out the blood.

'The X-rays and scans are clear,' the medic reiterated. 'And, as I said, other than some cuts and bruises—'

'Then why isn't she awake?'

'Head injuries are unpredictable, and when she does wake she might be totally fine.'

Joaquin heard the *'might'*.

'And if she's not totally fine?' His expression gave no clue to the fact that he had to force the question out—that this was a question he did not even want to think, let alone voice.

She had been in his car; he had been driving. Anything that happened would be his responsibility.

'Head injuries are unpredictable,' the doctor reiterated, lifting his hand as if to clasp the younger man on the arm and then changing his mind. He didn't have to be psychic to know he was dealing with a man who wanted facts, not empathy. 'After a concussion there can be some…confusion, but we are not anticipating any permanent cognitive impairment in your fiancée's case.'

Again with the word 'fiancée'.

What sort of world was it when you needed a ring to show you cared? He'd always cared about Clemmie and always would.

He looked at her face and felt emotion swell in his throat. He would have given everything he had in the world to see her open her eyes and grumpily tell him to stop making a fuss.

He could make more money.

There was only one Clemmie.

The last thing that Clemmie remembered thinking was that she didn't really want to die. Not yet, not here, not now.

She must have said the words out loud, because a reply floated into her head.

'You're not dying today.'

The corners of her lips tugged into a half-smile at the memory—or was it happening now?—and then faded.

She was alive, but what if Joaquin wasn't?

Had she dreamt Joaquin was there?

He was in New York.

Was this New York?

She tried to open her eyes, but her eyelids felt heavy. Finally they budged a little for her, and she looked at her hands, half expecting to see them clutching the car's leather armrest in a white-knuckled death grip.

Instead, she found that her hands were resting on her chest. She flexed her fingers. Her fingernails were broken and caked with blood. Then she saw the ring, her eyes widening when it caught the light.

'How…?'

The croak brought the attention of the occupants of the room to her bedside.

There were just two people—a young woman in white scrubs and…

As she identified the second figure some of the fear clenching in her belly let go.

He was alive!

Her head was spinning, but also aching.

Was any of this real?

Had there even been a car crash?

Now she wasn't sure. Her memory of the events felt like a dream…already fading, vanishing like smoke.

'Is this New York?'

'No, we were in my car.'

'Car? Why am I in New York in a car with you? God, do I look as bad as you?' Her eyes closed again. A moment later they opened, and she blurted with feeling, 'You look awful!'

'You are not in New York. This is Dorset.'.

He watched as she batted her hand at the nurse, who attempted to shine a torch in her eyes.

'I still don't know why you are here, Joaquin.'

'You rang and I came.'

'Did I? I don't remember that.'

'What do you remember?'

'All in good time—no need to rush things.' The medic, who had presumably been summoned by the nurse, walked across to his patient in the bed. 'I'm glad to see you are back with us. There might be a few gaps in your memory.'

He half turned to include Joaquin in the conversation as he continued, 'Your fiancée needs rest.'

Fiancée? There were three people in the car? Joaquin was engaged?

Emotion thickened in her throat, but the tears pricking her eyes were, she told herself, nothing to do with Joaquin's marital plans and everything to do with her weakened state.

They said she'd been in some sort of accident. Surely she was allowed to cry!

'Is she all right?' Clemmie asked.

'Is who all right?' asked the nurse.

Clemmie's heavy-lidded gaze shifted groggily from the nurse to Joaquin. 'Your fiancée?' She ran her tongue across the dry outline of her lips and told herself she was happy for him. 'Congratulations.' Clemmie closed her eyes. 'I'm a bit tired.'

'Of course you are. Do you have any pain?' the nurse asked, adjusted the IV dripping into her arm before smoothing the pristine white sheet beneath it. 'Such a beautiful ring...'

The comment tickled a hazy memory in Clemmie's head, but it remained frustratingly out of reach. There had been a ring—but she didn't wear rings. Her brow furrowed and she opened one eye, squinting at her hand. A moment later both eyes flew wide as she held up her hand and began to struggle to raise herself.

'That's not mine!' she cried as she collapsed back on the pillows in an untidy heap. She turned her glance of appeal to Joaquin, hoping for him to provide some sort of answer, but saw the doctor was speaking to him in a low monotone.

Joaquin had been listening to the doctor voicing soothing medical platitudes, with an expression of interest on his face, while most of his attention was focused on Clemmie's pale face. The pallor was now alleviated by twin bright red spots on her cheeks.

If he hadn't been so focused on her injuries he might have anticipated this situation, but he hadn't. Going along with the assumption they were engaged had seemed harmless enough, but less so now. There had been some vague idea in his head of the ring on her finger scenario being a story they would both laugh about on some later date over a glass of wine.

There was no laughter in her face now. Just confusion and, yes, alarm. Her response to the idea of being engaged to him appeared to be a combination of panic and horror.

Well, he always had been able to rely on Clemmie to puncture his ego, he reflected. But he was not smiling at the thought because she looked so anxious that he wanted to hug her.

'Joaquin...?' she said, as if she was registering his presence all over again. 'How are you here? Why are you here? You are in New York.'

'I came back.'

'You might have told me you were coming back. I would have booked a day or two off work.'

'There was car crash...we were in my car.'

'How was I in your car?' she croaked, her hoarse voice rising in panic. She shifted restlessly in the narrow bed and clutched her head with her hand. 'I'm in hospital... Oh, God, I can't be in this place.'

He moved towards the bed. 'Relax, Clemmie, there was an accident.'

'This isn't mine.' She shook her head and stared at the ring on her finger.

'It was my grandmother's. Don't you remember?'

She shook her head. 'No, you are in New York.'

'Well, he'll just have to propose again, won't he, darling?'

Ruth Leith stepped into the room.

'Mum?' Clemmie felt tears press at the back of her eyes. She sniffed. 'I want to go home. And Joaquin *didn't* propose to me. He is never going to get married; he promised me he wouldn't get married. Married people hate each other.'

Her mother swept across the room. 'Oh, your poor little face,' she said selecting an unbruised spot to kiss. There were tears in her eyes as she turned her gaze to Joaquin. 'You saved my baby. How can I ever thank you? When I saw the news report, I thought... Then the news reader said it was a miracle there were no fatalities.'

Struggling to follow her mother's emotional outpouring, Clemmie moved her gaze to Joaquin, who stood there looking uncomfortable.

'You saved me? Was I stuck up a tree?'

'You were coming home with Joaquin. There was a crash,' her mother said, enunciating the words slowly. She got to her feet and turned to the doctor. 'She seems very confused, Doctor,' she added in a worried aside.

Resting one hand on the wall above her head, Joaquin bent over her. 'Not a tree this time. We were in a car crash.'

Clemmie pushed into her memory, the struggle to recall anything feeling as if she was fighting her way through a cotton wool fog.

'You said that you remember...?'

'No, I don't think so, Joaquin. I'd know if I was in a crash.'

Over his shoulder, Joaquin threw a look at the medic that prompted the man to join them.

'Things sound a bit echoey to me...' said Clemmie.

'Same here, but I'm told it's only temporary. There was a loud bang.'

She looked at him blankly. 'After the crash...? Are you okay?' Then, as if seeming to notice for the first time, she added in a concerned voice. 'Is that why you look so terrible? You should be in hospital.' The comment seemed to wake her up to her surroundings once more. 'Mum, I can't stay here. I want to go home.'

Watching the interchange, Joaquin drew the doctor a little way apart.

'She knew what had happened when we were in the helicopter and when she woke up, but now she seems the be getting more confused.'

'It's not unusual for someone to blank out the trauma. I wouldn't read too much into this.'

'All this doesn't help.' His gesture took in the room. 'Clemmie is not good with hospitals.'

'Not many people like hospitals.'

Joaquin reacted to this patronising, pat-on-the-head tone with a forceful, 'Clemmie is not "many people".'

A flustered expression briefly slipped through the man's professional mask. 'Of course. Your fiancée is—'

His eyes flickered across to the bed, where Clemmie had drifted off to sleep holding her mother's hand.

'I have known Clemmie for twenty years,' said Joaquin, cutting across the man, his protective instincts in full flow and his impatience stamped on his lean features as he relayed her history in a tone devoid of the emotion the memory always kicked up in him.

'Shortly before we first met she lost her twin sister to cancer. She had spent weeks visiting her sister in hospital every day, watching her get sicker. I think the fact that she had been told by the well-meaning idiot doctor caring for her sister that her twin would get better added another layer to her grief when her twin died.'

He had learnt the full story only after Clemmie had reacted with tearful fury to the mocking comment he had made about a stuffed toy he had seen sticking out of her rucksack, not knowing the special meaning it held.

It had belonged to her twin.

'I think she is allowed to dislike hospitals,' he finished quietly.

'Of course, and I will make staff aware of her history.' The doctor hesitated, before saying formally. 'If you would like a second opinion…?'

'I would like a *first* opinion,' Joaquin cut back grimly. 'What is your diagnosis?'

'It's early days…' the man began, but his voice trailed away when he saw Joaquin's expression. 'You might be aware that confusion is not unusual after a head injury— even temporary amnesia?'

'You are saying she has amnesia…on what basis?'

Not used to people demanding facts like this, the man blinked. 'I am suggesting it is a *possibility*,' he continued carefully. 'One you should be aware of. Tomorrow, when she has rested, we will be able to—'

'I am assuming there are experts in this field?'

'Of course, but we—'

'I will arrange a second opinion. Could you make yourself available to consult tomorrow morning?'

The doctor blinked, his faintly patronising air evaporating. Feeling very much less in charge, he found himself agreeing without demur to the arrangements being made.

'Try not to worry. We'll give her something to help her sleep, and in the morning the world will seem a much less confusing place.'

* * *

After Joaquin had spoken to Ruth, arranged transport for her home, as she was clearly too upset to drive, and agreed to her suggestion that he spend the night at the manor, he contacted his PA, who had clearly heard the news.

'Congratulations! Is Clemmie going to be okay?'

Even though they had only ever spoken on the phone, his PA and Clemmie were on first name terms.

'We are not engaged.' He saw no reason to go into details.

'Oh,' his PA said, sounding disappointed. Then, more professionally, 'Do you want me to put out a press release to that effect?'

'No.'

Then he listed what he did want her to do, which was to arrange a team of consultants in the relevant specialities to provide second opinions, no later than tomorrow morning.

'And I need a car, and I need a fresh set of clothes here. Now. You can send the rest straight to Maplehurst. Oh, and also I'll need a new laptop. Anything else… I'll send the details with you.'

Leaving the practicalities in her capable hands, he made his way back to Clemmie's room. The light above her bed illuminated her sleeping face, highlighting the bruises, her blood-matted hair lying on the white pillow.

The palette of clashing emotions he felt as he stared down at her was as complex and confused as the multi-coloured bruise on her cheek.

It could have been worse, he told himself, not allowing himself to think of how much worse.

He didn't make it to the manor until three a.m., having fallen asleep in the chair beside Clemmie's bed. He fell on to the bed fully clothed and got a couple of hours' sleep.

It would have been too much to say he awoke refreshed, but a shower and a shave did make him feel slightly more like part of the human race.

He was anxious to be gone. With luck, Clemmie would have got her memory back. If not he would fill in the blanks. Hopefully she would see the funny side of it. Most women wouldn't—but then Clemmie was not most women.

He drank his coffee while choosing a clean set of clothes from the selection that had arrived before him. He hadn't expected Ruth to be ready, and she wasn't, but she had packed some of the clothes Clemmie kept at the gatehouse and they were in the hallway.

He explained to Ruth that a car and a driver for her use for as long as she needed would be arriving within the hour and then set off for the hospital.

His plan to get to Clemmie was thrown off course from the outset. When he arrived, the team of consultants ready to give second opinions were already on the job. He was met as he entered the building and directed to the medical director's office, where the consultant from the previous day had been joined by the three experts his PA had managed to get on site.

As he took a seat they explained that the results of the tests were in and they had all spent two hours with Clemmie. Apparently there was now a diagnosis.

Joaquin gave his attention to their individual contributions, which appeared to overlap.

There was a consensus.

Clemmie, aside from some bruising, was suffering only from mild concussion and amnesia.

'Temporary?' he asked.

On this there was no consensus—just a lot of options. He found the ambiguity frustrating.

'How can she have amnesia?' he asked, directing his question to the group and not just one individual. 'She knows who I am, and when she first woke up it seemed as though she knew she had been in an accident. Are you saying that now she doesn't? How is that possible?'

One of the experts responded. 'The brain, Mr Perez, has a way of protecting itself from painful trauma—physical and emotional—that it is not ready to deal with. Retrograde amnesia is often a protective mechanism. It would appear from our examination that she has no memory of the last six weeks.'

'What *does* she remember?'

'Her last clear memory is apparently from over a month ago, when she was helping clear away a Christmas display at the library where she works.'

Joaquin nodded.

'But...' The speaker hesitated, then, 'She has no memory of being engaged to you.'

'Well, that is not surprising. We are not engaged.'

A wave of collective shock went around the room.

Joaquin didn't notice; he was suffering from guilt. He had contributed to Clemmie's confusion and possibly even to her memory loss by allowing the mistake to stand.

The medics exchanged glances but if they were tempted to ask for further details they repressed their curiosity.

'It is my intention to clear that up right now,' he added, rising decisively to his feet.

The doctor on his home ground was the first to speak, though the others nodded agreement at his words.

'That might not be the best course of action at this stage.'

Another nodded, before voicing his support. 'There might be some danger at this stage in pushing things.

There is every chance that she will remember the period she has lost.'

'So, I am meant to lie?'

'You are meant to allow her to fill in the gaps in her own time.'

'What if she never fills them in?'

An image floated across his vision of him lifting a veil to reveal Clemmie staring up at him, her green eyes shining.

Weddings were the subject of his nightmares, but on this occasion he found himself not running from the preposterous image but allowing it to linger.

Someone laughed.

'Well, obviously this advice is a very short term. If her memory does not return, we will adapt to that circumstance.'

Joaquin did not ask what form this adaptation might take—he just felt the need to be out of there. He needed to see for himself that Clemmie was okay.

'In the meantime, our initial problem is… We were hoping you would use your influence… Your fiancée… Sorry, Miss Leith has discharged herself.'

'She has *what*?' Joaquin closed his eyes and shook his head before biting out. 'Of *course* she has. She is—'

He compressed his lips and felt sorry for the man who would marry her for real as he raked a frustrated hand through his hair.

'I am assuming you told her that was not advisable?'

'I told her that we would prefer she stayed with us for another twenty-four hours, but actually I had no power to stop her.'

'Well, I have!' Joaquin intoned grimly.

'I am not sure that would be a good idea. As she has

pointed out, all her tests are clear, and she might just as well "lie there staring at the ceiling" at home.'

'I can almost hear her...'

The medic's lips twitched at his tone 'She is a very determined woman.'

'She is mule-stubborn.'

'Her mother, who has just arrived, is also very determined.'

'Perhaps Ruth can make her see sense.'

'I would prefer not to see the patient distressed...and taking into account her hospital phobia...'

The other medics nodded in agreement.

'Of course she's distressed—she doesn't remember.'

And doesn't know there is nothing to remember.

His frustration rose. If he could fill in the blanks things would go back to the way they were before.

'We are simply asking that you do not put pressure on her...do not push.'

Joaquin sighed. 'I don't want to hurt Clemmie. I just want her memory to come back.'

'Excellent! Then perhaps you could speak to her mother? I am afraid she has upset our patient...especially after she insisted that her daughter *must* remember getting engaged.'

Thirty very uncomfortable minutes later, Joaquin stood between the two women who had at least stopped yelling.

'So, this is settled?' he said. 'Clemmie will come home and return for tests on Friday?'

'I've already had tests!' Clemmie pouted.

Give me strength, Joaquin prayed, as he forced a calm smile.

'And you have endured them with stoicism. However...' He flashed a high-voltage smile at her mother. 'As your mother has said, a full MOT will calm our collective nerves.'

Ruth hadn't said any such thing, but she looked complacent.

Clemmie glared at them both and pushed her feet into the furry slippers on the floor as she stood up.

In the midst of his frustration and guilt Joaquin found himself smiling. Five feet two in her fluffy slippers, with her hair its usual spectacular fiery mess and her small chin lifted aggressively, she looked—

The half-smile faded from his face. She looked like the sexiest female he had ever seen in his life: strong, brave and in-your-face furious, but so, so incredibly sexy...

'All right...' Clemmie said slowly, dividing her killer glare between her mother and her...her fiancé?

Even the thought felt wrong—on several levels. The transformation felt as though she had jumped from newborn to teenager in one hour! And, actually, she *had* had a terrible short-lived crush on Joaquin in her teens.

It seemed weird to know they were engaged when she couldn't even remember their first proper kiss, she mused, staring at the sexy curve of his mouth and feeling a quiver low in her belly.

She tried not to acknowledge it—then realised that she didn't have to ignore it now; she was allowed to lust after him.

God, this felt as if she'd started reading a story in the epilogue and had missed all the chapters that led up to it.

Realising she had been staring at his mouth for a long time, she lifted her gaze. 'It really is overkill,' she said.

Seeing that maternal love was about to make Ruth explode into deadly ire, Joaquin intervened. 'You're probably right, but these medics…it's best to humour them. Ruth?' he said, adding a full thousand volts to his smile. 'Am I being a total pain in wanting us to stay at the manor for the next few days?'

'Where else would you go?' she asked, looking offended.

'And I can't wait to meet your Harry. Clemmie has told me all about him.'

'She has?'

Clemmie reached for her bag and watched Joaquin do what he did best and charm her mum. It appalled her, but it was *so* convenient. She was utterly exhausted—too exhausted for a fight. It took everything she had to move from A to B.

The doctors had warned her that fatigue was a normal consequence, post head injury, but this this leaden-limbed, buzzy head feeling was like nothing she had ever experienced before.

It took half an hour to get from the hospital to Maplehurst, and Ruth Leith kept up a steady flow of chatter for the entire journey.

Clemmie, who appeared lost in her own thoughts, didn't say a word, and Joaquin, who produced a polite grunt or nod when required, was also mostly quiet as guilt continued to ride him—hard.

He was not in the habit of second-guessing his decisions, but his choice of following the medics' advice and letting this charade play out did not sit easily with him.

All well and good to wait for her to remember—but when would that be? He could not see his explanation that he had been following doctors' orders by not filling in the blanks cutting much ice with Clemmie. She was going to be as mad as hell and he couldn't blame her.

And what if she never remembered?

By the time they drew up at the gatehouse at the end of the manor's drive, Joaquin had learnt several things from the one-sided conversation. The most frequently mentioned being that short engagements were the best.

Clemmie, who hadn't said a word for the entire journey, seemed to come out of her trance-like state as the car came to a halt.

'We're here.'

'No, don't get out, darling,' her mother said, leaning forward from the back seat to press a kiss to her daughter's cheek. 'Stay in the warm. I'll see you tomorrow.'

Joaquin watched the confusion in Clemmie's eyes slide into realisation before her lashes fell to conceal panic.

'Of course. I'll…see you, Mum.'

Having seen Ruth into the cottage, Joaquin slid back into the car.

'You thought you'd be staying here with your mum, didn't you?' he said.

She turned in her seat and grimaced. 'Sorry. I just don't feel… I wonder why I didn't tell Mum about our engagement?'

He shrugged. 'It wasn't something we discussed.'

'Sorry, this must be hard for you too.'

'There is no need for you to be sorry.'

There was plenty of need for *him* to be sorry. He fought the need to tell her the truth; was that a selfish need to offload his guilt or genuine remorse? asked the cynical voice in his head.

He still didn't know how he'd managed to get himself into this situation.

Yes, you do. You said nothing.

'*The* doctor asked me what the last thing I remember is.'

'And what *is* the last thing you remember?' he asked, even though the doctor had told him.

'Dismantling the Christmas display at work. The pre-schoolers had made some lovely collages in one of the craft sessions we have at the library. I thought that was last week, but Mum has told me it was last month. I'm missing more than a whole month—or big bits of it. I'm scared, Joaquin. What if I never get that time back?'

Glancing at her stricken face, he pulled the car over, its wheels sending up flurries of gravel. He switched on the interior light, which illuminated her pale face and the bruises on her forehead and cheek, and felt a wave of protective warmth that made him want to reach out and drag her into his arms.

She shook her head. 'Sorry. I am not going to fall apart and cry on you. I'm not that sort of person. At least I don't think I am.' She gave a wild little laugh. 'Who knows? I might be. I mean, nothing could be weirder than being engaged to you.'

She looked at the heavy ring on her finger and felt nothing.

'Don't overthink it, Clemmie...don't force it.'

Her eyes lifted. 'Overthink? I can barely think at all.'

Joaquin felt a fresh surge of protectiveness, and extended his hand to push back the curls that had fallen across her brow. 'Do you still have a headache?'

He retracted his hand, his face clenched in a pained grimace when she went rigid.

'Did I hurt you?'

He cursed himself for forgetting the damage that was hidden under curls so abundant that the small area where the hair had been cut away to suture a scalp wound was totally concealed.

She shook her head and laid a hand on his arm, her face filled with excitement, not pain. 'No... No, I remember something!'

He tensed, his expression guarded. The moment he had wanted and also dreaded appeared to be here.

'What do you remember?'

Would she laugh or would she hate him?

Her nose wrinkled as she put the flashes of images and sensations into words, haltingly at first, and then with more confidence, afraid that if she didn't share what she was seeing and feeling the memory might vanish again.

'I was looking out of my bedroom window and I saw someone. I knew it was you, even though you were too far away for me to see your face.' A little smile flickered across her face as she looked at him. 'You move... You have a very distinctive walk. So I must have been expecting you.'

He felt the small fingers on his forearm tighten and swallowed. 'You were.'

She nodded. 'I remember watching as you got closer, and I remember feeling...' She pressed a hand to her chest and her wide, wondering eyes lifted to his face. 'I felt excited and kind of *nervous*...'

But it had been more than that. Her forehead furrowed and her eyes half closed as she tried to articulate the surge of emotions she experienced as she relived the moment.

The scene playing again in her head felt like real time, not a memory.

'Is that it?' he asked. 'Or do you remember anything else?'

'There's more... I know there is,' she said huskily, moistening her lips with the tip of her tongue. It was so frustrating. It was as if an open door had slammed in her face, just after she had opened it. 'But the next part is vivid.'

'What part?'

'I ran down the stairs and opened the door. You were standing there, and my heart was thudding and butterflies were kicking in my stomach.'

'What's the last thing you remember?'

'You smiling and me wanting to kiss you so badly that it was an ache. Did I?'

He shook his head. His body had reacted to this artless confidence with painful arousal and a fresh stab of guilt. If he had been able to find the words to bring this charade to a stop there and then, doctors' warning or not, he would have. He was rarely at a loss for the right words, but he was at that moment. The reason being that his brain was involved in creating a very detailed *what if?* scenario.

What if Clemmie had followed through with the impulse and kissed him?

Would he have kissed her back?

Where would it have stopped if he had explored her mouth and felt her warm body plastered up against him?

The thought shook free the memory that still surfaced regularly, of a very tipsy Clemmie, just eighteen, lying there, linking her arms around his neck and pouting as she demanded a birthday kiss.

He had done the honourable thing and pushed her away. He had seen the hurt in her eyes a little later, when she had been packing up the remains of their picnic. He had walked fully clothed into the lake, hoping an icy swim would relieve his agony. He'd pretended that when he had slipped.

Where was an icy lake when you needed one?

'No,' he said.

A sliver of sympathy flickered into her wide green eyes as she studied his face, the lines etched around his dark eyes and the deep grooves around his mouth. It looked likely that Joaquin was suffering the sort of headache that was drumming into her own temples.

'I wonder why?' she said, her voice vague, her thoughts drifting as she struggled to retain an interest in anything beyond the distracting pain drilling into her skull.

He realised she remained oblivious to the fact that she had taken the genie out of the bottle. The rules had changed. She had taken away the forbidden, leaving the attractively possible in the vacuum.

He couldn't stop the what ifs. It had always felt like an unspoken pact, what was between him and Clemmie, and it had been. It was safe that way... But now she had spoken out, in the mistaken belief that those barriers no longer existed.

He knew himself. He knew that he would never settle for one woman, that sex was nothing more to him than a physical outlet, and he knew—he had *always* known— that Clemmie would never understand.

The idea of hurting her was anathema to him, but there were parts of playing her fiancé he knew he would enjoy.

'I remember looking at your mouth...' Her eyes drifted in that direction as she spoke, lingering there. 'And wanting to kiss you... That's a good start, isn't it?'

His words were strangled in his throat as he looked into her eyes. He was helpless to control the fresh rush of arousal.

Clemmie couldn't imagine why she hadn't kissed him— unless they had fought, or she was the sort of woman who waited for a man to make the first move?

She really hoped she wasn't that sort of woman.

She wouldn't be that sort of woman.

A smile curving her mouth, she reached across, entwining her fingers behind his head as she dragged herself upwards and fitted her mouth to his.

The effort it cost him not to respond to those soft lips tapped into a better self he hadn't even been sure existed. Was this pain the cosmic payback for years of self-indulgence? He asked himself.

Hurt and confusion and embarrassment jostled for supremacy as inside Clemmie as she pulled back, looking at him with big, confused eyes. Presumably they had already shared wild, head-banging sex, but all she remembered was trying to kiss him and getting rejected—twice now.

'What's wrong?' she asked.

She looked so hurt, but he knew she would be more hurt if he followed his baser instincts; this was a lesser hurt.

'You are just out of hospital,' he pointed out, with a lightness he was far from feeling. 'And the general consensus is that you should still be there. I don't think making out in the back seat of a car would be medically approved.'

'It's not the back seat... But I suppose you might be right,' she conceded. 'Are you being noble because I don't remember?'

Noble? He stifled a bitter laugh. 'Memory loss or not, you know me better than that, Clemmie.'

'You did save my life. I watched the video.'

'Did they get my good side?'

She sighed. 'You don't have a bad side. You're a very beautiful man—though I've tried not to think of you that way.' She shook her head. 'I wish I knew what changed between us.'

He was sweating, and as for his control—he could almost see the single frayed thread that was holding it in place.

'I can't intimidate you…that much hasn't changed. If I could you'd still be in hospital.'

'I couldn't stay there.'

'I get that.'

'Have we spoken about having a family? I'd have to have a home birth—you do realise that?'

Out of nowhere, an image of Clemmie holding a baby to her breast flashed into his head, and he had to remind himself that childbirth and babies were not sexy.

Her breasts were, though.

He swore low, under his breath.

She heard and mistook the cause of his frustration. 'I do want to remember!'

'I know, but for God's sake cut yourself some slack,' he cried, wrenching the rear-view mirror around. 'Look!'

She did, and winced. 'I don't look very kissable, do I?'

'You look…' His throat worked as he swallowed. 'You are bruised and hurting. What you need is rest. Tomorrow you have your MOT.'

'You make me sound like an old banger…'

That drew a laugh from him, which faded as his dark glance slid over the lissom curves of her body, awakening in him an ache he could no longer pretend was not constant.

I've already had a load of tests,' she sighed out.

'That was the bargain. Your mum has more faith in the medical establishment than you do. It will make her less anxious.'

CHAPTER FOUR

'TRUE,' SHE ADMITTED at the reminder. 'But it won't make me remember, will it? What if I never remember?'

She couldn't keep the fear out of her voice as she saw a void of utter loneliness opening up in front of her.

The anguish on her face made things twist in his chest, and the unaccustomed feeling of helplessness made him struggle for a response.

'There are a few things in my life I wouldn't mind forgetting...'

'Oh? Like falling out of a nightclub drunk or losing your phone? I'm not talking about that I'm talking about... It's like losing a part of yourself, if that makes any sense.'

'It does—and I'm sorry. It wasn't my intention to make light of your experience, but you will make new memories.'

'Together?' She flushed. 'I mean...'

'I'll do anything I can to help.'

His jaw was taut as he brought the car to a gravel-spitting halt on the forecourt of the manor. In the gloom it glowed, the stone facade honey-gold.

As he switched off the engine the light-activated spotlights burst into life. Beside him he felt Clemmie's sigh.

'It is beautiful,' she said, staring up at the three-storey

building, with its mullioned and transomed windows. The sight of it always affected her on a visceral level.

'You love this place, don't you?' he said.

'I never get tired of this view,' she admitted, unwilling to admit out loud that the connection she felt to her old home made her feel close to her sister. She gave a self-conscious little shrug. 'Especially since your mother spot-lit it.'

'And ruined the dark sky view.'

Her smile was tired, and so far from the usual fearless and confrontational Clemmie that he experienced a heart-clenching moment of protective tenderness.

She had always touched a part of him that no other woman had—none could. Without Clemmie in his life that part of him might have died years ago.

'You're tired.' He reached out his fingertips, touching the bruise on her cheek.

She shivered. 'Post head injury fatigue, apparently.'

Maybe that was why she couldn't stop thinking about putting her head on his shoulder, which was so temptingly close.

They were engaged. It would be the most natural thing in the world to react to the impulse and feel his arms circle her, his fingers in her hair. She'd close her eyes and breathe in the clean male scent of him...

They were engaged.

No matter how many times she thought it, it didn't seem real—and yet at the same time it felt so right.

Frustration bubbled up inside her. How could she *not* know, not remember? Not remember being kissed or...?

Her glance drifted to his mouth...the firm, sensual line of his lips. Why should she feel guilty for staring? It wasn't as if she'd woken up and found herself engaged to a total stranger. She'd woken up and found herself engaged to her best friend.

How had it happened?

When had it happened?

She rubbed her forehead. The ache had started to dig in behind her eyes.

'Shall we go inside?' he asked.

She nodded.

At the doorway Clemmie braced herself; she always felt a tangle of emotions when she walked into her old home, and today the tangles were way more complex than usual.

It was a stupid situation. It hadn't been her home for a long time and it was just stupid sentimentality. So what if generations of her family had lived here? She knew you couldn't really feel a *connection to* a building, bricks and mortar, but it always took a few seconds for logic to re-assert itself.

She remembered the look of surprise on her mum's face when she had asked her how she coped with the fact that she saw this place every day—saw other people living here, in what had once been her home.

Her mum had laughed and said that all she felt was relief, explaining that she'd never felt like lady of the manor material, and that, to be honest, she'd felt a sense of freedom the day she handed over the keys.

It was also a massively inconvenient house, she had added.

Not as inconvenient now as it once had been, of course. The ancient plumbing was gone, and there were no leaks in the roof, but the new interior design was not exactly to Clemmie's taste. To her, it made no sense to buy an ancient building and then try and make it look like a new build.

'Luckily the historical listing and the conservancy people stopped her ripping *everything* out.'

Clemmie blinked; he had tuned into her thoughts so exactly that for a split-second she thought she had voiced her criticisms out loud. She realised he had not lost his uncanny ability to read her mind.

Did he read her mind when they were in bed, too?

The question came from nowhere, and opened a door to a subject she'd been carefully tiptoeing around. She still couldn't get her head around the idea that they were intimate. That he knew her body, that she knew his, that they had lain together in a sweaty, breathless, post-coital tangle of limbs.

The images in her head made the panic she was keeping at bay by sheer force of will threaten to overwhelm her.

'You all right?'

Her eyes skittered away from the concern in his.

'I'm not qualified to give an opinion on interior design, but everything looks...expensive.'

Her choice of words dragged a laugh from him. 'You hate it, don't you? Admit it. Don't worry—I won't be offended. The wallpaper in my bedroom makes me feel that I've woken up in a jungle populated by purple silk zebras. But at least the fabric of the building is intact, and the new refurb might be an improvement.'

'New refurb?'

'Apparently this is all "dreadfully dated" now, but the real reason is the that my father gave his last girlfriend an apartment as a parting gift. This refurb is my mother's way of hitting him where it hurts—his wallet. Oh, the joys of matrimony.'

His cynicism and distaste for marriage seemed intact—

which made her wonder why they were engaged. Was he already regretting it?

His phone buzzed, and after glancing at the screen he grimaced. 'Sorry, I have to take this.'

'No problem.'

By the time he'd finished his call, Clemmie had vanished.

He called her name, but all he got back was an echo. After a short search he eventually found her standing outside a bedroom door on the second floor.

She turned her head, sensing his approach. 'This used to be our room—mine and Chrissie's.'

'I know. It was mine for a while. You must have resented me.'

She shook her head. 'No, not really. I wasn't very happy when I lived here, but in this room we couldn't hear Mum and Dad arguing.' A sad smile tugged a corner of her mouth upwards. 'Once Chrissie took her piggybank down and told them they could have all her money if they stopped yelling.' Her smile faded when she saw his expression. 'Have I already told you that?'

'No.'

'I was not canvassing for the sympathy vote,' she cut back, wincing internally at the thought.

'I never thought you were. Do you want to see inside?'

She shook her head. 'This room holds no ghosts to exorcise for me... Well, not many,' innate honesty made her add.

But she could deal with the past, she thought. It was the present that she was struggling to get her head around.

'A good philosophy,' he agreed as he followed her to one of the windows in the gallery that led to the next wing of the house. It overlooked the garden, and on a clear day gave glimpses through the trees of the village church spire.

Clemmie's breath caught as his muscled thigh touched her own when he sat down on the wide windowsill beside her. She was aware of an internal battle between her instincts: one urging her to push into him, the other to shuffle away. It resulted in a draw. She stayed exactly where she was and hoped the quivering of her own thigh muscles was not obvious.

The internal battle was exhausting. Was this something she had already gone through and moved beyond? Well, she supposed she must have. They were intimate.

The thought of it sent prickles of sensation along her nerve-endings. It just seemed so impossible.

She was living her secret fantasy—she just really wished she could remember.

'It's a store room now, I think,' he said.

'I know. I used to help Mum in the holidays, remember? I also know that your current room is the one above the library, and—'

'Why do you pretend you don't *love* this place?'

She turned her head, the abrupt action sending a section of curls across her face.

'I... I... How did you know?' She had barely acknowledged the truth herself. 'Sorry. I know we must have shared that, and more, but I don't remember.' The utter futility of it all hit her. 'It's just a building...bricks and mortar...or stone and mortar, at least. But it makes me feel close to Chrissie.'

Her pallor was beginning to concern him. 'I should have made you stay in hospital.'

She flashed a smile. 'You can't make me do anything I don't want to...' She paused, her eyes dropping.

'You can have your privacy tonight, Clemmie.'

She nodded, relieved that she hadn't had to explain. 'I know that this must seem odd to you, but to me you are not my fiancé.' She frowned as she tried to pick her way through the minefield of wrong words in her head. Maybe there were no right words.

'Your mum will have made up my room—you take that.'

'Thanks.'

He shrugged, and had the immediate impression that her gratitude had made him tighten the guilt screw another notch. Because all he could think about was being inside her.

'Are you hungry?' he asked.

She shook her head. At this point just putting one foot in front of the other was an effort. 'I think maybe I just need to sleep for a while.'

Even though she said it was unnecessary, he shadowed her as she made her way to his room on the next floor.

He opened the door and looked down at her. 'Maybe you should have stayed with your mum tonight. Shall I call her?'

'No, I'm fine.'

'Can I get you anything?'

She shook her head.

Inside the bedroom there were no clues to the man himself—but then why would there be? He stayed here once a year, maybe. She wandered through to the bathroom and filled a glass with water, then returned to the bedroom and sat on the bed, before kicking off her shoes.

Suddenly she didn't feel tired at all. She lay down and wondered if she should ring her mum.

Sleep came before she had decided.

* * *

Joaquin chose the room a door down from where Clemmie was and went downstairs. An hour or so and several emails later, he made his way back to the top floor and, seeing the light under the door of his bedroom, he knocked.

There was no reply.

He fingered the card in his pocket that had come with her discharge pack. It listed the signs to look out for with concussion. Scanning them, he figured that checking someone was alive trumped the invasion of privacy.

Calling her name, he pushed the door open. The main light and the bedside lamp were on and the curtains were open. He walked across to the bed—his bed—where Clemmie was lying fully clothed, one arm flung above her head, her face turned into the pillow, exposing the bruised side of her face. Her chest rose and fell with slow breaths. Her colour seemed good.

As he looked down at her the surge of fierce emotion he'd experienced before gathered in his chest and he found himself reaching out, the action instinctive. His expression intent, he brushed a strand of her hair from her cheek, freezing as she shifted and murmured in her sleep.

When her breathing evened again he went to the chair set against the wall and took the folded throw that was there. He spread it across her and walked out of the room.

Twice in the night he returned to check on her. Both times she looked fragile and vulnerable, and he felt a total heel for wanting her.

The first time she was sound asleep.

The second time she opened her eyes and looked at him. 'Don't go...please stay.'

He did. Arranging himself beside her, he drew her into his arms and felt her sigh. Even after she had fallen asleep he stayed, stroking her hair. He recognised the irony; he had never stayed the entire night with a woman, and this one he had not even had sex with.

Clemmie was not a woman you just had sex with—she was a woman you made love to. And for the first time in his life Joaquin found himself regretting that he was not a man who made love. He was a man who had sex.

Clemmie awoke confused. She had no idea where she was. And then, as she moved and her bruises made their presence felt, it all came back. Well, not all—and that was the issue.

She sat up in bed and looked down at the cashmere throw that lay across her legs. She genuinely didn't remember how it had got there. Normally this would have bothered her, but compared with all the other things she had forgotten this was a very small thing.

She had dreamt that Joaquin was holding her last night. A dream so real she had half expected to find him there this morning. It had made her feel safe and warm.

How could her mind blank out sex...making love with a man like Joaquin? A man she had been pretending not to lust after most of her adult life—actually all her adult life. She was living her own fantasy and she had forgotten it!

She eased out of the clothes she had slept in and twisted around in front of the mirror to view the bruises that were developing. There was a particularly livid one along one shoulder, but at least that one could be hidden. Not so the one her cheek, which looked terrible.

She rifled through a bag she recognised—presumably packed by her mum—and was glad to find a selection of toiletries and make-up.

The shower eased some of her stiffness, and a judicious

application of concealer on top of her tinted moisturiser improved but didn't hide her facial bruises.

She knelt on the floor and selected linen trousers and a matching jacket that seemed appropriate for a hospital appointment.

Just thinking about it made her stomach quiver with apprehension. She told herself not to be a wimp and texted her mum before making her way downstairs, using the back route that took her through several interconnecting rooms and down one of the many staircases.

This one led directly to the kitchen, where there was a pile of warm croissants on a tray and the smell of coffee in the air. She poured herself a mug from the pot, buttered a croissant and stood eating it as she looked out of the window, envying the grazing sheep in the field who, it seemed to her, had an inner peace that eluded her.

Yes, she decided, rinsing her mug under the tap. *I have definitely lost it. I am envying sheep.*

She walked through several rooms to reach the hall and there was still no sign of Joaquin. She was sliding her arms into her jacket when he appeared, dressed in a pale grey suit, a white shirt and, she assumed as a concession to informality, no tie.

His hair was still wet from the shower and slicked back, dark against the even gold tones of his skin. Any cuts on his face had obviously been superficial, because they were scarcely visible this morning. He exuded a vitality that, considering the fact she felt terrible, was almost an insult.

I look like the morning after the night before without the fun, and he looks like a...a...sex god!

The ease with which *sex god* had sprung to her mind deepened her frown and made her blush—an irritating habit she ought to have long outgrown.

She took comfort from the fact that Joaquin couldn't know why she was blushing, and that it probably just blended into the bruises that the make-up she had applied didn't totally disguise.

Joaquin glanced at her, frowning in a way that she decided suggested he thought she looked terrible too. She took the silent insult on board and glowered.

'I'll take you,' he said, picking up the car keys from the table.

Clemmie shook her head, controlling her irritation with difficulty. 'I don't need you to take me. This is really overkill, you know. I feel perfectly well, and I wish you'd stop watching me as though I'm an unexploded bomb!'

'Someone got out of bed the wrong side this morning.'

Your bed, she thought—and therein lay the issue. She had never allowed herself to imagine sleeping with Joaquin...having sex with him. Because she knew that even if she caught him in a weak moment, it would mean the end of their friendship as she knew it.

And now she had woken to a world where it seemed she *had* slept with him—where they presumably had enjoyed wild and uninhibited sex. It was something she really found hard to imagine herself capable of, and she didn't remember a thing about it.

But that hadn't stopped her imagining last night—when at some point she had jerked herself into wakefulness, afraid of the nightmares she sensed were waiting for her—how nice it would have been to have him hold her. She had even imagined she could smell the scent of the elusive male fragrance that clung to him...

'If Mum isn't free, I'll call a taxi.' Well aware that she was behaving like a bit of brat, and yet unable to stop herself, she slid her eyes from his dark, knowing stare as she mumbled defensively, 'This entire thing is stupid anyway.'

'It was the deal we made. And if you call your mum she'll think we have rowed.'

She fixed him with an irritated, narrow-eyed glare. 'We haven't done *anything*! I mean… I didn't mean that sort of anything.'

'I feel frustrated, too,' he said.

It was true that he enjoyed sex, but this was something else. Last night when he had held her, the tenderness he had felt had been on a cellular level. This morning his body was still humming with a sexual pulse.

'You do?' she said, mollified slightly. And then, 'I won't be admitted to a ward.'

Clemmie didn't like the understanding that flickered in his dark eyes. His understanding made her feel vulnerable and exposed—especially as she didn't understand herself.

'When you get a clean bill of health your mum will back off.'

'What if I don't? What if they find something?'

She could still remember the school doctor, who had been doing routine school medical checks, pulling their mum to one side while she and Chrissie played. The expression on her mum's face…the fear—even though at the time she hadn't really understood what it was—was etched into Clemmie's memory.

'I think that is not very likely.'

'So, you think there is some chance they'll find something?'

A frustrated sigh whistled through his clenched teeth as he prayed for patience.

'Sorry,' she mumbled.

'If there is an issue, we will deal with it.'

The way the *'we'* had come so naturally sent a wave of unease through him.

This isn't real, a dry voice in his head reminded him.

He dropped the car keys into her hand.

Clemmie looked down at them for a moment and then shook her head. 'Actually, it might be better if you drove me.'

'Fine,' he said as she held out the keys. 'Hurts more when the bruises start coming out, doesn't it?'

She nodded, quite happy to encourage his assumption that her mood was totally attributable to her various bruises. Actually, she was more than happy to accept it herself.

'You too...?' she asked brightly. 'Actually, it's not just that. I haven't actually been behind the wheel since I passed my test.'

A look of shock spread across his face. 'You were seventeen! And wasn't the idea to give you independence?'

'I know. I always thought I'd have a little car by now. But it costs a lot to keep a car on the road, and I have been living in London. A car is not a priority...'

He looked at the hand still extended to him and after a moment reached out, but only to close her fingers firmly over the keys.

'If you are feeling up to it, you can drive me.'

'But your car is...'

The car that had appeared like magic to replace the one that had been written off in the crash was, if anything, even larger than the sports models she knew he normally drove. It was some sort of four-wheel drive, with a leather interior you could sink into and a wooden dashboard that looked as if it belonged in a space shuttle.

His shoulders lifted in a negligent shrug. 'It's a smooth ride.'

'I would have thought that one crash in a week would be enough for you.'

'You plan on crashing?'

'No, of course not!' she retorted indignantly.

'I always said you passing first time was a fluke.'

Her mouth opened and her eyes widened in outrage before her indignation melted into a lopsided smile. 'Don't try your pop psychology on me.'

He grinned back. 'Fine.' He held out his hand for the keys.

'I suppose you can afford to write off two cars a week,' she said.

'I've only one neck, though.'

He lifted his chin to reveal his brown throat, the warm skin dusted with the faintest shadow of stubble even though he had obviously shaved this morning.

Her stomach muscles clenched as she imagined what it would feel like to press her mouth to that warm skin and work her way to his mouth.

But she already knew—if only she could access those memories...

'You don't have to drive,' he said, watching her face. 'You don't have anything to prove.'

Except that I can go five minutes without wondering what sex is like with you?

'I know that,' she said, but her attempt at bright and breezy sounded a bit manic.

At least focusing on driving had taken her mind off the dreaded medical check-up ahead. As she parked up she snapped off her seat belt and swivelled in her seat to face him.

'How was that?'

The sarcastic comments, unwanted advice or even the odd wince had never come. But he had seemed lost in his own thoughts most of the way. She sensed a tension in him—as though he was the one getting tested, not her.

'Good.'

'You seemed zoned out. Or was that just fear because of my driving? At least I haven't forgotten how to drive,' she added, trying to get a response from him and feeling frustrated. Yes, it was a pretty feeble attempt at a joke, but he hadn't even smiled.

'Don't force it—that's what the doctor said.'

She felt a surge of impatience. 'Anyone would think you didn't *want* me to remember.'

He felt a fresh stab of guilt—maybe because there was a grain of truth in it. He wanted her to recover her memory—of course he did—but when she did he knew the friendship he valued, the trust that had existed between them, was going to need some repairing.

In the past, every time he had felt the tug of attraction he had closed it down. Filed it away in a box marked *Do Not Touch*. And now, because of a crazy combination of events, he was forced to deal with it.

And the fact he was, he wasn't dealing with it well.

CHAPTER FIVE

IT WAS HARD to imagine this situation ending in any way that would preserve their friendship.

He wanted her—and that want had steel claws.

She wanted him—which in itself was an aphrodisiac. And she wasn't hiding that want because she believed they were a couple, that he loved her, that she was safe.

Talk about a moral maze. He wouldn't wish this situation on his worst enemy.

The consultant greeted them in Reception.

'No, I haven't remembered anything,' Clemmie said, before the man had even finished shaking their hands. 'Well, not much,' she added, with a sideways glance at Joaquin. 'Nothing significant.'

'Don't rush it.'

Clemmie clamped her lips over a rude response. She was fed up with being told not to rush it—she wanted to rush it.

'Now, shall I talk you through the tests we are going to run?'

It was late afternoon before the tests were finished, and she was given a clean bill of health—along with some information that changed everything.

Joaquin was alongside her as they walked through the

revolving glass doors and out into the pale winter sunshine together.

For how much longer that *together* would last, given the bombshell information that had just been dropped on her, remained to be seen.

Clemmie angled a sideways glance at the tall figure beside her and took a deep breath before asking brightly, 'Did you manage to get any work done?'

During her trips to various departments she had caught glimpses of him sitting in an alcove, his laptop on his knee, apparently completely absorbed.

'Work?'

'I saw you were deep into it.' She glanced at the laptop bag he carried.

'Sure...most productive,' he lied.

'You drive back.' She threw the keys and he automatically caught them. 'I'm tired and we might hit rush hour.'

'So how did it go?' he asked, when they were seated side by side. 'You have the results?'

She shrugged. 'I have to wait for some of the blood test results, but everything else I passed with flying colours.'

'Your memory?'

'Except that one. And please don't tell me not to push it.'

'All right, I won't,' he responded. A voice in his head was telling him to proceed with caution. 'Something is wrong?' he asked.

She chewed on her full lower lip and didn't deny it. Because something was very, very wrong...but what it was she didn't know yet.

She had her theories, but mostly it boiled down to *was it her or was it him?*

'I do not want to discuss it here. Let's wait until we are back at Maplehurst.'

She thought for a moment that he was going to push her, but after studying her face for a long moment he just nodded.

She sat there immobile, and the longer her silence stretched the deeper into overdrive his imagination went. He didn't say anything when she took out her phone, but when she had finished with it, and slid the phone back into her bag, she explained.

'I was texting Mum. I had said I'd call in, but... Anyway, I've told her I've had the all-clear.'

'Sure you don't want to drop by?'

She shook her head. 'I'm tired,' she said gruffly. 'I'll see her tomorrow.'

Surging frustration gnawing him to the bone, Joaquin resisted the temptation to pull the car over and demand she tell him what the hell was the matter.

Ten minutes later they drove past the gatehouse. The lights were on.

'I think Harry is meant to be arriving tomorrow. Mum will probably be glad I didn't drop by. She'll be cooking and cleaning.'

Halfway up the long drive to the house a fox ran across the road in front of them before disappearing into the woods. Clemmie didn't even react to it.

Frustration and fear scraped his nerve-endings. Whatever she had learnt at the hospital must have been pretty devastating.

The sooner she told him, the sooner he could get her the help she needed.

'Do you want a drink?' Joaquin asked, studying the label on the bottle he'd pulled from a cupboard before pouring himself one. He had the feeling he might need it.

In the act of putting a match to the pile of kindling someone—probably her mum—had arranged in the fireplace, she shook her head.

'I might make myself a cup of tea, though,' she said as she straightened up, dusting her hands on her bottom as she watched the flames flare and take hold. 'I might get changed too,' she added, glancing down at her silk shirt and wide-legged linen trousers. The matching jacket lay over the back of the sofa.

He caught her arm. 'Not now.'

She sighed and nodded, not pretending to misunderstand his meaning.

'What is wrong? You can tell me anything—you know that.'

Anything beside the fact that she...

She blinked. She couldn't say it—she couldn't think it.

'After all the tests I asked the doctor about...' She gave a self-conscious little shrug. 'I asked him about birth control, and he said...he said—'

'What did he say?'

'He said that it was sensible of me to think about such things before beginning a sexual relationship.' She watched his face for reaction. 'I said that obviously I was already in a sexual relationship.' She sucked in a deep, sustaining breath. 'And then he said...'

Joaquin's patience snapped. He was thinking the worst by this point—not that he even knew what that was. But with this sort of build-up he was imagining something devastating.

'He said what?'

'That I wasn't. He said...'

'Get to the point, Clemmie.'

'He told me I was still a virgin.'

Her eyes were trained on her feet as she spoke, but she was aware of Joaquin across the room, downing the contents of the glass he held.

'It was a bit of a shock.'

Joaquin laughed. *Shock* didn't really cover what he was feeling—what had glued his feet to the floor. The idea that all the passion he had always sensed in her was untapped...

'So, this was news to you?'

'Well, I knew I once was, obviously.'

He watched a thoughtful expression drift across her solemn face.

'I suppose that's one of the reasons that I was upset. I couldn't remember my first time. I just assumed that...' She had assumed that her first time had been with Joaquin, and somehow that had felt right...like the last piece in a puzzle slotting into place. She extended her finger to look at the dull glitter of the multiple stones. 'Well, we're engaged. And sex is usually pre-ring, not post.'

She looked at Joaquin, who had been standing still, as he slammed his glass down on a table and flopped into a chair with less than his usual inherent elegance. There was a stunned expression on his face as he leaned back, dragging both hands through the dark hair that had begun to curl on the back of his neck.

'I really thought I was beyond being shocked, but you...'

His eyes drifted to her lips, to their full, passionate curve, and he shook his head. He had always prided himself on never making assumptions, but in his defence even to imagine that a woman with that mouth being *untouched*...

'So, I need to know,' she told him.

He watched as she straightened her spine and lifted her

chin, delivering to him a *Bring it on, I can take it* stare. The extraordinary colour of her eyes was emphasised by the dark smudges beneath them.

'Is it me?' she asked. Twin circles of colour stood out like flags on her smooth cheeks.

'Is that a trick question?'

She slung him a frustrated look and gritted her teeth. 'I've never been very... Well, not very *sexy*,' she admitted bluntly. Her eyes narrowed when he gave a short laugh. 'You think that's amusing?' she asked, her throat aching and scratchy with hurt.

Thinking of the testosterone-charged fire in his groin, he shook his head before stretching his legs out in front of him and linking his hands behind his head.

It was an indolent pose that sent her resentment spiralling.

'Sorry...a private joke,' he said.

'Were we about to split up when all this happened?' she hypothesised, thinking that if this was the Joaquin she had got engaged to she was surprised it had lasted at all.

'That was never discussed.'

'Am I frigid?'

She ticked the question off on one finger, as though it was high on the list of possibilities she had been compiling. Then she paused and cleared her throat, flashing him an apologetic look from under her lashes.

'Or is it you...? Do you have issues?'

Too stunned by her revelation to halt her stream of wild speculation, he stood there barely registering the comforting pressure of the small hand that had come to rest on his arm as she'd produced her last theory.

'If it is you...' Her lashes came down in a luxuriant protective sweep as she probed delicately. 'There is nothing to be ashamed of—'

'*Virgin?*'

Joaquin spoke the word with the inflection of someone pronouncing a word that had no meaning. Then he shook his head as if he was just waking up, messing up his hair as it he dragged his hand back and forth across his scalp.

'You are a virgin? *How?*' he demanded. 'Is that even possible? All this rubbish about you not being sexy and asking if you're frigid... You wonder why I laughed? Seriously—*how* are you a virgin?'

'Well, I kind of hoped you would have the answer to that one. I assumed that... Well... I thought it was a subject that would have come up between us.' She looked down at the ring weighing down her finger and tacked on drily, 'Considering.'

What *had* they spoken about? It would seem they'd had plenty of time for talking, because they clearly hadn't been doing anything else, she thought bitterly—which left open only that explanation that still didn't seem possible to her.

'There's nothing to be ashamed of, Joaquin,' she said gently. 'It happens to a lot of men.'

Joaquin shook himself free of his contemplation of her mouth as it finally dawned on him what she was suggesting. He laughed again.

'This is not a joke, Joaquin.'

'That is true. I have been called many things in my life, but impotent...?' *Only Clemmie.* 'And how would *you* know what happens to lots of men?'

The cruel taunt sent a rush of heat under her skin.

'There's no need to be so defensive,' she countered spikily.

Of all the options, this seemed the most likely. She

might never have set the world alight with her sexuality, but she didn't have any hang-ups, and her virginity had zero to do with moral principles. Frankly, anyone who could look at Joaquin and think *Let's wait for a ring* had to have serious issues!

'Defensive? You're the one changing the subject.'

She slung him a frustrated glare and suddenly felt in danger of forgetting what the subject was as his dark, heavy-lidded eyes slid downwards over her body, making her nipples tingle and burn.

Mortified that she had no control over her physical response, that her body seemed to have been highjacked by lust, she compressed her lips. 'It's better to discuss problems.'

'I don't consider your virginity to be a problem, as such. A mystery, maybe?'

'We are not talking about my vir— Don't change the subject.'

'I thought that *was* the subject.'

With one elegant motion he surged to his feet, and a moment later was standing close enough for her to feel the warmth of his body as he towered above her.

'You're feeling insecure because we have not consummated our—?'

She gave her head a tiny shake and pressed the flat of her hand to his lips to still the flow of words. When, a self-conscious moment later, she tried to withdraw it, his fingers curled like warm steel around her wrist, holding her hand against his lips for a long, lingering moment.

Fighting the hypnotic pull of his dark eyes, she tugged again and pressed her free hand to her chest, against her pounding heart.

Joaquin turned on his heel and put himself out of grabbing distance before he twisted back to face her.

'Don't deflect,' she hit back waspishly. 'I am not insecure—though I do think it might have been simpler all round if you had discovered you didn't fancy me *before* you put a ring on my finger! That's it, isn't it?' she accused, thinking that sometimes the simplest explanation was the most accurate.

He just isn't into you, Clemmie.

A spasm of exasperation washed over his perfect features. 'Will you stop putting words in my mouth?'

Of course now she couldn't stop staring at his mouth.

Her face was so expressive that he could almost *hear* her thoughts. His eyes darkened, the pupils expanding to almost obliterate the chocolate-brown of the iris. The pounding of blood in his eardrums was echoed by the pounding elsewhere in his body.

He recognised the natural physical response of his body when a beautiful, desirable woman made it clear she wanted him to kiss her. It was a dance he had enjoyed before, and it was always an extra turn-on when a woman was bold enough to let him know what she wanted.

But this was not any beautiful, desirable woman, he reminded himself. This was Clemmie, which made the rules of engagement different—or should have.

At some point the rules had changed.

They had an intimate bond that he had never experienced with another woman…an intimate bond without sexual intimacy. Which was why it had lasted.

Were there any rules?

Her eyes widened as Joaquin crossed the room, his purposeful panther-like stride bringing him to her side in seconds.

'Do us both a favour and quit with the conspiracy theories and the casting aspersions on a Spanish man's machismo.' He tilted his head to one side, considering the face turned up to him. 'Or was it meant to be a challenge? I enjoy a challenge...' he purred.

'Challenge...?' she parroted faintly. His proximity was having a powerfully mind-numbing effect on her.

Or it could be the after effects of her concussion.

She clung to this hope in the face of the strong kicks of lust in her belly and lower.

'A challenge to prove myself to you?' he asked.

It struck Clemmie forcibly that he was not looking or acting like a man who felt his machismo threatened. And then he took her chin between his thumb and forefinger, leaving her no option but to tilt her head back to look up into his face. Then she wished she hadn't. Because the nebulous *thing* that was prowling deep in the darkness of his darkly lashed eyes made her insides dissolve.

They had shared so much, but now—inexplicably—he seemed like a stranger. This was not the Joaquin she joked with, the man she debated issues they disagreed on with, from the profound to the just silly... But then how could anyone *not* like vinegar on their chips?

This was a dark, dangerous and exciting stranger.

I am Clemmie, short for Clementine—my mum couldn't stop eating them when she was pregnant. Who are you?

If she'd said it out loud he would have been justified in thinking she had lost her mind—and maybe she had? Bombarded by his overwhelming maleness at a cellular level, she quivered—and drew in a sharp breath as he dragged his knuckles gently across the softness of her cheek, making a detour around a bruise. The contact felt like raw electricity prickling along her nerve-endings, disconnecting her body from her brain.

The attraction of not being in control had always eluded Clemmie. She considered it a form of insanity, and it was scary to know that at this moment she was on the brink of embracing that particular form of insanity. But there was another part of her that wanted to retreat behind the safe security of her emotional excess filter.

Her nostrils quivered as she breathed in the scent of him greedily. Her eyelashes fluttered like trapped butterflies against the curve of her cheek as she put a fight against the sensory overload.

'I wasn't... I'm not...' she protested weakly, forcing the words past the aching occlusion in her throat. Her attempt at a laugh failed on every level, emerging as a strangled croak. 'I have a concussion...' she reminded him.

The glitter in his eyes damped down a few degrees. 'I thought they gave you a clean bill of health?'

The concern in his voice wrapped inside its interrogative harshness was at some level even more dangerous to her state of mind than the idea that he was going to kiss her... It made her ache for something and she didn't know what she yearned for.

'They did,' she admitted, fighting a sudden strong urge to burst into tears.

'Truth? Or is this you being stoic?' he asked, sounding scornful of this tendency.

'I'm fine...a bit sore. I don't even have a headache.' She sketched a smile. 'But the day isn't over yet.'

'So, you were suggesting that I have a problem?' he framed, and a mixture of hauteur and amusement quivered across his firm, fascinating lips.

Clemmie was rapidly ditching that particular theory.

She had always been aware of the inherent sensuality he possessed...the aura of maleness he exuded. You'd have to be dead not to. But it wasn't until this moment that she realised she had never experienced its full force—only a diluted *just friends* version.

She had been shielded. And now she wasn't. It was as if someone had just opened the door on a flaming furnace. She was no longer warm, but burning.

'You're right,' he murmured. 'I do have a problem. I have a very big problem.'

His devilish white grin flashed and she could feel the warmth of his breath on her cheek as he leaned down.

'But not the one you are talking about...'

He had been shifting his stance in slow increments as he spoke, moving closer, and he was close enough now for her to feel not just the heat of his lean, hard body but the quivering tension that was coming off him in waves, making her think of a stallion being held back at the starting line, all hard sinew and rippling muscles, strength and power restrained—*just*.

The perfect symmetry of his face, its slashing angles and hollows, all blurred as she was hit by a wave of dizziness. She could hear her heartbeat in her ears, its dull pounding like waves crashing and retreating onto a rocky shore, an elemental sound she had always found soothing.

Except Clemmie didn't feel soothed.

She felt out of her skin, simultaneously excited and scared.

His fierce, blatantly carnal smile sent her insides into meltdown. Her heart continued to hammer. Her legs felt as though they did not belong to her.

'Point p-proved...' she stuttered out.

'What point would that be?'

She shook her head. She had never seen that look of hard intent on his face before. A look that stretched the golden skin tight across his perfect bones and emphasised the sharp carved angles.

Joaquin didn't need to prove a thing. This was not about his fractured ego. It was about need. The sort of need that for the first time in his life sidestepped logic. The tabloid frenzy that frequently surrounded his love life made him the first to admit that love had nothing to do with it! But he was not indiscriminate. Aside from natural lust, there was always an element of cold logic to his choice of partners.

His parents' marriage, and the total lack of honesty involved, had given him a pathological loathing of hypocrisy and keeping up appearances. Even less cynically based marriages seemed to him ultimately to become prisons as the chemistry that had brought two people together faded, all too frequently turned to bitterness and dislike or even—in many ways worse—indifference.

He had never bedded a woman who expected more than he was willing to give. They didn't want a piece of him. They were not interested in what made him tick. They wanted sex and the boost to their profile that being seen with him would give them.

He could see the logic of that and even admire it.

Clemmie belonged to a different part of his life. Their shared past was not something that could be replicated. The only *honourable* thing he had ever done in his life was not acknowledging the physical attraction between them, let alone following through with it. It had been his way of protecting her and preserving their friendship.

He had always known the danger of blurring the line between friendship and sex: once you stepped over that line there was no going back.

But now, pumped up and frustrated, he knew the hormonal heat in his blood was in charge, and the danger warnings were silenced as he began to rationalise the situation. There could be an *afterwards*... Once the attraction faded there would be a route back to friendship. It just required their keeping things realistic.

The thing he was keeping in the back of his mind was still not front and foremost, and the option of not acknowledging this had been taken away. Nothing could muffle the screaming fact that he wanted this—he *wanted her*.

Once acknowledged and given oxygen, that want, that primal need, grew exponentially with each passing heartbeat. Heartbeats were the only time scale that made any sense in this sense-free zone. He breathed in the fragrance of her hair, wanting to bury his face in the soft, fiery mesh. The warning bell in his head was playing to a deaf audience. There was a hungry clamour singing through his blood, urging him to touch her.

A part of him recognised that it was crazy to feed this hunger, but his imagination was embracing the crazy even as it moved beyond touching, conjuring an image of him lying between her legs, watching her face, feeling her slim legs wrap around him, pulling him into her warmth...

She read the challenge in his deep-set eyes. It was mingled with something that seemed close to compulsion as he placed a hand on the small of her back, before stepping in to seal their bodies from the waist down, thigh to thigh.

'All right,' she croaked, striving for irony as wave after debilitating wave of warmth fluttered through her belly and her knees began to sag. 'Point proved. You are all man—no doubts at all.'

She was saved from crumbling ignominiously at his feet by the tightening of his hand on her waist. She gasped, her eyes squeezing tight shut, as she felt the carnal imprint of his erection grinding into the softness of her belly.

What would it feel like to have her tingling breasts crushed against his chest, skin to skin?

She clenched her hands into white-knuckled fists to prevent them crawling around his neck and finding out.

'I haven't proved my point. Not yet,' he slurred softly as he angled her face up to his.

His expression was intent as he moved his thumb, allowing it to trace the plump, quivering outline of her lips as he captured her wide green eyes.

Transfixed, Clemmie could only stare into his face. She forgot how to breathe as his eyes grew dark and deep, silver shards lighting the darkness drew her in, captured and held her. The air around them seemed hotter, matching the dancing flames in the stone inglenook fireplace.

She melted into him, aware of the hard maleness of his body as he dragged her closer, his hands sliding into her hair, dragging her head back and exposing the long line of her neck as he kissed his way down the elegant column until he reached the blue-veined pulse throbbing at the base.

Then he reclaimed her mouth. Clemmie was barely aware that the hands at her waist had lifted her until she found herself sitting on the table, with Joaquin standing between her thighs.

She gasped as he stepped in closer.

His grip on her waist loosened as he swore, misinterpreting her gasp. 'I knew you were lying...'

'I wasn't lying. It only hurts when I move my head too quickly. Or breathe. Just joking,' she added quickly, afraid that he might not kiss her. At that moment she wanted his kiss more than she wanted to breathe.

Oxygen was in very short supply.

So was sanity!

The first brush of his lips across her own was soft, almost a whisper, and then the darkness in his eyes intensified. She wanted to look away, but she was drawn in as he covered her lips with his. She reacted to the skilled sensual intrusion of his tongue with a low moan as the tenderness flicked into hard hunger, demanding a passionate response. The shocking liquid heat between her legs made her squirm against the hardness of his thigh, moaning as she kissed him back.

There is no right, said the voice in his head as he hesitated. *There is no wrong.*

There is. She thinks we are in a relationship.

There is no tomorrow or yesterday.

Above the primal roar in his blood a small, sane corner of his brain awoke.

Tomorrow she'll hate you for this lie—and this is all a lie. She thinks you are together. You might be a scoundrel, but you have never lied to a woman—and this is Clemmie.

It felt right. But it wasn't. Not on any level.

CHAPTER SIX

THE ABRUPT REJECTION as he stepped away felt like a warm shower turning ice-cold.

Clemmie shivered.

She felt physically sick.

'What?' she asked, pitching her trembling question at the figure who was now standing several feet away, looking...

At least he looked as if he was in pain, she decided, studying the darkness along the sharpened contours of his face. Hearing the breath whistling in and out of his parted lips. Pain was the least he deserved, she concluded, shaking with reaction.

'Sorry,' he said, in response to the voice in his head that was telling him he was a total fool in reacting to some misguided sense of chivalry.

Things changed, things moved on...they were both consenting adults.

She was a virgin.

That incredible fact alone should have put her out of bounds, but at some primitive level it aroused him more.

The idea of being her first lover...

He had never been anyone's first lover.

'That shouldn't have happened.'

It was the timing that was wrong, not the action, he decided. She still thought they were engaged. She thought that she was kissing the man she was going to marry.

No way in the world could he rationalise that.

Clemmie hid her profound hurt at this fresh rejection beneath a surface layer of anger.

'Well, it did! Was all that just to prove you don't have a problem?' Her eyes blinked wide, the sensual haze clearing as she bit out furiously, 'You don't want me. You are a piece of work,' she declared hotly, feeling the sting of utter humiliation.

She jumped down from the table, waiting a moment for her shaky legs to steady before she looked at him.

'What is wrong with me? Am I just a total—?'

'Nothing is wrong with you. You are...' His nostrils flared. As he covered the space between them he fought the urgent need that was taking bites out of his control. 'A virgin...' he said accusingly.

'Yeah? So what? Hasn't it come up in conversation during our engagement?'

He took a deep breath and took his hands off her shoulders, not really sure how they had got there. Desire was roaring like a furnace out of control, kept in check only by the knowledge that he was taking advantage of her ignorance. That she had bought into a lie.

Hurting her, taking advantage, was a low he could not sink to. So before his need outweighed his conscience, he knew he had to speak the truth.

The truth could not hurt her more than continuing this charade to its inevitable conclusion.

'There has been no conversation.'

'What do you mean?'

'There is no engagement.'

It took several heartbeats for this information to penetrate the sensual thrall she had sunk into, then a few more for her to fight her way clear of it.

'I don't understand…'

'You haven't forgotten we're engaged because we never were.'

She shook her head, as if she was trying to make sense of his words, looking so vulnerable he felt worse than ever.

'The ring…?'

He had lied to her. The one person she had believed would never betray her had.

'My grandmother sent me the ring, trying to guilt-trip me. I shoved the damned thing in the glovebox and you found it in there and decided to try it on.'

She held out her hand and stared at the ring, hating it and in that moment hating him as she realised the truth. 'It got stuck.'

'Before it could be unstuck we crashed,' he finished, delivering the basic sequence of events in a flat monotone.

'Say that again? No, don't. I get it,' she choked out as the scenario he'd described flashed through her head.

Unlike the idea of them being a couple, it seemed lot more feasible—a *lot* more!

'People *assumed* we were engaged at the hospital and I didn't correct them because you were unconscious. I didn't have a clue what was going on, and I knew a fiancé gets access and information. I thought that as soon as you woke up you'd put things right…or I would. Then the internet thing went viral and suddenly your mum was welcoming me into the family.' He hefted out a sigh. 'And you didn't remember what happened. It was a nightmare!'

Her lips pursed. 'A nightmare being engaged to me? Thanks a lot!'

Of course it was a nightmare for him. He had never hidden his belief that marriage was a trap. Why on earth had she imagined that *she* had made him think differently when all the beautiful women who had gone before her had not?

The sheer level of her self-delusion made her want to scream.

'I meant...the thing took on a life of its own.'

She took a step towards him and pressed both hands to his chest. Then she pushed as hard as she could.

Caught unawares, Joaquin staggered back, but quickly regained his balance.

'You make it sound like *you* were the victim!' she shouted. 'You lied—you betrayed me!'

'That was not my intention—and it wasn't my intention to continue this farce.'

Her jaw tightened as she stood there, hands on her hips, glaring at him, refusing to let the hurt show in her expression. 'Farce? Good to know what you think.'

He expelled a frustrated sigh. 'You know that's not what I meant. I had every intention of telling you yesterday morning, but the medics told me that I shouldn't.'

'Since when did you do what people tell you?' she countered.

'Granted. But you don't pay money to a cabal of expert medics and then ignore their advice. They advised me not to fill in the gaps in your memory at this stage.'

'They did?'

'According to them, amnesia can be the mind's way of protecting you from a painful memory—something you are not ready to face. And who was I to argue? Whatever the reason, it wouldn't have been helped by you waking up in hospital…which is the reason why I didn't push back when you wanted to come home too soon.'

His glance shifted to the bruise on her cheek that was more visible now the light covering of make-up she had applied earlier had faded.

'And this is too soon, Clemmie.'

Too soon for him to be kissing her, the inner voice of guilt reminded him. And yet it had been something he could not control. The need he had felt had talons; he still couldn't get his head around how that need had consumed him in a way he had never experienced before.

'Ignorance is not bliss. It is a lie and it's patronising. They told me Chrissie would be okay! My dad said he'd be back for the funeral!'

'I know…'

He watched her breasts lift as she inhaled, flicking her hair from her face with a shake of her head. It was a tiny characteristic gesture, and he had seen the action a thousand times before. So why was he only just noticing how erotic it was? The way her fiery hair whipped back to reveal the slender pale column of her neck?

And afterwards she always…

She licked her lips. Even though he knew it was coming, the tiny flicker of her tongue across her lips sent a rush of testosterone-charged heat through his body.

He had wanted normal back—but how could that happen when he wanted her this way?

'It wasn't your choice to make. Even if our engagement hadn't been a lie, it still wouldn't have been. I had to get out of there!' she cried through clenched teeth.

'I understand.'

'No, you don't.' She took a deep breath. 'So…okay. I can see why it's happened. But didn't you at any point think enough was enough?' An expression of dawning horror spread across her face. 'I told you... Oh, God, I told you that I wanted to kiss you...!' She groaned, her face contorting into a grimace of sheer mortification. 'I told you I was a virgin!' Swamped by the weight of sheer humiliation, she covered her eyes. 'I tried to kiss you...'

He watched as her head dropped and her shoulders hunched.

'Do you actually think that I didn't want to kiss you back? That it didn't...?' He raked a hand through his dark hair, and the words were seemingly dragged out of him against his will as he continued in an uneven voice that reflected the strength of the emotions surging through him. 'Hell, Clemmie, it *killed* me not to kiss you. And then I did—' he said, realising as he broke off that that action had put the *normal* he so wanted them to return to out of reach...maybe for ever.

Her head came up, and her eyes were instantly caught and held by his. The dark, burning heat in his gaze sealed the contact.

'You know what I think, Clemmie?'

'I'm sure you're going to tell me.'

'I think we're both guilty of self-delusion.'

'Speak for yourself.'

'I am. I've been dodging the fact that I want you because I was afraid of the fall-out. I didn't want to mess up what we already had. But it's out there now, so we have to deal with it.'

I want you.

The raw statement sent a primal shudder through her body.

He wanted her.

But he lied to you, the voice in her head countered

coldly. *The way your dad lied time after time to your mum, and your mum believed his lies.*

'I don't want to deal with this…this is just too much,' she whispered. 'I want things back to the way they were.'

'I think you want me more than you want that.'

The awful part was he was right.

She fixed her gaze on some safe, blurry point over his shoulder as if it was a lifeline as she fought off the suspicion that on some level she had already known the truth. She had known that it was impossible they were engaged, but she had gone along with it because she'd been enjoying living the fantasy.

She couldn't blame everything on the concussion—though that would be nice. The fact was, there had been some glaring inconsistencies in the timeline of their engagement staring her in the face the whole time. She was worried that she hadn't wanted to see them.

'The doctor said there might be a trauma I don't want to remember?'

He nodded.

'Do you know what it is?'

'No. I thought it was maybe just being in the hospital where your sister… That is the place where she was…' he hesitated '…treated?'

'Same hospital, different building. The old children's ward was replaced by a new building ages ago. It isn't that specific hospital…it's any hospital. It's the smell. The…'

She paused and sucked in a breath before shaking her head. There were too many painful memories she didn't want to revisit.

Playing with her twin and then later, when she was too tired and too ill to play, sitting beside her on the narrow bed, not wanting to let her go when it was time to go home.

The cycle of Chrissie's hospital treatment and then coming home, and the hope that had seemed to last for ever.

But then came the day when Chrissie had never come home.

The survivor's guilt had never truly left her.

Chrissie had been the brave part of her—the dominant twin. It made no sense even now that strong Chrissie was the one who had succumbed to that evil disease.

'So, what are you going to do now?' asked Joaquin.

She looked down at her hand. 'I'm going to get this bloody ring off,' she said, glaring down at it with loathing.

Half an hour later she left her room, a cool smile painted on her face and the ring still on her now red and swollen finger.

'You can do this,' she told herself as she walked down the carved staircase, trying not to look at the monster of a ring that seemed to symbolise this whole mess.

As she had scrubbed and tugged at the ring all she had been able to hear was Joaquin's voice saying, *'I want you.'*

Had he meant it?

The thought made her tummy muscles quiver.

It didn't matter if he had. Nothing was inevitable. It would be a disaster.

On the other hand, it already was a disaster!

What was the point in deciding anything? She knew full well that her resolve would crumble the moment he touched her.

She reached the bottom of the stairs and paused, listening, her ring-bearing hand on the ancient carved banister that had made Aria Perez furious because she was not allowed to replace it with something *'less dark'*.

Following the distant sound of voices, which seemed

to be coming from the general direction of the west wing, she narrowed her search to the open door of what had once been the library. It had once smelt of musty old leather, and the bookshelves back then had heaved with dusty tomes, but they were long gone, all stripped out during the refurbishment.

She hesitated for a moment. She could hear two voices—one obviously Joaquin's, the other female. For a split second she thought there was a woman in there. The feeling of furious betrayal only lasted a split-second before she realised that it was, in fact, a two-way phone conversation.

The fact that she had been on the point of charging in there in militant *gotcha* mode—that she had bought into this act so much that she had actually felt, even for a fraction of a second, like a betrayed fiancée—was a massive wake-up call.

She had to get herself under control!

She pasted an in-control expression on her face and, head up, walked through the door.

These days the room was dominated by a massive desk, pale wood and Scandinavian in design. The only reading material was the stack of glossy magazines arranged in geometric precision on its polished surface. Like the rest of the very expensive furniture, it would have looked good in many settings—but not this one.

Joaquin was standing with his back to her, so he didn't hear her enter or see the expression of hopeless longing she knew had appeared on her face.

So much for under control, Clemmie.

His phone was lying on the blond wood, on speaker.

'I saw the video...'

Clemmie immediately recognised the distinctive, rather nasal tones of Aria Perez.

'What were you thinking of, letting someone film you?'

'I had my mind on other things at the time.'

Despite everything, listening to Joaquin's dry response to his mother's complaint made Clemmie's lips twitch. She had watched the clip they spoke of several times. Her five minutes of fame and Joaquin looking like some sort of Hollywood hero in a big budget action movie.

'Are you *insane? She* is the *cleaner's* daughter!'

About to reveal herself, Clemmie froze.

'Housekeeper, Aria.'

'Do not talk to me in that manner. I am your mother, and it is disrespectful.'

'Isn't this what you've always wanted? Me getting married? I'd have thought you'd be pleased.'

'Do not be flippant. You cannot marry that girl—I forbid it!'

Forbid...?

Listening, Clemmie could not believe this woman's stupidity. Did she not know her son at all?

Do you? asked the voice in her head.

The answer a few days ago would have been a confident yes. But a few days ago, while she had always known he possessed charisma off the scale, she had not seen his sex god persona up close and personal.

Not that close, complained the voice in her head.

'Forbid...?' he echoed.

Though the response was not directed at her, Clemmie shivered. It was made of steel, with an inherent hauteur that made him a stranger—a dangerous stranger. She had caught glimpses of this side of him over the years, but she had never really appreciated that it was as much a part of him as his teasing humour—probably more so.

'You are normally so...fastidious, Joaquin,' his mother complained, and there was a note of pained bemusement in her penetrating voice. 'That girl...she is not even... She was always a positively feral little thing...'

'"*That girl*" is a woman. And she is and always has been the one authentic person I know. If anything, she is too good for me.'

There was a short silence while Clemmie stood still, emotion welling in her throat to hear his impassioned defence of her.

The silence was broken by a nasty little laugh that filled the room like a poisonous echo. 'Oh, my...she really must be good in bed.'

From where she stood Clemmie saw Joaquin surge explosively across the room until his nose was almost pressed against the big mullioned window. His fist was clenched and raised as though...

She gave a little sigh of relief when he lowered his arm. She had been afraid for one split-second that he was about to punch the glass.

He spoke then, but in Spanish—something sharp and short that drew a gasp from his mother that made Clemmie wish she could translate it.

'I sometimes wonder what I did to deserve a son who is so... How dare you? Can you imagine what people will think? Can't you just sleep with her?'

'What gives you the idea that I care about what people think? What you think...?'

'Fine—become a figure of fun. But at least get a decent prenup...' A sound of exasperation echoed down the line. 'And get her a stylist. I doubt the girl has ever seen the inside of a beauty salon—and that hair! I don't think she even combs it from one week to the next. Is she pregnant? Did she trap you?' she wondered out loud.

Clemmie bit her tongue quite literally as she fought the temptation to reply to this awful woman herself. Knowing her impulse was not an option, that left disappearing and pretending she had never been there, or alerting Joaquin to her presence.

'Mother, I think you should stop talking now. Before I say something that *you* will regret. My life is none of your concern.'

He snapped his fingers with an air of finality, but without any real belief that his words would get through to her. This was a message that had not got through for the last ten years, so he doubted it would get through his mother's narcissistic barrier now.

He was right.

'You have not thought this through,' she said. 'Look at the mother if you want to see your future. I'm not surprised the husband didn't stay around. The woman is nothing but a common tart. She beds anything with a pulse and floats around with her airs and graces as though she's wearing silk. But it's polyester. I only keep her on out of charity.'

This claim drew a grim laugh from Joaquin. 'You keep her on because she is good at what she does and she doesn't ask to be paid overtime.'

He knew his family, like many, had got to be rich and stay that way because in part they were mean.

Clemmie, who had walked up behind him during this last interchange, laid a hand on his arm. She felt the tension in his muscles and read the shock on his face as he twisted around.

Read it through a red mist, because she was fizzing with fury.

The woman could bad-mouth her—she could take it. If pushed, she could even respond in kind. But this was her mum, and *nobody* was allowed to do that!

'Oh, Aria *darling*…!' she said, injecting as much insincere adoration as she could manage into her raised voice, everything in her focused on making this hateful woman's day a bad one! 'Oh, gosh. I can't call you Mrs Perez now, can I? Do you prefer Mother or Aria?' she gushed, with an artificial titter.

She was aware of Joaquin shedding his tension like a skin, rolling his eyes as he fought off a grin.

'I'm so glad to have a chance to speak to you. I told Joaquin that we couldn't just invite ourselves, but he tells me that you can't wait to meet me and very much want me to be part of the family celebrations. How many years is it that you have been married? I just hope that Joaquin and I will be as blessed in our union. Also, you are right—I am *very* good in bed.'

There was a choking sound from the other end of the line before Joaquin ended the call, picked up his phone and slid it back into his pocket.

Lacking a plan, Clemmie just stood there.

Joaquin's face was unreadable; the light filtering through the half-closed window drapes cast his face half in shadow.

The adrenaline rush had receded, leaving her feeling shaky and anxious—probably with good reason, she decided, as she mentally reviewed her own words.

'I don't know what got into me…' she said.

'How long were you standing there?' He arched an ebony brow. 'Let me guess…long enough?'

She nodded. 'I didn't mean to eavesdrop, but she made me so mad. I know she never liked us being friends when we were kids, but honestly... *"The cleaner's daughter?"'* she said, adopting a close approximation of the older woman's voice.

There was amusement in his eyes as he watched her thumb her neat little nose and adopt his mother's exaggerated hip-swaying sashay as she walked across the room, running her finger across a polished surface and tutting as she surveyed it for invisible dust.

There was a sardonic glint in his eyes as he watched her performance, which became something harder as his glance rested on her taut, rounded bottom.

'I should have known we weren't engaged. I'd need to be out of my mind to marry into your family.

'So it's no longer marriage you're against, it's marriage to me?' he asked.

An image came to his mind of Clemmie floating up the aisle in white towards some faceless male waiting for her. The pain that centred in his chest, but was not limited to that area, caught him off guard. But reminding himself that his mother had probably been a beautiful bride, and before her his grandmother, helped soothe the pain.

Had she caught it, Clemmie might have wondered at the expression that flickered across his face, but she was still too furious to register much.

'And the things she said about Mum! I just lost it.' She heard her voice rising and made an effort to stop her temper going nuclear again.

'She has that effect. The fact is, she's jealous of Ruth.'

Clemmie's eyes widened. 'But she has all this!'

She allowed her gaze to trail round the room which, beneath the superficial change of décor, was still beautiful.

The bones of the place had not been touched, and it still had the power to clutch at her heart, no matter how many times she told herself it was just a building.

'Money can't buy her class.'

Clemmie felt distinctly mollified by the compliment, but viewed him through narrowed, wary eyes. 'You're not angry?' she asked, her attitude suggesting that if he was she could be too.

'You defended your mum. Why should I be angry?' The corners of his mouth lifted. 'Join the family celebrations? That was brilliant—a direct hit. The irony of course, is that it's a gig I've been trying to avoid for years. My mother has been trying to pull my strings all my life.'

'You think she'd have learned by now.' She could not imagine anyone believing that they could influence Joaquin.

'It is beginning to become tiresome... I might have to exert myself to teach them a lesson.'

'You could marry someone even worse than a *cleaner's daughter.*'

'Is that even possible?'

She fought off a smile and pretended to swipe at him. 'I'm not even sure if I'm talking to you.'

'You are talking.' And he liked the sound of her voice... always had. It had a husky, musical quality.

'Look, I didn't come to fight,' she told him. 'I just wanted to say that I understand why you did what you did—not that that makes it any easier.'

'What is not easy?'

She shook her head, forgetting that she had spent ten minutes—as it turned out a wasted ten minutes—lecturing herself in the mirror on the dangers of blurting out what she was thinking without some serious censoring when she was talking to Joaquin.

'It's never nice, making a total fool of yourself. When I think back to the things I said...' She screwed up her eyes and winced. 'You know that nightmare about being in a supermarket in your undies and not the good set, the mismatched greying bra and knickers? Times that by a billion.'

'I have no matching set of any colour, and I see no reason you should feel...vulnerable.'

'You are joking!' She snorted. 'How did things get so complicated?' she despaired.

She lifted a hand to her lips, which still hadn't lost the tingle left by his mouth.

'Sex,' she said.

'I'm not talking about sex.'

The patronising edge to his smile made her want to swat at him for real.

'Sex is not complicated, it is as basic as breathing,' he observed, staring at her mouth.

'Don't look at me like that.'

'I can't *not* look at you like that,' he said.

The devastatingly simple statement drew a sound of protest from her lips.

'You wanted the truth,' he reminded her. 'Doesn't mean you'll like it.'

It was beyond disorientating to have Joaquin talking about sex in this way to her.

'I wish I could go back.' She paused, took a breath, and lifted her eyes to his. 'I wish everything could go back to normal.'

With a despairing shake of her head, she threw herself down into one of the very uncomfortable armchairs that were set beside the window embrasure. She let her head drop and her hair fell like a flaming curtain against the ugly tapestry upholstery.

'To when, precisely?' he asked, staring at the exposed length of her pale throat, remembering how she had tasted. How she had smelt.

The strength of primal need to possess her was something he had never experienced in his life before. It was insane—a form of insanity that was pure Clemmie—but maybe that was why? He'd spent years thinking of her as *just Clemmie,* and now she had stepped outside the box in his head and become not 'just Clemmie' but a warm and incredibly desirable sexual woman.

He thought of the untapped passion in her.

Playing the part of her fiancé had felt a good fit, and he had found himself envying the man who would truly earn that title. The idea of anyone but him unlocking that passion felt like a dark cloud over his head.

His stare had the hallmarks of compulsion as he watched her shake her head, before straightening with a little wince. She drew her knees up, rocking on her behind as she pushed her fingers into her hair, cautious around the wound. Slim and pale, they instantly vanished into the fiery mesh.

Clemmie held her tongue. But she knew exactly when she wanted to go back to—the moment in the car when she had related her retrieved memories, the ones that revealed she had lusted after him.

She sighed. She *did* lust after him.

That was the moment it had all started to unravel and the nice, neat lines around their relationship had become a maze where one misstep could take you off the edge of a cliff.

'What a mess,' she said.

His broad shoulders lifted in an expressive shrug as he studied her downcast features. 'Looking backwards and wishing is not a very practical use of our time. How about we move forward? Accept this as the new normal?'

He made it sound so easy—but then it probably was for him, she thought, refreshing her resentment as she thought of the way he had just switched off the heat of that kiss like flicking a switch, while she had been left a bundle of frustrated, lustful longing.

'Do you want me to ring your mother back and tell her the truth?'

'She started it—you finished it. You wanted to teach her a lesson.'

She grimaced, but felt relieved. 'I suppose so.'

'I've frequently felt that way, but I've never quite... That was inspired,' he observed as he savoured the memory, Clemmie mad and fired up was better than any firework display. 'I'd love to see the family's faces if we did rock up for real, all loved up.'

She did not share his delight at this image. 'I'm glad you find this funny,' she said, directing a glare of simmering resentment at him. 'This new "normal" does not feel normal. Are we meant to forget what happened?'

'Who said anything about forgetting?'

Their eyes connected, smouldering brown on brilliant green, and she felt her heart try to climb its way out of her chest.

She shook her head, moistened her dry lips and decided to skip the *What do you mean?* section of this conversation. She was not sure she really wanted or needed to know, so she went straight to the practical details.

'Look, after what's happened I can't stay here—obviously. I'll move in with Mum. I'll have to tell her the truth…although not all of it.' She frowned, trying to work through an expurgated version that left her with a bit of pride intact. 'God, this is going to be a terrible holiday.'

'Probably.'

His rapid agreement earned him a glare.

'This time of year is usually terrible for me,' he told her. 'Celebrating not one but two toxic unions. Celebrating not just one but two unhappy marriages. It's kind of a given that things will go wrong. I reckon that marrying on the same day was not a good omen.'

'Will they expect you to get married on the same day and carry on the tradition?'

He mouthed the first Spanish swear word he had taught her when they were kids. He had told her it meant have a good day—it didn't, of course. Something she'd realised when she had said it in front of the Spanish-speaking wife of her deputy head teacher.

'Your grandparents' marriage was unhappy too?' she asked.

'Oh, their mutual loathing was much more civilised than my parents'. There was no swearing or smashed crockery, no hushed-up abortions arranged for girlfriends and then arriving the next day at Mass hand in hand. For my grandparents' generation it was all about never forgetting what was owed to the family name. They communicated in a civilised manner through intermediaries for at least thirty years before my grandfather died.'

Her eyes grew round. 'They didn't ever talk?'

'Not a word—which made family dinners quite interesting. Since my grandfather died, get-togethers are less entertaining as a spectator sport, but equally awful.'

'Why did they hate each other that much?'

'Who knows? I doubt if even they remembered.'

'But you still go?'

'Maybe I'm an optimist? Maybe I think one day we will play happy families?'

She snorted at the idea; Joaquin's cynicism went cell-deep. 'No, you don't.'

'True, I don't. But sometimes it takes more effort to break a bad habit than to go along with it. One week in a year…a few hours of my life… I suppose that was my mindset, but this year I decided to exert myself to break the habit.'

'Which is why you are here?'

He nodded.

'Actually,' he admitted, 'when my grandfather was alive, I went just to see him. He was an old curmudgeon, but I kind of liked him. He would have liked you,' he added unexpectedly.

She laughed, not hiding her scepticism. 'I find that hard to believe,' she retorted, thinking of all the up themselves, snobby members of the Perez family she had met, or rather encountered, over the years.

'That's why he would have liked you.'

She blinked. 'What do you mean?'

'That bolshy "screw you" attitude.'

'I do not have a—' She broke off, actually liking the idea that she might be an empowered in-your-face woman, but as her eyes drifted to Joaquin's mouth her sense of self-satisfaction took a hit.

The fact was her hormones must be desperately unlib-erated, or she wouldn't be thinking the thoughts she was.

But that was okay. Because she was in charge and not her thoughts.

'Could you give me a lift down to the gatehouse?'

'Look, Clemmie, there is no reason for you to leave.'

'Seriously...?'

'I agree this has all happened the wrong way around, and I take responsibility for that.'

'Big of you,' she snapped out, not having a clue what he was talking about.

'I should have explained about that ring straight off and *then* made love to you.'

She had always known his arrogance was eye-wateringly off the scale, but she had accepted it as *just Joaquin being Joaquin* because it didn't affect her directly.

She folded her arms tight across her chest. The affect felt pretty direct now—at least to her tingling nipples.

'Is that how it usually works for you, Joaquin? You say "I want you" and women throw their knickers in the air?'

His devil-on-steroids grin blazed out. 'They more slide them slowly and sexily down their thighs.'

She felt her cheeks burn. 'Well, I'm not doing a strip-tease for you!'

For starters she wouldn't know where to begin.

You could learn, suggested the voice in her head.

Joaquin's expression blanked as he breathed through the images her words had planted in his head.

Images he would have liked to explore.

He would like to explore Clemmie...

Allowing himself to think of the details as his gaze slid over her slim, supple body proved to a masochistic indulgence too far. He felt a groan swell in his chest and fought to contain it. He hadn't felt this out of control for... Not ever, he realised. Not even in his teens, when he had been all hormones.

He had fancied her back then, but then his hormones had not been exactly discriminating. When you were eighteen a two-year age gap put her out of reach. And by the time she was eighteen he'd had more sense than to mess up their friendship.

There were plenty more fish in the sea that weren't Clemmie. Fish he could throw back in. Once a man had Clemmie there would be no throwing her away—maybe that was what had made him back away?

She was a keeper.

She watched as his dark lashes lowered leaving just the glitter of his eyes showing as he shrugged, as if it didn't really matter to him one way or the other. Anger cooled her shameful level of arousal, and in the cooling her mood made a mercurial shift.

'You do that with everything!' she charged, her voice rising.

'I do what?'

'You act like nothing means anything to you. You could stop your family being total pains *that* easily.' She snapped her fingers to illustrate her point. 'But you're just not bothered enough to make the effort. If you had to exert yourself to get a woman you couldn't be bothered, because there would be ten more ready and more than willing to take her place. The only thing you put any effort into is making money, and I don't believe you actually care about that! Your entire life you've never had to make an effort to achieve anything. You were always the fastest on the track, the smartest in the room and too good-looking—and don't you know it!'

During her outburst Joaquin's expression had shifted from astonishment to anger, landing on fascination as she came to a gasping halt.

No woman—*nobody*—had ever called him out that way.

'Is that genuinely how you see me?' He arched a brow,

sounding more curious than crushed by her no-holds-barred analysis.

'I don't think you're vain.'

The grudging concession drew a laugh from him.

He stopped laughing. It shouldn't be possible to feel both fiercely possessive and tenderly protective, but when he met those aquamarine eyes he felt those things and more.

'Do I not have *any* redeeming features?'

'Does being the best person to have around in an emergency count?'

'Am I?'

'You did save my life.'

'Which time?'

'I would have got out of that tree on my own!' Her expression sobered. 'No, this time you really did save my life.'

His discomfort was palpable.

'Sure, I'm a hero,' he returned, self-mockery in his voice. 'They are minutes I would not like to relive,' he admitted, his eyes clouding as the chaos of the crash flickered frame by frame through his head. Those seconds when he'd thought he would not be able to free Clemmie would stay with him for ever. Followed by the dread that his split-second decision to drag her out had inflicted upon her irreparable damage.

'Why are you so scared of change, Clemmie?'

'I'm not,' she countered. 'I'd just miss you as a friend.'

'Sex doesn't have to change that,' he said.

He was not sure he believed his claim but, set against the fact he had never wanted anything more in his life than to take this new shrewish, sexy Clemmie into his bed, truth was a secondary importance.

'But it always does—and don't ask how I would know, because *I know.*'

'So, what is the alternative? You'd actually want marriage with some guy you'd gift your innocence to?'

His contemptuous mockery stung as she thought, *No, I want love!*

'I do still think marriage is a mug's game,' she said, 'but that doesn't mean I'll settle for casual sex. I want an emotionally satisfying relationship *and* great sex. Is that too big an ask? I don't know...?'

'You are making this more complicated than it needs to be. Do you really think we could go back to being platonic now and pretend none of this ever happened?'

'Casual sex—'

'I'm not a stranger you just met in a bar.' Dark stains of frustrated anger appeared across the slashing angle of his cheekbones, emphasising the knife-edge, the sybaritic carved slant.

'It would be casual because that is the only sex you do. I happen to want sex with a person who doesn't just have a convenient gap in his diary. I want him to be...'

The feelings she kept boxed up inside her beat against the protective self-restraint she had built up.

'To be what?'

She wanted so much to say *not you*, but she knew that it wouldn't be true. This was definitely an insight she could have done without at that moment.

'You say we're not strangers? Well isn't that the point? The sort of sex you are talking about would only work if I didn't care about you.' She swallowed. 'And I do.'

There was a short static silence.

'Some things don't need to be said.'

'Actually, they do. But do you know something? I think you care about me, but not in the right way.'

She stopped, her expression going blank. Those words had acted like a key opening a closed door, releasing all the memories trapped inside.

It hurt in a way that bruises and cuts never hurt.

How happy the doctors would feel to be proved right. She was one for the textbooks, a classic case, burying a painful memory, a painful truth she didn't want to own.

The truth that had been revealed when she had looked at the ring on her finger and thought about it belonging to someone else...about someone else belonging to Joaquin.

The intense sense of loss that had engulfed her had made it impossible for her to dodge the truth. This wasn't a sudden shift between friendship and love. She had always loved him. But she had buried the feeling deep, because she didn't want to spend her life longing for something that would be out of reach for ever.

She loved Joaquin.

Joaquin, who was so emotionally inarticulate that he couldn't even say he cared for her.

'Damn ring!' she cursed, tears starting in her eyes as she gave it another vicious tug.

He watched her struggle to pull the ring off her finger. 'Stop that—you'll hurt yourself.' He caught both her wrists, his eyes dropping to her hands, so small and delicate between his, and he felt the now familiar kick of guilt, mingled in with lust and protectiveness.

It was a tangle of emotions he had never experienced before.

Hurt myself? she thought despairingly. *That ship has already sailed.*

Her cynical little laugh brought his dark eyes to her face.

'So if we end up in bed, Joaquin, what would it mean? Would we both have other relationships and just hook up occasionally?'

A spasm of frustration crossed his lean face as he released her hands. 'Clemmie—'

Refusing to be diverted, she cut across him, grabbing his arm. 'Would it be a secret thing? Or would we laugh about it in company? And when one of us found someone else would—?'

She stopped, catching her full lower lip in her teeth. Suddenly tired of being logical, tired of fighting herself.

She wouldn't be finding anyone else, because she wouldn't be looking. She didn't *want* anyone else.

He saw her expression change and, recognising the shift in her mood, opened his mouth to push his advantage. He closed it again.

She was totally inexperienced, and he was a man who thought of sex as a pleasurable pastime that he happened to be good at. She was a virgin who was looking for a romantic partnership.

He could rationalise it as much as he liked, but the end would not be pretty.

'You're right,' he said.

Shock skittered across her face. 'I am?'

He nodded. 'Let's draw a line under it. Sex is… Well, readily available. A conversation with a woman isn't—for me.'

He was agreeing. He wasn't fighting. He was saying he preferred chatting to her.

'That makes me feel *so* special.'

Joaquin scowled darkly in response to her sarcasm. It would seem that no good deed went unpunished—though personally he considered the ache in his groin was punishment enough.

'So you don't want to talk and you don't want sex? When am I going to be able to do something right?'

To hell with being noble! She was not a violent person, but the fact that he had the cheek to feel let down made her want to hit him. But while she was rising above this base instinct she was uncomfortably aware of how irrational her response was.

He was acting the way she had wanted him to.

And she was acting out.

It would be irrational not to feel relieved—and she was not irrational.

The silence stretched and Joaquin breathed through flared nostrils as he tried to lower the emotional temperature in recognition of her fragile status.

There was a limit to how many allowances he would or could make.

Where was your concern for her fragile status a few minutes ago?

Ignoring the sarcasm of his internal critic, he made an attempt to return a little normality to the situation.

'Your mum texted earlier, to say she's left some food. I'm sure it's a banquet, knowing your mum. It's in the fridge and just needs heating up. We could sit in the kitchen.'

They had shared many meals at that table, or at least its predecessor, over the years.

'We could open a bottle of...'

He paused and backtracked, thinking, *Skip the wine.* He suspected his nobility would not withstand alcohol—or for that matter, her smile.

But she wasn't smiling at him.

The sparkling contempt glowing in her wide green eyes was sending a very different message.

'Wine might not mix with your painkillers,' he said.

'I'm not taking any painkillers.'

His rejection felt like the ultimate gut-punch.

He was talking about food.

Metaphorically, he had swatted her away like a bug.

'I'm not hungry,' she said coldly.

Actually, she was. But it was the principle of the thing. He'd seduced her with… Well, without doing much at all. And now he had turned off the sexy seductive stuff like a tap.

'Where are you going?' he demanded.

She turned, her eloquent brows swishing upwards. 'Upstairs—do I need to ask permission?'

He gave a weary sigh.

'Fine. I'll heat up the food.'

CHAPTER SEVEN

HE HEATED UP the rather delicious-smelling casserole that had been left in the fridge. He laid two places at the kitchen table—not the old scrubbed one that his mother had thrown away, but something designer, involving a 'river' of green epoxy between two slabs of oak.

He hated to admit it, but he quite liked it.

Possibly because he found himself comparing the colour of the epoxy with Clemmie's eyes.

He poured himself a glass of red wine and waited.

After twenty minutes he was on his second glass and he decided to eat.

The food was wasted on him. He stirred it around his plate. There were things aside from food that man needed to survive and stay sane, and Clemmie had lit a fire in him that still flamed hot.

He left the food on the table and wandered through to an opening that his mother had had cut through the wall to the orangery. Fortunately, the orangery itself had escaped the tweaks that jarred in so much of the rest of the house.

It was filled with light from the massive south-facing floor-to-ceiling windows that looked out on a Gertrude Jekyll–inspired garden, complete with manicured hedges and a long ornamental pond with fountains and carp.

His footsteps echoed in the cavernous green space as

he walked across stones worn smooth with age. They were still warmed by the original steam pipes, and the air was scented by the exotic plants that spilled out of raised beds. Rows of orange trees in deep ornamental tubs still lined the stone walls which were covered in carefully trained vines that provided a healthy crop of grapes. The trickle of water from several pools added to the soothing atmosphere.

Joaquin didn't feel soothed.

Casting his brooding glance over the tranquil scene, he decided that doing the right thing had never felt more wrong. Actually, who was to say it *was* even the *right thing*?

Even as the defiant thought was flickering through his head, he recognised the absurdity of ignoring a bunch of red flags.

In what world, he asked himself, *would sleeping with your best friend, who turns out to be a virgin and who is also suffering from amnesia, be considered right?*

Clemmie allowed the jets of water to wash the suds from her hair as she continued to work at the ring. No matter what she did, it remained jammed on her knuckle. Tears of frustration streaming down her face, she stepped backwards, hitting the tiled wall. With her right hand holding up her left, she glared at the ring, her thoughts drifting back to that moment in the library when the gaps in her memory had been filled in.

There had been no gentle transition from ignorance to knowledge. It had just hit her with a force real enough that even now she struggled to catch her breath.

Panic attack, diagnosed the voice in her head as her chest tightened.

She had imagined this moment—imagined relief, imagined the truth setting her free.

The opposite was true. This new knowledge made her feel helpless.

The low buzz in her head got louder.

Her legs were shaking.

She was shaking all over.

A whirl of black dots danced in front of her eyes as she stumbled out of the shower, her heart pounding so hard she thought it would burst out of her chest.

And then it was all a blur.

She didn't remember pulling on the silky wrap, but felt it flapping against her wet legs as she raced down the stairs.

The kitchen bore signs of recent occupation, but no one was there. Then, through the arch at the end of the room, she saw movement in the orangery.

'Joaquin!'

He swung back from his grim contemplation of the garden.

Clemmie was standing in the stone archway, barefoot, clad in a thin blue robe that ended just above her knees. Her hair was darkened with water that dripped over her face and left dark patches on the silky fabric of the robe.

'I've remembered. It's all come back.'

The confession came out in a rush.

She lifted a hand to her head, her brow puckering when it came away wet.

'I was in the shower...'

The getting out of it was not too clear.

'I was trying to get the ring off... Sorry I—' She broke off as she suddenly found it impossible to explain her panic and the impetuous rush to share, which already

seemed stupid. 'I don't know why I came to tell you…
you already know.'

He did know—but not everything. He didn't know the
truth that had been too painful for her to remember.

Her eyes went to the ring on her finger—the ring that
she had imagined on another woman's finger. And that
had made her realise that she didn't just love Joaquin as
a friend.

The searing truth that had hit her just before the collision was that she loved him, and that the idea of him
marrying another woman made her want to curl up in a
ball and hide away in a corner—which she supposed her
brain had achieved its own version of when it had blanked
her memory.

'I kept trying to get it off.'

She tugged at it, to illustrate how hard she had tried,
and at the first touch the ring slid off her finger and bounced
across the stone floor. Eyes wide, she watched it before it
vanished down a steel grating.

'Oh, my God. I'm so sorry!' she yelped, running over
to the grate and falling on her knees. 'I'll find it. I promise. Do you have a screwdriver or a…a crowbar?'

'Oh, let me see…' He patted his pockets. 'I knew I'd
forgotten something.'

Her head lifted, reproach in her eyes. 'This isn't a joke,'
she sobbed.

'I can see that.'

'That thing is probably worth a fortune.'

'Probably,' he agreed, crossing to her side and holding out a hand. 'You do know you look a little bit crazy
down there?'

'Well, your sensitivity lessons really worked, didn't
they?' she snapped, finally taking his hand. Not because

she would admit she needed it, but because she was suddenly very aware that she had nothing on under her robe, and covering all the essentials while getting up unaided would not be easy.

The way Joaquin was looking, and where he was looking, suggested that he was well aware that she was naked under the robe.

He removed his burning stare and his hand at the same moment, and as he took a step back she fought the magnetic tug that made her want to lean into him.

'As a general rule, I have no objection to women on their knees at my feet.' His smile deepened. 'But I do believe you are blushing all over.'

She stifled a gasp and brought her lashes down in a protective shield. 'The ring…' she pushed out in desperation, wanting to focus on anything but the internal shudder, the rush of liquid heat between her legs, the nipping contraction of her nipples.

'Is hideous. And, yes, extremely valuable. I will arrange for it to be retrieved and put in the back of a dark bank vault. Where it belongs. So, forget about the ring and relax. Take some deep breaths…not too deep,' he added, seeing there was a danger of her hyperventilating.

She sniffed and tightened the belt on her robe, thinking that being able to relax did not seem likely any time before next year—maybe longer. But despite her gloomy prediction she followed his advice, and felt the buzz in her ears recede.

'Excellent.'

On another occasion she would likely as not have told him where he could shove his pat on the head and patronising approval, but at that moment she was just happy that there were no black dots.

'Let it go.'

The hand on her shoulder and the thumb massaging her collarbone through the silk was not a recipe for further relaxation. Wearing an inch of armour would not have made her feel relaxed with him...wearing very little made it a laughable concept.

'Sorry for the drama.' She stepped back and felt his hand fall away before opening her eyes, not sure if she was going to laugh or cry. Luckily it turned out to be the former. 'All a bit OTT.'

She left a gap for him to join in with her laughter. But he didn't. He just carried on looking down at her in that dark, intense, hungry way that made the knot of helpless longing in the pit of her stomach tighten.

'I just wanted you to know that I had remembered.'

Pity you didn't remember to put any clothes on, she told herself. Though the cooling updraught on her heated parts was something of a relief...

'Not the part when you rescued me, because I was pretty out of it then, but I do remember you were in the helicopter. I remember your voice.'

She remembered clinging to it when she felt herself sliding into the darkness. She looked at his chest, at the wall of strength it offered, and wanted to cling again.

'You held my hand, I think?' she said.

Something flashed in his eyes. 'I did. I was terrified.'

'You...?'

The silence between them stretched, and so did Clemmie's tension.

'So, barring the cuts and bruises...' he ran a light finger over the fading bruise on her cheek '...and the loss of a little hair...'

He lifted a wet skein, rubbing it between his fingers

before allowing it to fall, allowing his thoughts to drift for a brief, indulgent moment to his private fantasy of wrapping himself in that glorious mane of hair.

With a sharp inhalation, he pushed it away while he still could. 'And let's face it, you can spare it. We are back to normal...'

Which of course was what she had told herself she wanted. But now he had come around to her way of thinking it didn't feel such a desirable outcome—or, for that matter, so normal.

Their 'normal' had definitely altered.

Their eyes met and she knew he recognised it too.

'What's normal?' she asked, and the seething frustration and spiralling out-of-control confusion she felt spilled out in words. 'How can anything be normal after I...?'

'Told me you were a virgin?'

Her eyes slid from his. 'I thought we were engaged—I thought there was a *we* when I told you that!'

'I'm glad you did. It would have come as something of a shock.'

Her eyes flew upwards, eyelashes fluttering as her breath quickened. 'You seem to be taking a hell of a lot for granted.'

'You're not going to have another panic attack, are you?'

'Is that what you ask every woman you make love to? Because if so I can imagine it being a bit of a turn-off. I am not having a panic attack!'

'Is that what you think I'm doing? Making love to you?'

She studied his perfect face. His expression seemed still and almost remote—until she connected with his molten dark stare.

'I don't know...' She hated the quavering note of appeal in her voice.

One corner of his mouth lifted in a smile that was both tender and fierce. 'Do you want me to?'

Her stomach muscles clenched as his words shocked and excited her.

He arched a brow as the silence stretched.

'All right,' she conceded huskily. 'Yes, I do. But I feel...'

She closed her mouth. They knew each other so well, but this was not the Joaquin she knew.

Hell, she didn't know herself.

His dark head dipped, his hands sliding to her shoulders to drag her in closer.

'Tell me how you feel,' he rasped, his breath wafting over her cheek, his glittering eyes snaring her wide green stare.

'I can't,' she breathed, suddenly hit by a wave of inadequacy as images of the women he'd dated flickered through her head.

He wanted her to be sexy and provocative and... And she was sure she'd just sound lame and stupid. If he laughed at her she might never recover.

'It's scary.'

'You're scared of me?' He drew back slightly, not sounding as if he liked the idea.

She lifted a hand to his stubble-roughened cheek and gave him a long, level look. 'Not of you—not ever.'

The total confidence in her voice smoothed the frown lines in his forehead.

'The way you make me feel is scary, though,' she admitted.

'How do I make you feel?' he asked, and his soft voice was sinfully suggestive as he placed his hand over hers to keep it there against his cheek for a moment.

When his hand fell away, she missed the warmth.

'You are fighting it,' he told her.

'There is no "it".'

'*We* are fighting it. Ask yourself why? It's not as if we don't already know things will never go back to the way they were.'

He acknowledged it out loud and she agreed with a wistful shake of her head, part of her acknowledging his candour, part of her resenting it.

'I wish…'

She stopped mid-sentence as his hands slid up her arms, ruffling the light silk covering and coming to rest on her shoulders. The action drew her eyes to his face.

'Do you want your first time to be with me?'

She swallowed, thinking, *I want my first and last time to be with you.*

That wasn't going to happen.

Get real, Clemmie. Just take what you can get. Make memories for when you are a sad old lady with cats.

No cats. She was allergic.

Her internal dialogue was a poor distraction from the driving need inside her. She could never resist Joaquin for the simple reason she didn't want to.

She wasn't sure if the truth equated with freedom, but it was a relief to acknowledge the facts.

'You're shaking,' he discovered, drawing her closer until her head rested on his chest. 'Sorry. I'm rushing this. Recovering your memory must be pretty mind-blowing—'

'No,' she said, burrowing in close, breathing in the scent of him, her breath coming in frantic little gasps. 'You're not rushing things… I don't want to wait and you're right—I want this.'

She lifted her face from the hardness of his chest and

tilted her face up to his. Her green eyes glowed half in plea, half in invitation, and he couldn't resist.

His lowered his mouth to hers, his tongue skimming its lush outline before claiming her lips. It was not a full-on assault. She sensed he was still holding back. It felt more like a question.

A question that she responded to by sliding her tongue between his lips and kissing him.

'Yes, Joaquin, I do want this.'

The level of tension quivering in his body did not lessen, but it altered as he took her chin between his thumb and forefinger, becoming more focused.

He made her feel as though she was the only person in his world.

He was so beautiful!

She squeezed her eyes tightly closed, suddenly unable to stand the sensory and emotional overload.

'This is really happening?'

'Only if you want it to.'

Her eyes flew wide. 'I do, Joaquin, I really do.'

Nothing had ever felt so right.

And then, without warning, like a cold gust of wind, she was suddenly attacked by a fluttering flock of insecurities.

'I don't know if...'

He brushed her lips with his again, kissing away her insecurities with a skill and a ruthless efficiency that left her breathless and aching for more.

'This is not about technique...this is about *feeling*.'

The words were confident, but they came from a place inside him that he hadn't known existed.

CHAPTER EIGHT

'IF YOU DON'T want this, this is the point where you tell me.'

'I do.' She couldn't take her eyes off his mouth as she strained to press her lips to the sensuous curve. 'I do want this. I want you.'

He kissed her back and the heat was instantaneous. It was a firestorm—and they were in the middle of it.

Holding her eyes, he pulled at the cord on her gown and slid it off her shoulders.

She closed her eyes.

'No, look at me,' he commanded, cupping her chin.

Her eyes flickered open and she looked into the searing heat of his stare. She stood there quivering with a need that rose up in her like a tide.

'You are beautiful,' he rasped, stepping back fractionally to allow his gaze free range over her body, from her small, high breasts with their plump rosy nipples to her soft belly and slim hips. 'Perfect.'

His hands on her waist, he picked her up, and Clemmie wound her legs around his hips, her hands in his hair, and returned his kisses with a hunger to match his.

Instinct was totally in control as she plastered herself against the muscular hardness of his chest. She was only vaguely conscious of him laying her down on one of the deep padded benches along the orangery wall.

His eyes never left hers as with one knee braced on the bench he fought his way out of his shirt before tossing it away.

She gasped, staring hungrily at the taut, defined musculature of his chest and belly.

He was the most beautiful thing she had ever seen.

He leaned over her, adjusting his position, inserting his knee between her legs, pressing against the aching core of her as he unfastened his belt and unzipped his trousers.

Clemmie reached up and tugged them down his narrow hips, revealing his muscular thighs and the black boxer shorts he wore underneath.

He stood up and slid them all the way down; a moment later the boxers joined them and were kicked away too.

Clemmie's awed gasp was both flattering and arousing, and it brought a fierce grin to his face as he pushed a bunch of cushions to the floor, to give him room to plant a hand on either side of her shoulders. Another cushion hit the floor, and the last one was about to receive the same treatment when he changed his mind and tucked it underneath her head.

As he lowered himself, their first skin-to-skin contact drew a low moan from her throat. He was like hot silk... and so hard.

He kissed her then, and she kissed him back, their kisses becoming a primal rhythm as his tongue plunged and retreated into the moist recesses of her mouth, exploring every crevice and secret corner. It became wild, teeth clashing, noses grazing, as she tangled her fingers in the dark silk of his hair and battled to increase the skin-to-skin contact as she arched her back under him.

'I'm going to kiss every inch of you,' he told her in a throaty whisper as he licked away the pool of salty moisture that had gathered in the hollow at the base of her throat.

She arched into the heat of him as he took one pouting nipple into his mouth, making her squirm and gasp beneath him. All the while his hands were moving over her body, touching, stroking, massaging in a restless exploration.

His gaze was searing as he watched her. She was trembling with the ache of a desire that was overwhelming. Her hands slid over his shoulders, loving the damp silk texture of his golden skin and the hardness of sinew and muscle, her fingers digging in when his exploration became more intimate.

She whispered his name over and over, panting as he parted her moist folds, his eyes never leaving her face for a moment. Rolling onto his side, he pulled her with him and, looping her leg over his hips, continued his exploration, sliding a finger into her as he led her hand to the silky iron hardness of his erection, murmuring words of encouragement as she tightened her fingers and cupped him.

'You're so tight...'

He groaned against her parted lips, pulled in a sharp breath as her fingers moved up and down his shaft. He was panting as hard as she was.

'And you're so...'

His nostrils flared. 'It'll be fine...don't worry,' he soothed. 'It'll be good. I promise.'

When he lowered her onto her back and moved himself over her, she grabbed his shoulders and pushed herself against his strategically placed knee to ease the ache between her legs. It didn't ease.

'I can't!' she cried in frustration as the sensations continued to drive her wild.

'You can. We're doing this together. Relax… I am very good at this.'

'You're so arrogant,' she said, biting his lip a little too hard.

He bared his teeth in a provocative smile, running his tongue over the pinpricks of blood. 'And don't you love that about me?'

'Yes!' she groaned out. She loved everything about him.

'Your voice is so sexy it hurts,' he crooned huskily. 'Now, wrap your legs around me.'

She did, her fingers tightening on his shoulders as she felt the imprint of his erection first against her lower belly and then, as he kissed her, lower still.

The external friction was exquisite and frustrating in equal measure.

'God, you *are* good at this.'

'Just relax,' he breathed, fighting the overwhelming urge to thrust into her. 'Let me do this…stay with me…'

She tensed a little as she felt his first intrusion, but quickly relaxed, sinking into herself as he entered her slowly. She took a little more of him with each thrust, until he slid a hand under her bottom and lifted her hips to take him fully.

She had never imagined anything could feel this way. She had never imagined the sheer, intense excitement of him inside her, the pleasure building and building, the sensation growing more intense until suddenly she wasn't staying with him. She felt as if she was losing herself. And then, just when she could not bear it, she was whole again, and the dam inside her broke, releasing wave after wave of toe-tingling pleasure.

She was conscious at some level of a feral groan as he sank heavy and hot against her...

Joaquin looked at her, marvelling at how anyone who looked so fragile could be so fierce and so strong. He waited for the post-coital sense of dissatisfaction to hit him. It didn't. And as he looked at her lovely flushed face he was conscious of a surge of possessiveness he'd never experienced before. But then he had never slept with a virgin before...

He rolled onto his side and pulled her across him until her head lay on his chest.

They lay there, the sweat on their skin cooling. And lying there naked, with the most beautiful man on earth, Clemmie thought she'd feel self-conscious—but she didn't. She just felt a glow and a sense of *rightness*.

'We don't want to fall asleep here,' said Joaquin.

'It sounds like a good plan to me.'

He laughed as she attempted to burrow into him. 'I think we should make it to the bed this time.'

Her head lifted. 'This time?'

'This time. Next time we'll play it by ear.'

Laughing at her expression, he thought he couldn't remember the last time he'd laughed in bed with a woman, or even smiled. It had all become a purely mechanical exercise, he realised.

He slid out from under her and stood there holding out his hand. She took it, marvelling at his lack of self-consciousness.

'I can walk, you know,' she said without much enthusiasm. It was not an unpleasant sensation to be lifted into the arms of a naked sex god.

'Humour me,' he suggested as he strode off, Clemmie

in his arms, through to the house, where the only sound was their combined heartbeats, the tick of a clock and the odd creaking floorboard.

Joaquin was just about to fall asleep when he heard a phone. He glanced at the time and grimaced. The sound of a soft grunt beside him came as a shock. He reached out and felt a warm, squirming body next to him, and he felt something that came close to sleepy contentment despite the screaming phone.

It took Clemmie a few seconds before she came fully awake too. With a gasp, she slid out from under his heavy arm and, rolling onto her side, reached for her phone.

He watched her dropping it. He lay back with a sigh. The view of her bottom, the dip of her narrow waist and the smooth elegant curve of her back was a good way to start the day—and it *was* day. The sun was filtering in through a gap in the heavy drapes, casting a pool of light close to her head, sparking fiery lights in her hair.

'Let me.'

He pushed up against her back, leaning over her to grab the phone and hand it to her before settling back, his face pressed to her neck and his body pressed hard against hers.

He allowed his thoughts to drift with gloating approval over the night they had shared.

'No, you didn't wake me, Mum,' Clemmie lied, glancing at the clock and repressing a guilty groan. 'Yes, I'm fine.'

'More than fine...' he whispered into her ear.

Then he dragged himself towards her, his body effectively pinning her legs down, and started kissing a wet, wandering path up her belly.

'No…what? No, Mum, I'm fine. Totally recovered this morning.'

She met the wicked eyes that held hers. With a sigh, she swivelled her legs over the edge of the bed.

There was a hesitation, and then her mother asked, carefully casual, 'Have you remembered anything?'

'Yes, I have, Mum. Things are coming back to me now,' she said, feeling wistful for her previous ignorance, when she hadn't known what the painful memory she'd been protecting herself from was.

She had paid heavily for that temporary blissful ignorance.

The only surprise was that the illusion she had built up had lasted so long. All it had taken to smash it to a million pieces was seeing the ring that was intended for another on her own finger.

She loved Joaquin—not just as a friend but as a man.

'Oh, darling, that is so marvellous. I can't wait to tell Harry.'

'Harry sounds like one of the good ones, Mum,' she said, feeling ashamed that she'd half wanted her mum's new love to be a loser, like his predecessors. She really hoped he wasn't. The Leith women deserved to be happy in love!

'Oh, he is, but—'

She listened, holding the phone so that Joaquin could hear as her mum explained that Harry, who had been due to arrive later that day, would now not be coming.

'Oh, that's a shame,' Clemmie said, meaning it.

'His mother is very elderly and quite frail. She's had a fall and she's in hospital awaiting surgery.'

'Oh, I'm so sorry.'

'He's suggested I go there and keep him company, but I've explained that that's out of the question.'

'I don't see why.'

'Because... Well, you need me here, Clemmie. You are only just out of hospital.'

Clemmie frowned—she could tell from her voice that her mum was torn.

'Good morning, Ruth... Yes, I *am* here,' Joaquin said, smiling provocatively as he ignored Clemmie, who was miming a frantic zipping motion across her lips as she held out her hand for the phone.

He evaded her attempts to snatch it from him by levering himself lithely out of the bed. And Clemmie sat there simmering as she listened to the one-sided conversation and tried not to be distracted by his state of arousal.

She failed.

'Yes, she is... I was listening in,' he confided, before laughing—leaving Clemmie wondering what the hell that laugh was about. She dreaded to think as he went silent, clearly listening.

'Oh, I agree,' he said after a long pause. 'Well, actually, Ruth, this could work out well. My mother has been in touch and she's invited us to go to the castle for the annual family party. Everyone is anxious to meet Clemmie. Yes... Obviously we said we couldn't, because Harry was coming, but now... Well, that's sorted, then.'

He fielded Clemmie's killer glare with an insouciant shrug.

'I can promise you she will keep you up to date, and if there is any issue we will contact you. In the meantime, I will look after her for you. Here she is now.'

He handed the phone back to Clemmie who, aware that

he wasn't looking at her face, dragged the sheet up over her breasts.

The rest of the conversation was short, as calling Joaquin a liar was not really an option when her mum sounded so relieved at the new arrangement.

'I told Ruth we'd pop down and see her after breakfast. When you're dressed. Are you cross with me?' he asked when Clemmie had hung up.

She sighed. 'Well, I am grateful. Mum obviously wants to spend some time with her Harry.'

'You've changed your tune. I thought you wanted Harry out of the picture.'

'I never— I just want my mum to be happy...'

'And you being away with me in Spain will achieve that?'

'Not *really* in Spain, obviously. Once she's gone the gatehouse will be empty.'

'Have you really thought this through? What if someone sees the lights on and informs the police? Neighbourhood Watch will consider it their duty to keep an eye on the place.'

'Don't be stupid.'

She knew she didn't sound as confident as she had intended. Community spirit, of which there was a lot locally, did have its downsides.

'We could simply go to Spain.'

'Your mother hates me.'

'I don't think she particularly likes me either. Aria is not really the warm, maternal type. What are you looking at me like that for?' he asked.

She shook her head, still picturing him as little boy with no one to hug him. These days he had plenty of hugs. A therapist might suggest that was why he seemed to be searching for love, but any therapist would ditch that theory after five seconds in Joaquin's company and diagnose a man who didn't believe in love. Let alone go out looking for it.

'Hate is a strong word,' he said now. 'But, yes, she would loathe it if we arrived. And I cannot see that being a bad thing. It is time I drew a few lines in the sand,' he said grimly.

'I never realised what a vindictive person you are.'

'That does put you in the minority.'

'If we turned up, we would be shown the door quick-smart.'

'No,' he said calmly. 'We wouldn't.'

'All right, *I* would be shown the door—you would be embraced as the prodigal son.'

'It's *my* door, Clemmie—did you not realise that?'

He felt a weird pang in his chest when he saw the confusion flashing in her eyes. She had always seen him in a way no one else did. But it was time that she saw him as he was if they were ever to have any sort of future.

He froze, his eyelashes flickering as he asked himself where that thought had come from?

Did he *want* a future in which Clemmie saw him as he actually was?

'What do you mean?' she asked.

'I mean that my grandfather left everything—the entire estate—to me when he died. I was twenty. Sure, Mum owns this place, but the rest of the property portfolio is mine. I was "the best of a bad lot"—and I am quoting. If anyone is going to be doing any throwing out it is me.'

'You own the *castillo*?'

Clemmie had seen photos, obviously, and the building was iconic. What it represented was outside her experience. The manor was big, but the place she'd seen photos of online and in magazines was on a different scale.

'Why did I not know this?'

'It must have slipped my mind to mention it. Or maybe we don't share everything?'

'I don't have any secrets.'

'You never revealed you wanted to kiss me!'

She lifted her chin. His taunt felt like a slap—a piece of deliberate cruelty. 'Been there, done that, and burnt the tee shirt!'

'Look, we both know that you're not comfortable with lies—'

'You make me sound like a freak! And that wasn't a lie!' she said, finding that she couldn't not look at his mouth when she said that.

'Freak? I wouldn't go that far. But it does limit you in normal everyday life. You must realise that at some point your mum will see past your telling her *I'm in Spain, Mum, having a great time* and will come rushing back. However, if you *are* in Spain?'

'You are not seriously suggesting...?' She gave a disbelieving laugh.

He didn't laugh back. He just shrugged. 'Why not?'

'Why *not*?'

'Think of it as a dirty weekend, if that helps.'

'It doesn't. You just want to use me to get back at your mother.'

'I am happy for you to use me back—especially if you are sitting naked in my bed. And you can't tell me you wouldn't enjoy a little payback for what she said about your mum.'

'I suppose...'

'That's settled, then.'

'What time did you say to Mum we'd drop in?'

'I left that open, so there's no rush,' he said, catching hold of the sheet she was still holding and dragging it down to reveal her unfettered breasts before leaping into the bed.

'Do you mind? It's cold!'

'I'll soon warm you up,' he promised, lifting the sheet in a billowing tent above his head and letting it settle over them as he slid down beside her.

CHAPTER NINE

IT WASN'T JUST the jaw-dropping luxury of Joaquin's private plane that struck her, it was the casual way he treated travelling in such luxury. She had only ever seen him on her home turf previously, but this was a glimpse into the life of a very different Joaquin, who enjoyed a lifestyle that few did.

A lifestyle she had been granted a peek into.

Don't get used to it, the voice in her head cautioned.

'You have gone very quiet,' he said.

She turned in her seat, pushing her head into the soft leather to look at him. 'Have I?'

'Well, you haven't babbled for at least five minutes.'

'Sorry. I'll try and be sophisticated and blasé the next time I fly on a private jet. I know it's like catching a bus for you, but this is my first.'

He stared at the lips that had delivered all the sensual delight he had imagined they would. 'You're fitting a lot of firsts in.'

His comment sent the heat to her cheeks. 'Have you ever caught a bus?'

He gave crack of laughter. 'Yes, several times.'

'Like royalty? With a security team sitting two rows back?' She paused before adding, 'I assume you do have security?'

'Only when strictly necessary, and always discreet.

Airports can be potential areas of concern, and lately the threat level has been...'

'You have a threat level?'

He mistook her concern. 'You are perfectly safe; I would never put you in danger.'

'But you have been in danger?'

'There was a rather determined stalker.'

The shocking admission chilled her blood. She could not believe how casual he was about it.

'These days anyone with a public profile is a target for threats. The trick is to be aware, not to be afraid.'

'I couldn't live like that.'

He opened his laptop and said nothing, although she decided he was probably thinking she didn't have to—she was just a visitor with sleeping rights.

She squared her chin and pushed away the thought. She was going to enjoy every moment and not allow thoughts of tomorrow spoil today.

'Work?'

His head lifted from the screen. 'No, the latest test match cricket results,' he said, closing the lid of the laptop and sliding his arm across her shoulders. 'You're nervous.'

'What makes you say that?' she asked, allowing her head to fall onto his shoulder.

Joaquin smoothed a silky strand of hair from her cheek and, hooking a finger under her softly rounded chin, brought her face around to his. 'You chatter like a five-year-old on a sugar high when you're nervous.'

'I do not—' She closed her mouth and mimed a zipping action.

In response, Joaquin bent his head and fitted his mouth to hers, flicking his tongue along the sealed outline as he kissed across the plump, generous curve.

Clemmie groaned. 'Cheating...' she whispered huskily.

'Like they say...' His smile was caressing as he kissed the corner of her mouth, her chin, the tip of her nose. 'All's fair in love and—'

She silenced him with a fierce kiss, closing her eyes to prevent the emotional heat of tears she felt press against her eyelids.

Love...the word he only ever spoke with sarcasm or irony. The word she didn't allow herself to speak. Most of the time she was okay with that, but sometimes it just hurt so much. Because since she had acknowledged it she wanted to shout it from the rooftops.

'Look, I might sit upfront for a bit, if you don't mind,' he said. 'Catch up with the pilot. He's a friend.'

'Go ahead. I'm fine. I've brought a book.'

When he returned half an hour later she had it propped up in front of her. The illusion that she was lost in the pages was ruined when he took it, turned it the right way up, and then put it back.

'Good read?'

'I was cloud-counting.'

'Did you miss me?'

His careless manner annoyed her so much that she almost blurted the truth, but managed to bite her tongue in time.

Maybe he sensed something. She was hoping not anything specific.

But then he dropped the teasing manner and just said, 'Time to belt up...we are landing.'

It was border control, but not as she knew it. The security check was literally a walk-through, and the waiting car was a chauffeur-driven limo.

She had always considered herself a 'feet on the ground and muck in' sort of person, but she realised as she pushed back into the leather upholstery and refused the offer of a glass of wine from the built-in bar, that it would be very easy to adjust to this sort of life.

'Wake up, sleepyhead we're here.'

'Mmm?' Clemmie blinked and lifted her head fractionally from his shoulder, claiming with a yawn, 'I wasn't asleep.'

'Then you have a serious drooling issue,' he said, patting his shoulder.

'We're here?' Clemmie cried, suddenly becoming aware of her surroundings as she jerked upright. 'How long have I...?'

She stopped as she took in the building they were approaching.

Maplehurst was considered grand by most people, but this place took 'grand' to a new level! Even though she had been prepared to be shocked, she stared in awe at the fortified castle that towered over them. It must dominate the landscape for miles.

'Welcome to Castillo Perez,' he said, watching her.

'It's not just that this is a *real* castle,' she whispered. 'I mean...the towers, the walls...it looks like a fortress.'

'Cosy it is not,' he inserted drily. 'It will not surprise you to learn that at one point in its history it served as a prison.'

She spun around in her seat. 'How old is it?'

'The templars built the original in the thirteenth century, on Moorish foundations. My family acquired it after the roof was destroyed by fire in the fifteenth century. Back then there were fifteen towers, but we have lost one since then.'

'Careless,' she said breathlessly as a sinister-looking metal gate opened across the porticoed entrance to allow their car to sail inside.

'This is yours? A bit big for one person, isn't it?' she suggested, hiding her sudden spike of nerves in flippancy.

'I haven't spent more than a week a year here since I inherited—I sometimes forget it's mine. Actually, several members of the family live here periodically, and they forget too.'

'And now you're here to remind them?' she speculated, finding the play of expressions across his face more fascinating than the courtyard they had arrived in.

'You could say that.'

Something in his voice made her add. 'Your mother does know we... *I* am coming?'

'Oh, she knows. We had a cosy little chat about it last night.' His lips twisted in an ironic smile as he replayed the conversation in his head.

Clemmie frowned as he exited the limo with his usual ineffable grace. Smiling at the uniformed figure who held her door open, she got out and walked around the car to join him. He was adjusting his tie and staring up at the building. Clemmie followed suit and tilted her head back.

'I don't believe this place...'

It was impossible not to be intimidated by the sheer size of the building that towered above their heads. She looked around, half expecting someone to greet them.

He correctly interpreted her action. 'There won't be a welcoming committee.'

'But they *are* expecting us?'

'You keep asking me that?'

'And you,' she retorted, 'keep looking shifty.'

He looked cool and remote. Almost like a stranger,

standing there, literally lord of all he surveyed, dressed in an immaculate suit and handmade leather shoes. Perhaps the difference was in the setting and not in him.

He laughed at her accusation, but she noticed he didn't quite meet her eyes.

With his mother's parting threat last night in his mind, Joaquin felt a faint scratch of guilt—which he dismissed as irrational. He hadn't told Clemmie the details of his conversation with his mother because he didn't want to believe she would follow through with her threat.

He knew she would.

His mother was a spiteful woman, who hit out when thwarted and frequently acted against her own best interests when she felt ignored or insulted.

Telling Clemmie about it would achieve nothing, and for him to successfully negate that threat and protect Clemmie she needed to be here.

He just hoped that the fact he had invited some guests that would require his mother to be on her best behaviour would save Clemmie from the worst of his mother's spite.

'This place looks deserted,' she said.

The men carrying their luggage had already vanished, and they stood alone amidst the carefully tended gardens of a courtyard garden, complete with fountains and statuary and hedges trimmed with surgical precision into the shape of leaping dolphins.

'Would that it were… I realise it can be intimidating,' he conceded.

'I'm not intimidated.'

'Fair enough.'

Clemmie smiled, grateful that he hadn't called her out on the obvious lie. The place was as scary as hell—on so many levels.

'I'll give you a guided tour later. It's basically a museum stroke art gallery—at least that's the way I think of it.'

'Not home?'

She was not surprised when he shook his head.

'Is it open to the public?'

'It is my intention that it will be. I expect the news to go down like a lead balloon. Sharing is not in the Perez family's vocabulary.'

'You really have come here looking for a fight,' she observed.

Was she to be stuck in the middle?

Her accusation drew from him the glimmer of a grim smile. 'My private apartments are in the bell tower,' he said, and tipped his head to a building on the far side of the courtyard they stood in. 'It is as far away as possible from the areas occupied by other family members. I took it over after my grandfather died. Not the furniture, though—his tastes were rather…erm… Gothic. Come on.'

Inside the building, she immediately understood his 'museum' description. The stone walls of the corridor he led her down were covered in what had to be priceless tapestries, and the vivid tiles underfoot were obviously ancient. Chandeliers hung from the dark wooden rafters overhead and the entire place had an almost ecclesiastical hush. There was no sound but the noise of their footsteps.

There was nothing Gothic about the suite of rooms that they ended up in. She got the impression of light and space. The furniture was antique, but not in a way that made you afraid to touch it, and books were haphazardly arranged in several bookcases. The walk-in closets in the main bedroom were vast and mirror-lined, and looking at the massive bed, with its Moorish carved headboard, made her imagination spike, causing her body to flush with desire as she imagined ending up there.

'I could live in that bathroom,' she called out, emerging from the first of two bathrooms, which boasted a massive copper bath set on a raised plinth. There was nothing ancient about the plumbing.

Joaquin, who had stayed in the salon while she explored, had poured himself a drink.

He offered her one, but she refused.

'Are you hungry? Dinner won't be before eight.'

She shook her head. She had eaten on the plane, choosing her food from a menu that had been prepared by a Michelin starred chef.

He put down his glass and walked across the room, coming up behind her to slide his hands to her hips and pull her hard against him.

She sighed, her eyes closing as he lifted her hair to kiss his way up her neck before he turned her to face him.

'You look good in this,' he said, tugging her cotton shirt out of her jeans and sliding his hands up her warm back. 'You look better without it, though.'

'Yes, I do,' she agreed, her voice a low, throaty purr as she felt his hand work its way around to her breast. Anticipation hardened her nipples.

'Talking of clothes...' he said.

She squirmed. He still hadn't got as far as her breast. 'We weren't.'

'I've bought you a dress for tonight.'

She was already backing away, tugging her shirt down. 'I already have a dress.'

He sighed. 'I *knew* you'd be like this!' he said, sounding frustrated.

She loosed an incredulous gasp. 'So you thought you'd

soften me up? You thought that if you got me into bed I'd be fine with anything you say or do.'

'Well, you've been fine so far,' he tossed back audaciously.

'I am not having you buying me a dress. I am not one of your... I refuse to be a *thing*...a *clothes horse* for you.'

Her occupation of his bed might have a short life span, but she had promised herself at the start that it would be on her terms. That she would be herself. That she would look back and not be sorry or ashamed.

That she would be sad was a given...

'I have a perfectly good dress; you saw me pack it.'

'Please stop acting like an oppressed teenager!' The frustrated words were out there before his brain actually kicked in.

She looked at him the way he imagined a volcano might look before it exploded, annihilating everything within a five-mile radius.

'It is a perfectly good dress, and you'd look incredible in a sack.' Her eyes were still narrowed, but she looked less ballistic. 'But tonight is... A few people besides my family might be there.'

'"A few people"?'

'A few politicians...a couple of church representatives—and we have a local celebrity.' He named a Hollywood legend and her eyes widened. 'Think of the dress as armour. When you look good, you feel more confident.'

'I am not scared of your family—and isn't dressing me up to look like I belong kind of negating the point you're trying to make?'

'Point?' His brow creased.

'The reason why I'm here. This is you sticking a finger up to your family, to show they can't dictate your life choices or who your sleep with.'

The fierce pride that shone in her eyes as she challenged him made something shift inside him. Automatically he tried to pull his emotions back, lock them away—only to discover he couldn't.

Soon this would be over.

The thought came from nowhere and echoed in his head as a sense of alien loneliness crept over him as he thought of a future without Clemmie in it.

'I know that you are tough and brave and beautiful...' he said, and then he stopped speaking.

'What is it?' she snapped out belligerently, one hand still fending him off, the other tucking her shirt into the waistband of her jeans.

He looked at her and saw her slipping inexorably away from him. He knew that he would do *anything* to stop that happening.

'You are a total idiot, Joaquin,' she said. She sniffed loudly and glared at him, her green eyes flashing. 'You know that?'

He nodded, still only half in the moment. His brain was playing catch-up with the emotions that had somehow slid through the wall he had built around them. 'Yes, I do,' he agreed, thinking he was not just an idiot, he was also a blind, arrogant fool.

Some idiots are born and others are self-made, he decided, and the taste of self-contempt was bitter on his tongue as he realised that he had found the thing he had been too cowardly to even acknowledge he craved and had almost thrown it away.

He had never thought to avoid love—why protect yourself from something that didn't exist, someone who didn't exist?

The level of his arrogance now seemed shocking.

'I've got a big family, Clemmie.'

'This I know,' she cut back, puzzled by the emotions she could feel rolling off him.

'But I've always been alone.'

She knew what he meant without him explaining. Their eyes connected and clung and the moment stretched, emotion buzzing in the air between them.

Was the longing she felt inside her or in his eyes?

Then the vibration of the phone in his pocket broke the spell.

Joaquin forced his taut facial features into something approximating a smile and ignored the buzzing.

'Wear what you like—and, yes, I know you will anyway. But it is a very nice dress...'

She stood there, her arms folded across her chest, wondering what had just happened.

'Just look at it,' he said.

She gave a tight nod as his phone started buzzing again.

'All right, I will look at it,' she said, showing that she could be a grown-up too.

It occurred to her to ask how he'd conjured up a dress, presumably in the right size, but thinking about the trip here, and her brief taste of the world he inhabited, it didn't seem worth the effort.

He snapped his fingers and things happened. Or more likely he just typed some terse instruction into his phone that ended *Make it happen*. And it did!

Joaquin acknowledged her concession with a nod minus any air of triumph and walked away to refresh his glass. 'I don't want to argue.'

He sounded… Not tired… He sounded… She couldn't quite put a name to it.

'No…?' she said.

'No, I want to make love to you.'

His stare she *could* put a name to.

Smouldering.

'That works for me,' she whispered, walking into his arms.

As much as part of her wanted to reject the dress she found wrapped in layers of tissue, with a discreet hand-sewn label inside, she knew it was beautiful.

Everything about it was beautiful.

The buttery silk texture, the colour—which was one shade deeper than her eyes—and the elegant simplicity of it. It was sleeveless, high at the neck, and dipping low at the back to reveal her shoulder blades.

It was simply a beautiful thing, and when she tried it on and saw that it clung in the all the right places, the bias-cut skirt swishing beautifully when she walked… Well, the choice was made.

But if he said a single word, or even gave her an *I told you* so look, she would wear jeans!

He hadn't mentioned the new shoes, which were soft silver leather, with a heel higher than she would normally have chosen. But the slim jewelled diagonal strap made them surprisingly comfortable to wear.

She sat down at the dressing table to add a second layer of gloss to her lips. She had kept her make-up to a minimum—just a touch of blusher to her cheeks and a swipe of mascara. She put the finishing touches to her hair, which she had chosen to pin up loosely. It was less about allowing tendrils to fall casually round her face and more a matter of going with the flow.

She had just finished when she heard a door in the suite open and close. Fastening a pearl stud in her ear, she walked towards the door and paused to view the back of her dress in the mirror.

She raised her voice to say, 'I still couldn't contact Mum. I'm starting to get worried.'

'She sent a message through my office,' he called back. 'Rose just gave it to me. Your mum is in a black spot. The phone signal is intermittent and there's no Wi-Fi connection to speak of.'

Clemmie, who had been checking her phone at regular intervals since she'd arrived, gave a sigh of relief.

'I hope you didn't mind me giving Mum your contact details for emergencies,' she yelled, then stopped as she found herself looking at his reflection in the mirror...tall and supremely elegant in his formal black tie.

Her senses leapt, making her aware of every nerve-ending in her body, and her pulses were madly racing as she spun around to face him, the silk of her dress swishing against the bare skin of her legs.

'I've sent back a message via Rose to tell her that you are here and safe...and looking very beautiful.'

She felt a flush of pleasure at the compliment that was reflected in the look in his dark eyes. 'Not the beautiful bit?'

'No...' He delivered the throaty admission with a smile that seemed strained.

'Did...did Mum say anything else?'

Like, Don't fall in love with men who don't love you back?

She pushed the thought away. He lusted after her, and while that lasted she intended to enjoy it and pretend that delicious, mind-blowing sex was enough.

CHAPTER TEN

THE DINNER WAS being held somewhere that Joaquin called 'the central keep', and the walk to where the dinner was being held took so long she joked that she wished she had worn her trainers.

Her first view was from a gallery level that was built into the stone barrelled roof. Stairs led down to the ground level, where guests congregated, their combined glitter competing with the row of chandeliers that illuminated the scene.

'The dining room is that way.' He nodded towards a wide Gothic arch. 'What are you thinking?'

Her eyes lifted to his face. 'I'm imagining what size the party will be when your mother celebrates us splitting up.'

His face went blank. Maybe he was regretting his decision to bring her?

'I'm assuming they will expect me to use the wrong fork, or offer to do the washing up?' she whispered behind her hand, her eyes travelling around as they approached the staircase. 'It looks like a film set!'

'My thought exactly.'

Joaquin arched a brow at the speaker. 'Always working, Allie?'

'You know me.'

A tall brunette wearing a dramatic red dress with a split

that was daringly high smiled at Clemmie and leaned up to kiss Joaquin on each cheek.

'Hello, stranger,' she said.

'This is Clemmie.'

'No introductions necessary. We all saw the movie. I'm Alice Betts.'

'Real life—not a movie, Allie. Allie is a set designer,' he said, by way of explanation to Clemmie.

'Not a movie *yet*,' the brunette cut back, with a sly look up at him. 'Maybe Rob could play you?'

Her gaze slid to the other side of the room, where the famous Hollywood actor was surrounded by people, mostly female, who were hanging on his every word.

'I should go and rescue him,' said Allie. 'He's jet-lagged... Who'd be married to a sex symbol? Well, you, I suppose,' she added, grinning at Clemmie as she skipped past them on the staircase before heading across the room towards her husband.

'This feels bad...lying to your friends.'

Joaquin's magnificent shrug suggested he did not share her guilt. 'The lie is not one of our making,' he reminded her. 'And not many people here are friends—just contacts and family.'

Now she was on ground level, Clemmie recognised a few faces of his family members from functions held at the manor, when she had been roped in to help, but she could not have put names to them.

'But we are perpetuating the lie.'

'Isn't it worth putting your moral scruples in a dark cupboard when you see how sick my dear mother is looking?'

Following the direction of his gaze, Clemmie saw Aria Perez, the diamonds at her throat giving the chandeliers that lit the dramatic barrel-ceilinged room a run for their money, bearing down on them, her face wreathed in fake smiles of welcome.

Dread tightened in the pit of her stomach.

'Oh, well…this is going to be cringey, isn't it?'

It no longer seemed like the harmless joke it had when Joaquin had suggested it.

As she angled a resigned look up at her escort she caught a strange look on his austerely handsome face. She was immobilised by the cold ferocity stamped on his features as he stared across the room at his mother.

Clemmie, who was not a 'revenge is a dish best served cold' sort of person—hers burnt bright and then faded— realised that, for Joaquin, it was not just cold, it was icily implacable.

Before Aria could reach them, they joined the people beginning to move en masse through to the dining room.

'You're here, Clemmie.' Joaquin held a chair for her. 'I'm opposite.' He looked from the place setting card to the man approaching. 'Rob will look after you.'

'Rob will be delighted.'

The American actor bared his perfect teeth.

There were actually several occasions during the meal when she was grateful for the American's presence, his quick wit and his ability to defuse a tense moment.

There had been a few of those, but Clammy had made it through to coffee without allowing her hostess to pro-voke her.

'Are there any more like you at home, Clemmie?' asked Joaquin's father, whose conversation had stayed only *just* the right side of inappropriate so far.

It was the third time he'd asked the question; it was also his third brandy.

'Just me and my mum.'

Aria raised her voice. 'Who is our cleaner at the manor.'

Six.

Clemmie, who had been counting, calculated that it was the sixth time the woman had managed to drop into the conversation that Clemmie's mum was their cleaner.

'Really excellent cleaner...such a good little worker. Husband left her, poor woman... It must be so hard being a single parent—they say the child always suffers.'

Seven.

She almost felt sorry for the older woman by this point. She didn't realise that her not very subtle attempts to embarrass Clemmie were backfiring. Clemmie was not at all embarrassed and a significant portion of the guests didn't like what she was doing.

'Wasn't there talk of a sister?' asked Aria now.

'I had a twin, but she died when we were children,' Clemmie said quietly.

The entire table had fallen silent, all aware of the malice in Aria's eyes, glittering behind the fake smile.

'I'd forgotten. Wasn't there some talk of therapy...?'

'Hasn't everyone had therapy?'

Rob, the man who was everyone's favourite Hollywood actor—or at least by this point in the evening Clemmie's favourite—broke the awkward silence.

He had turned out to be as charming in real life as he was on the screen. Clemmie mouthed a silent thank-you.

'Any time,' he said, and his low voice held understanding. 'In-laws...what are you to do? Though actually mine are pretty terrific.' His glance slid to his wife, who was talking animatedly, gesticulating as she spoke. 'I really got lucky. I was on my way to... Well, let's just say that Allie is one in a million.'

Clemmie smiled, her heart aching as she wondered wistfully what it would be like to have someone feel that you were his one in a million.

The actor cleared his throat. 'So, how long are you here for?'

'Not long. I need to be back at work on Friday.'

Back to real life, which would be a natural cut-off point for their fake engagement.

Her reply had coincided with a lull in the conversation around the table and all eyes swivelled her way.

Aria Perez responded for her.

'She works in a *library*,' she announced, as if she was revealing a guilty secret.

'You're a librarian?' asked Rob.

'A library assistant,' she said. Then, because the American's interest seemed genuine, she added, 'It suits me. And I love books, which helps.'

He joined in her laughter.

'The library is a real community hub. We have a group of "silver surfers" who meet up, craft sessions, story sessions for nursery kids... It can get a bit noisy. Sadly, for some people, it's just a place to come to stay warm.'

'Do you intend to carry on working when you get married?'

Caught off guard, she struggled to hide her embarrassment and glanced across the table to Joaquin.

'That is still under discussion,' he inserted smoothly, directing an intimate look towards Clemmie that was clearly intended for their audience, not her, but which made her heart flip anyhow.

'I'm sure your expertise would be an asset for Joaquin's literacy project.'

The actor flashed a questioning look across at Joaquin, who nodded.

'That had occurred to me. She's actually already helped a lot with ideas when I was launching the programme.'

'So, you two have known each other…?'

'I rescued Clemmie from a tree when she was eight and I was ten. She kicked me for my efforts.'

The American gave a delighted chuckle. 'So you were childhood sweethearts? I love it!'

At the end of the table Aria, in a voice that was penetrating enough to cut across all conversation, deliberately took centre stage as she launched into a long and detailed description of all the charities she supported. Clemmie relaxed slightly. It seemed to that Aria had run out of spiteful things to say.

'Of course, red hair is actually a genetic mutation…'

Clemmie couldn't repress a laugh. That would teach her to be an optimist.

'A very beautiful mutation,' Joaquin corrected, coming to stand behind her chair and addressing the room at large.

His caressing tone sent a shiver of helpless longing down her spine. She stood as he pulled the chair out for her, and then she felt one hand remain on the back as he leant down to speak to Rob, who was still seated.

Clemmie looked around the room, congratulating herself on having survived the evening with her temper intact.

Most people had left their seats, and there was a general rash of air-kissing, along with a few unsteady staggers from those who had partaken a little too generously when the port had been passed around the table. They made her smile.

It was a smile that became tinged with cynicism when

she saw Aria Perez, still enjoying her role as hostess, sur-rounded by guests and lapping up the attention.

Joaquin was still deep in conversation with Rob. Had she imagined she would be able to get back to his suite without getting hopelessly lost, she would have tried.

She wandered away and, drawn by the silence of the massive antechamber, went in. There was a row of deep-set, floor-length windows in square-cut embrasures along one of the stone walls. Seeing the fluttering of a light drape in the nearest, she walked across and discovered that the window behind it had been opened.

She stood there, eyes closed, breathing in cool air scented with pine. It was when that scent became min-gled with the heavy, cloying expensive perfume that al-ways cloaked Aria Perez that she opened her eyes.

The other woman was standing a few feet away, watch-ing her with a cat-like intensity that sent a shiver down her spine.

Clemmie chided herself for her reaction. There was nothing this woman could do to her.

'I came to say I am sorry.'

Clemmie's jaw dropped. Shock and suspicion fought for supremacy in her head.

'Sorry...?'

'I'm sure your mother will find another job easily enough... But one that comes with a home...?' She gave a sigh. 'Not so easy for a woman her age.'

'I don't know what you're talking about.'

'Oh, didn't I say?' she exclaimed, evincing surprise. 'I have decided to divest myself of Maplehurst Manor. The sale went through today, and I seriously doubt the new owner will want to keep your mother on.'

Clemmie felt the blood drain from her face. 'But...'

She looked past her wildly, instinct making her search for Joaquin. 'You can't do that.'

'Oh, I've been thinking about it for some time and—'

'When Joaquin finds out he will...' Her voice faded. If this was true. what could Joaquin do?

'Joaquin knows.' The woman searched her face and gave a crow of laughter. 'He didn't tell you? Oh, priceless! But that is the sort of man you are marrying, my dear. He knew this was going to happen. I told him that if he brought you here, if he did not break this connection with you, I would sell the place.'

Clemmie shook her head. 'I don't believe you!'

The older woman shrugged. 'Have it your way. I actually don't care. I'm just glad to be rid of the place...too provincial. I have my eye on a villa that has just come onto the market, right next door to...'

Clemmie stood there, watching the woman's lips moving, the rest of her words an incoherent static buzz.

Joaquin had known.

He had lied to her again!

'Excuse me, I must...'

She tipped her head to indicate the conversation was over. Her spine ramrod-rigid and her chin up, she painted an expression of serene calm over the chaos of her swirling inner thoughts.

She must have presented quite a picture, because she had the mild satisfaction of seeing an expression of thwarted confusion drift across the older woman's face before she walked away.

She had no idea where she was going... She just walked, her thoughts not on the stone floor, nor the priceless art, nor the curious glances.

She was just thinking of betrayal.

She had made Joaquin out to be someone he was not; she had fallen for an illusion. He was someone with the bare minimum of decent human feelings. And she hated the weakness in her that made it so hard for her to believe this.

It was a lie—it had to be a lie.

The Joaquin she knew would not do this...

Then the ice-cold in his eyes came back to her.

Could his need to punish his family really make him not care about the hurt he caused to others in the process? And not anonymous others, but her mum?

And he knew how much she loved the house...the memories it contained of her twin.

He had used her.

Perhaps she was leaping to conclusions...

Leaping to conclusions? How much more proof do you need? she asked herself contemptuously. *When are you going to wake up to the fact that people lie, that they betray?*

As she passed down the endless corridors her thoughts continued to tread endless corridors of their own, many with dead ends and many looping back in circles.

People nodded and smiled, but nobody questioned her right to be there—and then, when she wasn't even looking, she saw a landmark: a massive oil painting of a luminous Madonna and child. Surely she had seen it before?

Joaquin paced the salon of his suite. This wasn't the way he had planned for this evening to end.

Where the hell was she?

He had already retraced the route back to the dining room and there had been no sign of her.

He felt his panic rise even as he recognised there was no logic to it.

He had almost lost her once before; he had even recognised what he would be losing.

It couldn't happen again.

On one level he knew that he was overreacting—that she would be sitting in a corner somewhere, nursing a glass of wine and chatting, or else wandering down a corridor, totally lost. Neither scenario was life-threatening.

The knowledge didn't lessen the feeling of dread in the pit of his stomach.

'You lost your fiancée? Man, that was careless,' Rob, mellow after an after-dinner brandy, had joked when Joaquin had come across him with a group of guests.

It was a joke that had not made Joaquin smile, and he'd voiced his lack of appreciation—maybe not so politely. Not that Rob had seemed offended. And Allie had chased after him, telling how much they loved Clemmie.

'Me too,' he'd said.

Allie had squeezed his arm. 'Might be an idea to tell her that?'

He would, he decided, as he contemplated retracing his steps again, unable to rid himself of the idea that his mother had got to her.

He was tired of games. He'd been so proud of her tonight...of her dignity and humour in the face of his mother's snide comments.

He should have been there to protect her.

At last, he faced his biggest fear.

Could she have left him?

The door opened and she appeared, and his initial relief immediately switched to anger. 'Where the hell did you vanish to?'

When her green eyes lifted to him, his mood made another ninety-degree turn.

'I was worried. It's been an hour. People are looking for you... I was looking for you. Where have you been?'

'I don't know.'

'You got lost?' he said, struggling to moderate his tone. 'It's easily done. You should have waited for me.'

As he approached she raised her hands, as if to fend him off.

He stopped dead. 'What's happened?'

'Is it true?' she asked, amazed that she sounded totally normal.

'Is what true?' he said, playing for time.

He could see in her eyes that they both knew it.

'You knew that your mother would sell the manor and chuck Mum out of her home if I came here with you.'

She looked at him, willing him to say it was a silly misunderstanding.

'I wasn't sure she'd go through with it.'

His words sucked all the hope out of her body.

'You weren't sure?' she echoed, feeling sick as she searched his face, even now hoping for a sign of contrition. But there wasn't not even a hint. 'So you knew it was a possibility and you didn't care? You just had to show her and your entire family who was boss.' She shuddered. 'It makes you just like them.'

He took a step towards her. 'No, Clemmie, that is not how it is. Let me explain...'

'Save yourself the bother. I am not interested in anything you have to say!'

It was the contempt and hurt shining in her green eyes that cut him like a blade, not her words.

'Clemmie...'

He went to take her hands but she moved away. As her back made contact with the massive iron-studded door there was a loud urgent banging from the other side.

Clemmie stepped away.

His jaw taut, he wrenched open the door. The exchange in Spanish was short.

When the visitor left, Joaquin turned to her. He studied her face for a moment.

'I have to go. My father has had, they think, a stroke. He was in bed, and he wasn't alone.'

He delivered the information in a bleak monotone.

This time when he reached for her arm she didn't pull away. She struggled to reconcile the opposing desires to wrap her arms around him and to hate him.

To punish him for punching a hole in her heart with his betrayal.

To punish him for not being the man who, in a world where bad things happened, was the one person she could always rely on.

The man she had grown to love.

It felt like a bereavement.

His face was grave as he reached down and blotted the tear that was running down her cheek.

'Just promise me... Don't do anything or go anywhere until I get back. I can explain.'

She gave a futile little shrug as the fire went out of her like a snuffed candle.

'Where could I go?'

The sense of isolation she felt was total.

CHAPTER ELEVEN

WHEN HE LEFT, she found she was shivering. Instinctively she reached for the jacket he had thrown over the back of a chair. She lifted it to her face and inhaled. The scent of him filled her head and slowed her rapid heartbeat.

It was crazy to take comfort from something that belonged to the person responsible for her misery.

She felt empty of hope. He wanted to explain? She could not think of anything he might say that would make things right.

It was hard to imagine anything ever being right again.

She caught sight of herself in a mirror, looking lost and hopeless, and with a cry she switched off the lamp to blank the image. She stepped back into a bucket chair and drew her knees up to her chest, and sat there hunched inside his jacket.

She was still there when the door opened and the light came on. She watched as Joaquin entered the room, closing the door behind him. He vented a deep sigh and dragged a hand wearily through his hair, then began to roll down his sleeves, which had been pushed up to the elbows.

He was leaning his shoulders back against the wooden panels of the door when their glances connected. He immediately levered himself off.

To lessen the sensory impact of him standing over her,

she unfurled her legs, pulled the jacket off and handed it to him.

He shook his head. 'Keep it. You look cold.'

She slid the jacket back over her shoulders. 'Any news?'

'What would you like to know about? The hysterical naked girlfriend, screaming that she had never seen a dead body before?'

'He's...?'

'No, he's not dead—and she is no longer naked. My mother has wished he *was* dead on several occasions. She is very worried about the scandal and the potential cost of private nursing—such a warm woman. However, she is cheered by the thought that the stroke might put an end to his womanising. He's been airlifted to hospital, and she has gone with him. Not to hold his hand, in case you thought that was a bit out of character. She's trying to get him to give her power of attorney, in case he has another, worse stroke that makes him incapable. Her lawyer is meeting them at the hospital.'

'Oh, goodness!'

'I think *goodness* has very little to do with it.'

He studied her face, which was normally so luminous, and saw only shadow. Her pain felt like a stab in the heart. And knowing he was responsible hurt him at a cellular level.

He walked across to the bureau and poured two glasses of amber liquid from a decanter before bringing them back and handing one to her.

'What is it?'

'Does it matter?'

She decided it didn't, and swallowed it back in one gulp.

He waited for her to stop choking before he launched into his explanation. 'I did know about my mother's threat, but I wasn't sure she would follow through. Happily, she did.'

'Happily?' Clemmie choked.

'If my mother had known that I was the potential buyer she would never have sold—not even for an above-market valuation.'

'You've bought Maplehurst?'

He nodded.

'So, you own the manor?'

He shook he head. 'No, *you* own the manor, Clemmie.'

She watched as he opened a drawer in the bureau and pulled out a buff folder.

'These are the deeds.'

She reached out automatically and took them, then asked in a dazed voice. 'What are you talking about?'

'Maplehurst is yours—the sale is complete. The only person doing any throwing out is you. You love the place, and I wanted to make sure that… If I'd told you about my mother's threat you would have worried, and your mother would have worried. You belong there. I hope with me.'

This last husky addition and the look in his eyes sent her heart racing.

'What are you saying?' she asked faintly.

He dug into his trouser pocket, pulled out a box and handed it to her.

'I was planning to give you this after dinner tonight, but things did not go according to plan. I'm saying, Clemmie, that I'm asking you to consider marrying me. I know I've blown it, the way I've handled this, but I'm used to making decisions, sorting out problems on my own. It's hard to break the habit. If I have lost your trust, I'll do my best to win it back—for as long as it takes.'

Clemmie opened the box and saw a ring sitting there. An aquamarine surrounded by diamonds.

'It's the colour of your eyes.' He dropped into a squat

beside the chair. 'I love you, Clemmie. I think I always have. But I didn't see it because I was trying to keep things the same. I was paranoid about change. I never realised that my marriage wouldn't be like my parents' because *I* am not like my parents. You have always been the one constant in my life. I want you to be the one constant in my future. I want to share that future with you.'

He looked at her, a question in his eyes.

She shook her head. She couldn't speak. Her throat was choked up with emotion and with the joy that was singing through her veins as she slid the ring onto her finger.

'It fits perfectly and I never, ever want to take it off!'

She slid out of the chair and they both rose to their feet together.

Arms around his neck, she gazed lovingly up into his eyes. 'What happens now?'

'We go to bed?'

'That sounds like a plan. I have no idea what happens next, but I think we're going to have fun finding out.

Much later that night, as they were lying in bed, he spoke. 'I'll just throw this out there…how about we get married by special licence tomorrow?'

She was tempted… But, 'My mum would never forgive me. Nor your family.'

'My family are not coming.'

'We'll talk about it later.'

'No, we won't.'

Two months later…

'We must invite your family,' Clemmie said as they strolled together through the gardens, past a carpet of irises, towards the spot that afforded the best view of the manor and to the new carved oak bench that had been placed there.

Could a house look happy?

As she stared at the honey-coloured stone it seemed to Clemmie that Maplehurst did.

She and Joaquin had been staying in the gatehouse, which now boasted a high-speed internet connection so he could work from home. It meant they were close at hand to supervise the ongoing refurbishment of the manor. Her mum had stayed on with Harry, who really did seem to be a keeper, and was keeping her options open about returning full-time to the gatehouse.

It had been a busy few weeks. As well as turning Maplehurst into their permanent home, Clemmie had taken on an active role in Joaquin's literacy programme. She had accepted the job only on the understanding that it was a *real* job. It was indeed real, and challenging enough to take up a large part of her day. But the hard work was counterbalanced by the fun bits, like delivering books to school children in deprived areas.

'Why must we?' he asked now.

'Your parents would be humiliated if we didn't.'

He shrugged, but when he met her earnest green eyes the cynical twist of his lips smoothed. He touched her cheek and kissed her parted lips.

'We don't want to sink to their level,' she whispered against his lips as they drew apart.

She felt the laugh rumble in his chest.

'All right, invite them,' he said, philosophical about losing this war of attrition. His lip curled again. 'But be warned: my father is still pinching bottoms, even from his electric wheelchair.'

'You won't regret it,' she promised, stretching up to kiss him.

His arms circled her waist. 'I don't know what sort of husband I'll be, but you won't regret marrying me, Clemmie.' His voice thickened with emotion. 'I swear it.'

She touched the roughened angle of his jaw and smiled.

Joaquin felt warmth flow through him. A sense of rightness that he only felt when he was with Clemmie.

'I know I won't. I don't have any doubts, Joaquin,' she promised, her glowing eyes sending him a message of total certainty. 'Thank you for this home. I do love it. But you are my home...you are my heart.'

EPILOGUE

'YOU LOOK LIKE a dream.'

With a gasp, Clemmie spun round, the ivory silk of her dress swishing around her. Her breath caught as Joaquin's hot stare pinned her to the spot.

Joaquin—who was looking quite breathtakingly handsome in an impeccable dress suit—had materialised as if by magic in the bedroom that they shared.

Or had shared until last night.

'Where did you come from?' she asked.

Joaquin grinned. 'Don't you mean how did I get past the army of people downstairs?' He tapped the side of his nose and said mysteriously. 'I have my ways.'

'Not an army. Just the florists, the caterers and the string quartet. I hope they have arrived?'

'Either that or someone is being mean to a cat.'

'And—'

'All right, I get the idea. A large contingent of essential persons... You are so pedantic. Though I am not sure why they are deemed *essential*.'

'We agreed.'

He conceded this with a deep sigh. 'You caught me in a weak moment—namely flat on my back in bed—when you had me at your mercy. You took advantage of me.'

She gasped in mock outrage at the claim, but actually

she quite liked the idea of taking advantage of this gorgeous man...often by invitation.

'The power of having me at your mercy has turned you into a monster, Clemmie. A beautiful monster,' he conceded, his prowling gaze taking in the full glory of her dress.

'I didn't see you complaining.'

'Granted.'

The wicked glitter in his eyes faded as he reached for her hand and pressed it to his chest. She felt the heavy vibration of his heartbeat and felt a tidal wave of hot emotion flow through her.

She loved this man to distraction, and it seemed a miracle that he loved her right back. The knowledge had a healing quality. She still felt wistful when she thought of her twin, but she no longer felt guilty. She really believed that she carried Chrissie in her heart, and she certainly had enough joy for two.

'This is the only essential thing,' he said, his deep voice thick and husky with emotion. 'Just you and me.'

Clemmie blinked away the sting of tears. 'Don't make me cry. This make-up took me hours.'

Her determination not to take advantage of a professional make-up artist and hairdresser for today had been a point of contention with her mother and the wedding planner, but Clemmie had stood her ground.

It seemed to her that over the last few weeks she had been one of the only people there who understood the meaning of a simple country wedding.

She was prepared to let other people share the day, but it was not about looking like some perfect person who wasn't her.

'"Natural" is very popular at the moment,' the wedding

planner had agreed, when she'd realised her client was not for budging. 'But it's the hardest thing to pull off.'

Clemmie liked to think she *had* pulled it off.

She leaned into his long, lingering kiss.

'Better?' he asked, when they finally pulled apart. His glance slid to the tiny pearl buttons down the front of her bodice. 'Well, they'll be a challenge.'

'And we both know you love a challenge. Do I look as stressed as I feel?'

'It's not too late to elope,' he said, a smile glimmering in his eyes.

'We have been through this. Let people have this day. We have the rest of our lives together.'

Before he could react to this emotional statement her gaze went past him to the fluttering drapes and her eyes widened in comprehension.

'You actually climbed in through the window?' She gasped, thinking of the fifty-foot drop below the window.

He brushed a twig off his lapel and gave an irrepressible grin.

'And after being forbidden to do so on pain of bringing down dire cosmic retribution on our heads. Apparently, it is unlucky to see the bride in her dress before the wedding—did you know that?'

'Everyone knows that.'

'I am not superstitious. The window seemed the obvious solution to my being denied access to you.'

'Obvious? Only to a mad person,' she retorted, fighting back a grin as she clicked her tongue with mock severity. 'You can't climb through bedroom windows on your wedding day. And *why...?* There are doors. And I have never known you not to do something because it was forbidden before.'

'I thought you'd consider it a romantic gesture,' he admitted. 'Have I not earned a few brownie points?'

'It is not romantic to break your bones on your wedding day.'

'I had no intention of falling.'

She laughed.

Joaquin didn't laugh. His expression was brooding and intent, almost like a man in pain, as he stared at her.

'God, but you look beautiful!' he said, his voice smoky with emotion. 'I was persuaded to spend last night away from you against my better judgement, and I wanted... I *needed* to see you. I never want us to spend another night apart.'

The possessive warmth glowing in his eyes made her light up inside. 'I'm not sure how practical that will be,' she said lovingly. 'But I missed you last night too... Today has been...' She grabbed her hair in both hands. 'Look!'

'Gorgeous!'

'No, not gorgeous! Awful! Every time I practised putting it up it worked, and today...'

'Wear it loose. I like— All right,' he added quickly, when he recognised the signs of an imminent meltdown. 'Let me,' he heard himself offer recklessly.

'*You?*'

Sitting on the stool in front of the dressing table mirror, she discovered there was something almost hypnotic about watching his hands running through her hair, his elegant fingers massaging her scalp.

It was ten minutes later when he spoke. 'More relaxed?'

She opened eyes that had drifted closed. Her hair was still loose but, yes, she was relaxed, she realised.

Even though she probably shouldn't be.

'I am,' she admitted, meeting his eyes. She shivered as

his fingertips grazed her neck and he pushed her hair to one side to kiss her neck. 'Mmm... I should be getting... Joaquin... You can't...'

But of course he could.

He could always transform her into a helpless bundle of inarticulate longing.

They had reached the bed, and Joaquin was straddled across her, when the door opened.

'Oh, my God! Your dress...your hair! You should be ready, not...not...'

'Sorry, Mum, he was just leaving.'

Clemmie pushed at Joaquin, who did not look abashed as he sat on the side of the bed and straightened his tie.

'You look very happy, darling.'

'I am, Mum.'

'Harry and I have been discussing our next step, and we have decided there is no hurry for our wedding. I intend to stay in Yorkshire with him—at least until he has sorted through his mother's house and belongings. But I have told him that when you have children—no matter when that is—we will move back to the gatehouse. I want to be a very involved grandparent.'

Resisting the temptation to press her hands to her still-flat stomach, Clemmie smiled. She had only known for twenty-four hours, and for the moment she was hugging the news to herself.

News that would be her wedding present to Joaquin.

'That sounds like a plan. Now, my hair, Mum... Any ideas? At least we don't have to worry about rain, or the wind blowing my veil away.'

When the guest numbers had grown, the village church had been substituted for the great hall in the manor—the only space big enough to accommodate everyone and the masses of flowers that filled every corner of the house. After the ceremony the plan was for everyone to transfer to the marquees that had been set up in the grounds.

When Clemmie walked down the aisle, her mind was not on her hair—which had been arranged in a half-up, half-down style, the half-up part supporting an antique veil—her attention was totally focused on the man who stood waiting for her...

'Did that really just happen?' she whispered after the ceremony, as they walked hand in hand past the smiling guests.

'Don't tell me you've lost your memory again? Sorry, that's not funny,' he added with a wince. 'You're wearing your wedding present, I see,' he went on.

Clemmie touched the diamond studs that glittered through the strands of hair floating around her face.

'And I'm wearing my wedding gift to you.... Well, sort of...'

He looked down at her, bemused, and she watched comprehension dawning as she held his eyes and pressed both hands to her stomach.

'*Really?*' he said, sounding stunned.

She nodded, seeing joy, fear and awe flash through his eyes. The same emotions that she had felt when she had looked at her positive pregnancy test.

'I only did the test yesterday. It's still sinking in. Do you like your present, Joaquin?'

'I love my present—and I love you!'

Behind them the guests' cameras clicked, recording the couple kissing under the flower-bedecked stone arch as if they were alone in their own world.

* * * * *

AFTER-HOURS PROPOSAL

TRISH MOREY

MILLS & BOON

To you, dear reader.

Readers are a writer's best friends.
This one's for you. x

CHAPTER ONE

SUCCESS.

Dominico Estefan stared out at Melbourne's skyline and basked in the glow of his latest acquisition. Whoever said success was sweet was way off the mark. Success was more fundamental than that. More elemental. Success was like sex. Intoxicating.

Addictive.

Dom Estefan was seriously addicted. He loved it when a plan came together. After weeks of circular negotiations and knockbacks, his bid had finally been accepted, and at a much lower price than he'd been prepared to pay. Cooper Industries, the small but promising private pharmaceutical company that he planned to transform into a global powerhouse, was his.

He glanced at his watch. Barely past nine a.m. and already it was shaping up to be a perfect day. And later, once all the dust had settled and he'd completed today's meetings, there might be an opportunity to celebrate. He growled with satisfaction, and not without a modicum of anticipation. Because he might be in Melbourne, and half a world away from his home in San Sebastián, but he'd never had a problem finding willing, if not enthusiastic, company. In Dom's world, there was never any shortage of enthusiastic company.

And he liked Australian women. Or he had, once, a long time ago.

What was her name?

Marianne.

The name came to him on a tendril of memory, drifting up from the darkest recesses of his mind, the name as fresh and newly minted as the girl had been, still a teenager, a free spirit with wild blonde hair tumbling over her shoulders and lights in her vivid green eyes. Their few months together had been the highlight of his time in Sydney. It had bent him out of shape when he'd had to return to Spain, not that he'd had a choice, and while there was still that lingering residue of guilt, he'd also had a sense he'd dodged a bullet.

He rested one hand against the window frame and gazed down at a tourist boat chugging along the ribbon of river far below until it disappeared under a road bridge.

What would she be doing now? No doubt she was married with a clutch of kids and living somewhere close to nature like she'd endlessly talked about. She'd been a novelty to him, a dreamer with her head in the clouds, and so different from the daughters and nieces the society *señoras* back in Spain had steered his way.

He snorted. Not that anything had changed there, except that now it was their granddaughters they were shepherding his way.

His phone buzzed and he pushed away from the window. He glanced at the screen and his spine turned to ice. His mother's physician in San Sebastián calling? Now? One a.m. was far too late for a social call.

He swiped at the screen. *'Hola?'*

'I'm sorry to disturb you,' the doctor began.

'My mother,' Dom said, cutting to the chase. 'How is she?'

'I won't sugarcoat it,' the doctor said. 'The latest treatments haven't given us the results we hoped for. I'm sorry to tell you her condition is deteriorating. I'm going to recommend that her plan be changed to palliative care.'

Palliative care? But that meant…

'How long—' Dom began, his words turning to ash in his throat as he raked his fingers through his hair, mentally reckoning the time it would take to fly home. Forget about any kind of celebration. The last place he needed to be right now was the other side of the world when his mother needed him.

He'd known this moment was coming ever since her initial horrific diagnosis; known that it was inevitable that his mother would lose her battle with the inoperable cancer that was invading her cells and wasting her body. But that knowledge didn't mean he was ready to lose her.

'How long do you think she has?'

'I wish I could answer that. It could be weeks. On the other hand, it could be days. There is no telling.'

Weeks? *Days?* He wasn't ready for this. Knowing something was going to happen some time in the future was infinitely worse when there was a timeline attached to it, however uncertain that timeline might be.

'What are you two wittering about? Hand me that phone.'

Dom started as his mother's frail, yet still imperious voice rasped. 'Mamá?'

The doctor sighed. 'Rosaria insisted I call you tonight. She demanded she talk to you.'

'Surely she should be sleeping? It's the middle of the night there.'

'In a perfect world, yes. Instead, Rosaria dozes. Except tonight she refuses to settle at all until she's spoken to you.'

'Are you going to stop bleating and give me that phone?'

Normally Dom would raise a smile at his mother's haughty demands, but not tonight, when he knew that, for all her strength of spirit, her body was crumbling. It was unthinkable. To Dom, she'd always been a powerhouse, strong, indomitable. The only time he'd ever seen her falter was when his father had died, and she'd lost her beloved Roberto. She'd grieved then, long and hard, at times her grief threatening to overwhelm her. But slowly and surely, she'd come back from that. And instead of being crushed by her grief she'd grown stronger, adding the role of father to the already heavy burden of mother, lending her intellect to his while he grew into his new position as head of Estefan Inc. In Dom's book she was a force of nature, which made what nature was doing to crush her all the crueller.

'My son,' he heard. 'Is that you?'

'It's me, Mamá.'

She sighed. 'At last. I thought I might die before that damned physician handed over the phone.'

Dom pressed his lips together. His mother's condition was hardly a joking matter, but he wasn't about to tell her that. 'Dr Rodríguez is the best in the business, you know that.'

'That may be true, but that's not what I wanted to talk to you about.'

'What did you want to talk to me about?'

'I'm dying, Dominico.'

A dagger pierced his heart. 'Don't say that.'

'Why not, when it's true?'

'Because it's not what you should be focusing on.'

'I'm not focusing on it.'

'Then why mention it?'

'Because I want *you* to focus on it.'

As if he could focus on anything else right now, all thought of his most recent success blown out of contention.

'How do you know that I'm not?'

'Because otherwise you'd have already given me what I want. If you were a good son, you would have given me the grandchildren I have so longed for.'

'Mamá,' he protested, 'it is not because I have sought to deny you grandchildren. I did not know you would become ill. I cannot change that now.'

'No. What is done is done.' She sniffed. 'Or, in this case, what is undone is left undone.'

Dom dropped his head into one hand, his earlier high spirits deflated by both the physician's prognosis of his mother's worsening condition and her comprehensive evaluation of his failings as a son. It didn't seem to matter to his mother that he had taken the business his father had bequeathed him at the tender age of twenty-two and expanded it tenfold. The myriad successes he'd had along the way didn't seem to count. He had denied his mother the experience of becoming a grandmother and for that and that alone he was being judged.

'Dominico!' His mother's thready shriek was like a slap to his head. 'Are you there?'

'I'm here.'

'Good. Because I am asking this one tiny thing now. Before I die.'

He winced. 'Please stop talking that way.'

'Why should I? We're all going to die; I just have a clearer idea of when and why than most. But listen to me, that is why I'm asking you this.'

'What is it you want, Mamá?' he said, swallowing down on the lump in his throat.

She gave a long sigh, sounding suddenly resigned. 'I want to see my son married before I die.'

'What?'

'After all,' she continued, ignoring the interruption, 'you're not getting any younger. You're forty-two years old. It's not too much to ask, surely? It's not like you've not had plenty of time to find a wife. In every picture I see of you in the papers you're accompanied by some beauty. When are you going to settle down with one of them?'

Caramba! His mother had been angling for him to get married for more than a decade. It hadn't happened, despite the women shoved in his path. He hadn't been willing to marry any woman simply to keep his mother happy—not a woman more interested in the family fortune than him.

But there was more to it than that. He hadn't gone looking for it. He'd witnessed his mother's deep despair when his father had died. He'd seen the battle she'd fought to dig her way out of her life-sucking depression. He'd shared every day of it with her.

Why would he willingly want to jump into that shark tank? Why did he even need to? There were plenty of women who were more than happy with a brief fling—if not with the actual brevity...

But there was no point arguing with his mother now. No point upsetting her when she was already finding sleep difficult to come by. He schooled his voice to mellow. 'And who says I haven't found someone I want to settle down with?'

'You have?' His mother's voice sounded as if it had received a jolt of electricity. 'Why didn't you tell me?'

'Because it's early days and I don't want to frighten her off.'

'Who is she? Anyone I know?'

Good question, Dom thought. Who the hell was she? 'How about I fill you in when I get home? Meanwhile, it's late, and you should be sleeping.'

'You're really getting married? You've really found someone special?'

'You should rest,' he heard the doctor say.

'I can rest now,' she said on a weary sigh. 'My son is getting married.'

'We'll talk when I get home,' Dom said with a sad smile. 'I'll fill you in on all the details then. *Te quiero,* Mamá.'

'My son...*te quiero.*'

He heard the sound of the doctor gently taking the phone. *'Un momento,* Dominico,*'* he said, before settling his mother into the pillows. Dom heard the snick of a door closing before the doctor spoke again. 'Thank you for taking the call.'

'Are you sure that she's failing? She sounded much stronger than your prognosis would suggest.'

'Don't let that fool you. She is a strong woman and, if I may say, a woman on a mission. She refused to sleep until she had spoken to you and her efforts will have taken a toll. But Rosaria will sleep now, because of the assurance you gave her.'

But would Dom sleep? It was one thing to make a promise—another thing entirely to keep it when you had no idea how to make it happen.

'And can I add,' the doctor said, 'congratulations.'

'Gracias,' Dom uttered, through a throat that might have been filled with gravel. He put down the phone, his heart heavy. If the doctor suspected Dom's promise to his mother was nothing more than a cynical attempt at placating Rosaria and getting her to rest, he didn't let on. But then, why

would he care, so long as Dom came through and made his patient's final weeks and days more comfortable?

Dom sat back in his chair and put his hands behind his head, his mind assessing what he needed to finish before he headed back to Spain and to his mother's bedside for the however many days or weeks she had left. There was a meeting with his lawyers at ten to iron out any details, followed by a meeting at eleven that shouldn't take more than five minutes, meaning he could be on the jet by mid-afternoon. His team could take care of any loose ends here.

And in the meantime, he had to find himself a bride.

Simple.

He snorted. His situation would be laughable if it weren't true.

Because finding a suitable bride was going to be nowhere near as easy as finding a companion for the night. Sure, there were plenty of women he'd encountered who'd dropped not so subtle hints during their time together that the two of them would make the perfect couple, but none of them had convinced him and, frankly, their rank enthusiasm for the role of his wife had left him cold and more cynical than ever about finding a woman that he wanted to marry.

There were still more women he'd met who he knew would be more than happy to playact in the role of his bride for however long that took, especially if he offered the right kind of financial incentive. He'd be more than willing to compensate any woman handsomely if it meant his mother might go to her final rest without the worry of her son being left on the shelf.

But even that way came with complications. He didn't want complications. He didn't want a woman who wanted to be his wife, but neither did he want a woman who told him she was happy to act in the role, only to change her mind when her use-by date expired. Prenuptial agreements could only go so far, and he had no desire to have to resort to legal action to sort it out.

No, what he needed was a woman who *didn't* want to be married to him. A woman who would only do it under sufferance, persuaded to marry him only because of a decent incentive, whether financial or otherwise. A woman who would nonetheless be more than prepared to blow him off the first opportunity she got.

Where the hell was Dom expected to find a woman like that?

CHAPTER TWO

BY THE TIME Mari Peterson's so-called express train finally pulled into Melbourne's Flinders Street Station forty minutes late, she was fuming. She hated being late any day, but especially on a day as important as this one. Forget about grabbing a coffee on the way to the office, she'd barely have time to collect her papers let alone her thoughts before this morning's nine-thirty meeting with the bankers. Cooper Industries desperately needed this loan to fund its expansion onto the world stage. What kind of impression would it make if the company's own finance manager turned up late?

To be fair, Mari hadn't been in the best of moods when she'd boarded the train, but lack of sleep coupled with caffeine deprivation could do that to you. She'd woken after a fractured night, her mind still grappling with the fallout of yesterday's bombshell phone call from her sister's carer that she couldn't afford to stay on without a substantial pay increase and that she needed to find a new job. Where was Mari going to find another Valerie? Housekeeper, cook and faithful companion all rolled into one, the woman was a godsend. More to the point, Suzanne loved her. Valerie's departure would break her heart.

Not that Mari could blame the woman. Nobody was exempt from the cost of living crisis and Valerie hadn't had a pay rise in two years—because Mari hadn't been in a position to give it to her.

What the hell was she going to do?

Outside the station her tram was pulled up at the stop. She powered down the steps to catch the crossing, only to have the lights turn red and the traffic cop send her smartly back to the kerb.

'Good grief,' she muttered, her spirits taking another hit as the tram took off. Another delay. This day was shaping up to be a disaster.

Breathe.

Through the turmoil of her hammering heart and the constant roar of traffic filtered the calming voice of her grandmother. The steady voice she'd employed whenever a teenage Marianne had worked herself up over some real or imagined injustice, whether it be despair over their parents' tragic deaths in a country road crash, some despot in a land far away terrorising and holding hostage a civilian population, or even because her little sister was driving her crazy. Suzanne had always had a knack for driving her big sister crazy.

'*Breathe,*' her grandmother would say. '*Take a moment. Focus on what you can control, not on what you can't.*'

Mari took a deep breath and turned her face away from the impatient crowds jostling around her and up to the blue sky above, blocking out the ding of trams and rush of cars, instead focusing on her breathing, drinking in the autumn air. She was a long way from that excitable and passionate teenager she'd been more than half a lifetime ago, but her gran's advice was still just as sound now as it had been then. More than that, it was apt.

Because just like that impulsive teenager she'd been, she was working herself into a frazzle. Sure, she was late for work and missing her coffee fix and she'd have to sort a new carer for Suzanne and soon. But when all was said and done, Mari was already late and there was nothing she could do about that other than text the CEO with an updated arrival time and pass on her apologies. Likewise, while it might elicit a grimace, it probably wouldn't kill her to make use of the instant coffee in the office kitchen for once instead of the barista-made coffee she preferred. Finding a new carer for her sister would no doubt prove more of a challenge, but she would make that happen too.

Mari found a smile of thanks and sent it heavenwards. She'd needed that moment to calm the tangled mess of her thoughts and steady her racing heart. Any ideas that the day was ruined were overblown. Any sense of foreboding was entirely down to lack of sleep. A strong coffee—however sourced—would soon fix that.

She texted a quick update to the CEO.

Train finally arrived. Waiting on tram. Be there in ten.

An answer pinged back almost immediately.

No rush. Meeting cancelled. Fill you in when you get here.

Cancelled? What was that about? The bank had demanded this meeting as part of their deliberations as to whether they approved the loan. Forget that the statements had been audited, they wanted to quiz Mari and go through the financial statements line by line.

Unless the bank had already approved the loan? She refused to entertain the prospect that they might have knocked Cooper Industries back. The financial statements had been audited and together with the extensive reports

Mari had provided proved that the company's fundamentals were rock-solid. Any banker worth their salt could see that.

She stared at the message on her phone. Eric Cooper would be ecstatic if the loan had been approved, but it was impossible to read anything into his brief text. Unless he was wanting to share the good news in person? Yes, that was something Eric would do.

She exhaled as the walk lights turned green, feeling her spirits lighten as she headed to the tram stop. Because suddenly it didn't feel as if everything in her life was turning to custard. Even better, she actually had time to get herself a decent coffee. This day was getting better already.

Ten minutes later, aromatic coffee in hand, Mari pulled shut the cage on the ancient lift in the old red-brick warehouse and pressed the button for the third floor. The lift rattled its way upwards, past the ground floor that had been given over to delivery van parking, through the two levels of screened-off laboratories and up to the small mezzanine office level she liked to refer to as the penthouse suite. It was hardly anything as salubrious. But between the flash new apartment blocks and hotels that now populated the Docklands area, a slim window in her office offered the tiniest sliver of Melbourne's Port Phillip Bay.

She sipped her coffee as she stepped from the lift, ready with a greeting for Carol, but there was no one manning Reception, the space unusually hushed. She stepped into her office without encountering a soul. Today the sun turned the tiny glimpse of sea to dazzling, sparkles of light dancing as the surface of the sea shifted. She watched it for a moment, enjoying the play of light. Oh, yes, Mari loved working here.

'You're here. Good,' she heard behind her.

'Eric,' she said, smiling as she turned to greet the CEO. 'I'm hoping it's good new—' But something in her colleague's face stopped her in her tracks. Eric looked ten years older than he had yesterday, the lines around his nose and mouth turned to crevices, his eyes bloodshot, the corners of his eyes recessed, resembling black pits either side of his nose. He looked like he had the weight of the world on his shoulders. She swallowed. 'They turned the loan down.' It wasn't a question. What else could affect Eric this way?

He shook his head. 'No.'

'Then what…?'

He sighed as he sat down on the edge of her desk, before looking up at her sadly. Almost apologetically. 'I withdrew the application.'

'But why? We were so confident.'

The older man gestured with his eyes towards her chair. 'You might want to sit down. This is going to come as a shock.'

Mari swallowed as she numbly complied. She felt as if she'd been strapped into an emotional rollercoaster ride that had started last night with Valerie's phone call and that clearly wasn't about to end any time soon. 'What's going on?'

Eric sucked in air, as if he needed the fortification. 'There's no need for a bank loan anymore.'

'But the expansion—'

'Will be handled by someone else.'

'I don't understand. Who? You founded this company, it is your baby, your pride and joy. It was your dream to take Cooper Industries to the world.'

'*Was* being the operative word.'

She shook her head. 'But what's changed?'

'I'm sorry, Mari, but I've sold the business. As of nine this morning, I no longer own Cooper Industries.'

'What? I don't understand.' There'd been no hint of a sale in the offing. No whispers. As far as Mari was aware, the expansion plans were only waiting for a decision from the bank before they proceeded full steam ahead.

Eric shrugged, his body seeming to sag in on itself. 'I'm afraid there's no easy way to say this, so I'll say it straight. I've been diagnosed with pancreatic cancer.'

'No!' It was unthinkable. Unbelievable. Eric had been a father figure and mentor combined since she'd joined this company ten years ago. And Eric might be well into his seventies, but he was still running regular half marathons. 'You're the fittest man I know.'

He shook his head. 'I wish, but I went looking for a reason for these pains in my back I've been having, and I found it.' He gave a self-deprecating chuckle. 'So much for my powers of self-diagnosis. Turns out it wasn't the wrong running shoes after all.'

For all his attempt at humour, Mari knew that such a diagnosis might be a death sentence. She licked her lips, trying to form the words for her next question.

But Eric was one step ahead of where her thoughts were heading. 'Three months, maybe six if I'm lucky.' He attempted a chuckle, but it died in his throat. He blinked. 'Of course, Helen is hoping for at least six. She's been wanting me to cut back my hours and focus on home and family for years. She's got a list of things longer than my arm to get done. I have a horrible feeling I'll be busier in the next few months than I ever have been.' He gave up trying to smile and pulled out a handkerchief to bat at his eyes and swipe at his sniffly nose. 'Maybe I should have thought about winding back before now.'

Mari was fighting back tears too but losing the battle. 'Oh, Eric,' she said, blinking tears from her eyes, 'that's such dreadful news. I don't know what to say.'

He shook his head. 'There's nothing anyone can say. But I wanted you to know why I had to make the difficult decision to sell.'

She sniffed. 'I understand.' Wanting to spend whatever time he had left with his wife and family made perfect sense. Perfect, ghastly sense.

'Thank you, Mari, for not making me feel worse than I do. You've put so much of yourself into this company, and you put so much work into the loan applications and the reports. I feel like I'm letting you down.'

'No, you mustn't think that! You have to put yourself and your family first. I'm sure whoever is taking over Cooper Industries will see the potential it has. I'm equally sure it will go on to great things with whoever is at the helm.'

He leaned over and squeezed her hand. 'That would be something. Apparently, he's been watching Cooper Industries for the last twelve months but only showed his hand in the last few weeks, trying to convince me to sell.'

Her head snapped up. 'You never told me that. You never hinted—'

He shrugged. 'There was no point bothering you. There was no way I was going to sell. I was too invested—we all were—in securing that loan. That was my focus.' He paused. 'At least, that was my focus before my diagnosis.'

Mari nodded, even as he looked away from her and shook his head.

'Unfortunately, you think you're doing something for the best and then you discover that things might not work out like you planned.'

'What do you mean?'

'I thought I was selling the business lock stock and barrel, simply a change of ownership, all of the staff assured of keeping their jobs, but it turns out the new owner has a different vision.'

'Oh?'

'He wants to keep the lab staff on, at least for now.'

She swallowed, not really wanting to know the answer to her next question. 'And the admin staff?'

'He's bringing in his own team. When I found that out, I couldn't leave it to everyone getting a blanket email that their services were no longer required. I've been saying goodbye to all the staff as they've come in.'

Mari's throat tightened. She thought of Carol and all the admin staff he'd had to share the grim news with, staff who'd probably packed their belongings and left the premises in tears. That explained why it had been so quiet when she'd arrived. But Mari was admin too. Was that what this chat was about? That she was gently being let go too?

Please God, no.

Twenty-four-hour care didn't come cheaply, and she had no idea how much any new arrangement for her sister would cost. She couldn't afford to lose her job now. She blinked rapidly and stared blankly into her barely touched coffee, the very same coffee she'd been so desperate for not thirty minutes ago. Now a caffeine hit felt as enticing as a road accident. Now she felt sick. Because Eric Cooper—her mentor, her friend—was dying.

And the icing on that dreadful cake was that Mari was about to lose her job. What was she going to do? How was she going to pay for Suzanne's care now?

Eric's voice filtered through her troubled thoughts, thoughts that were suddenly more focused on her own situation. Guiltily, she turned her attention back to Eric in time to hear him add, 'He wants a meeting with you. Eleven this morning, at his hotel. He has a suite at the Langham.'

Her mind scrambled to catch up. All the admin staff were being let go. She was admin staff. What had she missed?

'Who are we talking about?'

'The buyer.'

'He wants to meet me?' she scoffed. 'Why, so he can sack me personally?'

'He wants you to walk him through the financial statements.'

'What? Mr Hotshot Takeover Merchant takes over a business but can't read for himself a set of financial statements?' Mari didn't have a lot of sympathy or time for someone who had swooped in and taken over the company, resulting in half the staff being let go without notice. Especially when her neck was next on the chopping block. 'I don't know that I care to meet him.'

Eric shrugged. 'I know where you're coming from and I don't blame you. By all accounts, he has quite the reputation. Ruthless is one word I've heard to describe him. Arrogant too; I've found that myself. But once he made his intentions about the administration staff clear, I asked him—well, actually, I insisted—that he make an exception in your case.' He held up his hands, almost apologetically, before his voice softened. 'I know how much you need this job, but that's not why I recommended you. I told him what I've always told you, that other people make excuses, whereas you make things happen. I told him he'd be mad to let you go.'

'Eric...' She had no words. The man had just learned that he had a terminal illness, and he was thinking of her? 'You shouldn't be worrying about me at this time.'

'Why not? You've always made things happen for this company. You've been far more than a finance manager. You've been my wingman—' he managed a chuckle this time '—wing *person*, I probably should have said. But yes, you've been there helping steer this company through the last ten years and setting up the finances for a global expansion. So, this could be an opportunity for you. If—*when*— the company goes global, who knows where it might take you?'

It was generous of Eric to go into bat for her, but Mari wasn't as confident. From what she'd seen and experienced during her time in corporate life, companies that were taken over and subsumed into larger conglomerates were always the losers, their systems and staff devalued and changed, if not dispensed with, to fit the larger corporation. It was no surprise the buyer wanted to keep on the laboratory staff—at least until his own scientists were up to speed with the technology—but admin staff? They were a dime a dozen, even good ones. She liked to think she was one of the good ones, but she wasn't so egotistical as to think she was any kind of world-beating talent, no matter the praises Eric heaped on her.

'I don't know,' she said, wondering how much the buyer really wanted to meet with her. He'd probably just been humouring the older man. 'Maybe I should just pack my personal belongings and call it quits. Jump before I get pushed.'

'No, no, no,' said Eric. 'Please don't be too hasty. Finding a new job in this market is going to take time. Surely, it's at least worth meeting him?'

Well, there was that. Eric was the only one in the company who knew where the bulk of her salary went. And he was right that finding a new job was going to take time.

Precious time when she should be sourcing another carer for Suzanne without worrying about the means to pay for her. And Eric had been good enough to recommend her. Given everything he had on his plate, it was generous of him to give anyone else a second thought. The last thing she wanted to do was add another crease to his already furrowed brow.

'All right,' she said, adding a smile just for Eric's sake, 'I'll meet him.'

'Excellent! I'll drop Estefan a note that you'll be there.'

The name was like a whiplash to her senses, adrenaline propelling her from her chair. 'Wait. What?' She stared unseeingly out of her sliver of window. 'Who did you say?' Her words sounded reedy and thin, as if all the volume in her body had been directed to her thumping heart, leaving only the thinnest filament for her voice.

Because she couldn't have heard that name. She must be mistaken. She must have misheard. *Misinterpreted.* Even with the way her luck had been running today, life couldn't be that cruel.

Could it?

'Estefan,' Eric repeated. 'Dominico Estefan. He's a Spanish businessman—a billionaire, by all accounts— looking to diversify into pharmaceuticals. Have you heard of him?'

Mari's blood ran with ice. Oh, yes, she'd heard of him. *She'd slept with him.*

'You could say that,' she muttered, shaking her head as she turned around.

A long time ago.

'Are you all right?' Eric asked, on his feet now. 'You look like you could do with something stronger than coffee.'

'I'm fine,' she lied, pasting on what she hoped would

pass as a reassuring smile. Eric was the one who'd received the devastating diagnosis. He should be the focus of her concern, not the other way around. 'I just…wasn't expecting to hear his name. I…um… We were at university together. For a few months.'

Eric's frown converted instantly into a beaming smile. 'Oh, so you're old friends, then. I dare say that will make things easier. He'll be sure to want to keep you on in that case. I'll text him now to let him know you're coming.' He pulled out his phone from a pocket. 'Shall I let him know you two know each other?'

'No, don't!' she said, putting voice to her first panicked thought. 'Please don't. I'd like it to be…a surprise.'

Eric chortled. 'A surprise. I like it,' he said, beaming as he put his phone away. 'Right, I've told him you'll be there at eleven. What I wouldn't give to be a fly on the wall when you walk in. You will let me know how you get on, won't you? If you can keep your job, it will be one bright thing coming from this deal.'

Her body was vibrating at the thought of meeting Dominico in person. 'There are no guarantees he'll offer me a job,' she protested. And once he knew who she was, there was no chance he'd offer her one.

Not to mention there was not a snowball's chance in hell that she'd accept it even if he did.

'I know, I know,' he said. 'But I have a good feeling about this.' He tilted his head to one side and smiled softly. 'Let me hold onto that.'

'I will,' she promised, even if she had to massage the truth a little. Because it was worth it just to see Eric smile.

'Okay,' he said, glancing at his watch. 'I've got an appointment with my oncologist in thirty minutes, I'd better run. Apparently, this is my life for the next however long.

That is—' he smiled at her over his reading glasses '—whenever Helen isn't running me ragged.'

The pair hugged, Mari squeezing her friend and mentor tight as tears once more welled in her eyes. 'I will see you again?' she asked as they drew apart. Whatever nightmarish treatments the coming months held for him, she couldn't bear to think that this might be the last time they'd meet.

Eric's lopsided smile confirmed her fears. He reached a hand to her shoulder and squeezed it gently. 'Let's keep in touch,' he said, making no more commitment than that. 'And let me know how you get on with Estefan.'

The mere mention of his name sent another bolt of electricity down her spine. Oh, yes, that undisputed pleasure was still to come.

CHAPTER THREE

MARI TOOK THE pedestrian underpass under Flinders Street Station and emerged into the sunlit morning on the northern bank of the Yarra River. Across the river the stepped hotel that was the Langham rose twenty-five floors between the taller towers that filled the skies over Southbank. Now only a bridge separated her from meeting the man who had torn her world apart twenty years ago.

Twenty years.

Normally, such an anniversary would be cause for celebration. Twenty years free. Twenty years during which she'd picked up the shattered pieces of herself, dusted herself off and made herself new. Sure, it hadn't been easy. She'd had her share of ups and downs along the way, but she'd made herself a success into the deal and put the past behind her.

Or so she'd thought.

Because as it turned out, twenty years was nowhere near enough to forget the past. Her memories were like rocks that had been in a rock tumbler all that time. By now, after so many years tumbling, all their rough edges—the elation, the despair, the abandonment—should be smoothed and rounded and gentle to the touch.

And yet there was nothing gentle to the touch about memories of her time with Dominico. Her emotions were

like those craggy rocks, not rounded through the tumble
of the years, their jagged points and edges merely blunted.
It had only taken mention of his name to return them to
their barbed glory.

She stood there staring at the hotel across the river,
being jostled by pedestrians rushing by, inconvenienced
by this woman turned statue in their way. But she didn't
care. She wasn't inclined to move. She didn't want to see
Dominico Estefan and every cell in her body was in ac-
cord. The thought of seeing him—of being in the same
room with him, of breathing the same air—made her feel
physically ill.

Because she hated the man with a passion.

She'd thought she'd come to terms with her past. She'd
thought she'd put this chapter of her life behind her. But just
the mention of his name had brought it all back. Brought
back the hurt.

And she hated him for what he'd done to her. Hated him
for promising her his heart and leaving her with a gaping
hole where hers should be. That hole ached now, pulsing
with the pain of loss as if it had been only yesterday that
he'd torn her world apart.

She wanted to turn and walk away. It would be so easy
to do. But the promise she'd made to Eric came back to her.
There was no way she could go back on a promise made
to him, this day more than ever. She had no choice but to
meet with Dominico.

She swallowed down on the roiling in her gut, the only
hope that he wouldn't recognise her. Why should he recognise her?

They hadn't seen each other for twenty years and she
was far from that nineteen-year-old girl with crazy hair and
stars in her eyes. She was groomed now. Wild hair tamed

into a sleek chignon. Loose cheesecloth shirts and floaty skirts swapped for buttoned down jackets over crisp white shirts and pencil skirts. She was as sensible as her court shoes, she was grounded and cynical, and not about to be blown away by a dark-eyed, dark-haired god with a chiselled jaw and even more chiselled body. Even her name was different.

Whereas, of course, she'd recognise him. There was only one Estefan. She'd seen his picture on the international business pages, seen his photo emblazoned on the society pages, attending a gala ball or a big-ticket charity event, and always with some beauty on his arm. He'd grown from a good-looking twenty-something into a drop-dead handsome man. Fully formed, assets at the ready. To charm. Convince. *Seduce.* Would he still wield the same power over her? Would he still be as commanding a presence, as magnetic?

No, she assured herself. Because that vulnerable creature had been Marianne. She'd been so young. She'd been so naïve and unworldly, and ripe for the taking. Maybe this was her opportunity to discover that he had no hold over her now, that it had all been a figment of her fevered teenage imagination.

And that had been before he'd betrayed her. Before she'd hated him.

Someone shoved at her shoulder, sending her feet stumbling forwards, a burly man wielding an oversized backpack who couldn't be bothered going around. 'Blasted tourists,' he muttered, as if she'd been standing there with a camera phone in hand.

She glanced at her watch—five to eleven. That shove was the wake-up call she'd needed. She sucked in a breath and mounted the steps, uttering a mantra to herself.

Maybe he wouldn't recognise her.

Maybe he wouldn't recognise her.

And maybe, if he didn't recognise her and he did indeed offer her a job, she could tell him exactly where he could shove it. God, wouldn't that be satisfying?

Dom had a suite, the concierge informed her. Well, of course he did, Eric had said as much. What Eric hadn't informed her was that Dom was booked into the Presidential Suite. Mari wasn't sure why she was surprised.

The Langham Hotel's signature ginger flower scent offered none of its usual calming magic as the lift climbed, her earlier bravado evaporating as the floor numbers lit up.

Twenty. Twenty-one, Twenty-two...

And when the lift doors opened to the twenty-third floor, Mari was once again assailed by conflicting emotions. Nerves, anger and, most of all, something she hadn't banked on—a niggling undercurrent of fear that twenty years had not dulled his magnetism or the power he'd once held over her.

Not a chance, she reinforced to herself as she stepped out. Her anger was both her armour and her superpower. They would make sure she would never fall victim to the siren call of that man's charms again.

A butler opened the door.

Of course.

He saw her into the room—*suite*—although even that word didn't do the space justice. There was a dining table to her immediate right, an adjoining kitchen into which the butler had melted away and a closed door beyond that. The bedroom, she presumed. There was a living room to her left, leading to another closed door. Another bedroom? Lordy, this place made her unit look like a closet.

And there, behind a gigantic timber desk, sat a man facing the window, studying the device in his lap. *Dominico...*

Her breath hitched, nerve-endings up and down her body sparked and fizzed. If he turned now, he'd see her frozen, a kangaroo trapped in headlights.

But he didn't turn to face her. He made no move to so much as acknowledge her presence. If he'd heard her come in, he didn't show it. He didn't so much as flinch as he sat with his back to her and stared down at whatever he was studying. And even though all she could see of him was his broad shoulders and the back of his dark-haired head, she was spun back in time. The broad shoulders she'd wrapped her arms around, the dark hair she'd splayed her fingers through as he'd gone down on her.

She turned her eyes up to the ceiling.

Don't go there. Think instead about what he did to you. Think about how he left you high and dry with your pain and your despair, without so much as a backward glance.

Just like he wasn't giving her so much as a backward glance now.

Charming, she thought, her nerves already stretched tighter than piano wire, *why not ratchet up the tension one more notch?*

Damn him, she might be a bundle of nerves, but she wasn't about to stand here cowering all day.

'You asked to see me.'

Dom had wondered how long it would take for her to speak. He'd sensed her nervousness, he was well used to that, but there was something else about her voice. A note. An inflection. Something he almost thought he recognised. He glanced around from the flight details his PA had just forwarded, and just as quickly looked back down again. A glance was all he needed. He'd been mistaken—there was nothing to recognise. She looked exactly like he'd expected. Like a mouse. Drab. Dull.

Beige.

'I did, but only as a favour. I don't have much time.' In his peripheral vision he registered her bristle. Seriously, what had she been expecting? A welcome party? Eric had insisted on this meeting—he'd all but begged for it, for that matter—but it didn't mean anything had to come of it. 'So, you're the accountant?' Of course she was, with her scraped back hair, sensible shoes and chain store navy suit. She was wearing the uniform of every low-ranking bean counter he'd ever met.

'Finance director, yes.'

'Right, like I said. Eric tells me I should keep you on. Tell me why I should.'

'Because I'm good at what I do.'

'That's it? Only *good*?'

'Very good. What else do you need to know? I can run through the financial statements if you like?'

Fabulous. As if he didn't know his way around a set of financial statements.

'All right, then. Astound me.' It might be entertaining to hear this one explain them.

Except it wasn't.

She'd made it all the way through the profit and loss statement and had started on the balance sheet when Estefan swung his chair around to face her. 'Enough!'

The woman jumped.

Dominico looked pointedly at his watch. 'I don't have time for this. I was told you were something special. I was told you were worth keeping on. And yet I see before me an everyday accountant, full of dull-speak and numbers.'

'It's a set of financial statements,' she said, jamming her glasses higher up her nose. 'Of course it's full of numbers. It's hardly a comedy routine.'

'Now, that was funny.' He raised an eyebrow and looked at her, more closely this time. Her cheeks were slashed with colour and under that navy jacket her chest was heaving. There was a surprise. She had a not bad figure hidden under that boring suit. He lifted his eyes to her face and was struck again with that flicker of recognition. Mad. But then he'd known a lot of women in his time, she was bound to resemble at least one of them.

'Okay, one last chance. Tell me why I should keep you on. You have thirty seconds.'

His phone pinged. Another email. The plane was ready to leave when he was. If he could tie this meeting up, he could be on his way to the airport in ten minutes.

It occurred to him that she hadn't spoken. 'Well?' he said, turning in his chair to face her. 'You can't think of even one good reason why I should keep you on?'

'Maybe it's because I can't think of one good reason I'd want you to. Thanks for your time, I'll see myself out.'

She turned to go.

'Wait!' he ordered, intrigued and not a little piqued. Nobody walked out on Dominico Estefan, least of all a drab little accountant he'd only agreed to see in order to get the old man to sign. People bent over backwards to get a moment of his time in order to push their latest project or seek some kind of favour. He was the one who would decide when he'd had enough. What was her problem?

She stopped, her back to him. She was angry, he could tell by the rapid rise and fall of her shoulders and the rigid way she held herself. His eyes drifted down her body. There were curves from this angle too, her jacket cinching in a slim waist before her skirt flared out over her hips. A decent designer could make the most of that shape.

'I get the impression, Ms—' he checked his email '—Ms Peterson, that you're not happy about something.'

Her head went back with a very unladylike snort as she spun around. 'You think?'

The surprises just kept on coming.

'Okay, so tell me, what is it that's made you so...prickly?'

'You really don't know?'

'I'm all ears.'

She sighed. 'Okay, so you take over a company where staff are more akin to family. Then you immediately sack half the staff without notice—'

'They'll all be well compensated.'

'That won't help them find new jobs—long-term jobs. And the remaining staff know that they are firmly in your sights, for whenever they reach their use-by dates.'

'You're being melodramatic.'

'Am I? Isn't that what you have planned?'

He shrugged. 'Takeovers can seem brutal. Ruthless even.'

'Apparently so. You took advantage of Eric Cooper. He didn't want to sell. He had plans to expand the business himself, plans that would have succeeded.'

He frowned. 'In that case, why did he sell?' He'd wondered at the sudden change of heart himself. He'd been rebuffed time and again by the old man.

'He didn't tell you? But then, why would he? You wouldn't have cared less anyway. All you need to know is that, on top of the disappointment of having to sell the company he had birthed and nurtured, you broke his heart by sacking half his staff and putting the rest on notice that their days were numbered. So did you seriously expect that would endear you to any of us, and that we'd all somehow become bosom buddies?'

His gaze flicked once more to her chest. She kicked up her chin and crossed her arms protectively under her breasts, as if she'd realised the mistake she'd made. But the gesture only served to accentuate her breasts. This meeting had been far more entertaining than he'd expected.

'Well,' he said with a shrug, 'I guess if you don't want to work with me, I'll just have to swallow the disappointment.'

'You make me sick,' she said. 'In all honesty, why the hell would anyone in their right mind want to work with you?'

He saw the flare of fire in her eyes as she turned to leave. Green fire, he realised as he received the full force of their savage glow.

And there it was again, not a spark of recognition but a bolt, that had first come in her voice and now appeared in her eyes, hurtling him back through the shrouds of time, decades ago, to when he'd been a student in Sydney.

And yet it couldn't be.

It was all wrong.

She was all wrong.

She was halfway to the door when he knew he couldn't let her go. Because it might just be right.

'Mari?' he called behind her. 'Mari*anne*?'

CHAPTER FOUR

MARI STOPPED DEAD. Or tried to. Because how did you stop yourself from trembling when every cell in your body was shimmering with anxiety? All the time she'd been here he'd not recognised her. He'd barely looked at her. He'd glanced her way and made her feel like something unpleasant stuck to the sole of his shoe. And that was good. That was what had given her the confidence to speak her mind. To tell him exactly what she thought of him.

So what that she'd have to find a new job? She'd manage it. Somewhere. Somehow. And it might be a struggle—no, it would be a struggle—and she might have to take on two jobs to ensure Suzanne's care, but that option was far preferable to sucking up to this man, being forced to beg for a job.

She wouldn't beg. She hadn't begged. She'd honoured Eric's desire that she meet with Dominico and she had. She'd satisfied everything that was expected of her and she'd survived the experience.

She'd survived and she felt all the stronger for it. Because she'd changed. Twenty years had seen her change. She'd grown. She'd made something of herself.

Dom had changed too. But not in any way that was an improvement. He'd become a horrid, despicable man. So arrogant, exactly as Eric had said. So full of his own importance. So different from the man she'd known all those years ago.

She'd caught his gaze lingering on her breasts. She'd felt that laser focus burn right through the fabric of her jacket. She'd felt her nipples peak and ache. And then she'd cursed herself for bringing his attention back to her breasts again with that stupid comment.

Bosom buddies.

Big mistake.

And yet still she'd been less than five metres from disappearing back into her less than perfect but Dominico Estefan free life. Until he'd called her name.

Her whole name.

She'd put Marianne behind her when she'd left university and started applying for jobs. When she was looking to be taken more seriously. She'd straightened her hair and taught herself how to tame it into professional-looking updos. She'd given up cheesecloth and cotton and colour and bent herself into monochrome Mari. Nobody called her Marianne now.

And twenty years on, here she was, in all her serious accountant get-up, the suit and glasses and sensible court shoes, and still he'd recognised her.

It occurred to her that she could just keep on walking. Open the door. Take the lift down. Get out of his life like he'd once left hers. Let him think that he was wrong because she had no idea what he was talking about.

But something about him knowing was even more delicious. Now there was no need to temper her words, no need to hold back. He knew who she was and now she could unleash what she really thought about him.

She spun on her heel. 'I'm surprised you even remember.' Contempt dripped from her voice.

'Marianne?' He was on his feet now, making short work of dispensing with the barrier that was his desk, his eyes intent on her face. Searching. Seeking. 'Is it really you?'

Mari swallowed. His voice until now had been just the same as she remembered. Caramel over granite, with a barrel-load of the gravel of irritation underlying it. Now there was almost an element of wonderment to it. Something that she remembered was a part of him. Something that maybe his arrogance and ruthlessness hadn't stamped out completely. Not that it helped to soften her attitude towards him.

'Is it so unlikely?' Once again, her heart was pounding. It had been bad enough when Dom was sitting behind the desk ignoring her, but now he was standing in front of her a mere metre away, all tall, dark and unbearable.

His features were still compelling, maybe more so with the passage of time. She'd thought his twenty-two-year-old self a man then, but that had been her teenage view. This was the real man before her—a man in his prime. She could feel the heat emanating from his body along with his signature scent that she recognised as uniquely his. It hurtled her back through the decades, to a time when he'd lied and told her that he loved her. She pressed her eyes closed to try to block out the memories, but they kept rushing back. Of picnic lunches in Sydney's Botanic Gardens, of falling asleep in Dom's arms after making love, of waking up to his kisses and making love with him all over again.

'But you,' he said, looking her over. 'You became an accountant? You, who was the original earth mother.'

Her flush of courage suddenly felt over-egged. He was too close. He was before her. A full head above her, overwhelming her. He was so close that every cell in her body hummed with his proximity, drawn to him, just like they always had been. Twenty years after his betrayal and abandonment and, curse them, still her cells betrayed her.

'Somebody has to pay the bills. You're probably not familiar with that concept.'

'I pay the bills in my family.'

Her chin hitched. 'Slightly different circumstances, I'm sure.'

'Exactly. Which is why I'm wondering why you can afford to throw this job opportunity in.'

'I'll manage. I'll look after myself. I always have.' Like when he'd abandoned her twenty years ago and she'd had no one to fall back on but herself. There was no way she'd take a job from this man. There was no way she'd ever rely on this man again. She'd well and truly learned her lesson. 'Goodbye, Dom.'

Where was the invisible butler to let her out? Never mind, the door was at her back. All she had to do was take the handle and let herself out.

'You can't just disappear,' he said. 'We haven't seen each other in what, twenty years.'

'You're missing the point,' she breathed. 'Why would I want to stay with you a moment longer than I already have?'

'Why?' he said. 'Because I took over Cooper Industries? Or because of what happened twenty years ago?'

She didn't answer and he knew which it was.

'We were kids, Marianne. Little more than kids. You can't still be holding a grudge after all this time.'

A grudge? He thought she was harbouring a mere grudge? It was like rubbing salt into wounds he'd just scraped clean of their scars. It was almost as if he looked back on those days with a degree of nostalgia and was looking to reconnect as if they were meeting at a class reunion.

He paused. 'It wasn't like it meant anything.'

His words sent shards of glass into her heart. She shook her head. Because no, it meant nothing. Nothing at all.

'Do you really hate me that much?'

What kind of question was that? Memories overwhelmed her. Of loss. Of betrayal. Of a lover who'd turned his back on her when she was at her most vulnerable.

She untwisted her lips long enough to speak. 'You have no concept of how much I hate you.'

Dom considered her outburst dispassionately. He was still coming to terms with stumbling across Marianne again—what were the chances when they'd met in Sydney and here they both were, twenty years later, in Melbourne?—but something else occurred to him then. Something else that could provide a convenient solution to his problem.

'Then I have one question.' In spite of her professed hatred for him—or rather, because of it—he raised one eyebrow and allowed himself a smile. 'Are you married?'

CHAPTER FIVE

'WHAT?' WHAT KIND of a question was that? The man was mad. Whatever else had happened in the last twenty years, and however successful he'd become, it was clear that he was losing his marbles.

'It's a perfectly simple question. All it requires is a yes or no answer. If it's yes—your name would suggest you could be—you were Marianne Wheeler back then, if I remember correctly—and then, as much as I'd love to catch up with you and talk over old times, you're free to leave.'

Mari licked her lips. 'And if it's a no?'

'Then I have a proposition for you. One that you might want to hear. One that will profit you generously.'

'I want nothing from you. I already told you: I won't work for you.'

He cocked his head to one side. 'Which would seem to indicate that your answer would be no, and that you're not married.'

She opened her mouth to speak, and just as quickly closed it again. Because he was right. Because if she'd said yes she'd already be out of here.

'That still doesn't mean I'm open to offers.'

'Then maybe you might want to reconsider. What if I offered you a little inducement? How does one million dollars sound?'

Her mind boggled. Her accounting brain got to work. What could she do with one million dollars? What would it mean to her? No desperate rush to find another job, for a start. Money to give Valerie that raise she'd been so patiently waiting for. Maybe even some much-needed upgrades to Suzanne's house. Sure, it wouldn't last for ever, but it would be a good start until she could find another job.

But Mari knew that there was no such thing as free money.

She swallowed. 'And what would I be expected to do for this windfall?'

'Nothing illegal or unpleasant,' he said. 'All you have to do is marry me.'

Mari laughed. The sound started on a hiccup before swelling up from deep in her belly, long and loud and maybe even a little bit hysterical. Because the idea was hysterical. It had to be a joke. The man could not be serious.

'Marry you?' she managed when finally she could breathe again. 'I'm sorry, but now it seems you're the one writing the comedy routines.'

There was a glimmer of steel in his dark eyes. He didn't like being laughed at. 'I assure you it wouldn't be a permanent arrangement. I need a temporary wife for a few short weeks, that's all.'

'I don't care what you need. You're asking the wrong woman.'

'I seem to recall that once, a long time ago, you might have been more amenable to the suggestion.'

Her spine stiffened. How dared he bring that up? It was almost as if he was taunting her. 'Like you said, Dom, we were both kids. And twenty years on, be it temporarily or otherwise, I wouldn't marry you—'

'If I were the last man on earth?'

'In the universe, more like it. And now, can I go?'

He smiled. Not the reaction she'd been expecting. 'So, let's make it more interesting. What if I offered you two million dollars?'

She shook her head, trying to make sense of the conversation and finding none. 'This is madness. Why are you even talking like this? Why would you even ask me?'

'Because you're perfect. Because you hate me. And because my mother is dying and wants to see me married before she dies.'

Forget the ridiculousness of his offer. Her fingers clutched at the jacket over her chest. 'Rosaria is dying?' The blows just kept coming, first Eric and now Dominico's mother.

'You remember her name?'

'Of course I do.' Mari had met both his parents, if only briefly. They'd been visiting family in Australia when Dom had introduced them at a dinner shortly before they'd returned to San Sebastián, leaving Dom to complete a second semester at university. The Spanish woman had struck Mari with her beauty and elegance and her deep love for her Australian husband. She'd been adamant that her son should stay on to study and learn more of his Australian heritage, even when her husband had preferred Dominico go home with them to learn the family business. 'But she's so young,' Mari said. 'She can't yet be seventy.'

'Sixty-nine,' he said. 'And she wants to see me married before she dies.'

For a moment Mari wavered. What must it mean to have your one final wish fulfilled? But no, Mari told herself in the next moment, don't fall for that. This was Dom's problem, not hers, no matter how much she'd liked the woman. No matter how sad the news.

Her backbone stiffened. 'And she wants you to marry someone who hates you? How bizarre.'

'No, I want to marry someone who hates me. My mother is wanting the whole fairy-tale scenario. You'll have to pretend to love me when we're in Spain until...well, until she dies. And, given you clearly hate me, the divorce will be both a release and relief for the two of us.'

This was bonkers. He was bonkers.

'Do you know how crazy you sound?' Once upon a time she'd been crazily, totally in love with Dom, but there was no way she could pretend to be in love with him now, not after what had happened. There was no way she could convincingly pull off such a farce.

'I know, but my mother has weeks to live, if that. Why wouldn't I want to make her last days happy?'

That, at least, made sense. She was here, wasn't she, at the behest of her mentor, Eric Cooper, promising to meet the man she'd least wanted to meet. You'd do such a thing for family or a good friend.

And this was Dom, who'd taken off from Sydney the moment he'd heard his father had suffered a heart attack. Family was important to them both. Except, it seemed, for the family they'd been growing together...

The family he'd been all too ready to discard.

She couldn't do it. There was too much pain in going back. Too much pain in being anywhere in the orbit of this man. There was too much raw hurt. There was no way she could turn a blind eye to what he'd done and—what? Marry him?

What a joke. She'd dreamed of marrying him back then. She'd dreamed of making a family with the man she'd loved.

And what had happened to those dreams?

They'd turned to dust.

The man before her was still waiting for her answer.

'No,' she said, resolute. 'I can't be the only woman on the planet who wants nothing to do with you. I'm sure there's quite the queue. Find somebody else who doesn't want to have anything to do with you.'

'Two million dollars isn't enough? Then what about three?'

'You'd pay someone that much money to pretend to be your wife? Notwithstanding the fact that you'll be deceiving your mother. Lying to her in her final weeks or months. Expecting me to lie to her too. What if she finds out? What if she learns that her duplicitous son was trying to trick her? How do you think she'll feel?'

His jaw tightened. 'She won't find out.'

She shrugged and turned, reaching for the door handle. So close to escape that she could taste it. 'Good luck with that. But you're going to need a better actor than me.'

'Five million,' he said.

Her hand hovered over the door handle. Could this day get any weirder? Bad news, a late train, even worse news, a lost job and then a ridiculous offer for her to marry the man she least wanted to. Surely this must be some kind of *Alice in Wonderland* dream? What the hell had she eaten last night?

'Well,' he said, 'is five million dollars enough to convince you to marry me?'

She heard the hum of a vacuum cleaner in the corridor outside. She heard a helicopter returning joy flight tourists to the helipad on the river. That signature ginger flower Langham scent was still there with every breath she took. So no, she wasn't dreaming, but it was clear the power was firmly in her hands. She abandoned the door handle and turned back to face him.

Mentally, she totted up the yearly costs of Suzanne's care, costs that would escalate year on year. Costs that she'd find near impossible to cover on even a decent salary. It was a lot. And then she added a margin for error. A fat margin.

'All right. You want my price to faux marry you? I'll do it. But it will cost you. I want ten million dollars.' She waited a moment. 'Or no deal.'

A nerve in his jaw popped. His eyes bored into her. 'I never figured you for a gold-digger, Marianne.'

'I never figured you for a ditherer. Do you want to cement this deal, Señor Estefan, or should I just leave now? I'm perfectly happy to leave right now.'

She reached a hand for the door handle again.

'No,' he said. 'Ten million dollars it is.'

CHAPTER SIX

'HOW SOON CAN you be ready to fly?'

Mari was still reeling from his easy acceptance and his question didn't register. What had just happened? She'd half expected him to flatly turn down her request. Ten million dollars was a ridiculous amount of money to pay anyone to pretend to be their wife. But clearly ten million dollars was not ridiculous enough because he'd agreed. And maybe she'd secured a great pay day, but she had a gut-churning feeling that she'd just made a deal with the devil.

'Fly?' she said, as his words filtered through. 'Fly where?'

'San Sebastián,' he said, back at his desk and busily barking instructions to whichever poor soul was at the other end of his phone. He looked up. 'Oh, hell, you do have a passport, don't you?'

She thought about lying. If she didn't have a passport, she couldn't fly internationally. But already the prospect of being paid ten million dollars to temporarily marry Dominico was worming its way into her brain, boring holes in her reservations.

Ten million dollars.

It would solve so many of her problems. It would be the answer to Suzanne's ongoing care issues—for years. All she had to do was pretend to be his wife—his real wife—

but only temporarily. A pretend wife to a man who had abandoned her to her grief and despair.

Temporarily.

She had no doubt that he'd be done with her as soon as he had no more need of her. That was the rock she clung to.

Numbly she nodded.

'Good,' he said. 'And do you have some decent clothes to bring?'

'Decent?' She had her working wardrobe. It wasn't haute couture, but it served its purpose. She looked down at herself. 'What's wrong with this?'

He sighed and barked some further instructions into his phone. 'Right. We'll fix that. Is there anything else you need to take care of before we go? Do you have a cat or dog that needs looking after?'

Oh, heavens, how could she go anywhere? Not a cat nor a dog, but a sister. *Suzanne.*

'How long will I be gone?'

'A matter of weeks. Two months tops.'

'Then yes, I have…um…something to organise.'

'All right. I'll have a car pick you up downstairs. Get your personal effects—don't worry about your clothes, someone else will take care of that—organise what you must and meet me back here.' He glanced at his watch. 'Will one hour be enough?'

To get to her flat in Chelsea and then to Suzanne's house, see her settled and ensure there was nothing she'd overlooked.

'More like three.'

He grimaced. 'All right. Get on with it.'

He took a call, turned to the window and only when he turned back, saw her still there. 'What?'

She licked her lips. 'We haven't talked about terms.'

'You'll have your money. You needn't worry about that.'

'I need an advance. To make the arrangements I need to get in place before I can leave.'

'How much does it cost to put a pet or two in kennels?'

She lifted her chin. She wasn't going to sound like she was begging. He was the one asking for favours. Without her usual pay packet, she still needed the means to pay for a carer for Suzanne for however long she was away. And maybe—just maybe—there was a chance she could persuade Valerie to change her plans and stay on if she offered her a decent inducement.

'One million dollars should tide me over. For now.'

'*Tide you over...?*'

He rubbed the back of his neck and sighed, and Mari knew she had him and that she was now the one calling the shots. 'All right. I'll need your bank details in that case. Is that it?'

'Not quite. Because there's something else we haven't discussed.'

This time his sigh was less resigned, more aggravated. 'There's nothing complicated about this, Marianne. It's a simple contract. You pretend to be my ever-loving, happy wife for however long you're needed, and I pay you ten million dollars. That's not a bad deal from where I'm standing.'

She shook her head. 'Not bad, perhaps. But not complete. You see, I'll marry you, Dom. I'll take part in this farce and play the loving wife in public, but I won't sleep with you. There will be no sex. This marriage will never be consummated.'

He took a few moments to consider that. A few moments where she wondered if he wanted to call off the deal. And then he rose from behind his desk and came closer. Much closer. Until he was standing right in front of her again. Until she could feel the heat emanating from his body, his signature scent filling her every breath, the drumbeat of the heart in his broad chest like a siren's call to her.

'And yet,' he said, raising one hand to a loose tendril of her hair, winding it around his finger, 'if I remember correctly, we were so good together.'

She swallowed, the sensation of him touching her hair, the gentle pressure from the curling motion, threatened to undo her. Threatened to make her forget what she'd demanded. *Almost*.

'Past tense,' she said firmly, stiffening her spine against the onslaught to her senses. 'We're not good together now or evermore.'

He looked down at her intently, at her eyes, at her mouth, lingering way too long on her lips. He let go of her hair and didn't touch her again. He didn't have to. She felt him in her peaked nipples and the humming vibration between her thighs.

'It seems to me,' he said, 'that I'm paying an awfully hefty sum for this arrangement.'

'You're paying me to play your wife. You're not paying for the right to sleep with me. You want this marriage easy to unwind? Not consummating it will make it a piece of cake.'

A nerve in his cheek twitched. His eyes grew colder. 'You're absolutely certain about this?'

'Dead certain.'

'Well,' he said, his eyes still hard but with a smile that could only be described as a challenge accepted. 'We'll see.'

She threw him her own smile in return. 'Won't we just?'

Arrogant man. Mari stewed all the way to her flat. Stewed while she changed out of her suit and into jeans, a clean T-shirt and pulled on a navy blazer. She gathered up the rest of her belongings she might need in a suitcase. She wasn't sure what Dom had meant about someone else taking care of her clothes, but she wasn't about to leave packing them to someone else. With her suitcase packed and her peace lily, the one indoor plant she'd never quite managed to kill, tucked under her arm, she closed the door. Her flat would take care of itself while she was gone, there was enough money in her account for the rent to be paid. It was leaving her sister that worried her the most.

'Suzanne, hi!' said Mari ten minutes later as her sister opened the door.

Her sister looked from Mari's face to the pot plant in her arms. 'This is a surprise. Did you get the afternoon off?'

She leaned down to give her sister a hug. 'Something like that. How are you?'

'You know,' she said, wrapping one arm around Mari's shoulders, the slur in her voice more pronounced today. 'The same. What's happening in your world?'

I just agreed to pretend to be someone's wife.

'Oh, you know,' Mari said, dodging the question until she could work out a way to share the bizarre events of the day. Where would she even start?

'God, we're a boring pair, aren't we? Come on,' said Suzanne, struggling to negotiate a three-point turn in her wheelchair to turn around, 'let's have a cup of tea.'

Mari's heart broke as her sister's electric chair carried her into the kitchen. The house had originally been Marianne's, but she'd swapped it for the unit Suzanne had bought five years ago when she'd moved to Melbourne to be close to her sister. The home swap had seemed a good idea at the time, but the layout of the two-bedroom house was less than ideal when you factored an electric wheelchair into the space, and as Suzanne's disease progressed and her condition deteriorated it would become increas-

ingly problematic. Soon, though, if she could carry out her
end of the deal, Mari should be in a position to provide her
sister with something more suitable. All she had to do was
complete this deal with the devil.

Simple.

Mari sucked in a breath. If only. She was under no illu-
sions that these next few weeks were going to be the hardest she'd ever endured. Even harder than those godawful
weeks and months when she'd paid the price for falling in
love with Dominico Estefan.

In the kitchen it was Mari who filled the kettle and
turned it on. Mari who found the mugs and teabags and
found the milk in the fridge. Mari knew that, on a good
day when her pain levels were low, Suzanne could do it,
but still she hated her guests waiting for minutes for her to
do things that would take them seconds.

'Actually,' Mari started as she sat down opposite her
sister, mugs of tea and an open packet of biscuits between
them, 'something did happen today. Eric Cooper sold the
company.'

Suzanne frowned as she wound the fingers of one hand
around her mug's handle. She knew what Mari's job meant,
not just to Mari, but to them both. 'So that's why you're not
at work. But what does that mean?'

'It means the buyer is keeping the lab staff on, but he's
bringing in his own team to cover administration.' Mari
held up one hand. She could see Suzanne adding up A
and B and coming up with C, when the answer was actually D. 'The good news is that he offered me another role
in the business.'

'Wow, what a relief. How lucky is that?' She reached for
a biscuit. 'What's the new job, then?'

'Less accounting. More of a support role for the boss,'
she said, massaging the position. Instantly she berated her-

self. Do not think about massaging. Do not think about positions.

There would be no positions.

'The annoying thing is it's going to take me overseas for a little while. That's why I was hoping you could look after my peace lily.'

Her sister looked at the plant and back to Mari. 'How long will you be gone?'

'I'm not entirely sure. It could be a few weeks, but I've been told no more than a couple of months.'

Suzanne frowned. 'Are you sure about this? It sounds a bit dodgy to me.'

'I know it sounds odd.' Because it sure did, even to Mari. 'But it pays well with a really good bonus.'

'In that case,' Suzanne said with a sniff, 'I'll miss you.'

Mari reached out to take her sister's hand. 'And me you. But at least I'll know my peace lily will be in good hands.'

The same butler let her back into Dom's suite, relieving her of her pull-along suitcase. Dominico was looking out of the window, phone in hand, the other hand behind his head, and just the view of his broad shoulders, the pull of his shirt over the muscled arm triangled behind his head, was enough to ramp up her heart rate. He ended the call and turned around, his eyes fixing on her immediately. 'Change of plans,' he barked. 'There's no way we can get married in Spain, or even in Australia for at least a month from now. The licence conditions don't allow for it.'

'Oh. So, the deal's off?' Mari wasn't sure whether to be disappointed or relieved. Relief had a slight edge, but then there remained the issue of repaying the million-dollar advance she'd asked for.

'No, nothing's off. But we can't wait four weeks. We have no choice. We leave for Las Vegas first thing in the morning. Once we're married, we'll head to Spain.' He glanced at the suitcase the butler had in hand. 'What's that?'

'My things. My clothes.'

'I thought I told you not to bother with that. The stylist is in your room waiting to outfit you.'

'My room?' He was talking nonsense. 'What are you talking about?'

He pointed to his left, to the door, now open, beyond the dining room. She saw racks of clothes inside and a bevy of women sorting through them. 'That's your room. You've got work to do.'

She looked back at him. 'What is this? I don't need someone to dress me. I'm thirty-nine years old, not twelve. I hardly need a dresser.'

His gaze raked her up and down, now wearing what she'd imagined would make for comfortable travel wear, and nothing about his gaze was complimentary.

She bristled, her spine pulling tight. 'You think that insulting me makes me more amenable to playing your wife?'

'I'm not insulting you. I'm just pointing out that you need to look like someone I might be interested in marrying.'

'Instead of some commoner you dragged off the street?'

'If you want to put it like that.'

'How would you put it?'

He sighed, as if bored with her protests and that she had no right to be offended. 'I move in certain circles. I want people to believe that we're married and for that you need to look the part. That means no chain store suits or ripped jeans. Now, there's an entire boutique full of clothes that's been shipped into your room waiting for you. I've given them an outline of what you'll need. And don't take too long. The hairdresser arrives in two hours. Dinner's at nine.'

She stood stock still, hating him more than ever right now. He knew nothing about her or about her life or the choices she'd been forced to make. Sure, it would have been lovely to blow her salary on posh designer clothes, but she'd thought she'd done okay outfitting herself on a budget when her first priority had been ensuring her sister's needs were met.

'Yes, sir,' she said, giving him a mock salute. 'We can't have you looking like you're slumming it.'

His slate-grey eyes gleamed with an icy fury. Was he starting to regret the deal he'd made with her? Because that would almost be amusing. If it hadn't been for the money she'd be walking away with, that would make two of them.

She stalked into the room that was apparently assigned to her and was met by a gaggle of women and an overdose of perfume. Racks of designer clothes lined the walls. An empty rack sat waiting for what Mari presumed were her purchases. Somewhere under a vast display of shoes in the centre of the room, Mari guessed there was a king-sized bed.

The door snicked shut behind her, while a posh, matronly voice announced, 'Our client is here, ladies. Let's get to work.' And then she looked at Mari. 'I'm Audra Valentina,' she said, offering a high school prefect's smile, 'from Audra's of Melbourne. And today is your lucky day. You can get undressed now, my dear.'

'What?' Mari looked around. The women looked like they'd come stamped out of the same factory from wherever Audra had been fashioned. Stick thin, highly varnished and all standing to attention, their hands clasped meekly before them. All but one young woman, who was standing to one side looking uncomfortable. 'What is this?'

The older woman preened. 'I am your style consultant and I believe we only have a short window of time. But I can only help you if you are prepared to help me. Now,' she said, her ruby lips narrowing, 'don't be shy. Please take off whatever it is that you're wearing.'

'I don't think so. I don't want this. I don't need—this circus.'

'Nonsense. What girl doesn't want to play dress-ups?'

'This *woman*, that's who.'

'But Mr—Señor Estefan—'

'Might like to think he's Richard Gere playing in a remake of *Pretty Woman*, but this woman has other ideas. Now, he told me you have a list of what I need. Give it to me and I'll find the outfits myself.'

'But...' her eyes raked over Mari's casual outfit '...you'll need expert help.'

The woman could have saved her breath. Mari had read the sentiment in her eyes.

'Then leave her,' Mari said, pointing to the young woman who seemed to be the outsider. 'She can help me choose.'

'But she's not qualified. She's only here to observe.'

'Then she can get some on-the-job training. Everyone else can leave.'

The woman stalled. 'Well, this is highly irregular.'

'There you go, I knew we'd find something to agree on.' She pulled open the door. 'Don't worry, I'm sure your young colleague will help me spend lots of Dominico's lovely money.'

'We'll wait in Melba's, Ella,' she said. 'Let me know when you're finished.' And then, with pursed lips, the woman handed over a list and marched her team minus one from the room.

'Relief,' Mari said, her back to the closed door. 'That was all kinds of a freak show.'

The young woman hid a smile under her hand. 'I don't think that's ever happened to Madame Valentina before.'

Mari smiled. 'I'm sure she'll get over it eventually. And now, Ella,' she said, putting the list Dom had supplied down on the only part of the bed not covered in shoe boxes, 'it looks like we've got work to do. First item on the list is a wedding dress—Las Vegas suitable.' She regarded the young woman seriously. 'Hmm, do you think Audra has anything in the Elvis Presley impersonator line?'

The next two hours passed in a blur of colours, fabrics, but best of all, laughter. It turned out Ella was a great choice of consultant and Mari was glad she hadn't banished everyone from the room. She might be the work experience girl, but Ella had an eye for design, colour and fit, and for making an outfit stand out, from the right foundation garments right through to the accessories.

When a knock came on the door to inform her that the hairstylist had arrived, Mari was back in her jeans and T-shirt going through the list with Ella, doing a final check that they'd covered all the bases. The once empty rack was now filled with hangers, the rack below covered with shoe boxes. Mari couldn't imagine how much it would all cost, the total of her purchases had to be an eye-watering amount, but if Dom wanted her to look like someone he wanted to be with—*like someone he wanted to marry*—then he'd just have to pay the price. That was his problem.

In a way, she mused, as her hair was given 'sun-kissed highlights', she should be grateful to Dom. She'd never be able to afford designer clothes made from such fabulous fabrics and it would be a treat to wear them for however long this charade lasted.

She *should* be grateful to Dom.

Except no amount of couture clothing, no amount of pampering, could ever make up for Dominico's betrayal all those years ago. Nothing would ever compensate her for the pain he'd put her through.

Nothing.

CHAPTER SEVEN

WHERE WAS THAT WOMAN? Dominico paced the length of the suite. The hairstylist had left thirty minutes ago, the dinner booking was set for five minutes' time, and yet Marianne's door remained firmly shut. The woman was infuriating. To his horror he'd learned she'd banished the boutique consultant and most of her staff. Clearly madness when she so desperately needed help with her wardrobe. God only knew what kind of outfits she'd chosen.

Dinner tonight was supposed to be the test. To see if she could pull off the role of his partner. His fiancée. They were headed to Las Vegas tomorrow. They would be married in twenty-four hours.

Could she pull it off? She had to pull it off. His mother was expecting him and he had no other option. But sure as hell there would be words if she looked anything less than acceptable.

He heard the snick of a door and spun around.

And it looked like Marianne, except...

She was wearing a long-sleeved black off-the-shoulder mini dress in some kind of rib knit that hugged her waist and flared out over her hips before exposing those legs. And what legs. Long and lean, they ended in perilously high heeled strappy sandals. The dress had a white bow neckline over her breasts and her hair, that he'd only seen tied up in some kind of knot behind her head, now spilled down over her bare shoulders. Sun-kissed hair with chestnut highlights that added a pop of radiance to her otherwise monochrome outfit.

Another pop of colour, because she'd ditched her glasses and her eyes looked bigger and more vividly green than ever.

'Marianne?'

'Who were you expecting?' She sounded breathless, her voice a little husky, and maybe just a little nervous. 'What's wrong? Am I late?'

He shook his head. Partly because she wasn't late. Partly because he couldn't believe the transformation. And mainly because his loins were suddenly paying attention. His little beige accountant might well have been a caterpillar that had just emerged from her chrysalis, transformed into a bright and beautiful butterfly.

'So,' she said, trying to sound confident but still with that slight thread of nervousness. 'Will I do?'

Interesting. She was seeking his approval.

Very interesting.

'You'll do,' he said glibly, not bothering to disguise the fact that his voice was suddenly an octave lower. 'Let's go.'

Heads turned as they entered the restaurant, following the maître d' down the steps towards their table overlooking the Yarra River. Dominico was used to heads swivelling to follow him, women's eyes, some men's too. Hungry eyes. But tonight, he noticed the eyes following Marianne. He saw glances flick to her face, her figure, her legs. He saw their gazes turn to him but only to show their envy. He got it. She was making the right waves to be a partner to him.

He just wasn't sure he was entirely comfortable with it.

'You're making quite the impression on people,' he said as they were seated.

'Because I'm overdressed?' she asked.

'Because you look beautiful.'

For a moment she stiffened. Before she relaxed herself enough to say, 'You can thank your team of fairy god-mothers for that.'

'Not all of the fairy godmothers, apparently. I received an earbashing from one of them protesting your high-handed insistence that she and most of her cronies' services weren't required.'

'Audra called you?'

'If that's Madame Valentina, she certainly did. She made no secret of the fact she was unhappy.'

He didn't share the fact that he hadn't been wholly im-pressed with Marianne going rogue either, but frankly, Hydra or Audra or whatever the hell her name was had terrified him. She'd arrived with her entourage looking every bit like a crocodile wearing pearls. He for one had been relieved she wasn't dressing him.

'Lucky for me, Ella was fabulous. Not to mention your expense account. I imagine this afternoon's adventures have put a decent hole in your finances.'

'It's worth every cent,' he said, 'to see you looking this way.'

A waiter appeared, proffering a bottle of champagne for approval. 'Sir,' he said.

Mari frowned. 'Did we order that?'

'I did,' said Dom, glancing at the label and nodding at the waiter to proceed.

The cork was duly popped, a taster poured and declared perfect, and two flutes of the golden wine poured.

He raised his glass to hers. 'I'd like to propose a toast. To you, Marianne, the next Señora Estefan.'

He took a sip of the straw-coloured wine, the tiny bubbles dancing on his tongue like the anticipation fizzing in his veins. 'And along with a toast,' he said, pulling a small box from his pocket and snapping it open, 'I'd like to present you with your engagement ring.'

Mari's hand flew to her mouth. The ring winked up at her, boasting a massive champagne-coloured diamond that perfectly matched the sparkling liquid in her glass. The toast she might have expected. But a ring the size of a planet she hadn't seen coming.

'But why?' she said, shaking her head. 'It's too much. Besides, there's no need for it. I've already agreed to marry you.'

'There's every need. Because there's no way I wouldn't furnish the woman I am about to marry without a physical token of love.'

Her mouth twisted under her hand. *Love?* Did he not realise that every reference he made to love was like a hammer blow to her heart? Once upon a long time ago they'd exchanged words of love and she'd believed he'd meant them. As she had meant them. Little had she known that he could bandy words of love around and that they'd be as meaningless as this farce of a marriage.

'What's love got to do with it?'

'All right,' he whispered while wearing a smile that spoke of love but which carried an edge of menace. 'So wear it because people will expect you to wear my engagement ring. Like the people watching on at the tables nearby who think I've just proposed and who are right now awaiting your reaction. A positive reaction unless I'm very mistaken, so maybe it's time you started acting.' He pushed the ring box closer to her. 'So, what's it to be?'

So, what's it to be?

So very not romantic. So unlike the proposal she'd once yearned for. Something personal and private. But then, why would this be personal and private? It was a fake engagement to precede a fake wedding and she was one of the leading actors and the last thing he wanted was for her to take it seriously. The least she could do was get with the programme. But did he not realise that it would take her time to pretend that all was good between them—that what had happened twenty years ago meant nothing and could be swept under the carpet with the mere application of dollars, wallpapering over their fractured past?

But she'd accepted his expensive wallpaper so she could at least make an effort.

She shook her head as she gazed at the ring with as much wonder as she could muster. 'Yes,' she gushed. 'Yes, of course I'll marry you!'

The occupants of the nearby tables started applauding and despite knowing the truth, their delight was infectious. Mari felt herself blushing, nodding in acknowledgment, when she felt Dominico take her hands and pull her to her feet, slip the ring on her finger and draw her into his kiss.

Dominico's kiss.

She'd been there before. Experiencing the magic of his kiss. Being swept away by the hotbed of his mouth, the tangle of their tongues and the magical taste and feel of him.

But they were in the middle of a busy restaurant, and she couldn't afford to let herself get swept away today. She'd keep this short. They didn't need to make a spectacle of themselves.

At least, that was her intention.

But twenty years evaporated in the heat of his mouth and the sensuality of his lips until old hurts slipped into oblivion as she found herself lost in sensation. She clung to him for fear her knees would give out and she'd fall to the floor. She clung to him for fear that he'd let her go and she'd never feel him against her again. This was the kiss she knew, the kiss she'd missed—and yes, the kiss she'd longed for. For too many years until she'd thought she was over him.

Except, apparently, she wasn't.

He pulled out of the kiss before she did, taking her hands and smiling down at her as if he'd known she'd been unable or unwilling or both to pull out of that kiss first. Curse the man. Another reason to resent him. And now it seemed every table in the restaurant was applauding, the sound a muffled roar over the sound of the blood still rushing in her ears.

She eased out of his arms, breathless and shaken, before clutching the back of her chair so she could settle into it rather than collapse. 'What was that for?' she whispered.

'Sealing the deal with a kiss,' he said with another of those smug Cheshire cat smiles, raising a glass of the golden liquid to her. 'That's all.'

Was it all? Because it had sure felt like more. It seemed as if he was wanting to prove something, as if she wasn't immune to him, and smugly liking that she'd fallen for it.

Okay. Well, forearmed was forewarned. He'd blindsided her with his sudden move and his unexpected kiss. She'd let down her guard and he'd taken her unawares. She just had to make sure that he didn't take her unawares again.

She raised her glass to his and managed a smile she didn't feel in return before turning her attention to the menu. She needed to focus on something else and stop thinking about that kiss.

'Tell me about your husband.'

Whoa. Where had that come from? That wasn't the something else she needed to focus on. Her knees were no longer shaking, the warmth of his kiss evaporating. She blinked and looked up over the menu.

'Ex-husband, you mean.'

He nodded, smiling as if he'd just asked her what she might be partial to on the menu. 'Him. Tell me about him. Who was he?'

She smiled back. Two could play at that game. 'Does it matter? He was someone who seemed nice at the time. Someone I thought was a friend.' Who had acted like a friend when she'd been grieving and alone, when she'd seriously needed a friend. He was a widower who'd been married to an old school friend of Marianne's, and who was struggling to raise a baby and a toddler. Her gran had encouraged her to start babysitting for him to earn some money and because she was so concerned that Mari was collapsing in on herself and thought it would cheer her up.

He reached over and took one of her hands. Pressed it to his lips adoringly and asked, 'Did you love him?'

She resisted the temptation to pull her hand free and laughed instead. 'Did you ever love any of the women you've been pictured with?'

A warning light flared in his dark eyes, but he didn't let her hand go. 'I didn't marry any of them. So, did you?'

'Does it matter? It's over.' She looked back at the menu. 'What are you having?'

'And children?'

'Because I'm not sure,' she said, ignoring him as he had done her. She didn't want to go near the children question.

'I'm partial to the lobster medallions but then the Wagyu beef sounds tempting.'

'Why won't you answer? What are you so afraid of?'

She purposefully placed her menu down on the table. 'Why should I be afraid of anything? Why do you need to know?'

He shrugged. 'I'm naturally curious. Of course I want to know about your past. We're about to be married.'

A sham marriage and yet he still insisted on knowing about her past? She shook her head, his questioning heading ever too closely to one of the reasons she'd ended up married to Simon. But not close enough that she couldn't fire back.

'Good point. When you put it like that, I'd like to know about your past too. Just how many women have you slept with in the past twenty years?'

His jaw clenched, a muscle in his cheek twitched. Right before the smile returned. 'You're avoiding the question.'

'So are you. But okay, if it shuts you up, he married a friend of mine from high school and they had a couple of kids before she was killed in a crash.' She shrugged. 'He seemed nice enough at the time and I thought we might make a go of it, except we didn't, and no, there were no children. He already had two—and he didn't want more.' And she hadn't either, not after what she'd endured. It had seemed the perfect arrangement, her reluctance to have children meshing perfectly with his insistence that two was enough. At the time she'd been grateful to find some-one she wouldn't disappoint, because she couldn't bear the disappointment. Someone who was happy just to have her. She was lucky, everybody told her, to find someone who professed to care for her when she'd been so close to rock bottom. At the time it had seemed a second chance, almost too good to be true.

As ultimately it proved to be.

Because it turned out she did disappoint him in so many ways. Only occasionally at first, but then more and more frequently, until it seemed that hardly a day went by when she didn't do something to annoy him, whether it was buying the wrong brand of tinned tomatoes, or stacking the dishwasher the wrong way, or failing to cook meat loaf exactly the way his mother did. And she realised that all he'd really wanted was someone to manage the house and his kids.

She paused. 'And now, can we order?'

'That's a shame,' he said, still smiling. 'I always thought you would make the perfect mother. You seemed such an earth mother back then. All these years I imagined you with a clutch of children living on a farm somewhere close to nature. I'm sorry it didn't work out.'

Mari's senses were stretched razor-thin. She closed her eyes against the barrage of pain. They were both performing. Acting. Pretending to voice lines of romance and love to those around them while instead interrogating each other.

But the knowledge that he'd imagined her with a clutch of children... All these years? When had he even given her a second thought? But yes, he was happy to state that he was sorry her marriage hadn't worked out. And he seriously wondered why she hated him so much. The man had no clue. But why did he have to bring that up now, when they were supposed to be sitting here celebrating and drinking champagne? Why did he have to remind her of the pain that had sliced through her, the pain that they should have shared, but she'd had to bear it alone?

'I'm sorry he hurt you.'

Her gaze met his eyes. Slate-grey eyes that held a trace of empathy, but there was also a hint of smugness in his smile. As if he'd rescued her, and she was now in a better place.

She gave up any pretence of smiling and studying the menu and put it down on the table. 'You'd think I would have learned something, wouldn't you?'

A question mark might just as well have appeared in his eyes. 'I never hit you.'

'I never said he hit me. There are other kinds of hurt. Like the hurt when you left me. Like the hurt of you telling me that you'd been delayed. And then months and months later getting a phone call saying it would be best if we called it quits.'

He sighed, raking the fingers of one hand through his hair, his smile all but gone. 'Come on, Marianne, it wasn't like that.'

'Mari,' she interjected. 'It's Mari now.'

'Look, it was twenty years ago. We were just kids.'

'I was nineteen. You were twenty-two. Not quite kids.'
Not too young to make babies together.

'And my father had a heart attack. You knew I had no choice but to go back to Spain. You insisted I went.'

'Of course I did. And you told me to wait for you. That you'd be back. Only when you told me to expect you, you weren't on the plane.'

'How was I to know that my father would have another heart attack? How could I get on a plane and leave my mother then? I'm sorry I was too busy to let you know. I've always been sorry I was too occupied at the time to let you know.'

She nodded. 'So, you didn't come back. Instead, you call me months later and tell me that you have no idea when you might be able to get back so we should call it quits. That it's probably for the best.'

God, she hated the way she sounded, but this conversation had been waiting to be unleashed ever since she'd walked into his suite. If he hadn't recognised her, if he'd let her go then, let her walk out like she'd wanted, this conversation need never have happened. But proximity had brought it to the surface, like a boil waiting to burst and spill its putrid contents, or a volcano about to erupt and unleash its core of molten lava. And then he'd had to go and say he'd imagined her with a clutch of children living somewhere close to nature and it had pulled the pin on her grenade.

'Did you really think this conversation would never happen? That we could make this deal and that you could brush what happened all those years ago under the carpet and pretend it had never happened? Surely the great Dominico Estefan is not that much of a fool?'

All pretence of smiling was abandoned. His spine stiffened, his eyes flared, sparks on metal. 'So much for a celebration of our engagement.'

'Was that what tonight was meant to be? It seemed more like performance art to me, you playing to a crowd.'

He glowered. 'Are you going to be like this the entire time we're together?'

'Don't blame me. You're the one who wanted to marry a woman who hated you.'

'I'm paying you,' he said. 'Ten million dollars—'

'To marry you and pretend to your mother it's a love match. The hatred comes free of charge.'

He stared at his untouched glass. 'I don't see any point extending this dinner date.'

'At last,' she said. 'Something we agree on.'

He tossed his napkin on the table and beckoned a waiter. 'My fiancée is feeling indisposed. We'll take dinner in the suite.'

'Of course,' he said with a bow. 'Did you wish to order now, and we'll have it sent up?'

'Yes. My fiancée will have the lobster medallions and the Wagyu beef.'

'And for yourself, sir?'

'Nothing for me. I'm not hungry. Not anymore.'

'Was that completely necessary?' Mari demanded as the lift whisked them up to the twenty-third floor, each of them standing in opposite corners.

'Was what completely necessary?'

'That ridiculous order.'

He shrugged and loosened his tie. 'You said you couldn't decide. I made an executive decision.'

Mari scoffed and crossed her arms. She should make an executive decision right now. She should tell Dom exactly where to shove his deal. No faux marriage. No pretending to love him so he could keep sweet with his mother. He wouldn't be out of pocket much. He could probably ignore Audra's invoice and return all items—mostly—unworn and with labels attached. Most of all, he wouldn't have to put up with her any longer.

A win-win solution.

It was tempting. Sorely tempting.

Except...

He'd already advanced her one million dollars. She'd already spent quite a chunk of it and there was no way she could repay it.

She swallowed as the lift doors slid open.

She was trapped.

* * *

He closed himself in his sprawling room within the suite—more a suite within a suite—and left Marianne to her own devices. There was a deal firming up in Brazil and he could work in the private study without distraction.

And Marianne was distracting. She'd emerged from her room in that cocktail dress with her hair sleek and burnished bright and he'd been blindsided. The Marianne of twenty years ago had been spirited and free, her hair wild, her outfits composed of colourful cottons. She'd been a teenager, even if vivacious and beguiling and the most exciting creature he'd ever met.

Whereas the Marianne of today was a woman, fully formed, and looking every bit like the kind of woman he liked to be seen with. It had been a pleasure to take her on his arm and escort her to their table amidst the looks of envy from other diners, both men and women.

And then he'd kissed her, and the years had fallen away. He'd been in danger of losing himself in the kiss. It was only knowing that she was more affected than he was that he'd been able to take control and enjoy her vulnerability.

And it made him feel more powerful. Because for all her protests of hating him, she wasn't unaffected by his kiss.

And that gave him a degree of satisfaction that, despite tonight's disagreements, he could make this work, that ultimately he would bend Marianne's resistance to his purpose.

His phone buzzed and he took the call. Things were moving fast, the messenger relayed. Negotiations were moving along, and the paperwork could be ready for Dom's attention within the next twelve to twenty-four hours. He could look it over on the plane.

Perfect.

Just like the way Marianne had looked tonight. A shame

she'd had to ruin it with her obfuscating. Sure, Marianne's memory was right as far as it went. Dom's father had suffered a heart attack and Dom had headed home on the first flight he could get, promising Marianne to return as soon as his father's condition had stabilised. And just when it looked like his condition had stabilised and Dom was about to board a flight back to Sydney, his father had suffered a second massive heart attack, this time requiring surgery, and Dom had meant to let Marianne know he hadn't made the flight, but things had developed so quickly that he'd waited too long.

Game over. And Dominico had been hit with the responsibility of being the sole heir, while caring for his mother, suddenly a grieving widow, and there was no way he could have got back, not immediately. And there was no way he could have abandoned either role, not in the short-term. It hadn't seemed fair to keep Marianne endlessly hanging on, so he'd called her, just like she'd said.

Marianne had those things right.

But there was one thing that Marianne didn't know. A year after that phone call, the one where he'd told her that he didn't know how long it would be until he could get back, that it was unfair to expect her to wait for him and to go on with her university degree—one scant year later, when the dust had finally settled after finding himself the owner and CEO of a major business—he'd found himself wondering about Marianne. How was she doing? Was she still at uni?

He'd never felt good about the way they'd parted, even though there'd been no choice about any of it. He'd still felt rotten about it. Part of him had still felt as if he'd lost a limb.

So he'd tried calling, but the phone rang out. Her absence

had played on his mind. Sure, he'd told her to get on with her life. But where was she, if she wasn't at her uni digs?

A gap in his timetable had given him the window of opportunity he needed. He'd turned up at her old university accommodation and knocked on the door. A singlet-topped student had opened the door. 'Yeah?'

'I'm looking for Marianne Wheeler. She used to live here. Do you know where I might find her?'

He'd looked his caller up and down before he pulled a face. 'Never heard of her, mate. Sorry.' And slammed the door.

Dom had stood there a moment. How was he going to find her now? This was the only address he had. He put his hand against the wall and breathed deeply, thinking he'd made a terrible mistake. He'd told her to move on with her life, when what he'd really been hoping for was that she would be here, waiting for him. It would have been unfair for him to expect that of her, but it was what he'd wanted more than anything.

God, what a mess.

The screen door of the next door flat had swung open, a pram with a crying baby emerging, followed by a man Dom recognised. He'd been part of the crowd of student friends that Marianne mixed with.

'Hey,' he said. 'I'm looking for Marianne. Do you know where I might find her?'

The man didn't look up. He was too busy paying attention to the fussing baby. 'Shh...shh,' he said, trying to wrangle a dummy back between the child's lips. 'Let's give your mummy a break.'

'Marianne—she used to live here. Do you know where I might find her?'

'Not sure where she is now,' the man said, giving up on

the dummy and rocking the pram by the handle instead. 'But I know where she was last weekend.'

'Where?'

'At her wedding, out of Kempsey. It was a really good bash.' The guy looked up and recognition popped in his eyes. Recognition along with a frown and a measure of hesitation. 'Hey, weren't you and Marianne a thing back then? That is you, isn't it? Everyone thought you'd be the first of us lot to get hitched. What happened?'

'Life happened,' Dom had said before turning away. Marianne hadn't taken any time to replace him. There was no point him hanging around any longer.

Because life happened, and sometimes life sucked. He remembered how he'd felt then as if it was yesterday. As if he'd lost a part of himself, a part he was hoping he'd only just put in abeyance until he was ready to come back.

Sure, he'd offered Marianne her freedom.

But he hadn't expected her to take it.

He hadn't expected to lose her in the process.

Especially not so quickly.

Dom's phone buzzed again, jolting him out of his thoughts.

There was a problem, his Brazilian project manager messaged, could Dominico, with his experience, offer any insights?

Hell, yes, Dom thought. Because it was so much easier to untangle business problems than it was to unsnarl the tangles that were Marianne.

Mari managed just a fraction of her lobster medallions and Wagyu beef before giving up on the idea of dinner. She declined the butler's offer of dessert and decided to take coffee in her room.

Her room.

That was a laugh. A room in the Presidential Suite in Melbourne's prestigious Langham Hotel overlooking the Yarra River and the lit-up buildings of the city of Melbourne, and she was referring to it as her room.

She was becoming quite the diva.

She found a message from Suzanne as she was turning in and so she called her.

'I saw an article online about Cooper Industries being sold to a Spanish businessman.'

'Oh?'

'By the name of Dominico Estefan. And I got to thinking, isn't that the same guy who did the dirty on you way back when?'

'Suzanne, listen—'

'But that's not all the article says. There was an update on the story—the weirdest bit is where it says that you're engaged to be married. To Dominico Estefan of all people. What's gives, Mari? What the hell is going on?'

Oh, hell, Mari hadn't counted on the news getting out yet. She'd really hoped it hadn't got out at all.

'I know it makes no sense. I'm just doing him a favour. It's part of that job I told you about.'

'Getting married is part of the job? What kind of weird job is that? I told you it sounded dodgy.'

Well, yeah, there was that. But a pay packet of ten million dollars made a whole lot more sense of it.

'It's a short-term deal, Suze. I'll be home before you know it.'

'You're crazy. I remember what a mess you went through when he left you high and dry before. And then there was the mess you went through with that awful marriage to

Simon. I don't want anything like that to happen to you again.'

Mari swallowed back on a sisterly bubble of affection. Because here was Mari doing this for Suzanne, and yet here was Suzanne looking out for her.

'I love you,' she said. 'You're the best. But it won't happen again. This time it's different. This time he's paying me a lot of money to pretend to be his wife.'

'And you trust him? You seriously trust the man after the way he left you before?'

'I know it makes no sense,' she said, 'but right now I don't have any choice.'

Silence met her words. And then, 'You're doing this for me, aren't you?'

Mari didn't have to think before responding. 'I'm doing this for the both of us.'

It was only after she'd ended the call that Mari thought about her words and wondered where they had come from. This deal was all about ensuring security in Suzanne's ongoing care arrangements. That was why she'd agreed.

Except there was more to it than that. There was another reason Mari was here, doing what she was doing.

Because twenty years ago Mari had been at rock bottom. She'd lost the man she'd thought was the love of her life. She'd lost two tiny babies, and she'd lost herself in the process.

And maybe, just maybe, peeling back the layers of the past might offer a way to find herself again, and to finally lay the ghosts of her past to rest.

CHAPTER EIGHT

MARI HAD NEVER before been delivered by limousine direct to a waiting aircraft. Not that it was like any aircraft she'd ever flown on. It was sleek and white with a blue underbelly and tail and at least half the length of an Olympic pool. It was like a smaller version of a passenger jet, just more beautiful.

'Did you charter this?' she asked, as the car slowed.

'No,' he said, pocketing his phone after a call. 'It's mine. Or at least it belongs to the business.'

Right. And given Dom owned the business, that meant it was his. She should have realised he would have his own private jet. Didn't the man do business all over the world? No wonder he'd made flying first to Las Vegas to get married and then on to his home in San Sebastián sound so straightforward. Mari chewed her lip. Dom's world was so very different to hers. How had she ever imagined she would fit into his? She'd been so naïve back then. She'd thought love would conquer all.

But maybe they'd been doomed from the very beginning. Maybe it never would have ended well.

She shook her head. It was pointless even thinking about it.

The chauffeur opened her door, a black umbrella held aloft to protect her from a passing shower of rain as he walked her to the foot of the stairs, where a smiling cabin attendant was waiting with another umbrella to welcome her and see her up the steps. So, this was how the other half lived? Impressive.

But not half as impressive as the interior of the cabin where all similarity to an everyday passenger jet ended. There were no rows of seats. Instead, there was a scattering of large armchairs upholstered in white leather with tan headrests and trim either side of the wide aisle, and serviced by glossy parquet timber tables jutting out from the walls. Further back she could see long leather sofas lining the walls of the plane, and all of it set on a latte-coloured carpeted floor.

'You have a lounge room on board?' she asked Dom, who'd entered the cabin behind her.

'Of course,' he said, brushing raindrops from his shoulders, as if everyone had a private jet that could double as a palace. 'There's a dining room, bedroom and shower room on board too.'

'So where do I sit?'

'Up front for take-off and then anywhere you like. Feel free to explore once the seat belt sign goes off. I have work to do. The flight time is around seventeen hours although we'll have to stop to refuel along the way.'

She was glad he had work to keep him occupied. He'd been on the phone endlessly this morning, seemingly engaged in more negotiations, words like 'contract' and 'conditions' and 'terms of agreement' being bandied about, swirling around the suite. He'd barely communicated with her other than to acknowledge her existence with a nod while she'd taken breakfast at the dining table. He hadn't smiled. After last night's disastrous dinner date, she hadn't expected him to.

But at least if he was busy she'd be spared another prying twenty questions session.

The wide leather seat proved as comfortable as it looked, the leather buttery soft.

Outside the rain splattered hard against her window, while inside, the cabin attendant offered them a pre-take-off drink. Dom waved away the champagne, selecting sparkling water. Mari elected for the champagne—she didn't have to work and she was going to enjoy every little luxury going so she could recount each and every one of them to Suzanne when she returned home—and sipped it while watching the rivulets of rain run down her window. She certainly wouldn't miss Melbourne's changeable weather. It would be a pleasure to be somewhere warmer for a change.

The plane took off and Mari watched as the city shrank below, before the view was swallowed up by the clouds. Across the aisle Dom was already intent on whatever he was working on. Mari had seventeen hours to fill. Time for a movie or two before she could do some research of her own. A few hours later, she pulled out her laptop and opened a real estate site and started searching. She knew what she was looking for, a home with wide doors and passageways, enough bedrooms for Suzanne and any live-in carer, a big shower room and a kitchen with low benches and cabinetry—although she might have to get that custom-built. And no steps throughout—step-free was a must.

If she could get all that not far from her present location, just a few minutes away from Mari, that would be perfect.

'Shopping for a new house?'

Mari jumped. She'd been so focused she hadn't noticed Dom's approach. She closed her laptop. 'Just browsing.'

'You probably don't feel like sleeping but you might want

to take a nap. We arrive in Las Vegas in five hours—it'll be eight a.m. there, and we'll hit the ground running. We'll need to be back on the plane by two p.m.'

'What about you?'

'Are you offering to share?'

'No!' she said, feeling her cheeks flare.

He smirked. 'I'll be fine,' he said, and headed back to his seat.

Dom went back to his seat thinking about what he'd seen on her screen. She'd been looking at real estate—and not bargain-basement real estate either. She sure wasn't wasting any time working out how to spend her millions. She didn't even have the money yet and she was looking to spend it. She'd be able to set herself up nicely with a sum like that.

Then again, it would be her money, she could spend it how she liked. Why should he care how she spent it? He opened his laptop and just as quickly closed it again.

Sure, she could spend it how she liked, but the money thing grated. Marianne had never seemed bothered about money. He remembered her wanting the simple things in life—that was one of the things that had attracted him to her. She was so unlike the society women he knew back in Spain—so unspoilt and carefree.

But that was twenty years ago and the girl he'd known then had clearly changed. The girl he'd known then had seemed as far away from accountant material as you could get.

It was a shame. That Marianne had been fun.

The bedroom boasted a queen-sized bed with its own toilet and separate shower room. Seriously, a shower room in a plane? Luxury. She wasn't really tired but the bed did look inviting.

She hadn't thought to pack nightwear in her carry-on, so she stripped down to her silk camisole and underwear, slipped between the covers and dimmed the lights. The sheets were whisper-soft, the duvet like a cloud, what little sound the engines made more a white noise that settled any concerns about what she was doing.

Bliss.

The chief steward advised Dom the plane would be landing in forty-five minutes—did Señor Estefan wish him to advise the *señora*?

'No,' Dom said. He could do with a stroll; he'd been sitting for hours. 'I'll do it myself.'

He rapped softly on the bedroom door. There was no answer. He knocked again, harder this time. Still no answer.

He snicked open the door. 'Marianne?'

The room was dimly lit, the shutters down, and Marianne was asleep in the bed. Her arms were flung out wide, her head turned towards him, her lips parted as she slept, her hair spilling across the pillow.

She'd tossed back the duvet at some stage, exposing her chest. She was wearing some kind of silk slip in a soft green and that gently rose and fell with her chest.

His loins stirred. Dom had to force himself to remember why he was here. They were landing soon. He'd come to wake her up.

He should wake her up.

But he was transfixed by the beauty in the bed. She looked younger as she slept. She looked like the Marianne he remembered waking up to.

His Marianne.

And it hurled him back two decades—to when he'd wake up and watch her sleep beside him. Of waking her with a kiss, of feeling her smile under his lips and wrapping her arms around him and pulling him to her.

He remembered—and he ached.

She stirred in her sleep, murmuring something indecipherable. She was dreaming.

'Marianne,' he said softly. 'Wake up, we're landing soon.'

Still, she slept on.

There was nothing else for it. He sat down on the side of the bed, reached out a hand and tapped her gently on the shoulder. 'Marianne.'

She smiled and stretched out her arms and muttered something that sounded suspiciously like, 'Dom…' Then her eyes snapped open and she saw him and sat bolt upright in the bed, pulling the duvet up to cover her chest.

'What is it?' she said, brushing hair out of her eyes.

'We're landing soon. You've probably got ten minutes if you want to take a shower before we need to buckle up again.'

'Oh, thank you. I was dreaming.'

I know, he thought. 'I'll leave you to it,' he said in a gravelly voice, and closed the door behind him. Once upon a time he would have stayed and watched her rise from the bed, slim-waisted and long-legged. Once upon a time he would have showered with her, lathering her sweet curves. Once upon a time he wouldn't have stopped there.

But those days were in the past.

She wasn't his Marianne anymore.

CHAPTER NINE

'LOOK,' MARI SAID as they made their way along the Las Vegas strip, pointing out yet another wedding chapel in a city that boasted dozens, this one a squat white building with a sign out front, 'there's another one. "Heavenly Wedding Chapel. Where happy new beginnings are guaranteed."'

She regarded it critically. 'I see they're not so confident about the happy-ever-afters.' Her head swung around. 'Maybe you should have booked that one.'

Dom bristled. Clearly, she'd slept a lot better than he had. And okay, so this wedding might be fake, but he really didn't need Marianne joking about it. Right now, he was wound tighter than a coiled spring. He was so close to achieving what he'd set out to do, but he was wondering if he'd made a huge mistake. Why had he ever imagined this plan would work? It had seemed so simple at the outset. Find someone to marry, preferably someone who would be all too happy to get divorced in short order. Someone who had no expectation or desire to stay married.

Enter Mari. The perfect candidate, he'd thought, with her grievance dial turned up to ten and her professed hatred of him off the scale. And she'd agreed to marry him, even if he was paying mightily for the privilege.

But something supposedly so simple was turning out to

be a whole lot more complicated. Being anywhere near her was like wrestling with sandpaper. She was aggravating, uncompromising and prickly as hell. And all because of what? Because of something he'd done—or rather not done—half a lifetime ago. Because their relationship had fizzled out, the geographical separation and the business and family responsibilities he'd assumed on the death of his father making the continuation of their relationship an impossibility. There was no way he could have left his grieving mother.

He'd explained all that to Mari at the time. And no, it hadn't been easy, it had just about torn him in two, but it would have been unfair to keep her hanging on for his return when he didn't know when that might be possible. She was better off finishing her university degree and getting on with her life.

It was the only sensible thing to be done. It was the grown-up thing to do.

He'd thought she'd understood. She'd voiced no protest or argued that she'd wait for him, however long it might be. There were no tearful pleas for him to reconsider. Instead, she'd quietly agreed that it was probably for the best. And it was, but it had hurt like hell that she'd so readily agreed.

So quiet, so self-contained that he'd half wondered after he'd hung up whether she'd already found somebody else.

Something that he'd subsequently learned to be true.

And yet she was mad at him? The woman he'd once thought such a free spirit sure could hold a grudge.

It was infuriating.

She was infuriating.

The limousine from the Bellagio Hotel that had picked them up from the plane delivered them to the Clark County Marriage License Bureau to obtain their Nevada marriage licence.

The wedding industry in Las Vegas was nothing if not slick. In a little over two hours they'd be man and wife.

Could Marianne convincingly play the part of loving newlywed—enough to convince his mother that they were in love and truly married? Would this work? It had to work. He knew that they could make it work. He knew that they could look convincing. Because he remembered the sex they'd once shared. Marianne had been explosive in bed. He'd loved watching her face when she climaxed. He'd loved the feel of her body against his. They'd been good together.

They could be good together now if she bothered to make an effort. He knew that. He'd proved it when he'd kissed her in the restaurant. She'd all but melted in his arms and she'd felt and tasted so good. Just like she had back then. Just like he remembered, and he was more than curious to find out if grown-up Marianne was anything like the responsive lover the teenage Marianne had been.

No sex, she'd stipulated.

Ridiculous. They were adults and it was just sex, and she'd be far more relaxed around him if they got the bedroom business out of the way. She'd be far more convincing playing her part.

A marriage in name only.

That was what Marianne had insisted upon, even though it made their job of looking connected—in love—harder. What if his plan didn't work? What if his mother saw through the plan and discovered it was all a lie? She'd be gutted. Betrayed by her only son in her final days and weeks. And Dom would never be able to hold his head up again.

The chauffeur was waiting to open Dom's door, but Dom held up one long-fingered hand in a stop gesture. He wore his tension like a pressing weight, like he was being crushed by it. And for the first time Mari felt sympathy for him, trying to fulfil his mother's impossible dying wish the only way he could and getting stuck with Mari into the deal. And she regretted her joking and making light of something so important to him. She felt for him, and felt the weight of the pressure upon him.

'Are you sure you want to go through with this?'

The clench of his jaw and the tic in his cheek told her he wasn't, then he put down his hand and let the chauffeur open his door. 'I have no choice,' he said.

The dry desert heat rushed in to fill the vacuum he'd left behind, air that was now infused with the scent of the man who'd surged through it. Dominico with a triple serving of heat.

The scent transported her back in time to when they were both students. The day had been blisteringly hot, the sun a molten ball in the sky, and like most of Sydney, or so it seemed, they'd made their way to the crowded Bondi Beach to cool off in the surf. Dom and Mari had emerged from the waves exhausted and collapsed onto their towels, panting as they lay on their backs, arms over their eyes to block out the sun, when he'd rolled over and kissed her, filling her mouth with the taste of summer. Hot, salty and delicious.

'What was that for?' she asked when he lifted his head, curling her arms around his neck to keep him close.

'Just to remind you that I love you, Marianne,' he said, raining kisses down on her nose and cheeks and lips. 'For ever and a day.'

'I accept,' Marianne said, grinning up at him, blissfully happy but for the one cloud on the horizon that loomed ever closer. 'I just wish you didn't have to go home so soon. What are we going to do when you return to Spain?'

'I've been thinking about that,' he said, sweeping a salty tendril of her hair from her forehead. 'I'm going to ask my parents if I can stay for one more semester—make it a full gap year.'

Hope flared in her chest. 'Do you think they'll agree?'

'Papá wants me back to learn the business, but he's the one who wanted me to experience the Australian lifestyle. Besides,' he said, kissing her again, 'he knows how important you are to me. And six more months together means six less months until you finish your degree and can join me in Spain. I'll call him tonight.'

And that one cloud on the horizon burned off in the blaze of a summer sun and a future filled with promise. A future filled with love.

Dom lay down next to her, placed his arm under her head and nestled her close to his body.

She breathed his scent in, long and hard. Before Dom she'd never associated the aroma of a man's body with anything positive. But Dom's particular scent wasn't just alluring, it was addictive. A heady combination of salt and sweat and a body grown up on the best Spanish olive oil. 'Nobody in the world ever smelled as good as you,' she told him, drinking in the musky tang of his skin.

He chuckled. 'You're crazy,' he said, pressing his lips to her hair.

'Yeah, crazy,' she agreed, nestling closer against him. 'Crazy in love. With you.'

So crazy in love she'd been. Now she was just crazy. This whole plan of Dom's was crazy. But he was doing it for all the right reasons. He was doing it for his mother. Even if it was insane, he was acting out of love.

Maybe she could try to be a bit more cooperative. After

all, it wasn't like there was nothing in it for her. Whenever Rosaria succumbed to her disease and there was no need for this marriage, Mari would walk away with her millions of dollars and never have to see Dom again. It wasn't for ever. Maybe if she thought more about making Rosaria's final wish come true it would ease the torture of being with him now.

Dom rounded the car and opened her door, reaching out a hand to her. She took it and felt his fingers wrap around hers, felt the jolt of recognition like a muscle memory as she alighted from the car. His jaw was still clenched, his eyes hard. He was hating this, hating the whole charade, hating that his perfect plan had a downside and that marrying someone who hated him was never going to make for a comfortable ride.

'It'll be all right,' she said. 'It'll work out, you'll see.'

He frowned at her, as if trying to work out who this new Marianne was—a Marianne who didn't snarl and backbite and add bricks to the wall the past had built between them.

Then he turned. 'Come on. We have a marriage licence to procure.'

It was a fifteen-minute drive from the marriage licence bureau to the Bellagio Hotel where Dom had told her he had booked a suite for them to freshen up and dress. Their wedding would be held in the intimate East Chapel.

A suite for less than four hours in one of the fanciest resorts in Las Vegas.

A marriage in one of their posh chapels.

Dom was not sparing any expense.

Did Dom not know that he could have booked a drive-through wedding and saved all the fuss, along with a fistful of dollars? Not that she was going to mention it. She was done with making light of it. He'd been thoroughly unimpressed with her comment about the Heavenly Wedding Chapel.

And then she saw the curved white walls of the Bellagio Hotel, a central tower flanked by two wings. It rose from the desert like a standing butterfly holding its wings aloft.

And Mari knew why Dom had chosen this venue. Because sure, this might be a Las Vegas wedding, but it was no cheap wedding chapel affair. Dom wasn't splashing a fistful of dollars for nothing, but because nothing but the best would be enough to satisfy any doubters that their hasty Las Vegas wedding was anything but genuine.

The two-bedroom penthouse suite Dom had booked was opulent and sumptuous and looked out over the Bellagio's famous fountains, not that there was any time to enjoy the view. The wedding planners at Bellagio had thought of everything. They'd organised a hairdresser who coiled Mari's hair into a sleek updo before the make-up artist took over. Finally, a dresser arrived to help Mari into her ivory gown, a minimalist sleeveless design with freshwater pearl beading to the shoulders and draping across the open back. A small train pooled at her feet.

Her team declared her done, cooing their approval as they packed up their gear. There came a knock on the door.

'Marianne,' Dom said, 'are you ready? It's time.'

Mari blew out a breath and took one last look in the mirror. She almost didn't recognise herself. The make-up artist had done something clever with her eyes, making them appear larger, the eye shadow shade accentuating the green of her eyes. Her hair was styled in a romantic updo, tendrils framing her face, the clever chestnut highlights added in Melbourne gleaming under the lights. She stood while her dresser went to the door. 'She's ready,' the woman said. 'Come take a look.'

She opened the door wide so Dom could see inside the room, to where Mari was standing, waiting for his reaction. Hoping for his approval. After all, he was spending a lot of money and she wanted him to be satisfied. She wanted to think she looked the part, not for her own sake but because of Rosaria, she told herself.

Dom didn't speak. He just stared, looking her up and down and up again.

'Breathtaking,' he announced. Her team squealed with delight while Mari's every cell shimmered. Because Dom was his own kind of breathtaking, in a snowy white shirt, dark suit and a charcoal-coloured tie at his throat. And that was just what he was wearing. His gaze hadn't left her, dark eyes filled with wonder. Wonder, and something far more elemental.

'But I think there is something missing.'

'What?'

He crossed the carpet between them and pulled a box from his pocket.

'Surely we'll do wedding rings at the service.'

'Not a wedding ring,' he said. 'A gift for you. I found them downstairs.'

Them?

'No,' she said, afraid of what was inside. 'You've already spent too much on this wedding.'

'It's a thank-you gift, nothing more.'

He held open the box and Mari's eyes opened wide. A pair of exquisite Edwardian chandelier earrings met her gaze. She looked up at him. 'Please tell me they're not—'

'Diamonds? What kind of wedding gift would it be if they were not diamonds?'

'But it's too much.'

'It's exactly the right amount of much.'

She shook her head. What he'd just said did not make sense. None of it made sense.

'Try them on,' he said.

'All right.' She removed her favourite shepherd hook pearl earrings she'd been wearing, thinking they would do perfectly, and replaced them with the diamond chandelier earrings before turning to the mirror.

Oh, my. The earrings with their stunning Edwardian design perfectly complemented her minimalist gown, the faces of the rose cut diamonds glittering in the light. 'They're beautiful.'

'As are you,' he said, his voice sounding deeper. He coughed, as if clearing the army of frogs that had taken residence in his throat. He held out his arm and passed her the ribbon-wrapped bunch of roses that was her bouquet. 'Are you ready?'

They created quite the stir as they made their way to the East Chapel. Guests parted and made way for them, the women beaming and clutching hands to their chests, everyone offering good wishes and congratulations. If only they knew, thought Mari.

'Look at the bride,' a young girl said as they passed. 'She's so pretty.'

'Uh-huh,' the mother said, and Mari smiled because the mother's eyes were firmly fixed on Dom.

The good wishes followed them all the way to the chapel where the formalities took just a moment before they were in the chapel proper. A smallish room, high-ceilinged with chandelier lighting, panelled walls and gold curtains half opened over tall arched windows to let in more light. The pews were decorated in antique gold, the carpet in rich burgundy and gold swirls adding a richness to the decor. Flowers decorated the ends of the pews, their one hired witness sitting waiting.

Mari felt a sudden flutter of nerves. Focusing on the details—the dressing, the hair and make-up—had taken her mind off what was happening. But this was it. Pretend or no, she was about to walk down that aisle and marry Dominico Estefan. Once upon a time she'd dreamed of this moment. She'd dreamed night after night that it would happen. Until her dreams had turned to nightmares and her world had collapsed.

And yet, twenty years later, here she was, in a wedding chapel halfway around the world marrying the man she'd once most wanted to, the same man she least wanted to now.

The man who'd been the father of her babies. The man waiting at the altar with the celebrant. The man who looked like he half wanted this marriage for real. The man who had gifted her diamond earrings as if he wasn't already paying her enough. Why the kindness? Why a gift that she didn't deserve? It was impossible to read him. She knew he just wanted this done and to be over. He wanted to get back to Spain and show his mother that her dying wish had been fulfilled. That she didn't have to worry about him any more. That was all he wanted.

But he was waiting right now to marry *her*.

The past collided with the present and it was too much.

Halfway down the aisle her steps faltered. A sound like a sob escaped her mouth, two fat tears escaped from her eyes and ran down her cheeks.

And the man waiting for her frowned and took a faltering step towards her. 'Are you all right?'

She sniffed and nodded, regaining her composure, and forced her feet to resume their journey.

'You're crying,' he said, his eyes searching her face.

'I'm okay,' she said.

But then he touched the pads of his thumbs to her cheeks to sweep the tears away. She closed her eyes as his thumbs glided across her skin. She couldn't look at him in case he saw what was in her mind, all because of a touch that reminded her of how he'd once treated her: like she was the most precious object in the world.

A touch so gentle that her breath hitched, and she almost came undone again.

Because it was wrong. It was cruel. It was so unfair of him to hurl her back to the *before*, when everything had been perfect between them, when she needed to focus on the *after*. She so desperately needed to remember the after.

She opened her eyes to see him looking down at her, his brow creased, as if he actually cared.

'Okay now?'

'I'm fine,' she said, even though she felt a long way from fine.

'In that case,' said the celebrant, 'perhaps we might proceed.'

There was talk of the meaning of marriage, the question of intent and then it was time for the vows and the rings to be exchanged, before the final pronouncement came. Dominico and Mari were married. It had taken longer than twenty years to happen and yet the ceremony had lasted less than fifteen minutes.

'You may kiss the bride,' the celebrant invited.

This was the part Mari was dreading. He'd kissed her until she was boneless at the restaurant. She couldn't afford for him to have that kind of power over her, and yet...

And yet part of her wanted to feel that magic of being swept away again. Nobody had made her feel that way after Dom and it had been so long. Why wouldn't her traitorous body respond? Dom's kiss was like a drug she knew she shouldn't take, and yet she couldn't stop herself.

She braced herself for the onslaught of his lips. But what met hers was softness, tender and sweet and infused with the scent of his skin and the taste of his breath. He didn't rush, he didn't pull away early, he lingered, his tongue gently sweeping the line of her lips as his fingers stroked her bare back. And if anything, it was more impactful than the kiss he'd given her in the restaurant, when he'd taken her unawares and ramraided through her defences.

This kiss was bittersweet and poignant.

This kiss was perfection.

And once again two tears rolled down her cheeks. She was married to Dominic Estefan, not in the way she'd once imagined and hoped, but legally married.

It wasn't the way she'd always imagined, it might be a faux marriage, but once this deception was over and she wasn't needed any more, and once she'd returned to Melbourne to resume her average unglamorous life, she'd remember these moments for ever. The tenderness of his kiss, the gifting of the diamond earrings. Both things Dom hadn't had to do—and yet he had.

It was only when she turned to walk back down the aisle on Dom's arm that she saw the photographer clicking away, capturing it all, and cynicism kicked in again. Okay, so the earrings were a nice thought, but the kiss was just as much performance art as the dinner kiss, fodder for the photographers. Even if it had been the best kiss she could remember.

God, she was a sucker.

Her cynicism hit pay dirt when they moved to the terrace with the famous Bellagio fountain as backdrop for the money shot, and still, in spite of her cynicism, Mari found it impossible not to buy into the fantasy. The setting was so fantastical, so magical, that it was impossible not to be carried away by the moment. Dom was in high spirits, so different to how he'd been after they'd landed. From relief or something else? Mari couldn't tell, but he looked as if the weight of the world had lifted from his shoulders.

The photographer clicked away, Dom and Mari together in front of the fountain, Dom's arms around her, Mari's arms around his neck, when Dom suddenly dipped her low to one side. She looked up at him in surprise at the sudden move—she knew she was safe; he wouldn't let her fall—but she hadn't been expecting it.

'Are you happy with your wedding, Señora Estefan?'

He was so unexpectedly light-hearted that Mari couldn't help but answer, 'I can honestly say it's the best wedding I've ever had.'

He chuckled, his eyes locking on hers, before he brought his smiling lips closer.

Mari's focus was torn between watching his eyes and his mouth. She wanted to drink him in, all of him. And damn it, if Dom was after a money shot, she wasn't about to object.

Not if it meant he would kiss her again.

She could act as much as he could.

CHAPTER TEN

TWO HOURS LATER they were back on the plane and winging their way towards San Sebastián. Mari's head was spinning, jet lag tugging at her senses. While Dom with his boundless energy continued to work, she snagged the bedroom for some more sleep. But this time she set an alarm on her phone. She wasn't about to be woken by Dom again.

Not that sleep came easily.

She was a married woman. *Again.* And she wasn't sure how she felt about that. Married but not married. A wife and yet not really a wife.

When she'd married Simon she'd felt—nothing. Not delight, not relief, just a feeling of numbness, that this was the life she deserved, that she would be the sandwich-cutting wife of a small country town clerk for life. Oh, her grandmother was beside herself, and Suzanne thrilled to be her bridesmaid, and those things had permeated the numbness she'd felt, massaging the misgivings she'd had.

She'd so firmly believed that all she'd needed after her disappointment and despair was the love of a good man and a sensible marriage. It might have been a sensible middle-class marriage, but the good man turned out not to be, and as for love? 'You'll grow to love him,' her grandmother had assured her whenever she'd expressed her doubts. 'Give it time, you'll grow together.'

But for all her grandmother's assurances, love had never come into it, not on Marianne's part. And instead of growing together, they'd grown apart.

Again, she'd been a wife, but not really a wife. Not a life partner, but a housekeeper, cook and nanny rolled into one.

Memories and feelings so different from the first time she and Dom had made love. That had been a revelation. Not only the smorgasbord of new sensations and new emotions but the knowledge she was no longer a virgin. She'd guarded her virginity through her high school years. She'd always promised herself that she would never squander it, that she would share that special moment with a man she truly loved. That man had been Dom, and the act itself momentous. She'd half expected choirs of angels and a host of trumpeters to herald the news on high.

And now she was married to that man.

It should have been a cause for joy. Once upon a time it would have been a cause for joy. Now it was just a cause for regret.

The plane landed around ten a.m. at Hondarribia airport, where they were whisked away by a waiting limousine direct to San Sebastián, some twenty-five kilometres away.

'We'll go by the villa first,' he explained, 'and give my mother the news. Then we'll head to my apartment to freshen up, if you need.'

If she needed? Sure, she'd slept on the plane, but nowhere near enough given her tangled thoughts, and right now she was all kinds of confused. They'd departed Melbourne at eight a.m. and arrived in Las Vegas at eight a.m. the very same day. If that hadn't been mental enough, after a whistlestop Las Vegas wedding, they'd been back on the plane by two p.m. Eleven hours later it was apparently mid-morning, and her body clock was complaining about too many time zones in too little time, the jet lag starting to drag.

'Sounds good,' she said, covering her mouth while she yawned.

'And Marianne?'

'Yes?'

'This is important to me. I want my mother to be happy for whatever time she has left. Don't ruin it for her.'

'Why would I ruin it?'

'I don't know. Because you profess to hate me and so you might be planning to make me look bad in the eyes of my mother.'

Mari snapped. 'You are kidding me!' After all she'd done, after all she'd agreed to, she could not believe what she was hearing. They'd spent the best part of two days confined to a flying tin can, admittedly a very luxurious flying tin can, they'd been married in Las Vegas and even kissed, without threatening to kill each other.

Why now, when they were landed and heading to see his mother, did he feel the need to doubt her, and let her know he didn't trust her to fulfil her end of the deal?

'Do you seriously believe that I would fly three-quarters of the way around the world to tell your mother that her son loves her so much he's spent ten million dollars plus to get married to the woman who least wanted to marry him, just to make him look bad? What kind of person do you think I am?'

His jaw clenched. A muscle popped in his cheek. 'It's important, Marianne. That's all.'

'I know it's important. It's important to me too. I'm here, aren't I? And I'm hardly going to give up the chance of collecting nine million dollars to spite you, am I? I know what I have to do. Can't you just trust me to do it?'

She turned her attention out of the window, preferring to drink in the views of the hilly Basque countryside than put up with any more of his judgements. The colours were vibrant here, green trees and bushes bright against the clear blue sky.

'You're right,' he said, his voice gruff, as if it was costing him to get the words out.

Her head swung around. 'What?'

'Of course you're right. I'm sorry.'

Dominico Estefan was apologising? To her? Wow. His mother's condition must be really getting to him.

She nodded an acknowledgment and turned to look out of the window again. It was hard not to feel empathy for the man. She had no quibble with that. But increasingly, there were times when she almost felt like she liked the man.

And that was way more problematic.

Where was the hatred when she needed it? Where was the resentment and the cold, hard fury? He was still the man who'd fathered her twins and then abandoned her to deal with their loss alone. He was still the man who'd taken over Eric Cooper's business and sacked half the staff. He'd proved both his ambition and his ruthlessness. And yet the man wasn't made of stone. That had been the man the young Marianne had fallen in love with, and these glimpses that he still owned a heart were undermining both her resentment and her resistance.

Truth was, the more time she spent in his company, the more the hard edges of her hatred were dulled. She felt as if she was facing the ghosts of the past and still not knowing how to deal with them.

And then he went and twisted the knife and reminded her of all the things she hated about him.

Good.

The car pulled into a driveway with tall ornate gates that swung open to a circular turnaround with a massive marble fountain at its heart. The house behind sat tall and proud, the walls the colour of clotted cream, with white shutters on the windows and white balustrades framing the balconies. The house was grand without being ostentatious, and as Dom led her through the maze of rooms to his mother's room Mari could see that the classic good looks of the outside followed through to the interior. High ceilings, exposed timber rafters, arched timber doorways and terrazzo tiles on the floor, the home was beautifully appointed.

'You grew up here?' she asked, as he led her up an ornately carved timber staircase.

'Yes.'

'But you don't live here now?'

'No, I have an apartment in town, overlooking La Concha beach.'

Of course he'd have an apartment, Mari realised, following him up the stairs. He'd hardly want to bring his woman friends to the family home. She wasn't envious of them, she told herself. Dom hadn't chosen to marry any of them. He'd chosen to marry Mari. Temporarily, sure, and under duress, certainly. But because he'd trusted her to leave when she needed to. Because she wouldn't hang around hoping for more.

Mari wouldn't hang around. The moment this deal was done, she was out of here.

Dom had been in touch with the doctor en route. The nurse was expecting them and, after a few words to Dom, ushered them in to visit her.

'Mamá,' he said, leaning down to kiss her cheek.

His mother opened her eyes, blinked in confusion, before breaking into a smile. 'Oh, you're home!' she said, taking his cheek in one hand. 'Oh, my son, I am so pleased to see you.'

'And me you,' he said. 'I'm sorry it took so long to come home. I had to make a diversion along the way.'

'Oh, but you're home now, my son, and all is right in my world.'

He took her hand and kissed the back of it. Gently, because the skin looked bruised and paper-thin. 'I am hoping that things might get better in your world. I have a surprise for you, Mamá. I have someone I want you to meet. She's waiting just outside if you're up to meeting her.'

'Who is it, Dominico?' she said, struggling to sit higher on the bed. Dom gently put his arm around her back and eased her higher, slipping another pillow behind her. 'I'm not in a fit state for visitors. How do I look?'

'You look beautiful, Mamá,' he said, blinking moisture from his eyes. She'd lost more weight since he'd seen her last. Her shoulders were no more than jutting bones and he could feel her ribs and the individual vertebrae of her spine through her nightdress. She was shrinking by the day. 'You always look beautiful.' Even with her sunken cheeks and the dark circles around her eyes, she would always look beautiful to him.

'Tell me, who have you brought?'

'My wife.'

His mother stared up at him in shock. 'You're married? How can that be? Who did you marry?'

He squeezed her hand. 'Do you remember Marianne, Mamá? You met her once in Sydney when I was studying there.'

'Marianne? Marianne?' His mother was shaking her head, looking for answers. 'Not that beautiful girl you utterly adored?'

'The very same. We met up again in Melbourne when I was there, and—'

'And you fell in love all over again.' She crossed her

hands over her chest. 'It's just like a fairy tale ending, Dominico. It couldn't be better.'

It was indeed a fairy tale, if not exactly the way his mother believed. But she was happy, and his heart swelled. This was what he'd wanted. If his mother was happy, if she believed in this marriage, then it was worth every euro it had cost him. It would even be worth the grief he'd borne from the intractable Marianne.

'Something like that.'

'Oh, well, what are you waiting for? Bring her in, bring her in. Are you sure I look all right?'

He smiled. Because his mother was smiling, the light shining brightly in her eyes. 'You look perfect,' he said, and went to open the door to collect Marianne.

Dom took her hand, his eyes seeking hers as he drew her into the room. She expected them to contain a warning to her again to play the part of happy newlywed, but rather what she saw was almost a plea, a plea that, if nothing else, she get this right. Mari sucked in a breath. This was the moment of truth.

The large room was both masculine and feminine, the chunky timber furniture balanced by soft curtains, all dominated by the big king-sized bed. It had an elaborately carved timber headboard and, above that, a wedding portrait of Rosaria with her Roberto, painted many years previously, their love for each other shining out from their eyes.

Dom drew her to the bedside. 'Mamá, here is Marianne, my wife.'

'Marianne!' his mother said from the bed, patting down the covers beside her. 'Come sit on the bed, dear, so that I can see you properly.'

Rosaria was barely a bump in the bed, little more than a ripple in the bedclothes. Her once long black hair was now silvered and plaited down over one shoulder, and her face looked gaunt, the skin pulled tight over her bones. But nothing could erase her strong features and the beauty she'd once been. The high cheekbones were still regal, her eyes still piercingly bright.

'Hello, Rosaria,' Mari said softly as she sat down on the edge of the bed. 'It's good to see you again.'

'I remember,' she said, finding and clutching on to Mari's hands. 'I remember you. I used to think you were such a pretty girl. Now I can see that you have grown up into a beautiful woman.'

Mari dipped her head. 'Thank you.'

'And now Dom tells me that you are married.'

'It's true,' she said. 'It happened more quickly than we would have preferred, but it's true.'

'Didn't I tell you,' Dom said, 'that there was someone special? That person is Marianne.'

Rosaria beamed. 'I'm so delighted for you, but however did you find each other again?'

'A chance meeting,' Dom said quickly.

'Serendipity,' said Mari. 'We were in the same place at the same time, our paths crossed, and well, here we are.'

'Serendipity,' Rosaria said approvingly. 'I like the sound of that. But I still don't understand how you could get married so quickly.'

'We didn't want to wait the weeks it would take before we could be married here,' Dom said. 'So we flew to Las Vegas and made it official.'

Rosaria's eyes stared blankly at the wall behind Mari. And then she nodded as if she'd realised why. 'That was thoughtful of you both,' she said. 'Except...' She turned her gaze on her son. 'A Las Vegas wedding? It won't do, you know. It won't do at all.'

Dom frowned. 'Why won't it do? I thought you wanted me married. I'm married.'

'It's *not* what I had in mind. You have cheated me out of a wedding. The wedding of my only son. Why would you do such a thing?'

'Mamá, I thought you would be pleased.'

'Yes, of course I am, and I'm happy for you both, but I would have hoped to be there to witness my only child get married.'

Dom muttered something under his breath as he raised his eyes to the ceiling. Mari smiled. How Mari loved Rosaria. She loved seeing this less than pint-sized woman cut the ground from under her billionaire son's feet in a way nobody else could.

'Perhaps we could have a blessing ceremony?' Mari suggested. 'Maybe a party. It would be lovely to celebrate our marriage with you and all the family and friends here in San Sebastián. It would be right.'

'That's a wonderful idea,' Rosaria said, sounding animated. 'We'll have another ceremony, won't we, Dominico? And we'll invite everyone.'

'Mamá,' Dom interjected, 'are you sure you're up to this?'

'What?' she said imperiously. 'You would deny your dying mother a party to celebrate her son's wedding?'

'Of course not,' he said, while sending a glare in Mari's direction.

Rosaria leaned back on her pillows. 'You've made me so happy,' she said. 'Both of you.' Tears welled up in her eyes. She sniffed as she batted them away. 'So happy.'

And Mari, who'd been so opposed to the whole faux wedding idea, realised just what it meant to Dom's mother and, in turn, what it meant to Dom. He knew he was going to lose his mother, but he loved her so deeply that he would go to impossible lengths to fulfil her final wish. His plan wasn't perfect. Their marriage was a sham. But seeing Rosaria smile, seeing how happy Dom had made her, what else could he have done?

The older woman closed her eyes and looked as if she was drifting off.

'We should leave you and let you rest,' he said.

'Yes,' she said, blinking. 'I'm tired. But later, please come visit me again, Marianne.'

'We'll both come,' said Dom.

'No. Not you, Dominico,' Rosaria said. 'I want to talk to Marianne. I want to get to know my new daughter-in-law.'

Dom looked helplessly from his mother to Mari and back again. 'But surely—'

'No,' Rosaria insisted. 'You have work to do. You have a wedding party to organise. Marianne, you'll be fine to come by yourself. I promise I don't bite.' She smiled then. 'Unless it's my Dom. My nurse will let you know when I'm awake again.' She gave a blissful smile as she nestled back into her pillows. 'And now I'm going to dream about weddings and parties and celebrations. Right now, I think I must be the happiest woman in the world.'

Dom let the nurse in and closed the door behind him with a sigh. 'You did well,' he said, his voice thick and gravelly. 'She's happy. She likes you. She always has.'

'I'm glad. She's remarkably strong-willed for someone so ill. She certainly knows what she wants.'

'Oh, yes,' Dom said, his eyebrows raised. 'And don't I know it. Come on, we'll go to the apartment. We can freshen up and have some lunch while Mamá rests.'

Mari was entranced by the vibrant city, Dom pointing out the local sights as their driver weaved his way through the busy streets. Everywhere she looked there seemed to be another attraction, and even where there wasn't, the streetscape was an attraction all by itself. There were no skyscrapers, the character buildings seemed to top out at four or five levels, with balconies adorning almost every window. Dom pointed out the old town, the city hall and the Buen Pastor Cathedral before the car turned onto a street that bordered probably the most beautiful beach that Mari had ever seen: a sandy bay with mountains either side and the jut of a treed island in between.

'The Isla de Santa Clara,' he explained, naming the other peaks as Monte Urgull on the right and Monte Igueldo on the left. 'You can take a funicular up to the top of Mount Urgull, and there's a ferry that will take you out to Santa Clara Island.'

Mari was overwhelmed by it all, by the beauty of the sparkling bay, the mountains protecting it either side and the island nestled in between. 'I thought Bondi Beach was something special,' she said.

'It is special,' Dom agreed. 'But this is better.'

No false modesty there, thought Mari, but he was right. How could anywhere on earth compete with this glorious setting?

The driver pulled into a garage in a stately building with a classic sandstone façade. A lift took them up to the top floor, where the views were even better. Of course Dom would have a penthouse apartment with unobstructed views overlooking the entire curve of the bay, taking in the mountains and the island. Another window boasted a view over a park towards the city hall.

Dom showed her around. The vast apartment had the high ceilings of the villa but it was clear that it had been updated at some stage, to retain the charm of the original while giving the interior a more contemporary vibe. It was clear Dom had stamped his style all over the apartment. There was marble aplenty and terracotta tile floors, but it was elegance without fripperies. It was streamlined, masculine and functional.

'And this,' he said, flinging open a set of double doors, 'is our suite.'

Mari stopped dead. Inside she could see a massive bed. From the doorway, that was all she could see. 'Our suite?'

He smiled. 'That's up to you.'

She took a step back. 'You are joking. I told you that sex isn't part of this deal.' She licked her lips 'Maybe I could stay at your mother's house.'

'That would hardly come across as very newlywed, would it?'

'Extraordinary times call for extraordinary measures. I'd just be seen as a caring daughter-in-law.'

'You'd be seen as a runaway wife and the staff—and my mother—would wonder what you're running away from.' He moved closer, reaching for her hands. 'I thought you might be softening by now. Don't you remember how good we were together, Marianne?'

Her hands held captive by his, she closed her eyes. Against the feel of his long-fingered hands, against his heat, against the scent that was peculiarly his. The scent that now wrapped beguiling tendrils around her senses. Because of course she remembered how good they'd been together. She remembered all too clearly their lovemaking long into the night and then into the next morning. She remembered the feel of him entering her. Filling her. Completing her.

'We're both grown up, Marianne. Why can't we enjoy each other while you're here?'

Mari wavered. It would be so easy. Sex with Dom was

so alluring. So tempting. That was if she only remembered the good times.

But then there were the bad times. The times of loneliness and despair when Dom, for all the talk of them being good together, hadn't given her a second thought. When she'd gone through heartache and pain nobody should ever experience alone.

'You make it sound like some kind of sport.'

'It is, if you put it like that.'

She pulled her hands from his. 'Then I'll find a hotel. Thanks all the same.'

He wheeled away towards another door. 'Come on, Marianne, surely you can't blame a man for trying?'

'Yes, I can.'

'All right. If that's what you want, I'll show you to *your* room.'

He opened another doorway. 'It's through here.'

Mari regarded the room suspiciously—it looked fine, grand even, with its own bathroom with shower and bath—except... She pointed to another door. 'Where does that go?'

'It's an adjoining door to my suite. But I won't come in unless you ask me to.'

She glared at him. 'Don't hold your breath.' She took a closer look. 'Is it lockable from my side?'

Dom sighed. 'You'll be safe. I promise you.' He turned. 'I'll leave you to freshen up. We'll take lunch on the terrace before we head back to the villa.'

He left her then to talk to his housekeeper about lunch, growing increasingly frustrated with Mari's obstinance. What was it with her insistence that they didn't have sex? It wasn't as if she was a virgin; he knew that for a fact. And he knew for a fact that she wasn't immune to his touch. He'd felt her resistance crumbling when he'd kissed her. He'd felt her body start to yield to his. There was no way she couldn't recognise it for what it was. Desire. Mutual desire. And he knew for a fact that she'd be more relaxed and convincing with him if she only gave into it. So why was she fighting it?

It was baffling.

Infuriating.

And the maddest thing was, it only made him want her more.

It was late afternoon when Dom received a call from his mother's nurse that she was ready to see Marianne again. Dom ignored his exclusion from the invitation. Marianne might have made a good impression on her at their earlier visit, but he wasn't about to trust her to talk to his mother on her own. Too much was at stake.

Once again, the car delivered them to his mother's villa, and it was a relief to get there.

Marianne had changed since their visit this morning into a white slim-fitting dress with giant ink spots, the style accentuating the curves of her body. She wore her hair loose, tumbling over her shoulders. She looked cool and sophisticated and a million miles away from the buttoned-up mouse with an axe to grind who had turned up in his suite a matter of days ago.

She looked amazing, and that was hard enough to deal with when space separated them. But every time they were in close proximity the tension between them seemed to grow. In a private jet separated by several metres was one thing. The back seat of a car was entirely different. It wasn't just his problem; it was clearly hers too. She had scooted as far away from him on the back seat as she could get. She was clearly affected by his presence. So why was she holding out on him?

* * *

The nurse invited Marianne into his mother's room.

'I'll come too,' said Dom.

But the nurse barred his way. Rosaria, she said, was insistent that she only wanted to talk to Marianne. And Dom had no choice but to cool his heels outside.

Marianne entered the room. This time she received Dom's glower as she passed him. This time there were no gentle pleas. This time his eyes held a threat—*Don't get this wrong.*

As if she would.

Rosaria was propped up in the bed on white lace-edged pillows, her hair newly washed and fluffed. She was still tiny, her eyes closed, but as Mari approached the bed those eyes opened clear and bright, brightening even more as she saw her visitor.

'Oh, Marianne,' she said, patting the bed beside her. 'Come and sit here next to me on the bed. It's high time I had some girl talk.

'I've been so worried about Dominico,' she continued. 'I thought he would never settle down. I am so glad he's found you again, Marianne. I am so happy for you both.'

Mari smiled, and gently patted the older lady on the hand. Tiny hands, skin like parchment blotched with bruises and stretched over bones and knuckles so tightly it looked like it would tear at the slightest touch.

And Mari knew that, however long it took, she would keep up this pretence of being Dom's bride, because it made Rosaria so happy.

'I was married to an Australian, you know. Well, an Australian of Spanish descent, but still an Australian.'

Mari nodded. 'I do. I met him that time we all had dinner together in Sydney.'

'Oh, of course you did. That was such a fun night. Ro-

berto liked you, you know. He told me that he half suspected Dominico might ask you to marry him. Which is
why he agreed for Dominico to stay another semester in
Sydney. He didn't want to set up a potential conflict with
his son. He wanted him to enjoy his youth while he could.'

She sighed. 'Of course, that was before he had his heart
attack.' She shook her head, her eyes misting over. 'That
changed everything.'

Mari reached over and took her hand, squeezing it gently.

'Oh, listen to me, getting all maudlin. Silly, when I'll
be back with Roberto soon, but it's Roberto I want to talk
about. He had Spanish heritage, you see, and he was travelling through Spain, due to return home in a week when
he came to San Sebastián and met me. And the rest, as
they say, is history. It was a whirlwind romance. We were
married in three months, and so, so happy. He was such
a handsome man.' She sighed. 'So tall, broad-shouldered
and handsome and so very sexy.'

Mari was startled. She had not been expecting that.

Rosaria chuckled. 'Did I shock you, my dear? It's not
unusual, surely, that we find our husbands sexy? In fact,
it makes marriage all the more pleasurable. Don't you find
your new husband sexy?'

Mari did so not want to go there. She didn't want to think
of Dominico and sex in the same conversation, let alone
the same sentence. She wanted to keep the subjects far, far
apart. But she couldn't say that to Rosaria. But neither could
she deny that what Rosaria said was true. Because there
was no denying the appeal of the man, the intensity of his
eyes, the strong lines of his nose and mouth and the hard-
packed strength of his body. Even when he was glowering
he was beautiful—devastatingly, masculinely beautiful.

The man was sexier than he'd ever been when she'd last
known him as a young twenty-two-year-old. His shoulders

had broadened, his body had filled out, his perfect features had been aged by experience that only accentuated them. That was the danger the man posed. Here she was trying to rid herself of the ghosts of her past and her ghost had just turned himself into a living and breathing reason why she should take notice of him all over again.

'Oh, my dear,' Rosaria said, 'I can see I've put you on the spot and asked a question a mother shouldn't ask. I don't expect you to answer that. I just hope that you have a happy marriage, as Roberto and I did. For so long I've been worried about Dominico. For so long he seemed to reject any chance of becoming emotionally involved with any woman. I'm so glad that he's finally decided to settle down. You will have a good marriage, I can see.'

Oh, please. Mari turned her gaze to the ceiling as guilt piled on guilt. She was pretending to be in love with this woman's son and Rosaria was lapping it up. She should be congratulating herself that she and Dom were pulling this pretence off.

Except it was all so false. All so fake.

Except if Rosaria was happy, did it matter? Making Rosaria happy was the whole point of this farce.

'Dominico is so important to me, I want him to be as happy as his father and I were. He was my only live birth, you see.'

'Oh?' Mari said, discombobulated by this sudden change in the conversation's direction. The topic of losing babies was dangerous territory. She swallowed. 'That's entirely understandable.

'You see, I lost three babies before I delivered our Dominico. He was our miracle baby. Our gift from God.'

Mari was blindsided, Rosaria's tragedies bringing back the horror and despair of her own loss.

'Three? I'm so sorry. I didn't know. Dom never told me why he was the only child.'

'It was so hard to bear,' Rosaria said. 'It was harder every time to go back and try again when I knew I had miscarried, but of course I wanted to try. I had to try. I was desperate to give my Roberto children. After Dominico was born, Roberto refused to let me try again. He said we had our miracle baby and we should be satisfied, but of course I knew it was because he couldn't bear to see me suffer the anguish of losing another child.' The bony shoulders under her fine cotton nightdress rose a fraction in a shrug. 'Who knows if I would have miscarried again, but Roberto loved me too much to let it happen again.' She sighed. 'He was such a wonderful man.

'I would so love Dominico to experience the wonder of having a child. And selfishly, of course, I would have loved to have met my grandchildren. Alas, the latter can't happen now.'

Mari couldn't bear it any longer. She broke down on a sob, one hand over her belly, the other over her face.

'Oh, my dear, I've made you cry. I'm so sorry. I shouldn't be bothering you with all this rubbish. It's ancient history now.'

'It's okay,' Mari said. 'You see, I had a miscarriage too,' she admitted, her voice breaking. 'I miscarried at five months. I lost twins, a tiny boy and a tiny girl.'

'Oh, Marianne,' Rosaria said, patting Mari's hand. 'That's dreadful. I can't imagine losing two at once. I can't imagine anything worse.'

But it wasn't the worst, Mari knew. The worst was that she hadn't just lost her twins, she hadn't just lost Dominico's babies, but she'd lost Rosaria's grandchildren too. The grandchildren she'd so wanted. The grandchildren Rosaria would never meet.

They would be twenty years old now. Adults who would have had twenty years to delight their grandmother growing up.

And it was so wrong. It was all kinds of wrong.

And along with her despair came the familiar guilt. What if she'd done things differently? What if she'd taken more care of herself, eaten better, worried less? What if there was just one tiny thing that would have resulted in a different outcome? The medical staff had been wonderfully supportive of course, assuring her that she'd done nothing to cause the loss of her babies, but then, Mari had been inconsolable. And after all, the staff were hardly going to tell her she'd done something wrong.

Rosaria took Mari's hand in hers and squeezed, a surprisingly strong grip for one so frail. 'Did you ever try again?'

She shook her head. Losing her twins had been devastating. She never wanted to leave herself open to that kind of anguish again. But that was hardly what Rosaria wanted to hear.

'I...' she started, before finding a better way to answer. 'My then husband and I divorced. It didn't happen again.'

'So, it's not too late for you now, is it? It's not too late to give Dominico children.'

'Oh,' Mari said, blinking. This was not a question she'd expected. Of course, Rosaria would expect that Dominico and Mari had talked about the issue of children. 'I'm thirty-nine. I don't know.'

Rosaria nodded. 'There's time then. Can I ask you a favour?'

'Anything.'

'If you have a son, would you name him Roberto in honour of his grandfather?'

Mari sobbed quietly as she took Rosaria's hand in hers.

'Of course.' A bittersweet promise. An empty promise. And the easiest promise she'd ever have to make because Mari knew it would never happen.

'Thank you, my dear,' Rosaria said. 'I'm so glad Dominico found you again. He went looking for you, you know.'

Mari sniffed. 'Who?'

'Dominico. I told him he was wrong to let you go. He wanted to look after me because I was such a mess. He wanted to look after the business because there was so much to learn. He was trying to do everything right, but he was so miserable, I could see. He was missing you, and finally I convinced him that I was well enough and that he should go and find you.'

'He did?' Mari felt sick. 'When?'

'A year after he called you. He told me about that call, about finishing the relationship. He thought it was the right thing to do at the time. But later he regretted it, I know. So Dominico went with my blessing. He was angry when he returned. Angrier than I'd ever seen him before.'

A year after that call. Mari was reeling. She knew exactly what he would have learned. Her gut clenched. Her throat turned desert dry. 'He found out that I was married.'

Rosaria nodded sadly. 'He did.'

Mari squeezed her eyes shut. Dom had come looking for her. Not when she'd needed him so desperately, not in the midst of her anguish, but he had come back.

And she'd been gone.

Married.

The tectonic plates beneath her feet shifted and buckled, sending all she'd ever known about Dom's abandonment and indifference into a range of mountain peaks that sharply challenged everything she'd ever assumed.

How had Dom felt when he'd discovered she'd married?

How she wished she could go back and do things differently. Except she'd never known.

'Was he angry with me,' Mari asked, 'because he found me married?'

'No. He was upset that you'd married. But he was angrier with himself, for taking so long to go back and find you. He blamed himself.'

Mari swallowed. 'I loved your son,' she said. 'I missed him so much.'

'I know. It's no wonder you sought solace elsewhere.' Rosaria softly patted Mari's hand. 'And that's what makes you and Dominico marrying now all the more magical. It's like love finally got it right.'

Mari squeezed the older woman's hand. 'Thank you for telling me that Dom came looking for me,' she whispered. Because while love hadn't figured into her marriage with Simon and it didn't come into the current state of her relationship with Dom, it was good to know that Rosaria didn't judge her for not waiting for her son to make up his mind. 'It means the world.'

Rosaria asked, 'Did Dominico come with you this afternoon?'

Mari found her first smile of the day. 'He insisted on coming. He's waiting outside. No doubt pacing, wondering what we're talking about.'

Rosaria chuckled. 'I bet he is. Would you send him in, please? I'd better talk to him; I want to know how he's going with the party plans. He'll no doubt need help with the guest list.' She sighed. 'And then it will be time for another nap. That's all I seem to have the energy to do these days.'

Mari stood up from the bed, leaned over and kissed Rosaria's brow. 'I'll see you later.'

The woman in the bed smiled and squeezed Mari's hand. 'You sweet girl. I'm sorry I made you cry.'

I'm sorry I lost your grandchildren.
I'm sorry Dom didn't come to find me earlier.
I'm so sorry.

But Mari said none of those things. She simply smiled and said, 'I'll visit you again later.'

Dom looked at his watch. Again. What the hell were they talking about in there? Why did his mother need to get to know her new daughter-in-law when they'd met twenty years ago? What more did she need to know? And what was so private that he had to be excluded?

Marianne had played her part well this morning—if you didn't count that ridiculous party suggestion that his mother had taken to like a duck to water. He'd been on the phone to party planners ever since, all of them asking questions. How many guests? Day or evening? And music and menu choices.

How the hell was he supposed to know this stuff? Weren't they supposed to be the party planners? And given his entire team down to his PA were either fully employed on either the Melbourne takeover or the Brazil deal, he couldn't even shunt it to an underling.

Hopeless.

The door to his mother's room opened, and Mari emerged. 'She wants to see you now.'

Well, good. He wanted to see her too. It was on the tip of his tongue to ask Mari what they'd talked about, when he noticed the shadows dimming the vividness of her green eyes, as if someone had pulled down the shades. And now that he looked closer there was a smudge under one of her eyes. For the life of him, he couldn't remember it being there before. He put one hand on her shoulder and lifted a thumb to her cheek.

She flinched but didn't pull away. 'What?' she said.

'There's something under your eye.'

'Oh.' He felt her tremble as he gently ran his thumb along the tender skin. 'Oh, yes, I had an eyelash in my eye. I must have smudged my mascara.'

'Dominico!' a thready voice called from inside the room. 'I haven't got all day.'

He smiled as he stepped away. 'That's my cue.'

He kissed his mother on both cheeks and pulled a chair closer alongside her bed. 'How are you, Mamá?'

'Better now I've had a chance to talk to your delightful wife.'

'Really? What did you talk about?'

She chuckled, and it caught in her throat, turning into a cough.

He reached for her water, waiting while she sipped it from a straw.

'Are you all right?' he asked.

'It's you,' his mother said. 'Marianne said you were probably pacing outside, wondering what we were talking about.'

It seemed a fair question to ask from Dom's point of view, even though apparently it was amusing to the women.

'Oh, we had a lovely visit. Marianne and I have so much in common.'

Alarm bells went off in Dominico's mind.

'Oh? Like what?'

She patted his hand. 'Girl business, you know.'

Dom didn't know. He had no clue.

'But I'm so sorry I made her cry. Please apologise for me.'

And suddenly the smudge under Mari's eye made some kind of sense.

'What did you say to make her cry?'

'I made her remember something sad. It was thoughtless of me. Now, how are you getting on with the plans for the party?'

He spent the next ten minutes getting answers to all the questions the party planners had asked him. His mother reeled everything off as if it were the easiest thing in the world, which made a kind of sense seeing she'd spent a lifetime organising events from parties to gallery openings to festivals, leaving him wondering why she'd tasked him with the project in the first place.

But by the end of it he even had a half decent guest list.

'Now,' he said. 'We have to talk about dates. When would you like the party?' There was no point telling his mother the sooner the better, she knew that.

'What's today?' she asked.

'Wednesday,' he said.

'How about Saturday?'

'This week?'

'Are you busy this Saturday?'

'No. I'm not busy. But other people might be.'

'Then Saturday it is. And if that's all, please send my nurse in. It's time for my pain relief.'

'Is it bad?' he asked.

'It comes and goes. And then it comes and comes. But don't worry, she'll make it better.'

'Oh, Mamá,' he said, leaning over again to kiss her on the cheek. 'I'll send her right in.'

The light was leaching from the sky by the time they headed back to Dom's apartment. Marianne sat quietly and he wondered if her mood had anything to do with her conversation with his mother. In the car, curiosity got the better of him. 'What did my mother say to make you cry?'

'She told you that?'

'She said to apologise to you. What did she say?'

'Oh,' Mari said, her head swinging away from him, her attention suddenly taken by something they were passing in the street, something he'd obviously missed. 'She was talking about you and explaining why you're so important to her. She told me about the miscarriages she suffered before she managed to have you.'

'And that's what made you cry?' Her story didn't match up with what his mother had said. She'd said she had made Marianne remember something sad.

Her head swung back, an expression on her face he couldn't read, a flash of defiance in her eyes and—something else—something that looked entirely more defensive. 'Don't you think it's tragic?'

'It's sad, but it doesn't seem like the kind of thing that would reduce you to tears.'

'Don't you wish you had family? Brothers and sisters, I mean.'

He shrugged. 'It's hard to miss what you don't know.'

She nodded and turned her head away again. She looked like she had the weight of the world on her shoulders.

He watched her a while, waiting for her to turn back around, but she kept her gaze fixed out of the window as if she didn't want to engage with him. Definitely defensive. There was more to the story of her tears than she was letting on.

But *'girl business'* his mother had said.

Maybe he didn't want to know.

His phone pinged. It was good news. The Australian takeover was all but through the governmental jumps and hoops, the Brazilian deal was moving apace, and without needing his intervention. Which was good news, because he had more than enough to deal with here.

Frankly, his mother was enough to deal with. Right now,

her needs were foremost. But then there was Marianne, who couldn't help but challenge him at every turn.

He looked back at Marianne, who was still staring fixedly out of her window. Her silence annoyed him. What was she hiding? He was growing sick of her secrets.

And then he found an opening. She'd been the one who had brought up the subject of brothers and sisters after all.

'So,' he asked, 'as someone who doesn't know, tell me— what's it like having a sibling? I seem to remember you having a younger sister. I can't recall her name.'

Her head swung around. She took a moment before she answered, as if she was wondering whether she even wanted to. 'Suzanne.'

He wasn't sure why she sounded so defensive. 'And what's it like having a sister?' he coaxed.

She licked her lips before turning her head to stare out of her window again. 'It's good. She's my best friend.'

'Do you see a lot of each other?'

'We do.'

'She doesn't live in Sydney then?'

'She lives in Melbourne now.'

Dom stared at the back of her head. So much for making conversation. It was like trying to extract honey from a brick.

'Is she married? Does she have any kids? Do you have any nephews or nieces?'

'No,' she said, suddenly turning back. 'Is that it? Are we done?'

'What's wrong, Marianne?'

At first she said nothing, her back straight, head held rigid.

'Marianne?'

Her shoulders slumped on a sigh. 'Sorry, I'm a bit distracted. I guess there's no harm in telling you. Seven or

so years ago Suzanne was engaged to be married. Everything was set. And then she was diagnosed with early onset
multiple sclerosis. Her fiancé, instead of supporting her,
decided that he didn't want to be "lumbered with a crip-
ple"—his words, said to Suzanne's face—and that was it,
the wedding was off. We didn't see him for dust.'

'He was a creep. He didn't deserve her.'

'So we discovered.'

'How is she now?'

'She's coping, some days better than others, but she has
a progressive form of MS so her symptoms will get worse
over time. That's why she moved to Melbourne.'

'To be closer to you.'

She gave a small shrug as if it was self-evident. 'I'm her
only family now. I couldn't do anything to help her if she
were still in Sydney.'

'I understand.'

'It's cruel,' Marianne said. 'She was so happy, so in love.
And then to have the rug pulled from under her feet like
that. It was a double whammy.'

'I'm sorry. It must be hard for you, too.' And he'd just
made it harder by whisking her half the world away from
her sister.

'Oh, take my word for it, it's way harder for her.'

He nodded. 'Who's looking after her?'

'She has a carer, but she'll need more full-time help
soon. Along with a bigger house with more space to accommodate all the equipment she needs. I'll know it when
I find it.'

A bigger house.

She'd been looking at real estate on the plane. He'd assumed Marianne had been looking for a house for herself.
Not for her sister. No wonder she hadn't been satisfied with
his offer of one or two million dollars. He had no idea what

the kind of property Suzanne needed cost, not to mention her ongoing care, but Melbourne real estate didn't come cheap. Little wonder Marianne had demanded such a sum.

And the million dollars advance she'd asked for? Did that have something to do with putting arrangements in place for Suzanne to cover Marianne's absence?

Steel plates shifted in his gut, grating against each other, telling him he'd made a mistake, that he'd been wrong. He didn't like being wrong. His business success relied on him being right, of making informed decisions, even educated guesses. It was just as well he didn't rely on assumptions in that case.

Because, by all accounts, Marianne wasn't the gold-digger he'd assumed her to be.

Maybe the Marianne he'd known twenty years ago hadn't changed that much after all.

She'd settled into silence, staring at her knees. Wondering about her sister back in Melbourne? Who could blame her?

And now it wasn't just his mother that had made Marianne sad. Now it was Dom.

The driver turned onto Zubieta Kalea running along La Concha beach, and Dom had an idea.

He asked the driver to pull over.

'Why are we stopping?'

'I thought we could do with some fresh air. Do you fancy a walk on the beach?'

'Now?'

He shrugged. 'No time like the present.'

She gave a hint of a smile, the first he'd seen since getting in the car. 'All right.'

The driver opened Dom's door and Marianne scooted over. He offered his hand and she took it without thinking.

'It's so beautiful here,' she said, content to stand a moment, drinking in the beauty of the curved bay and its guardian mountains, the silvering sea dotted with small boats at anchor. Beyond the Isla de Santa Clara the sky was streaked with red, lighting up the wispy clouds to slashes of pink in the darkening blue.

They shucked off their shoes and stepped onto the cool sand. It squeaked underfoot and tickled their toes and made him wonder how long it had been since she'd been to the beach and enjoyed the simple pleasure of walking on sand.

'You're lucky,' she said, 'living so close to this beauty. I bet it never gets old.'

'It is a good place to come home to,' he agreed.

They walked hand in hand along the shore. She'd let him take her hand and he wondered at her easy acceptance of his hand hold. No bristling, No fighting.

And he relished the companionable peace between them.

People were packing up and heading home, the beach becoming more and more deserted, the lamps on the walkway flickering into life as the night drew in. Mari thought the coming night would have erased the beauty of the bay, but somehow the lights only seemed to accentuate it. The whole city seemed to light up, glowing gold in the darkening sky, golden light reflecting in the shallows of the bay. She heard music coming from somewhere, a beguiling sound, violin over accordion and drums, a sound that tugged at her. She knew enough to recognise that she was hearing some kind of tango, but she'd always associated tango music with drama and passion and speed, whereas this music was more purposeful, with a poignant depth, rich with emotion.

And there on a terrace overlooking the sea she found the source, a small group of musicians making music that could have been a homage to the sunset, because both were equally beautiful.

She stopped to listen as the violin rose to even sweeter heights.

'Dance with me, Marianne.'

The words were so unexpected she turned her head, expecting to see him smiling as if he were joking. But he wasn't smiling. Instead, his dark eyes held an intensity that caused Mari's breath to hitch.

'But—'

'It would be a sin to waste such beautiful music, don't you agree?'

'I don't know how.'

'Then let me show you.' He was still holding her hand, but now he was moving, his feet gliding across the sand, coaxing her to follow. Then he lifted their hands and spun her around, stepping towards her as she came back to him so that they were chest to chest. 'You see?' he said. 'You do know how.'

Before she could form a reply, he'd whirled her away again, except this time Mari felt the music, rather than just heard it. Felt the music in her limbs, in their movements, felt the music deep in her veins. The violin wrung emotional intensity from the air, and Dom harnessed the sound and used it to mould her to his every step, his every move. And it was intoxicating, moving with a rhythm that felt timeless, and yet also only theirs.

They'd always moved well together.

But here, dancing on the sand to a tune that stirred her soul, this was something different. This was a whole new experience.

This was magical.

The strains of the violin faded away, the notes evaporating on the night sky as Dom reeled her in one last time so her back rested against his chest, his arms wrapped around her waist.

Her entire body was tingling. On fire.

And she was breathless, not from the effort but from the fairy dust that someone must have sprinkled over her. Because here she was dancing on La Concha beach at sunset with the most handsome man in the world—and being paid for the privilege.

Forget all the baggage of the past. Forget all the reasons she shouldn't be dancing with this man. She just wanted this moment to pretend that all was right with the world. A moment to savour. A memory to take home with her and take out whenever the world sucked.

He kissed the top of her head, his hips gently swaying, rocking her with him.

'I want you,' he murmured in her ear.

And all the reasons she shouldn't want him vanished. All the reasons, like they'd had their time and this was nothing more than a blip. A chance encounter that had let memories bubble back to the surface. Bubbles that could well pop in the harsh light of day.

And yet, would it be so bad to admit she wanted him too? Would it be so bad to make love? What was she protecting herself from? From being afraid that he would once again discard her after rediscovering how wonderful he was in bed?

He'd come back for her.

Rosaria's news had shaken Mari to her core. He hadn't forgotten her all those years ago. He'd come back for her. Not when she'd been so anxious for him to return and share her news Not when she'd been in the depths of despair at both the loss of their twins and the loss of the man she loved. He'd come looking for her, only to learn she was married to someone else. And one of the pillars upon which she'd built her hatred for him shattered and crumbled into dust.

Why had she insisted that this marriage would not be consummated? Why else, if not to punish Dom for the sins of the past—for abandoning her in her moment of greatest need and turning his back on her love?

But he had come back for her and found her married and suddenly she found herself on shaky territory. Was it any wonder he'd relegated their affair to a meaningless summer fling when clearly—it had seemed to him—it had meant so little to her?

Why was she still holding out?

Because she wasn't just punishing Dom.

She was punishing herself.

Mari turned slowly in the circle of his arms, wrapped her arms around his neck and looked up at his beautiful face, his strong jaw, the masculine beauty of his lips, the intensity of his dark eyes, now looking quizzically down at her. She allowed herself a smile, anticipation already fizzing in her veins.

'I want you too.'

CHAPTER ELEVEN

DOM GROWLED, a low guttural sound of victory, a sound that rumbled into Mari's bones as he dipped his head to sweep her into his kiss. And this time she went willingly. This time it wasn't Dom driving the kiss. It was Mari that wanted it. Because she'd been wrong on so many levels—wrong to deny them both the passion and the pleasure she knew they would find together, wrong to waste so much of what little time they had. She took everything that he offered and hungered for more.

He delivered, wrenching his lips from hers to blaze a trail down her throat and setting her flesh alight under his heated mouth. He was hot. So hot, turning her own need to combustible. Dialling up her own desire to the max.

And his hands, his strong hands, were everywhere, cupping her behind and moulding her to him, leaving her in no doubt of his arousal, further ratcheting up her need.

'Come,' he said, breathing hard as he took her hand. They half stumbled, half danced their way across the sand, their progress slower than either of them would have preferred, but only because they couldn't get enough of the touch, the feel, the taste of each other.

Because it was the same as it had been twenty years before, except it was better. Twenty years better. Somehow, they made it to Dom's apartment building and into the private lift that would take them to his penthouse. Mari found herself wedged in the corner, Dom's hands busy shimmying her skirt up her legs, his leg inserted between hers, while his mouth and his seeking tongue plundered hers. It could have been uncomfortable—in other circumstances it would have been an outrage—but right in this moment there was nowhere in the world Mari would rather be. The lift rose, taking the temperature of Mari's blood with it until it was simmering, and she was threatening to combust.

The lift doors opened behind Dom and they spilled out, leaving a trail of clothing as Dom steered her towards the bedroom.

Such a big bed. It was a crime to have waited so long to enjoy it.

Why had she waited so long? Why had she tortured herself? Those questions tumbled through her mind as they tumbled together onto the bed, mouths locked, kisses deepening, the emotions of the past week unleashed in one furious tangle of bodies and mouths and limbs.

And then the questions stopped, and all Mari had the brain space to do was feel.

Hot breath intermingling, their bodies driven by desire, it was a desperate battle to remove what few clothes remained, a frenzied and furious race to achieve skin-to-skin contact.

The feel of Dom's ribbed chest beneath her hands, the hard-packed belly of his abdomen, the feel of his erection jutting into her as she lay with her leg across him. Her inner muscles clenched with anticipation, muscles long neglected and forgotten for too many years, but muscles that had been merely lying in wait, ready to be awakened again.

And who better to awaken them than the man who'd set light to them in the first place? Dom. Her first love. Her best love.

Her only love.

Dom looked down at her, now naked on the bed, his hand smoothing her hair back from her brow. 'You're even more beautiful than I remembered,' he said. She looked up at him, at his dark eyes still overcome with grief, but now burning with something more urgent, more primal.

She recognised it because she felt it too.

Need.

And then he dipped his head to take one peaked nipple in his heated mouth, drawing her in, his tongue circling her nipple, before he sucked on that bullet point. Exquisite torture, pain and pleasure intermingling as her back arched on the bed. Her other breast was already screaming for equal treatment when he turned his attention there, torturing her further, the buzzing need between her thighs growing more insistent. More needy.

Her hands were in his hair, her fingernails raking his scalp as he rose up to claim her mouth once more.

He slipped a hand lower, smoothing over her belly and lower still, over her mound and between her pulsing lips. Her breath hitched. Because he was touching her *there* and it was as if every dream she'd ever had of making love with Dom, every memory she'd ever had, was rolled into this moment. It was as if the world began and ended where his fingers shimmied. It was suddenly the most important thing in her life. The only thing in her life.

'So slick,' he murmured into her mouth, while one fingertip traced the outline of her opening.

'Dom,' she begged, not knowing what she was begging for, knowing that only Dom could give it to her. Before his fingertip alighted on that tightly packed nub of nerves, gently circling, gently toying, each pass, each touch building on the other until there was nowhere to go but to fly.

He barely had time to sheath himself before he was inside her. Inside her and filling her and grinding his hips against hers, lifting one leg higher as he plunged deeply into her. She cried out with the exquisite intimacy of it. Cried out with their perfect fit, their matched rhythm, the memories of the past melding with the newly made experience of now. And still he took her higher until Dom cried out with one final lunge.

Mari came apart in colours, an out of body experience of bright and shimmering light that drifted down from the heights in time with her heartbeat.

She clung to him, her breathing ragged, her senses reeling.

Because she'd had sex with Dominico.

No, she'd *made love* with Dominico.

And it was perfect.

It was everything she hadn't wanted and everything she had.

It was agony.

Mari and Dom were both still lying, their limbs intertwined on the bed. It should have been the perfect post-coital moment. That moment of post lovemaking bliss where they just luxuriated in their closeness and the warmth of the intimacy they'd just shared, sharing breath and kisses and the feel of satiated flesh against flesh.

It should have been perfect.

Except Mari knew it wasn't. Not until she knew.

'Why didn't you tell me you'd gone back to Australia looking for me?'

He stirred next to her. 'What?'

'You went back to Sydney.'

He wiped a hand over his face and sighed. 'My mother told you that?'

She nodded. 'Why did you go looking for me?'

'It was a mistake,' he said, his voice gruff. 'I quickly learned that.'

And Mari didn't have to ask him why. Because she knew he'd learned she was married and had so evidently slammed shut the door on her past.

There was no point trying to defend herself. She knew she'd be trying to defend herself against the indefensible.

'Why are we talking about the past,' Dom said, reaching for her, 'when we're both here now, in the present?'

Again, she thought, so soon? And Mari wasn't even sure she was in the mood after their latest discussion. Until Dom's mouth met hers and his hand swept down her side, lighting fires under her skin, and she forgot about the past in the passion of the present.

And Mari gave herself up once again to the pleasures of the flesh. Gave herself up to the pleasures of Dominico. Because that wall of resistance had fallen, and now there was no way she could say no.

Foolishly, naïvely, she'd imagined on a repeat performance, excellent as it had been, that Dom couldn't take her higher than he had before. She'd imagined that because he was older he would flag. She'd imagined wrongly. She hadn't imagined a man in his prime who knew how to extract every bit of joy from the act of sex, that he knew how to bestow it. It was like being gifted a masterclass in making love.

It was a gift.

Afterwards she lay panting, the heated passion of their union giving way to the chill of truth. Because now she could no longer fight the truth—the truth she'd been fighting ever since she'd stepped into Dom's suite at the hotel in Melbourne. The truth that she'd tried to deny by keeping her distance. The truth she'd buried under an avalanche of hatred—hatred that wasn't entirely as well founded as she'd imagined.

The truth—that there was a part of her that was still in love with Dominico. A tiny part, no more than a smoking spark that had refused to be extinguished, no matter his crimes against her, no matter the passing of the decades. A spark that, if she wasn't careful, could flicker into life and consume her, as it would if she fell in love with Dominico all over again.

And it terrified her.

Because she knew that it was pointless. That their contract had an end date and that she would be expected to leave. He'd demanded it and she'd been only too happy to agree. She'd promised she would leave him at the first opportunity.

And now she knew she had to, before Dom could get rid of her.

Marianne was avoiding him. Dom didn't understand how this could be possible when they spent their nights locked in passion together in his bed. He'd thought things had changed between them since that night on the beach, but time and again Dom went looking for her in the apartment, only to find her missing. At first, he'd assumed she'd gone for walks along the beach. But when he'd investigated further, it was to discover that she'd taken the car to visit his mother. And not just to talk, but he'd learned from her nurse that she'd been reading to his mother too, from the extensive library of books in both Spanish and English that she'd shared with Roberto.

Not that he had a lot of time to worry about Marianne.

Between the Brazilian deal coming together and arrangements for the party, Dom had been well and truly occupied.

In fact, it was a miracle they'd been able to pull off the party. Despite the rush, somehow it had all come together—the guest list, the catering and, best of all, the joy of his mother, watching on from her wheelchair. She looked beautiful tonight. Her silvery hair had been gently styled into soft curves that framed her face. Her make-up covered the worst of the dark rings around her eyes and highlighted her noble, high cheekbones. Her lips were painted her favourite shade of red, adding vitality to her otherwise faded features.

The celebration had begun with a ceremony performed by the local priest, blessing the marriage of Dom and Mari. A serious ceremony where the hushed crowd had watched on while they'd exchanged their vows again and the priest had blessed their marriage, hoping it to be full of love and fruitful, and to bear children.

And while Dom knew those words to be empty wishes, through it all, he witnessed his mother looking beatific, sunken eyes and shrunken body in her wheelchair perhaps, but beaming in her lace finery, the party lights reflected brightly in her eyes. She was in her element.

And all the lies and pretence were worth it, he knew. To see his mother this happy, it was right.

He saw Marianne surrounded by a crowd of guests, he saw her smile, saw that she was holding her own, and mentally applauded her for it. And then he saw one woman sidle up to the group: Isabela, a divorcee who'd advertised her availability to Dom every time she'd had the opportunity.

If Isabela had been a shark, she'd be a white pointer, taking no prisoners, and Dom wanted to intervene. Except his mother took hold of his hand and he couldn't leave her side.

'Isn't this the best party ever?' she said. 'And now your marriage has been blessed I'm sure that you will be blessed with children.'

'There's no rush,' he said.

'Of course there's a rush,' his mother said. 'You're not getting any younger, and your bride is almost forty.'

Dom's plan hadn't encompassed children. He'd wanted to see his mother's dying wish satisfied. He hadn't thought about what would come after, beyond Marianne going home. But what came after a wedding?

Children.

Of course, he needed to provide an heir to the business his father had begun and that he'd turned into a global powerhouse. He knew that. At least, he knew that in the back of his mind, where he'd parked the concept until he was older.

Except now he *was* older, and what was foremost in his mind was something else entirely. Because after Marianne left, as she would, what then?

There was no end of women who would sacrifice themselves on that altar, he knew. Finding one that he wanted to spend the rest of his life with was the issue. He hadn't found one in all the years since he'd left Sydney. What were the chances now? Settling with someone who would suffice?

'It's so sad that she lost her babies.'

His head swung around. 'What?'

'Marianne's twins. It's very sad that she lost two babies. I can't begin to imagine. You have to treat her gently. It's no wonder that she'd be wary about getting pregnant again.'

The shocks kept coming. Dom had the feeling he'd been sucked out of this world and spat out into a parallel universe. 'What are you talking about?'

'Oh, you don't have to pretend. It's all right, Marianne told me.'

Girl business, Dom remembered. So that was what they'd talked about.

His head swung around to locate Marianne in the crowd. She wasn't hard to spot. She was luminescent, her beautiful face animated, her emerald-green gown glowing. She was a bright light surrounded by moths all wanting a piece of her, all wanting to find her secret, how she had ensnared Señor Estefan, the most eligible bachelor in San Sebastián.

He'd assumed Marianne had been crying that day because she'd learned that Dom had gone to Sydney looking for her. Because she'd learned that if anyone had cause for grievance it was him.

But… She'd lost two babies? No wonder she hadn't wanted to talk about her marriage.

Except that didn't make sense either. Mari had told him that her husband hadn't wanted any more than the two he already had.

It didn't mesh. None of it made sense. Unless she'd had a pregnancy after her divorce in a relationship that she hadn't told him about?

Maybe that was it. Twenty years was a long time. She could have had any number of relationships between her divorce and meeting up with Dom again.

'But she's still young enough,' his mother said.

His head swung back.

He realised she was talking about babies. His mother wasn't about to settle for a marriage. She wanted grandchildren. Even knowing she was dying, she was wishing him children.

'I'm sure they'll happen in due course,' he said.

'They may,' his mother said, 'but take care of Marianne. It's going to be hard for her.' She squeezed his hand. 'Promise me you'll take care of her.'

He gently squeezed his mother's hand in return. 'I promise,' he said. And he would, knowing Marianne would be departing with another nine million dollars. And sure, she'd be spending a wad of it on a house for her sister, but still, Marianne would be well taken care of.

Mari felt very much the outsider as she was introduced, very much the odd woman out. A crowd of women surrounded her, all wanting a piece of her. There was one woman in particular who kept glancing at Dominico all the time she was trying to engage with Mari. Finally, she had her chance. 'So, are you truly married?'

Mari admired her directness—forget congratulations and happy wishes, why not cut to the chase?

'Dom and I were married this last week.'

'But in Las Vegas, I understand.'

She made a wedding in Las Vegas sound like something undesirable she had stuck to the sole of her Louboutin sandal.

'That's right. At the Bellagio Hotel. Have you been there?'

The woman's nose wrinkled. Her brow, Mari noticed, didn't. 'But Las Vegas. Isn't it a bit...tacky?'

'Clearly, you've never been to the Bellagio. But of course, when time is of the essence, you don't care where you make something happen. Just that you make it happen.'

Mari's answer clearly displeased the woman, not that she was about to give up any time soon.

'And yet a whirlwind romance, a whirlwind marriage—one might think that this was all an exercise in *time is of the essence*. I've known Dominico for more than ten years. Why would he choose to marry someone nobody knows, unless it's all make-believe?'

Ouch! How could the woman possibly entertain such an idea?

'A whirlwind romance, Isabela? Didn't Dom tell you that we first met twenty years ago? We were at university in Sydney together.'

The woman blinked. Clearly this was news to her. 'So, you knew each other back then?'

Mari smiled. 'Oh, yes. But back then we didn't merely know each other. We were lovers. As, of course, we are again now.'

The woman's eyes opened wide. She took a step back to regain her composure. 'In that case, congratulations. I was beginning to think that it would never happen, that Dominico would never marry.' She made a sound that could almost have been a laugh, if it hadn't sounded so false. 'There have been so many women that have tried and failed. I wonder what your secret is.'

Ten million dollars, Mari thought, along with a promise to agree to divorce as soon as his mother succumbed to her illness and Dom didn't need a fake wife any longer.

Mari smiled knowingly. 'I guess you'd have to ask Dom that.'

It was an hour later that Dom found her and pulled her aside. 'Did you tell Isabela that we were lovers twenty years ago?'

'I did. Why? I figured you wouldn't want me telling her that you'd paid me ten million dollars for the privilege. I told her the truth after all, though maybe not the whole truth. How did you know?'

He grinned. 'Because word is getting around. Before the night is out, everyone here will know we were once lovers.'

'Is that a problem?'

'No, it's good. Better than good.' He swept her close with an arm around her waist, swirled her around and placed a kiss on the tip of her nose. 'It's actually perfect.'

She laughed, clinging onto his shoulders. This was the Dom she'd known at university. Playful and spontaneous. The arrogant businessman mantle banished. 'What was that for?'

But the laughter died on her lips, her breath hitched when she saw the way Dom was looking down at her, his dark eyes intense, the same way he'd once looked at her. The way that had awakened her senses and her desire.

'Dom,' she whispered, sensing that something had changed. That everything had changed. The sounds of the party evaporated around her, the room shrank until there was just them, his dark eyes above hers and his arms around her, a buzzing in every cell and a humming ache between her thighs.

He was going to kiss her, she knew. He was going to kiss her.

And this time she sensed it wasn't a performance.

His lips drew closer, deliciously closer. So close. And then they were on hers. Blissfully on hers. Tender. Firm. For a moment she was lost in sensation. The feel of him in her arms, the taste of him in her mouth. It was intoxicating.

She was intoxicated. Carried away on her body's reaction to the man she'd always loved. The man she'd loved and who she'd believed had loved her.

The man she loved anew.

Oh, hell.

The realisation came as something else intruded on her senses. A noise, rising in intensity. She tried to block it out, to ignore it, too busy with her startling discovery to focus. Because the thing she'd most feared had happened. That tiny spark her heart had nurtured had caught alight, erupting into a blaze that lit up the words burning so brightly across Mari's mind's eye. She'd fallen in love with Dominico Estefan again.

Maybe he'd registered the thunderbolt that had coursed through her because he pulled back from the kiss, relaxing his embrace to wave to the crowd.

Applause, she realised, the noise registering. Cheers.

He waved to the cheering crowd while Mari's cheeks burned. If Isabela had any doubts remaining that they were truly in love, their kiss had put those doubts well and truly to bed.

And there, amongst the crowd applauding, sat Rosaria, beaming. Dom took Mari's hand and they crossed to her, kissing her cheeks.

'You've made me so happy, my son. Both you and your beautiful wife.'

Late that night Dom stood at a window overlooking the golden-fringed bay, reflecting on the evening. His mother had been almost radiant tonight. So happy. And he wasn't fooling himself, because it was Marianne who had made her happy. Marianne, and her gentle soul, convincing his mother that she was truly in love with her son.

And it was Marianne, now sleeping quietly in the bed, who had made him feel like it might even be possible. Tonight, his lovemaking with Marianne had moved to a new high. Not just the thrill of rediscovery, but the feeling that he was coming home. And it had felt good. It had felt right.

He had half a mind to make their arrangement more permanent. He didn't know how it might happen—he knew their contract had an end date, and he knew that Marianne had a responsibility to her sister—but he only knew that he had to try. That he couldn't let her go. Not again.

The call came in the early morning, just before dawn, the sound rousing Dom out of a restless sleep where he'd tangled with his thoughts as much as he'd tangled with his sheets.

He swung his legs out of the bed and clutched his phone, not bothering to look at the caller ID.

'Dominico...' he heard a voice say. Dr Rodríguez.

And ice slid down Dom's spine. 'Tell me,' he said.

'I'm sorry to tell you that your mother peacefully passed away in her sleep during the night.'

Dom squeezed his eyes shut. He'd known it was going to happen. Hadn't he been warned that it could happen at any time? But still, knowing that it could happen was no preparation for the sheer gut punch of when it did. The knowledge that hit him like a blow from a sledgehammer. Rosaria was gone.

'No,' he said, because there was comfort in denial. There was hope in not acknowledging that it was true. Even though he knew in his heart of hearts that there was none.

'I'm so sorry,' said the doctor. 'If it's any comfort, she died with a smile on her face. I've only ever witnessed that one time before. Clearly you made her very happy in her final days and hours.'

The words washed over Dom, all some kind of gobbledegook he'd have to unravel later, because all that mattered now was that his mother was gone. And sure, he'd been by his mother's side when his father had died, but right now his mind was a blank.

'Tell me what happens next,' he said, up on his feet and

heading for the shower, unable to think beyond getting over to the villa. 'Tell me what I need to do.'

Mari slept late, the bed beside her empty and cold. Last night's party had finally wound down in the early hours of the morning. It had been two a.m. before she and Dom had made it back to the apartment, so clearly Dom was feeling more sprightly than her.

She showered and made her way to the kitchen, the apartment eerily quiet with no sign of Dom. She found María, the housekeeper, there, quietly sobbing as she prepared eggs for an omelette.

'What's wrong?' she asked, which only sent María into new floods of tears.

'It's Señora Estefan,' she said, sniffing. 'She died overnight. Dominico is there now.'

Mari collapsed into a chair, a wave of grief flooding down her spine. Closely followed by a wave of empathy. *Oh, Dom.* He must be devastated. Nobody could have expected that the party to celebrate Dom and Mari's union was the party to see his mother out.

She remembered Rosaria's elation last night, her delight at the blessing of their marriage, her strong spirit allowing her to partake in the joy of the celebrations and be part of it. She'd been so happy. So beautiful, her joy lighting up her painted face. And yet suddenly she was gone, a bright light extinguished. It didn't seem possible.

'What can I do?' Mari asked, feeling helpless, moisture leaking from her eyes.

The housekeeper sniffed. 'Dom said for you to stay here. He'll be back when the arrangements are made.'

Mari nodded. Of course there would be arrangements to make. Arrangements for the body. Arrangements for a funeral. All to be made while he was still reeling and numb from his loss. Of course, he wouldn't need Mari there.

He didn't need Mari anywhere.

The thought slammed into her like a fist into a punching bag. She was his pretend wife. A wife to convince his mother that her son was finally settled down and married, for the term of his mother's existence. And now his mother was gone. Mari was surplus to requirements, a wife he didn't need any more, their contract at an end.

She sipped on the strong coffee with two sugars María had insisted she needed and had placed in front of her. María had been right. She needed the coffee's strength. Right now, she needed to be strong.

Dom would want her gone quickly, she presumed. He would want her out of the way. He would be busy with the funeral and with the legalities of winding up Rosaria's estate. He wouldn't need a reminder of the deal he'd made to convince his mother he'd finally found love. He wouldn't need a reminder of their deception.

And Mari didn't want to be here. Not now. Not after last night's realisation. How could she stay, knowing she loved him when he would soon want her gone?

She finished the coffee she hadn't realised she'd needed. Thanked María for it with a hug. She might not be able to help Dom right now, but at least she could help herself. She might as well make a start on packing.

CHAPTER TWELVE

MARI WASN'T PLANNING on taking anything he'd bought for her. The wedding dress she'd worn in Las Vegas? She didn't need that. The gown she'd worn at their marriage blessing likewise. And where would she wear a designer cocktail dress when she was back in her humdrum life in Melbourne? An interview suit would be more useful, given she had to find herself a new job.

But the silk underwear—she was nothing if not practical. What would be the point in leaving that?

'What are you doing?'

Mari spun around. 'Oh, Dom.' His face looked drawn, his eyes tortured. 'I'm so sorry.'

'She was smiling when she died,' he said, the words grating, as if talking were a struggle. 'Imagine that. My mother died happy.'

Despite her grief, Mari's heart warmed at the news. 'Her parting gift to you. A thank you for making her final days happy.'

He shook his head. 'Not just for me, but also for you. Because of you,' he said. 'Because she truly believed I was happy. That we were happy together.' His face twisted with incomprehension. 'And yet,' he said, 'I return from my mother's deathbed to find you, suitcase open and rifling through your wardrobe like you can't wait to get away.'

She jerked her chin up. He didn't sound angry. He sounded broken. She swallowed. 'I didn't think you'd need me anymore. I thought you'd want me gone. Our contract—'

'Damn the *pinche* contract! You thought wrong!' he said. 'Because I've never needed anyone more than I need you right now.'

'Dom—' she said, slowly shaking her head. This wasn't part of her escape plan. Couldn't he see that there was nothing to bind her to him any longer? She'd satisfied—more than satisfied—her end of the contract. He'd as much as admitted it himself.

So much for her newly found resolve.

There was no way she could say no. No way she could resist. Because Dom was hurting. Broken. She walked up to him, put her arms around his waist and hugged him close, nestling her head into his shoulder. 'Like that?' she asked.

'Like that,' he said, wrapping his arms around her and dipping his head against hers. For a moment they stayed that way, and then she realised he was sobbing. Silently shaking with long racking sobs, his body pressed against hers. And it fractured her heart into tiny shards.

'It's okay,' she said, hugging him close. 'It's okay.'

'I'm sorry,' he said.

She waited for the racking sobs to ease before she took his head in her hands, kissing his forehead, wiping the tears from his eyes with the pads of her thumbs.

'It's okay. I get it.' Losing someone who meant the world to you was never going to happen without that same world buckling beneath your feet. 'Even when we know it's going to happen, it's still a shock.'

He rested his head down on her shoulder and for a while she just rocked him. Trying to tell him with her actions how much she cared by just being there. By holding him. By consoling him.

She was there for him. That was all it was. That was all it was meant to be. She'd talk about her plan to leave later, when he wasn't so emotionally drained. He'd soon see that she was right. He'd see it made sense for both of them.

Almost imperceptibly there was a change in him. He lifted his head on a sigh, thanking her for her support and pressing his lips to her cheek, and it seemed the natural thing to do, to kiss him on the cheeks in return.

Except she never made it to the other cheek, because she found his mouth, his beautiful, sad mouth.

But even that was okay. Just a light touch of her lips against his, a butterfly touch to show her empathy. To show she cared. And God, she cared, because when her lips meshed with his there was no pulling away. There was no escape.

And neither did she want to.

He drank in her kiss like a man who'd been stranded in a desert. He clung to her as if she was a lifeline. She held his face between her hands and kissed away the moisture on his cheeks. It was always inevitable that they would end up on the bed although, looking back later, Mari couldn't remember when or how it had happened. Just that they were there and slowly and surely peeling away each other's clothes.

And it was so different to their first fevered coupling after the tango on the beach. So gentle. So tender.

So right.

They didn't need to talk. There was no need to exchange words. Their eyes and bodies did all the communicating as they slowly and languorously undressed each other, every removal of a piece of clothing, every piece of skin revealed deserving of worship and adoration, the press of lips, the lave of a tongue.

She soothed him. She comforted him, every touch stoking the fires building inside them.

And when he moved over her—positioned his legs between hers—and filled her, it was so poignant, so beautiful, so tender and sweet, that it was her time for tears. Tears for Rosaria. Tears for Dom. And tears for herself, because she was lost.

Tears that turned to stars as he sent her over into the abyss.

'You're crying,' he said as their bodies floated down from the heights of their lovemaking. 'Did I hurt you?'

'No,' she said, because it was nothing he'd done, and everything she had. She'd known the risks when she'd taken on this role. She'd known that she was susceptible, but the lure of filthy lucre and the wall of hatred she'd erected between them had turned her head and convinced her that she was impervious to him. A wall without substance, bricks laid without mortar.

And Dom was dismantling them, one brick at a time.

'You weren't serious about leaving straight away, were you?' he said.

Oh. She'd been going to talk to him about that.

'There's no need to rush off. At least stay for the funeral.'

She turned to him. 'Is there any point? I'll still be leaving.'

'What will people say if you're not there? Five minutes ago, everyone was celebrating our wedding, and the next minute you disappear, nowhere to be seen.'

Mari knew it sounded every kind of callous, but what did he expect when he'd been the one to set the contract conditions? And she was the one in danger here, and the longer she stayed, the harder it would hurt when he was finished with her.

'Wasn't that the point of our agreement? You wanted a temporary wife, and you got one. There was nothing in our contract about staying for a funeral.'

'How heartless are you? I thought you liked Rosaria.'

'I loved your mother! You know that. And she was happy. That's all that matters. That's what counts.'

'Then think about me. Think about a funeral when, instead of everyone celebrating the life and mourning the death of the deceased, everyone is focused on why the son's brand-new wife isn't there.' He looked earnestly at her. 'Do you really want to turn my mother's funeral into some kind of gossip fest?'

Mari turned away and rose from the bed, lashing a robe around her. It was not fair that he insisted she be there to attend Rosaria's funeral. He had no idea why she wanted—no, needed—to get away. He had no concept. He was trying to protect his image. She got that.

Whereas Mari was trying to protect herself.

'I thought… I was thinking…that things had changed.'

She knew immediately what he was referring to. God, what a mistake it had been, falling into Dom's bed.

'Because we had sex?'

She heard him rise from the bed. 'We made love. You know that. And it was just like it used to be. Amazing. We made love again just now. Why would you throw that away?'

And the answer came back to her, crystal-clear.

Because sex was one thing we always did right. Love, not so much.

And she wouldn't put herself in a position where her love meant so little to him again.

'Grief sex,' she said with a shrug. 'You were upset, I tried to console you, and it got out of hand.'

'Grief sex. That's all it was to you?'

No. It was much, much more. But she wasn't about to confess that to the man she needed to get away from. And neither was she as heartless as her words made out. She imagined a funeral without Dom's so recently celebrated new wife in attendance. She could almost hear the snarky comments being exchanged when the guests should be focused on Rosaria's life and loves. She couldn't do that. She couldn't reduce Rosaria's funeral into a hotbed of gossip. Mari owed the woman that much after the grand deception they'd pulled off and that she'd been party to. More than that, Mari needed to pay her respects. She swallowed.

'When do you think Rosaria's funeral might happen?'

'Will, not might. The chapel is booked for two days' time.'

Mari closed her eyes and gave thanks. Soon then. That at least was some kind of relief.

'I'll stay.' She turned then to face him. 'But then I will hold you to our contract. I will be leaving.' Adding a moment later, 'Suzanne needs me.'

Dominico made it through the next forty-eight hours running on a mix of grief, strong coffee and a goodly dose of Destilerías y Crianza del Whisky. He wasn't seeing things clearly, he knew that, but he didn't understand Marianne's resistance to him. He didn't understand her urgency to get away from him. He'd kept her away from her precious sister less than two weeks and, despite the words they'd had at the start, she couldn't pretend she hadn't enjoyed the time they'd spent together.

At one time he'd even imagined they could turn this arrangement into something more permanent. But if she was so determined to get away, clearly, he'd misread the situation. If she had a problem with being with him, so be it. He wouldn't impose himself upon her again.

But at least she'd agreed to stay for the funeral. At least he wouldn't have to field endless questions as to her whereabouts. It would be bad enough after the funeral, when he appeared in public without Marianne on his arm.

Then again, theirs wouldn't be the shortest marriage in history. The questions and gossip would soon die down.

And yet still he had the sense that he was missing something, but his brain was too full of grief, strong coffee and whisky to work out what it was.

Mari stood alone in the funerary chapel clutching her glass of sparkling water. The funeral had been poignant but wonderful, a true celebration of Rosaria's life, and now Dom was busy doing the rounds of the guests, something he seemed content to do without her. So perfectly content that she wondered why he'd insisted on her being here at all.

He hadn't made a move on her since she'd told him she was leaving, even though they still shared the same bed. It was as if, as far as Dom was concerned, she'd already left. And while part of her mourned the loss of his touch, another part of her was grateful. He wasn't making it harder for her to leave. She was merely here at the funeral to avoid any uncomfortable questions. So be it. For her own part, she was here to pay her respects to Rosaria, and she was glad she'd stayed. She was heading home tomorrow. She could hardly wait to get away from the endless tension of being in Dom's orbit.

'Señora Estefan…' said a man beside her. Rosaria's physician, she realised. He shook her hand. 'Such a beautiful service,' he said.

'Rosaria deserved it,' Mari said.

'She died smiling,' he said. 'Did Dominico share that with you?'

Mari smiled. 'He did. It warmed my heart to hear it.'

'You know, when Dominico assured his mother that he was getting married, I didn't quite believe it. I thought he was telling her that merely to make his mother happy. But then, barely a week later, you appeared by his side, and I can see now that he was speaking the truth. I'm so sorry I doubted him. You both did so much to make Rosaria happy in her final days. Thank you for that. My condolences to you.'

He bowed and excused himself. And Mari thought then that it was true. She and Dom had convinced the entire world that they were destined to be together. The pity of it was, the only people they'd failed once again to convince was themselves.

CHAPTER THIRTEEN

MARI HAD SAID that she was perfectly fine taking commercial flights to get home to Melbourne. Dom, however, had insisted that she take his private jet, he wouldn't be using it. A dig, because he'd be busy mopping up after his mother's funeral, of course.

A private jet was even more private when you were the only passenger on the plane. Twenty-something hours on a flight gave a person way too much time to think, even with the real estate searches and property inspections she was planning when she got home, even with the necessary sleep time. And who needed a film when twenty-something hours on a flight gave a person way too much time to replay every detail of every scene that she had shared with Dom?

Dom had been so cold to her the last two days, but she'd done the right thing, she knew. The longer she'd stayed, the more of a mess she would have been when he'd discarded her again.

She'd done the right thing.

But she didn't understand why doing the right thing hurt so much.

Melbourne's weather was doing what Melbourne's weather did best. Change. A day after her return home, Mari had swapped sunglasses for umbrella and back to sunglasses before a sudden gust of wind had almost torn them off her face. She knocked on Suzanne's door. Valerie opened it.

'You're back,' Valerie said, giving Mari a hug as she entered. 'How was the trip?'

Mari wasn't sure how much Suzanne had shared with her carer. 'Productive,' she said vaguely. 'And I've found some promising properties to take a look at. If Suzanne isn't up to visiting, maybe you'd like to come along with me?' She looked around. 'Where is Suzanne?'

'Here!' her sister said, beaming as she negotiated her wheelchair around the corner from the kitchen. 'I just put the kettle on.'

Mari rushed over, leant over and buried her head in her sister's neck. 'It's so good to see you,' she said.

'Hey,' Suzanne said, 'you've only been gone a fortnight or so. Anyone would think you'd been away a lifetime.'

'It felt like it.' A lifetime of revisiting her past. A lifetime of discovery. All packed into the blur of a few short weeks. She tried to push back the tears that threatened to launch themselves upon her unsuspecting sister.

'So how was it?' Suzanne asked.

'Interesting,' Mari said, peeling herself away, but not before Suzanne caught sight of her eyes.

'Oh, right. So maybe you want to show us these properties,' Suzanne said, 'that you're so excited about.'

Mari swiped her cheeks as she and Valerie pulled up chairs to the table, a space for Suzanne's wheelchair in between so they could all see the pictures on Mari's laptop. She was ready to make a bid for any of them, as soon as Suzanne and Valerie agreed. She'd woken in the morning to a notification from her bank that a large deposit had been made to her account, currently awaiting clearance by the authorities. She'd opened the bank app to see it bulging with a dollar amount unimaginable just a few weeks ago. So even in the midst of his grief for his mother, even at his displeasure that Mari would leave him, Dom had managed to fulfil his end of the deal.

To be done with her? Perhaps. When all was said and done, did it even matter? She had the means now to make her sister's life better.

And this ache she felt in her heart, that she had left something or someone behind in San Sebastián, was dulled with sister's excitement as she looked over the photos and floor plans and as the three made plans to do house inspections.

And Mari knew in her heart that she had been right to leave Dom when she had. Because right here in Melbourne with her sister was where she belonged.

Dom stared out of the window overlooking the bay that made San Sebastián internationally famous, and yet he registered nothing. Because there was a package on his desk. A package containing the divorce papers he'd had the lawyers prepare when the contract had been arranged. He'd thought of everything, down to the preparation of the divorce papers to dissolve the convenient marriage on his mother's death.

And now they'd been duly delivered. Ready for signing. Ready for the dissolution of his and Marianne's marriage.

He should sign them. Sign them and send them by courier straight to Marianne. The matter—their divorce—should be settled within a week.

But he couldn't sign them.

That day, that one day, when he'd arrived from his mother's deathbed needing her, she'd been there. She'd consoled him. Taken care of him. Made love with him so tenderly that it was bittersweet to even think of it. Made love to him so tenderly that it haunted his dreams.

Every time, the sex between them had been amazing, but that day, that one day, she'd taken care of him. She'd soothed him. She'd gifted him her body and given him solace.

She couldn't have done that if she hadn't felt something for him.

Once upon a time, long ago, he'd let Marianne slip through his fingers. He'd been busy. His father had died, and running and building the family business had fallen on his shoulders, along with supporting his grieving mother, and he couldn't afford to take the time to go back like he'd promised. Time and time again he'd put off going back, until he couldn't see when he'd get a break and it didn't seem fair to keep Marianne hanging on any longer, and so he'd called off their relationship, thinking he was doing them both a favour.

Except he wasn't. And then, when he'd gone looking for her a year later, it was to find her already married. And it had made him so angry.

Angry with himself. Because he'd waited too long.

Damn it.

He had lost her once. Was he prepared to lose her again?

Mari slammed her keys down on her table, collapsing into a chair. Three weeks back, three job interviews down and she was feeling no closer to finding herself a new job, despite the high-powered dresses and suits she'd treated herself to. She wasn't about to rely on any more of the money from Dom—that money was earmarked for Suzanne's care— but at least instead of looking like she'd just walked out of a chain store she looked like she meant serious business.

Not that it was doing her any good.

She hadn't made a shortlist once, despite a glowing reference from Eric, and despite believing her qualifications and experience satisfied the job requirements to a T. She was either told she was overqualified for the position or the interviewers said they were looking for someone younger, someone who was fresh and new.

Since when was thirty-nine years old no longer fresh and new?

Mind you, she didn't feel fresh and new. Her muscles were sore and she had a headache. She felt as if she was coming down with the flu.

Please God, no. Mari stood up, poured herself a glass of water and found herself some paracetamol. She didn't have time for flu. It was stress, she told herself. She was making herself feel ill through worry—about finding a place for Suzanne, about finding a job and, most of all, about whatever Dom was doing back in San Sebastián.

What was he doing? Had he found solace with one of the women lined up and all too ready to offer him comfort? Had Isabela wormed her way into Dom's affections? The woman had made it clear that she wanted to be in Mari's place as Dom's wife. And she was stunning. They would make an amazing couple—the perfect-looking couple—what if Dom had taken up with her? He was grieving. Who could blame him for seeking consolation wherever he could find it?

It shouldn't matter, it shouldn't concern her, and yet somehow it did.

God, she was torturing herself. It made her stomach roil anew thinking about it.

But there was hope on the horizon. She had another interview tomorrow morning. Sooner or later, one of them had to come good.

* * *

Mari had set her alarm clock early, to give herself time to get ready. Her body clock had set itself even earlier. She woke sensing…knowing…that she was going to throw up.

Nerves, she told herself as she clung to the porcelain bowl. It wasn't as if she'd eaten anything to throw up. She was nervous because she'd blown three interviews so far and she didn't want to mess up this opportunity.

She would not mess up this opportunity, she told herself as she patted her face dry in the mirror. She was going to be the very best version of herself she could be. She was going to knock this one out of the park.

But the smell of her favourite coffee was suddenly re-pugnant to her, her attempt at toast to settle her stomach making it rebel again. This time when she patted her face she stared in the mirror. What the hell was wrong with her? This wasn't like any flu she'd ever had.

It hit her like the blow from a sledgehammer. She saw her eyes widen in the mirror with the impact. Widen with fear. Widen with panic.

No, not that, she pleaded, *please not that.*

Her brain scrambled to count the days and weeks since her last period. Because it couldn't be. She was probably just peri-menopausal. That would make sense. Because the alternative would be too cruel. Too unfair.

But the horrible possibility refused to be ignored.

Because no. Her instincts told her that it wasn't flu. It wasn't menopause or even peri-menopause. It was some-thing way worse.

Mari made it to the interview, but afterwards she couldn't remember a word she'd said. Her mind had been fixated on the pregnancy test she'd be buying the minute she got out of the interview, a test she tried to convince herself she was buying to rule out the unlikely possibility.

Forget waiting until the visit to the toilet in the morning, like the box recommended. The moment Mari got home, she headed for the bathroom. She took one of the sticks and peed on it.

Negative, she projected with her thoughts. It had to be negative. Flu was infinitely better. Peri-menopause would work a treat too. Full-blown menopause even better.

Except it wasn't flu.

And it was the furthest thing from menopause you could get.

Two pink lines stared back at her. Bold pink lines, as the test all but screamed positive.

And for the second time in her life the bottom fell out of Mari's world.

Because once again she was pregnant by Dom.

For too long the divorce papers lay on Dom's desk, burning a hole in it. Once again he circled his desk, regarding them warily. He could sign them. He should sign them and get them off his desk and on the way to Marianne. That had been their deal. A quickie marriage. A quickie divorce. Piece of cake. End of story.

Except signing a paper to terminate their marriage wasn't half as easy as he'd imagined it would be.

Strange. He'd been worried that whoever he married might want to hang around and prove difficult to get rid of. Ironic that he was the one dragging his feet.

When he'd signed their contract, he hadn't wanted anything more than a temporary arrangement. That was the deal he'd stipulated and that was the deal she'd accepted.

Except he hadn't realised just how temporary it would be.

He hadn't been ready for his mother to die.

And he hadn't been ready for Marianne to leave.

He'd married her because she professed to hate him. She'd been the perfect choice because of it. But she didn't hate him, she couldn't have, or she never would have made love to him like she had.

So why had she taken off in such a godawful hurry?

What was she so afraid of?

He looked at the papers on his desk, awaiting his signature. Sure, he could sign and send the papers.

Except, damn it, he couldn't.

He'd have to deliver them to her himself.

Mari's ultrasound appointment was scheduled, her ride-share booked and expected at any moment. The knock on the door came as a surprise. The drivers usually texted their arrival.

She pulled open the door. 'Thanks for the courtesy,' she said, smiling, expecting to see her driver. Except it wasn't her driver.

'Dom?' she said, every cell in her body heading south. 'What are you doing here?'

'I came to see you.'

Her heart stuttered. Her brain scrambled. Her stomach swirled.

'Why?'

'I brought the divorce papers.'

She swallowed. 'And you couldn't just have posted them? Like any normal person would have.'

He blinked. Of course, he was far from normal. 'I could have.'

A car pulled up a little way down the street. Her phone

pinged. 'Oh,' she said, looking at her phone screen. 'That's my ride. I have to go.'

'Where are you going? I can take you.'

'Um…no.' There was absolutely no chance of that. 'I don't think so.'

'Why?' he asked, scowling. 'Are you meeting a man?'

She scoffed. 'And if I was? Why don't you just leave the papers here and I'll sign them and get them back to you?' She looked down at his hands, but they were empty. 'Where are the papers?'

'In my car.'

Her phone pinged again. Her driver waiting for her appearance, if not a response. 'Look, I have to go.'

'And I said I'd take you.'

'No.'

'If you want the divorce papers—'

'I thought you wanted this divorce! It was you who insisted on it.' Her phone pinged again. 'Look, I have to go.' She tried to step past him but he shot out an arm, preventing her egress.

On the street the driver was out of his car and looking towards the pair on the doorstep. She lifted a hand in acknowledgment. 'I'll be right there,' she called.

But Dom turned, saw the driver and was on the path and bearing down on him in an instant. There were few words exchanged, but multiple bills were handed over, and the driver waved, gave a beaming smile and happily drove away.

'Why did you do that?' she asked when he returned.

'You don't need a driver,' he said. 'Not when you've got me to take you where you need to go. Now, where are we going?'

Mari recited the address of the clinic without disclosing

what it was. Twenty years previously she'd never managed to tell Dom that she was pregnant, let alone with his twins. She'd been eagerly awaiting his return to share the news, to share the joy. But his return had been delayed, first by the death of his father, and then by the increasing responsibilities he'd had to shoulder. She'd tried to tell him by phone, thinking it might motivate him to return, but he'd begged off the call and asked her if it could wait, something was happening, and the precious secret she'd held was never divulged.

Until the day, four months too early, that her waters had broken.

And then Dom had rung to say that he was snowed under with the business, that he didn't expect her to wait for him, that it wasn't fair, that she should move on with her life.

And there was nothing left for her to say but to agree with him.

This time she'd vowed to tell Dom that she was pregnant, if today's scan revealed that all was well. He had a right to know, even if they were divorced. But she hadn't figured on him finding out this way.

'You're very quiet,' he said, as he followed the GPS directions through the busy streets.

She looked around the car, hoping for a distraction so she didn't have to explain why she might be quiet. And there on the back seat sat an envelope. She reached back for it. 'These are the divorce papers? Maybe I should just sign them now and you can drop me off and you can go home. That's why you came, right?'

He snatched the envelope from her hand before she could open it, and flung it to the back, where it landed on the back parcel shelf.

'I thought you wanted me to sign those.'

'First of all, we need to talk.'

'Oh, we do, do we?'

'We do.'

'So right, what would you like to talk about?'

He pulled into the car park of the address he had plugged into his GPS navigation.

'What is this place?' he said, frowning as he looked at the signs.

'It's a clinic where they do all kinds of testing. Ultra-sounds. MRIs. X-rays.'

'Why are you here? Is there something wrong with you?'

'I hope not.'

'Then why are you here?'

'I'm here for an ultrasound, Dom.'

'What for?'

'Because I'm pregnant.' She let that sink in for a moment. Watched the reactions flicker across his face—the shock, the disbelief, the inevitable questions that swirled around his eyes. 'And before you ask, it's your baby I'm carrying.'

CHAPTER FOURTEEN

'WHEN WERE YOU going to tell me?'

He was opening the door to the clinic for her. To give Dom credit, he'd recovered more quickly than she had when she'd learned the news.

'After the scan. After I learned everything was all right.'

'You say that now.'

'You know differently? How insightful of you,' she said, and brushed past him, giving her name at Reception and taking a seat in the waiting room. What she really wanted to do was head to the bathroom, her bladder was filled to bursting, but the main cause for her aggravation had just sat down alongside her.

He put his elbows down on his spread legs, his hands clutched under his chin. 'And you're sure it's mine?'

She rolled her eyes, sent him a blistering look and angled herself away. Tried to cross her legs and then gave up when it only put more pressure on her bladder.

'If you're trying to convince me not to sign those divorce papers,' she hissed, 'you're barking up the wrong tree.'

'I don't know who you've been with.'

'Likewise. Has the beautiful Isabela managed to weasel her way into your bed yet?'

He cocked an eyebrow. 'You care?'

'No,' she said, cursing herself for giving herself away.

'I left, didn't I? Would I have left if I'd cared? If I'd given a damn?'

'It felt like you cared.'

His voice was deep and measured and she knew exactly what he was remembering. The sex they'd shared. The sex that had resulted in this little one residing deep inside of her.

Her name being called saved her from answering. She sprang to her feet and approached the sonographer. Dom did likewise.

'No,' she said, except the sonographer got in first.

'Ah, is this your partner? Lovely,' she said, and Mari got the sense she was remarking about Dom's looks rather than the proud father-to-be he presented himself as. 'Come on through.'

She directed Dom to a visitor chair while she got Mari to lie on the bed. 'So, not your first pregnancy?' she said, looking at the notes while she positioned the equipment.

'Second,' Mari said. 'Twins. Miscarried at five months. Twenty years ago.'

She pressed a hand to Mari's shoulder. 'So unfair. Let's take a look at this baby and check everything's okay.'

Mari bared her belly for the gel and the transducer. The screen on the ceiling was turned away. There was no point watching that, so she closed her eyes and tried to ignore Dom sitting beside her, tried to put him out of her mind. The gel was cold, the transducer pressure on her belly she could have done without, but the sonographer was efficient with her work. Moving the transducer over her skin, searching for angles and finding them, clicking to take measurements and even more measurements. It might have been twenty years ago, but Mari had been there before.

The sonographer stopped clicking. 'Can you excuse me?

I just have to check something with my colleague. I'll be right back.'

'What's wrong?' asked Mari, but the woman was gone. Mari looked at Dom. 'Something's wrong. Why would she leave like that?'

'Because she had to check something with a colleague.'

'About what?'

'I don't know. Why do you think there's something wrong?'

'Because otherwise she wouldn't have to check. She says it's a colleague, but she means a doctor. They only do that when there's something wrong. Otherwise, she'd show me the pictures and send me home with a photo.'

'You don't know that,' he said.

'I know it. Something's not right. Something's wrong.'

He reached out a hand to her and she took it, clinging to it with both hands like a lifeline. And for the first time she admitted that she was glad that Dom was here, because this wasn't just her child but Dom's too. He needed to be here.

The sonographer reappeared, together with another white-coated woman who identified herself as a doctor.

'What's wrong?' Mari asked. She was thirty-nine years old—a geriatric pregnancy as some called it, where any number of things could go wrong. Especially following a previous miscarriage.

The doctor smiled benevolently. 'Don't worry. Just checking a few things. It won't take a moment.'

She took the transducer, moving it over Mari's skin. Mari flinched at the pressure of both an overfull bladder and things unknown. When the hell would they let her pee? When the hell would they stop torturing her and tell her what was wrong? She was thirty-nine years old. She wasn't a child that needed to be protected. If something was wrong, she wanted to know what it was.

A minute later the doctor nodded to the sonographer as she pulled the device away. 'I'm sorry to put you through that added stress, Ms Peterson, but we needed to be sure as it's sometimes difficult to determine at an early stage. But my colleague here was right. I'm hoping this might make up for what happened in the past. Congratulations,' she said, wiping the gel from her belly with paper towels. 'There are two heartbeats. You're expecting twins.'

Shock ricocheted through her.

'No!' she heard herself calling as she curled into a ball on the bed. If she could squeeze her eyes shut long enough, she might wake up and find this had all been a dream, a horrible, ghastly dream. Discovering she was pregnant, Dom turning up on her doorstep unannounced, learning that she was pregnant with twins.

Again.

History was repeating itself. Mocking her. Congratulations had no place in the circumstances. Condolences would be more appropriate. One baby was bad enough, but two was akin to scraping away the scars of the past with a box grater and rubbing salt into them.

'No,' she said, tears streaming down her face. 'I lost them before. I can't go through that again!'

The doctor patted her shoulder. 'I understand, but there's no reason to think that what happened before will happen again. You were unlucky, that's all. You'll have the best possible care, I can guarantee it.'

'But twins…'

Dom reached for her hand. 'Our twins.'

But Mari just turned her head to the wall and sobbed.

* * *

Dom took her home to her flat. Put her to bed, tortured by the sound of the soft sobbing coming from her room.

Marianne was pregnant with his twins.

And didn't that change things. Those divorce papers in his car were going nowhere. Everything had changed. Divorce was out of the question, even Marianne must re-alise that.

The evening was closing in, soft rain falling outside, spattering against the windows when Dom took Mari a tray with a bowl of warm soup from a can he'd found in the pantry, along with a handful of crackers. 'You have to eat something,' he said when she shook her head.

Her cheeks were puffy, there were dark circles under her eyes and her hair was a mess, but even so, she was still the most beautiful woman he'd ever seen. She always had been. Even more so now because she was carrying his babies.

He gathered pillows to put behind her back, placing the tray on her lap and sat down on the side of the bed. 'Do I have to feed you?' he asked gently.

'No,' she said, so softly it was little more than a whisper. She picked up the spoon, dipped it into the soup, and took a sip. 'I'm afraid,' she said, resting the spoon back on the tray.

'Of course you are, but you heard the doctor. There's no reason to think that what happened last time will happen again. Come on, eat.'

She stared into her soup. 'That's not the only reason I'm afraid.'

Her words barely made sense.

'Why else would you be afraid?'

She licked her lips. 'I miscarried my babies.'

'My mother told me. She truly felt for you.'

She lifted her gaze, her eyes sorrowful, searching his.

'Twenty years ago,' she said. 'Doesn't that mean anything to you? The twins I lost—they were your babies, Dom.'

Dom was reeling with shock. He stood up and gazed out of the window to the wet streetscape beyond, car headlights sending blurry beams along the bitumen.

His babies. Marianne had said as much to the sonographer, but his brain hadn't let him connect the dots. He'd assumed that she'd been pregnant with her husband's twins—that something had gone horribly wrong and he hadn't wanted Marianne to try again. That he'd been happy with the two children he'd already had. Twenty years ago, she'd told the sonographer, and the babies had been five months gestation. And it was twenty years ago that Dom's father had suffered his first heart attack and he'd returned to San Sebastián temporarily—until his father had died and temporarily had become permanently, and he'd put off his return to Australia again and again. Why hadn't she told him? Why hadn't he known?

He'd never had an inkling that she was pregnant. Why hadn't she told him? If she'd told him he would have moved heaven and earth to get to her.

But he hadn't known. And he'd lost her. He'd lost an entire family he didn't know he had.

'Where are they?' he asked.

'Sydney,' she said. 'Where I lost them. They're buried together in a cemetery overlooking Bondi Beach.'

And Dom knew he had to go.

'Take me there. Show me.'

CHAPTER FIFTEEN

THE SLOPING CEMETERY ended in cliffs that overlooked the Pacific Ocean. It had glorious views along the dramatic coastline and out to sea, the sound of waves pounding and roaring against the mighty cliffs and the call of gulls providing the soundtrack to the otherwise hushed space.

Grass-covered paths separated the plots, all manner of headstones, from simple slabs of stones to crosses to angels, rising from the ground.

'Why here?' he asked as she led him quietly along the path, two small colourful posies in her hands. 'Why this cemetery?'

She stopped and pointed along the coast. 'Do you remember that day we spent on Bondi Beach? I think that day I was the happiest I had ever been. I wanted our babies to have somewhere beautiful to rest, near the place that had made my heart sing.'

Our babies.

He swallowed down against the lump in his throat. He couldn't speak. He simply nodded.

'This way,' she said. 'It's not far.'

She stopped in front of a tiny grave, edged in marble rail. A small white stone comprising twin hearts stood at its head, on which two birds carrying a ribbon heavenwards were engraved.

Along with two names and an inscription.

Laura Marianne and David Dominico
Beloved babies of
Marianne and Dominico
Born before their time. Lost but never forgotten.
Sleep well, our tiny babies, sleep well.

'You gave them names,' he said, his voice thick with emotion. Both of the babies were acknowledged as his children. 'Our names.'

She gave a shrug as she knelt down, pulled a tiny weed from the grave and tenderly placed a posy next to each heart. 'I couldn't give them life. I had nothing else to give them.' She sniffed. 'Laura and David were my parents. I thought it appropriate.'

'It's beautiful,' he said. 'I'm so sorry you had to go through all of this alone.'

'It's my own fault,' she said, taking his proffered hand as she rose. 'I wanted to tell you, I was so excited to tell you, but I wanted to tell you face to face, not over the phone, not in a letter. And you were coming back, you told me, so I waited. And when, finally, I tried to tell you over the phone, you asked if it could wait. And then it couldn't, and I'd waited too long.'

She hauled in a breath. 'And then one of my waters broke. It was too early and there was nothing anyone could do, but they assured me that it didn't mean I'd lose both babies. Except they were wrong. I don't know why—nobody could tell me why, nobody could explain it—but it happened again, the second baby's waters broke, and I lost them both. They were so tiny, Dom, tiny like dolls, but they were beautiful. Perfect with legs and arms and the tiniest of fingers and toes. They died in my arms. They were too tiny to survive with their lungs underdeveloped. And then it was too late to tell you anything. You were already not coming back and I had nothing to tell you.'

He had been coming back. He'd meant to come back.

Over and over, he'd told her he was coming back.

'It's not your fault,' he said. 'I should have come back.'

'You called the week after I lost them, said you couldn't see your way clear, and you didn't want to keep me waiting endlessly, that maybe it was better if we ended it. That it was for the best.'

'And you agreed,' he said, his voice hoarse as he remembered, guilt piling on guilt that he'd imagined for one moment that she'd agreed with him because she'd already found someone else and moved on. Guilt piling on guilt that when he finally had come looking for her and discovered that she was married he'd believed it.

Tears stained her face. She looked up at him beseechingly. 'Are you angry with me, for not telling you?'

'No. I'm angry with myself, for ever imagining that work was more important than following my heart. And I'm angry with myself for not figuring out why you hated me so much. For believing that you had no right to hate me when you have every right in the world. Can you ever forgive me, Marianne?'

The waves crashed into the cliffs, sending spray high into the sky and salt-tinged air on the breeze.

She looked up into his face, taking in the dark, tortured eyes and clenched jaw. The breeze toyed with the ends of his hair, the movement at odds with the severity of his features and his plea for forgiveness.

And Mari felt that same breeze move through her and lighten her own soul. So much pain and hurt they'd caused each other. So much unnecessary resentment, and yes, even hate over the years.

'I already have,' she whispered. 'What happened to us was the result of circumstances outside of our control. It was the result of bad timing and bad luck. You never meant to hurt me, you thought you were doing me a favour releasing me, and I never intended keeping our babies secret for ever. And yet we fell through the cracks of our own bad decision-making.'

He took a deep breath, his eyes softening, his jaw relaxing. 'Thank you.'

She licked her lips. 'But I have a question. What happens now?'

'What do you mean? We're married, Marianne. You're pregnant with our babies. What do you think happens?'

'I don't know,' She closed her eyes and breathed deeply. 'You're the one who insisted this marriage be temporary. You're the one who arrived here with a wad of divorce papers for me to sign.'

'And then I discover that you're pregnant.'

She opened her eyes. Seeking her forgiveness—being granted it—was one thing, but assuming that all of a sudden everything had swung back one hundred and eighty degrees when he had clearly come looking for her to sign divorce papers?

No, no and no.

She put one hand to her head, the other low over her still flat belly where her babies resided, battling to make sense of it. 'So now you want to forget about the divorce? Is that what you're saying?'

'We're married,' he growled, as if she didn't already know. 'And you're having my babies. What would be the sense of getting divorced now? You can't shut me out again.

I refuse to be shut out. Can't you see it's for the best if we stay together?'

For the best.

And that was the only reason?

This time Mari turned away, gave a final nod of respect to the headstone at the top of the tiny grave and headed back down the grassed path. Because it was the wrong answer and there was no point continuing the conversation.

'Marianne,' he called, chasing after her. 'Surely you see it makes sense.'

Mari ploughed on, her hands plunged deep in her jacket pockets. Maybe his words did make a kind of sense, if you were other people in different circumstances, but they didn't make the right kind of sense to her.

'It's Mari!' she called over her shoulder. 'How many times do I have to tell you?' Because she wasn't that naïve young woman she'd been back then. And the jigsaw pieces of a horrible parallel between twenty years ago and now were starting to fit together.

Twenty years ago, Dom had professed his love for her, and yet abandoned her, now saying if only he'd known she was pregnant he would have been at her side in a heartbeat.

And now he'd turned up with legal papers to divorce her and to terminate their rushed marriage. Only to relent when he'd discovered she was pregnant.

Then and now.

Maybe those disparate situations weren't that far apart after all.

Marianne was on a mission, striding away as if she had the devil himself behind her. What the hell was wrong with her? Dom was no devil. Hadn't he said he'd be there for her and for their babies?

He finally caught up with her close to the cemetery gates.

'What did I say?'

'Will you please just take me home?'

'Seriously, Marianne. One moment you're telling me you're forgiving me for past sins—that we were both responsible—and in the next I've made some kind of heinous mistake.'

'Yes,' she said. 'And now can I go home?'

They hadn't made it to the car when Mari took the call. The caller ID told her it came from Eric Cooper, but the voice was female. But not Helen, his wife. Sandra, the caller identified herself, Eric and Helen's daughter.

'Mari,' she said, is that you?'

Mari's heart lurched. Her feet stumbled on the path. Please God, no, she thought, anticipating—*dreading*— why this woman would be calling her. Surely not already. Not so soon.

'It's Dad—Eric,' Sandra said. 'I'm so sorry to call you, but Dad passed away peacefully two days ago. You were on his list of people to contact with the news.'

Mari stood stock still, listening as Sandra filled her in with the details of Eric's upcoming funeral.

'I'll be there,' she said, her throat choking. 'I'm so sorry for your loss.'

'Who was that?' Dom asked.

'Eric Cooper's daughter,' she said, bitterness infusing her words.

'What's going on?'

'Eric died two days ago.'

A pause.

'I'm sorry,' Dom said.

'Are you?' she snapped. 'What do you even care? You

went after his company and you succeeded. You won, right? So don't pretend you give a fig.'

'I know what it feels like to lose someone you love. That's what I meant.'

Mari put her head down, a concession to a nod. That was fair. This was the man who'd so recently lost his mother.

'The funeral's tomorrow,' she said, licking her lips, tasting the salt of her tears. 'I need to be there.'

'You'll be there,' he said. 'I'll make sure of it.'

'Don't you have somewhere else to be?' she asked. 'A deal going on somewhere else in the world that you need to take care of? A company somewhere that you need to take over?'

'Marianne,' he said, trying to get through to her, trying to break down this invisible barrier that she'd erected between them, 'if there's one thing I've learned from my years of experience it's that I have to be in the place where I'm most needed at the time. Right at this moment, that place is here with you.'

She was quiet on the plane back to Melbourne, lost in her grief for the loss of a dear friend, her answers and comments to the cabin crew monosyllabic. He ached for her. He wanted to ease her burden. He wanted to put right whatever he'd done wrong. He wanted to comfort her, like she had comforted him in those dark hours after his mother had died. But she didn't want his comfort.

She didn't want him.

And that was the hardest thing of all.

The funeral chapel oozed empathy and compassion. The decor was muted, a lectern to one side, and there, on the dais, sat the flower-topped coffin, arrangements of flowers standing either side.

Dom held back, not sure that he'd be welcomed by the

family when Mari hugged Eric's wife and then his daughters, before taking a seat. Dom sat beside her, even though it was an all too painful reminder of the so recent funeral of his mother. But he had to remind himself that he wasn't here for himself today. He was here for Marianne.

She was broken, he could tell. Eric had meant the world to her. He'd been both her mentor and a father figure to replace the parent she'd lost when just a young child. Knowing that he'd added to her pain by whatever stupid thing he'd told her at the cemetery, he hated himself.

If only he knew what he'd done wrong.

The funeral service moved on. Prayers and readings and a eulogy delivered by his daughter that brought everyone to tears. And finally, the heart-wrenching kicker—the photographic display set to Leonard Cohen's beautiful 'Hallelujah' that spanned Eric's life, from when he had been just a baby and then a toddler and a schoolchild and onwards through his life, his marriage to Helen, his children, until he was CEO of Cooper Industries, and there were photographs from business and Christmas lunches, awards he'd won, and snapshots in which Marianne appeared, leaning down and smiling, her arm around Eric's shoulders, or when Eric was dressed up as Santa, his arm around Mari's shoulders.

Mari quietly sobbed beside him as each new picture flashed up on the screen. He reached a hand over to hers where they were clutched in her lap, but she pulled them away.

The interment was just as moving. Just as much an ordeal. While Eric's widow and daughters softly sobbed as the coffin was lowered into the grave, Marianne was contained and stoic, her emotions clearly held in check as she stood swaying ever so slightly at the graveside. But he could feel the pain vibrating through her, he could see the pain etched on her beautiful features, and her pain was his pain.

Afterwards there was a small reception for everyone to mingle and take refreshments. Helen Cooper was doing the rounds, shaking hands with and thanking everyone for coming, when she approached Mari and Dom.

'It was a beautiful service,' said Mari. 'Eric deserved every bit of it.'

'Thank you, dear,' she said, taking Mari's hands in hers and pressing her cheek with a kiss, before turning to Dom beside her. 'Mr Estefan, I believe,' she said, and she shook his hand. 'I'm sorry I didn't recognise you earlier. Thank you for coming.'

'I hope you don't mind,' he said. 'I wasn't sure—'

'Oh, no,' she said, waving his concerns away. 'Thank you for buying Cooper Industries when you did. I know it was his passion but I only wish Eric had sold it years earlier. These last few weeks have been such a gift. I will cherish the precious time Eric and I had together for ever.'

'He was so looking forward to spending time with you,' said Mari. 'I didn't expect we'd lose Eric so soon.'

Helen gave a wan smile. 'Nobody did. But he didn't suffer at the end so that's something to be grateful for.' She gave a wan smile. 'I just selfishly wish there'd been more time to enjoy having him to myself, but perhaps it's for the best.' She patted the back of Mari's hand. 'And now I must move on. Thank you both for coming.'

For the best.

There was something about those words, something that snagged in Dom's mind.

'Take me home,' Marianne said, sounding tired.

She closed her eyes in the car and rested her head back on the head rest, so quiet that Dom thought she'd fallen asleep.

But then she asked, 'When do you fly home?'

Her words were like a body blow. He looked over at her, her eyes still closed. 'You want me gone that badly?'

'What is there to stay for?'

'I can think of a couple of reasons.'

'I've been thinking about that. We can share custody.'

She sounded so logical, as if this were a simple accounting problem involving numbers that she could find an easy solution to, the reconciliation of a problem, but one that didn't involve any kind of reconciliation between Marianne and Dom at all.

'And before they're born? What if something happens and I'm not here?'

Her beautiful mouth pulled into a grimace. 'The doctors say it shouldn't happen again.'

'And if it does? *Dios*, Marianne, do you hate me so much that you would exclude me from watching my babies develop and grow? What is this, some kind of payback for me not being here first time around? The first time I didn't even know you were pregnant!'

She opened her eyes. Turned to him, her emerald eyes misty with tears. She looked sad. Desperately, achingly sad. 'How else can we make it work?'

He looked away. 'I don't know.'

Marianne said goodbye when he walked her to the door. There was no invitation to come in, just a thank you for escorting her to the funeral.

He didn't push it. Instead, he asked, 'You'll keep in touch? Keep me informed with what's going on?'

She nodded. 'I will.'

And Dom knew that he'd blown his chance with Marianne again.

CHAPTER SIXTEEN

MARI CLOSED THE door and leant her back against it, the action a trigger for her tears. She was exhausted, emotionally wrung out, first with the funeral and saying goodbye to Eric. Secondly by saying goodbye to Dom, the man she loved but who didn't love her.

Oh, he wanted her, but as the mother of his twins, not as the woman he loved. She couldn't bear having him within reach and yet not having him. It would kill her. It would eat her away inside until it destroyed her. Loving a man who didn't want her had destroyed her before. Better to have him safely on the other side of the world or flying around the globe doing his deals. Better to have him as far away as possible.

They'd work something out about the babies. She was barely seven weeks pregnant. It wasn't as if there was any rush.

She took a deep breath and pushed herself away from the door, throwing her keys on the table where her recently reclaimed peace lily sat, looking healthier than it had for months. Mari allowed herself a mocking smile. Maybe she should sign a contract to marry a billionaire more often.

Dom was halfway to the airport. There was no point staying any longer in Melbourne. His team had the Cooper Industries acquisition under control, and he was needed in Brazil, to finalise matters there. He tried to focus on the latest emails he'd received from his team there, tried to get his head back in the game, but something else kept on intruding, those few words that Helen Cooper had uttered that had snagged in his mind. That phrase—*for the best*—still grated.

More than grated. It wormed its way into Dom's psyche, slicing into his memories, conversations tumbling and tumbling over each other until he recognised the words he'd voiced himself, opening the floodgates to everything he'd said—thinking he was doing right, when all he'd done was wrong. Time and again he'd done wrong.

Starting with that ill thought out, ill-timed phone call twenty years ago, when he'd decided it was unfair to keep stringing Marianne along month after month and that it was probably for the best that they called off their relationship. Being adult, he'd thought. Grown up.

Stupid.

He'd destroyed Marianne with that thoughtless call. She'd already lost her twins, and then he'd taken away her hope.

And then, yesterday at the cemetery, at the grave where their tiny babies were buried, he'd done it again. He'd told her that they shouldn't divorce, that they should stay married because she was expecting their twins, that the babies needed them both, that it would be for the best.

And Marianne hadn't just looked appalled, she'd looked stricken. She'd withdrawn into herself, like a tortoise retreating into its shell, leaving nothing but hard defences, impossible to breach, impossible to reason with.

Why couldn't he have admitted to himself what was plain all along?

Why else would he not have posted the divorce papers or sent them by courier? For weeks they'd burned a hole in his desk. For those weeks they'd been the elephant in the room, glanced at only to ignore, another day, another week. Why had he felt the compulsion to deliver them in person when there was no earthly need? She wouldn't have been offended by their arrival, she would have been expecting them. She would have signed them and got them back to him by return mail.

And there, in a nutshell, was why he hadn't had them couriered over to her.

Because he didn't want her to sign them.

He didn't want to divorce her.

Because he loved her.

Dios! Why the hell had it taken him so long to realise? As a twenty-two-year-old he'd had no problem telling Marianne that he loved her. When had the word disappeared from his lexicon? When had he forgotten how to say the word?

When he'd learned that women wanted him for his fortune and not for himself? Or because he'd always been looking for another Marianne? Someone who might take the place of the woman he'd loved and abandoned, only to lose her to somebody else.

The papers.

He turned his head, searching for the envelope, spying it on the parcel shelf, remembering that he'd tossed it there when Marianne had threatened to sign them then and there on the way to the clinic.

And he knew what he had to do.

Mari tied up her hair and treated herself to a bath, trying to relax her body if not her mind. Sadness seemed to infuse her every cell, the sadness of farewelling a loved one, the sadness of losing another one—one who was destined never to be hers.

It was only early evening, but Mari donned her night-gown and sheepskin boots and wrapped herself in a cosy dressing gown, ready for a night in front of the television. It didn't matter what was on, it wouldn't register. She just wanted something inane to blot out the gaping hole in her heart.

The knock on the door was as unwelcome as it was unexpected. She settled in deeper to her sofa. She wasn't about to open the door to some stranger while wearing her pyjamas. Not a chance.

The knock came again, more insistent this time. More reason to ignore it. Mari crossed her arms over her chest and tried to blot out the interruption.

Whoever was at the door wasn't taking no for an answer, and this time there was another sound, something that sounded like '*Marianne...*'

Nobody called her Marianne, nobody but... She sat up.

'Marianne, it's Dom.'

A shudder skittered down her spine. He was back? But why? She could keep pretending that she wasn't home. But something about the urgency of his pounding and the sound of his voice made her curious.

She pulled the sides of her robe closer around her and tightened the belt around her waist, her hand hesitating on the door handle. She pulled it open and Dom was standing there, his arms spread wide, resting against the doorframe. His eyes looked tortured, his features drawn, an expression that transformed immediately when she pulled open the door. Because suddenly she saw hope.

He smiled. 'Marianne,' he said.

'What are you doing here?'

'I found these in the car,' he said, pulling down his hands from the doorframe. He was holding an envelope in one. She recognised it. The divorce papers.

'Oh.' Of course he'd want to mop up the details of their deal, now that he knew that she didn't want him in her life. She held out one hand. 'I'll sign them now.'

But he didn't hand them over. 'I have a better idea,' he said, taking the envelope between both hands and tearing it in half, and then in half again, and again and again, before he threw the scraps in the air. They fluttered on the breeze, scattering to the ground.

'What are you doing?'

'We don't need divorce papers. You don't want to be divorced.'

'What are you talking about?'

'I finally worked it out. I worked out what I'd said that was wrong, the words that hurt you so much yesterday in the cemetery. Then I worked out what it was that I hadn't said, and that was even more important.'

Marianne started to protest.

'No,' he said. 'I know that I hurt you. I saw it. I felt the defences go up when you didn't get what you needed. Because you weren't looking for someone who wanted to stay married to you because you were pregnant. You wanted someone to stay married to you because they loved you.

'And as it happens,' he added, 'I love you.'

'No,' she said, shaking her head. 'Why should I believe you? It's just another attempt to keep me close. To keep our babies close.'

'Marianne, listen to me. Why do you think I delivered those divorce papers myself instead of couriering them? I could have posted them if I didn't give a damn. I would have. But I didn't. Because I didn't want you to sign them.'

She started to protest and he cut her off. 'And that was before I knew about the babies. I couldn't bear the idea of being without you. It's you I came back for. It's you I want to be with. It's you that I love.'

* * *

Mari searched his eyes. She so desperately wanted to believe him. 'How can I believe you?'

His expression softened. 'Maybe, if you let me show you?'
'How?'

He reached a gentle hand to her chin, lifting it and dipping his face to her lips. 'Like this,' he said. He pressed his lips to hers, so gently, so poignantly that it almost broke her heart at the same time it was tearing down her defences.

He drew back. 'I love you,' he said, and that was when she saw the tears in his eyes. Tears that mirrored her own. 'I'm sorry it took me so long to realise the truth. I'm sorry I caused you so much pain and sorrow. I'll make it up to you, I promise. I'll spend the rest of my life making it up to you.'

She blinked away the moisture sheening her eyes as she crumpled his shirt in her fist and pulled him through the door, shutting it behind him as she led him to her bed. 'You know I'm going to hold you to that?'

'I want you to.'

He was naked in her bed, the sheet covering his loins, his beautiful chest exposed. He'd made love to her so tenderly that he'd plucked her heartstrings like he'd been playing a harp, and now she lay panting and satiated in his arms.

'It's a miracle,' he said, 'finding you again.'

It had to be some kind of miracle. Luck or happenstance didn't come close.

'Serendipity,' Mari said, thinking of the word that had appealed so much to Rosaria, the thought followed by instant regret. 'I'm sorry,' she said, 'for making out that I didn't want to stay for your mother's funeral. Every time we made love, I knew that I was falling deeper for you. Every time, I realised I loved you and I couldn't stay, knowing that the longer I stayed, it would only get harder to leave you.'

He looked down at her, his dark brows furrowed. 'That's why you were in such a hurry to get away? Because you'd discovered you loved me?'

She nodded. 'I couldn't tell you. I dare not tell you. Because I feared that history would repeat itself, because you didn't want a wife, and I'd end up alone and broken again.'

He dropped his head, pressing his lips to her shoulder. 'I thought things had changed between us too. I thought things might be different. But I was too stupid to realise what I had. I'd buried my feelings so deep inside me that I didn't recognise it for what it was. I'm so sorry.'

He rested a hand on the slightest curve of her lower belly, where their babies lay nestled deep below. 'And here we have history repeating itself, but only the good bits, and you'll never be alone again.' He leaned down to kiss her nose, her mouth, her chin, and then he leaned down to kiss the almost imperceptible swell of her belly before lifting his face to hers again. 'I love you, Mari. I've wasted twenty years. I promise never to waste another moment.'

Mari smiled up at him, at this man she'd loved in another life, this man who loved her now, and she believed him. 'I love you,' she said, 'so very much.'

Her heart soared. And it was so liberating to be able to put voice to her emotions. It was so liberating to be able to admit it to the man she loved.

He looked at her, his eyes wide. 'That's the first time you've actually said the words to me.'

She wrapped her arms around his neck. 'I know. I promise it won't be the last.'

'I love you, Señora Estefan. I love you, Mari.'

She smiled under his beautiful mouth. 'Marianne.'

EPILOGUE

MARIANNE APPROACHED THE five-month mark of her pregnancy with mounting trepidation and concern, fearing that the past might revisit her, sending her back into that dark place where she'd been twenty years before.

But her team of physicians and midwives was there to monitor her and assure her all was well. And above all, Dom was there to hold her close through day and night and promise that she would never be alone again.

And five months turned into six and then seven. When eight months clicked over, her medical team got together with Marianne and Dom. Marianne had turned forty and was considered to be a woman of advanced maternal age. So together they worked out a plan of how best to deliver her babies comfortably and safely for the babies and for Mari.

Two weeks later, the twins were delivered by Caesarean section, Dom holding Marianne's hands while their dark-haired twins, a baby boy and a baby girl, took their first breaths.

Dom watched on in wonder as the babies were gently towelled down, before being laid one after the other on Marianne's bare chest.

'They're perfect,' Marianne said, 'so perfect. Look at them, Dom.'

Dom was looking. He had never seen a more perfect vision than the sight of their newborn twins nestled face to face atop their beautiful mother.

He stroked Marianne's hair with one hand and reached out his other to pat the babies' backs, each of them no wider than his hand, and down one downy arm to the tiny hand curled in a fist. The hand opened briefly, closing over Dom's little finger and gripping tighter than should be possible for something so tiny and vulnerable, and melting Dom's heart in the process.

'How is it possible to love them so much already?' he said, his voice thick.

'They're a blessing,' she said. 'Like you were to your parents. A gift. How could we not love them?'

'A girl and a boy,' he said, marvelling at the mirroring of history. 'Now that you've seen them, have you settled on names?'

'Almost. Your mother asked if we had a son, that we call him Roberto to honour your father. I agreed. And I think we should call this one,' she said, stroking their baby daughter's head, 'Rosaria. Rosaria Suzanne.'

He nodded. 'Good choice. Rosaria Suzanne and Roberto—Roberto what?'

'I don't know. I haven't got that far.'

'I do. We should call him Roberto Eric, because it was Eric Cooper who insisted I should keep you on and who brought you back into my life. What do you think?'

'Oh, Dom,' she said, tears springing to her eyes, 'I would love it.'

He smiled and leaned over to kiss Marianne on the lips, before kissing each of their babies' heads in turn before settling back down in his seat. 'And while it might not have been the job he imagined I'd give you, it turns out

Eric was right. My wife and the mother of my children. But more than that, the most important job of all, the love of my life. I love you, Marianne. I promise you that you'll never be alone again.'

By now tears were streaming down her face. Happy tears. Tears of joy and bliss. But her arms were full of babies and she couldn't wipe them away. She sniffed.

'I love you, Dom, so much, and you better get your mouth back over here again because I seriously need to kiss you again.'

Their kiss was warm and all shades of wonderful, filled with respect and love, the past left behind in the promise for the future.

And Marianne knew that Rosaria had been right when she'd uttered those fateful words the day she'd arrived in San Sebastián after their marriage. It might not have been one hundred per cent right then, it hadn't been ten per cent right, but it was certainly right now.

Love had finally got it right.

* * * * *

Were you swept off your feet by After-Hours Proposal*?
Then don't miss these other dazzling stories
by Trish Morey!*

Bartering Her Innocence
A Price Worth Paying?
Consequence of the Greek's Revenge
Prince's Virgin in Venice

Available now!

MILLS & BOON ®

Coming next month

BILLION-DOLLAR RING RUSE
Jadesola James

'Am I that obvious?'

'Weren't you trying to be?'

'Don't be so eager to rush a beautiful thing, Miss Montgomery.'

'Val,' she corrected, her heart thumping like a rabbit's. If this was happening, she couldn't let it happen with him calling her *Miss Montgomery* or, worse yet, Valentina. Not with his liquid, rich voice simply dripping with all the dirty things she presumed he could do to her—it was bringing to the surface something she wasn't ready to explore. Not with him.

And yet, her thoughts were going in directions she couldn't control, while she sat in the booth, heart thudding, mentally grasping at them as they floated beyond her fingertips into places that sent back heated, urgent images that took her breath away with their sensuality. His mouth on her neck, his lips on hers, the softness of his breath on her ear. His hands on her breasts, hips, bottom, thighs. Stroking. Exploring.

Gripping.

Her face bloomed with heat, and it left her body in the softest of exhales before he *finally* kissed her.

Continue reading

BILLION-DOLLAR RING RUSE
Jadesola James

Available next month
millsandboon.co.uk

COMING SOON!

We really hope you enjoyed reading this book.
If you're looking for more romance
be sure to head to the shops when
new books are available on

Thursday 27th March

To see which titles are coming soon, please visit

millsandboon.co.uk/nextmonth

MILLS & BOON

LET'S TALK

Romance

For exclusive extracts, competitions and special offers, find us online:

- 🅕 MillsandBoon
- 𝕏 @MillsandBoon
- 🅞 @MillsandBoonUK
- ♪ @MillsandBoonUK

Get in touch on 01413 063 232

For all the latest titles coming soon, visit
millsandboon.co.uk/nextmonth

Afterglow Books is a trend-led, trope-filled list of books with diverse, authentic and relatable characters, a wide array of voices and representations, plus real world trials and tribulations. Featuring all the tropes you could possibly want (think small-town settings, fake relationships, grumpy vs sunshine, enemies to lovers) and all with a generous dose of spice in every story.

♪ @millsandboonuk
📷 @millsandboonuk
afterglowbooks.co.uk
#AfterglowBooks

For all the latest book news, exclusive content and giveaways scan the QR code below to sign up to the Afterglow newsletter:

SCAN ME

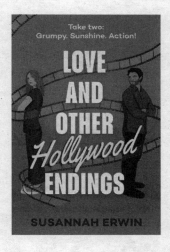
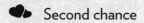
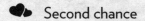

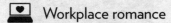